PRAISE FOR THE
RILEY O'BRIEN & CO. ROMANCES

"A sassy debut, delightful!"
—Lori Wilde, *New York Times* bestselling author of
I'll Be Home for Christmas

"Jenna Sutton crafts a sweet and sumptuous read, as sexy
and comfortable as a favorite pair of jeans."
—M. J. Pullen, author of *Regrets Only*

"A sexy, sweet, fun read."
—Tracy Solheim, author of *Sleeping with the Enemy*

"Sweet romance, steamy sex, and emotional drama."
—*Publishers Weekly*

"A wonderful, delightful, steamy, and fun romantic story . . .
[Sutton] has a wonderful career ahead of her."
—The Reading Cafe

"Peopled with complex, believable characters, and set in an
interesting business, Sutton's debut novel is a sexy, sassy, and
hot hit."
—BookPage

"If you like tension filled and chemistry charged romance,
this is the series for you. I want more of Riley O'Brien &
Co. right now!"
—Book Briefs

"This series and author are a true gem in the Contemporary
Romance genre!"
—The Book Reading Gals

"*Coming Apart at the Seams* is a love story done just right!"
—The Sassy Bookster

"*Coming Apart at the Seams* was fresh, unique, and left me
totally smitten. I'm loving the O'Brien clan and can't wait
for more."
—Herding Cats & Burning Soup

Hanging by a Thread

JENNA SUTTON

BERKLEY SENSATION, NEW YORK

BERKLEY
SENSATION

An imprint of Penguin Random House LLC
375 Hudson Street, New York, New York 10014

HANGING BY A THREAD

A Berkley Sensation Book / published by arrangement with the author

ISBN: 978-0-425-27997-7

PUBLISHING HISTORY
Berkley Sensation mass-market edition / June 2016

PRINTED IN THE UNITED STATES OF AMERICA

10 9 8 7 6 5 4 3 2 1

Penguin
Random
House

Chapter 1

CHASTE. UNTOUCHED. MAIDEN. PURE. INNOCENT. THE WORDS
that described a virgin might sound pretty, but the truth was
downright ugly, at least in Bebe Banerjee's opinion. She was
convinced her virginity was the reason her heart raced, her
breath seized, and her palms sweated whenever she was near
Cal O'Brien.

Bebe surreptitiously studied Cal, trying to ignore the wave
of lust that surged over her. If she'd had some experience
between the sheets, she was sure she'd be able to handle the way
he made her feel.

If she had gotten naked with a few guys, maybe she
wouldn't obsess about his glacier-blue eyes and his thick, dark
hair. Maybe she wouldn't notice the way his jeans clung to his
tight behind and long legs. Maybe she wouldn't fantasize
about his lips, his smile, his big hands . . .

Bebe desperately wished she could just avoid him, but his
little sister, Teagan, was her best friend. If she wanted to
spend time with Teagan, she had to put up with Cal. She said
no to a lot of Teagan's invitations to hang out because of him,
and she had to be very careful not to offend her best friend.

That was why the object of her X-rated fantasies stood
next to her in a club-level suite at PacBell Park. The San

Francisco Giants were in the playoffs, battling against the Atlanta Braves to win the National League pennant, and Teagan had invited her to attend the game in the Riley O'Brien & Co. suite.

Founded by Teagan's great-great-grandfather, Riley O'Brien & Co. was the nation's oldest designer and manufacturer of blue jeans. Americans had worn Rileys for nearly two centuries. In fact, Bebe was wearing a pair right now.

Teagan and her brothers were involved in the day-to-day operations of Riley O'Brien & Co. She managed the company's law department, while her oldest brother, Quinn, served as president and CEO, and Cal handled global marketing and communications. Even Quinn's wife, Amelia, was involved in the company, heading up the women's division.

Beside her, Cal shifted slightly and took a pull on his Shiner Bock. He was close enough to touch, and she clenched her hands into fists just in case her fingers suddenly decided to act out her secret fantasies. He didn't even look her way, and he probably wouldn't unless he felt the need to toss an insult at her.

"How was Antigua?" Cal asked, directing the question to his sister and her new husband, Nick Priest.

"It was the most amazing place I've ever been," Teagan said, her blue eyes shining and her glossy lips turned up in a smile.

Teagan and Nick had just returned from their three-week honeymoon to the Caribbean island. Both of them were glowing from their tans and their newlywed status.

"We were lucky we had our own private beach because Nick is apparently an exhibitionist," Teagan added with a lustful gleam in her eyes.

Nick was a former professional football player, and he had been voted one of the "Sexiest Men Alive" by *People* magazine. With his blond hair and bright green eyes, he was gorgeous, no doubt about it. But in Bebe's opinion, he wasn't nearly as gorgeous as Cal.

No one is as gorgeous as Cal.

Nick leaned down and whispered something into Teagan's ear, something that was obviously naughty because her face turned the color of cherries. When he straightened to his full six-five and saw her red cheeks, he chuckled.

"You're so bad," Teagan muttered, lightly slapping Nick's chest. In response, he grabbed her hand, hauled her up against him, and kissed her . . . with tongue.

Cal made a gagging noise. "Jesus Christ," he groaned, "do you have to do that in front of me?"

Teagan pulled away from Nick. "*Please*," she shot back, her voice full of disgust. "Do know how many times I had to listen to my high school friends talk about you and your big—"

Much to Bebe's disappointment, Cal covered his sister's mouth with his hand and cut off the rest of Teagan's sentence. She tried to pull his fingers away, and finally she got free by elbowing him in the stomach.

Laughing, Cal stumbled sideways into Bebe, almost knocking her over. He grabbed her forearm to steady her, his hand hot against her skin, and she gasped. Even the slightest touch from him made her pulse pound, and she tugged her arm to get away from him.

Instead of releasing her, his fingers tightened. She looked up . . . way up. He was almost as tall as Nick, and he loomed over her by more than a foot. He was a little leaner than Teagan's husband but still solid muscle. His faded Giants T-shirt showed off his broad shoulders, impressive biceps, and ropy forearms. He'd paired the shirt with ancient Rileys that fit him like a glove and well-worn boots.

"Sorry about that, Cookie," Cal apologized offhandedly.

"I told you not to call me that," she snapped, trying to jerk her arm free.

She *hated* it when he called her Cookie, and he knew it. Of course, that was why he did it.

He had come up with the nickname right after he'd found out she had a medical degree in addition to her MBA and law degree. He'd claimed it was a better moniker than Bebe, since she was such a smart cookie, but she knew it wasn't a compliment.

"I thought you liked nicknames." He smiled angelically and widened his eyes to look innocent. "You call Teagan *kanya* all the time."

Kanya was Bebe's nickname for her best friend. It meant "girl" in Hindi, the native language of her Indian ancestors. She had been born and raised in the United States, but using Hindi words was one way she stayed connected to her heritage.

"Teagan and I are *friends*," she pointed out.

He got her message loud and clear because his eyes got all squinty. "I can be friendly."

Yes, he could be friendly. In fact, he was friendly to *everyone* but her. He never had anything nice to say to her, and she returned the sentiment.

She wasn't sure who had struck first, probably her, but now they launched verbal missiles at each other with frequency and precision. He went out of his way to be rude and antagonistic, and she did the same.

Bebe knew the real reason she acted like such a bitch around Cal. She liked him, and she didn't want him to suspect how she really felt. She didn't want to be the pathetic geeky girl with a crush on the hot guy.

Before Cal, she had never been attracted to any man. She'd never even experienced a high school crush because she had entered the ninth grade when she was twelve and had graduated when she was fifteen. She had immediately headed off to college, and she'd obtained two bachelor's degrees in three years.

By the time she had been able to vote, she had been in her first year of medical school. She'd become accustomed to being viewed as a study partner rather than a sex partner.

She wasn't oblivious, though, and over the years, she had noticed good-looking men. But she had never felt that zing of sexual attraction until she had met Cal four years ago. She hated the way he made her feel: gauche, nervous, and overstimulated. When he was near, sounds were louder, colors were brighter, and smells were stronger.

Right now, she could smell him, a panty-soaking aroma of warm male and expensive cologne. It was so delicious, she could barely concentrate on the conversation swirling around her.

"Even though Antigua was amazing, I'm glad to be home," Teagan said, ignoring Cal and Bebe's sniping. "I missed everyone. Mom and Dad. Quinn and Amelia. Bebe. Letty."

"You didn't miss me?" Cal asked, feigning hurt feelings.

Bebe knew Teagan had intentionally excluded Cal, trying to annoy him. The O'Brien siblings teased one another mercilessly. Their relationship was so different from the one Bebe had with her older brothers.

She rarely talked with Pritam and Ranjit, and when she did, they definitely didn't tease her. They didn't even call her Bebe. They insisted on referring to her by her full name, Bindu, which she hated.

"No. I missed Kim more than I missed you," Teagan replied, referring to the woman who did her nails at the swanky spa she frequented.

Teagan's snarky response made laughter well in Bebe's throat. Before she could choke them back, giggles escaped her. Cal stiffened next to her, and she mentally prepared for their next verbal battle.

Ready. Aim. Fire.

CAL TRIED TO IGNORE BEBE'S SOFT LAUGHTER, BUT THE MUSIcal sound washed over him, and his cock twitched. He shifted away from her, annoyed with his unruly body.

Bebe didn't bother to hide the fact that she couldn't stand him. She was pretty much the only woman who *didn't* like him, and he didn't know what he'd done to make her hate him.

He had told himself a million times he didn't care, but he was lying. It bothered him . . . *a lot*. It bothered him so much that he acted like an asshole anytime he got within fifty feet of her.

Cal slanted a sideways glance toward Bebe, who was staring at her feet. Her shiny hair, the same color as his favorite dark roast coffee, was in its usual bun. He had never seen it any other way, and he'd spent more than a few minutes thinking about what it would look like down around her shoulders. He had imagined holding it in his hands while she knelt in front of him.

A few wispy tendrils clung to the nape of her neck, and he wondered if they were as soft and silky as they looked. Everything about her looked soft and silky, from her smooth, golden skin to her full, pink lips.

He felt Teagan's gaze on him, and he pulled his attention from Bebe's lips. His little sister was way too observant, and he had a feeling she knew exactly why he was rude to her best friend.

"Nick and I have decided to throw a Halloween party to show off the house," Teagan announced.

After Priest had retired from the NFL at the end of last season, he'd taken a job with Riley O'Brien & Co. and moved to the Bay Area. He'd bought a historic mansion in Pacific Heights, and the two-story Italianate-Victorian had been under renovation for months.

Cal was surprised Priest had agreed to host a party, since he tended to avoid situations where he was expected to talk. He went to great lengths to hide his severe stutter, and most people didn't even know he had a speech impediment.

Teagan leaned against Priest, and he pulled her closer, squeezing her waist. Suddenly Cal realized why they were throwing a party: his new brother-in-law would do anything Teagan asked.

"Costumes will be mandatory," Teagan added. "I think Nick should be a Greek god."

Priest groaned dramatically, and Cal chuckled, imagining the other man in a white bedsheet. "Which one?"

"Zeus," Teagan answered promptly. "The king of the gods."

Cal took a swig of his Shiner Bock, and as he lowered his arm, his hand accidently brushed against Bebe. She jerked away from his touch, and irritation rushed through him. She acted like he was a fucking leper, and it pissed him off.

What the hell is her problem?

"I bet I can guess what you're going to be," he said, pointing his beer toward her.

Since she was looking down, she didn't realize he was talking to her. He tapped her on the shoulder with the neck of the bottle, and she jerked her head up.

Her eyes were the same color as the gold that his Grandma Violet's ancestor had found during the California Gold Rush, luminous and ringed with long, dark eyelashes. She blinked slowly and licked her lips, leaving them shiny and wet.

He gritted his teeth as his cock thickened behind his fly. What was it about her that made him so hot?

"Did you hear me?" he asked, his voice nearly a growl.

She shook her head, and he repeated what he'd said. She frowned.

"Oh, really?" she snarked. "What am I going to be?"

He bared his teeth in a semblance of a smile. "Since you're so smart, I figured you'd go as a dictionary." He snapped his fingers. "Or maybe an encyclopedia, since you think you know everything."

Priest gave a muffled laugh, and Cal met his eyes. The other man raised his dark blond eyebrows, and Cal flushed. He just couldn't seem to stop himself from acting like a jerk.

"That's a good idea." Bebe smiled brightly, but there was an edge of anger behind it. "I have a suggestion for your costume, too. Since you're such a jackass, why don't you go as a donkey?"

It took him a second to process the insult because he was fascinated by the emotions swirling in Bebe's eyes. When he realized what she'd said, he couldn't help but laugh. He *was* a jackass when he was around her.

Teagan snorted. "Come on, Nick," she said, grabbing her husband's hand. "I'm tired of hearing my best friend and my brother hurl insults at each other. And I'm thirsty."

His sister stalked off, dragging Priest behind her. Bebe shifted to face him, and he took another swallow of beer, studying her as he did so.

She was so petite, the top of her head was even with his chest. She was even shorter than Quinn's wife, Amelia, who was a couple of inches over five feet.

He doubted Bebe weighed more than a hundred pounds soaking wet, but she was slender rather than skinny. In fact, her breasts looked like a nice handful under her orange Giants T-shirt. He wouldn't mind finding out if they would fill *his* hands.

She tucked a loose strand of dark hair behind her ear, and the movement drew his attention to her small hands. Thin gold rings covered every finger, wrapping around the slender digits like delicate metal vines.

She probably had a hundred rings on her fingers, and the sight of them glimmering in the sunlight mesmerized him. They made him think about what her hands would look like on his body, wrapped around his cock, stroking him to orgasm.

He let his gaze wander lower, lingering on her narrow waist and the subtle curve of her hips. She wore a pair of Rileys, and satisfaction trickled through him. He loved seeing his last name stamped on a nice ass, and he'd stared at Bebe's enough to know hers was more than nice.

The sound of Teagan's laughter filtered to him, and Cal

pulled his gaze from Bebe. He searched for his sister and found her across the room with her new husband. Priest was perched on the back of one of the leather club chairs, and Teagan stood between his legs. His hands clasped her hips, and a huge smile lit up her face.

Bebe looked over her shoulder, her gaze landing on the newlyweds. After a moment, she brought her attention back to Cal.

"I was worried that I'd never see her again," he admitted.

When Teagan had come back from Boston a few years ago, after completing her MBA and law degree at Harvard, she'd seemed like a completely different person. The funny, loving sister he had grown up with had turned into a sarcastic, angry woman. Cal hadn't known, but Teagan had been suffering from a broken heart. Now that she and Priest had worked things out, the sister he had adored was making a comeback.

Bebe tilted her head, her eyes intent on his face. She obviously understood exactly what he meant because she smiled slowly—a real smile—and his heart kicked in his chest.

"I was, too," she replied softly. "And I'm really glad she's back. I missed her."

Cal nodded. He had missed her, too.

They stared at each other, and he realized it was the first time he and Bebe had managed to have a conversation that didn't involve sly digs and over-the-top insults. He didn't want her to walk away, so he tossed out the first thing that came into his head.

"How's the new job going?" he asked.

"Great. It was a smart move for me."

Earlier this year, Bebe had taken a position at Generation Global Biotechnology, GGB for short. Its headquarters were located in downtown San Francisco, just a few blocks from Riley O'Brien & Co.'s high-rise.

When Bebe had lived in Boston, he'd seen her only a few times a year. He had always looked forward to her visits but had dreaded them, too. Each time, he'd hoped she would miraculously like him, and when it became obvious she didn't, he would provoke her just so she wouldn't ignore him.

Now that Bebe lived in San Francisco, he saw her all the time. Teagan invited her to most of the O'Brien family gatherings, and Bebe dropped by Riley Plaza to see his sister at least twice a week.

He knew he should stay away from her, but he always sought her out, whether they were at a barbeque, a baseball game, or Sunday brunch. And he always found a reason to stop by his sister's office when Bebe visited. He picked and poked and prodded until her golden eyes narrowed in anger and her sharp tongue slashed into him.

Deep inside, he knew the real reason he fucked with Bebe. He did it because he couldn't do what he really wanted to do: fuck her.

Chapter 2

IT WAS TIME FOR BEBE'S MONTHLY VIDEO CHAT WITH AKASH, SO she logged on to Skype and hit the Call button. Within seconds, her fiancé's face filled the computer screen.

"Good evening, Akash," she said, leaning back in the leather chair.

There was a twelve-and-a-half-hour time difference between San Francisco and Delhi, India, where Akash lived. They had scheduled their chats so Bebe could do them in the privacy of her loft before she headed to work.

"Good morning, Bindu. How are you?"

"Fine. Thank you for asking," she replied, trying not to show her annoyance that he persisted in calling her by her full name just like her family. "And you?"

"Quite well," he answered in his precise, formal English.

Even though they had been engaged for more than ten years, their conversations were stilted and uncomfortable. They weren't friends, and they definitely weren't lovers. They had never even kissed.

Their engagement had been arranged by their parents, and they'd both had their own reasons for agreeing to it. Arranged marriages were still relatively common in India, especially among the upper class.

Bebe's family had been connected to Akash's family for centuries, even though no Banerjee had ever married into the wealthy, powerful Mehra family. While the United States had the Kennedys, India had the Mehras. The family was not only politically active, but also involved in commerce, controlling everything from telecommunications and transportation to retail and real estate.

Bebe had been in her second year of medical school at Johns Hopkins University in Baltimore when her parents had suggested marriage to Akash. She had been desperate to gain their approval, and marrying one of the Mehra heirs hadn't seemed like too high a price to get it.

Akash was handsome, wealthy, and well-educated. He had attended Oxford and the London Business School, and he would eventually control Mehra's real estate holdings, which were scattered around the globe and worth billions of dollars.

While Bebe had chosen to become engaged to Akash, he'd been forced into it. In order to take his place within the family company, his parents had demanded that he accept the bride of their choice.

In addition to the connection their families shared, Akash's parents had been impressed with Bebe's intelligence. Moreover, they viewed her American upbringing as a plus, given the global nature of their business interests.

Akash leaned closer to the video camera, his darkly handsome face filling the screen. Despite his good looks, Bebe wasn't attracted to him, and she knew the feeling was mutual. In fact, she was pretty sure he found her unappealing in every way.

"In truth, Bindu, things are not quite well," he admitted with a loud sigh.

Since they rarely discussed anything personal, his comment surprised her. Their chats were purely obligatory so he didn't have to lie to his parents when they asked if he and Bebe had spoken recently.

"My parents are increasingly eager for us to marry," he continued. "Our engagement ceremony only made them more determined to see us wed. They want us to set a wedding date."

Akash's parents had become impatient with their son's long engagement, and he had been confident an engagement ceremony would appease them. At his request, she had flown to India in January and spent three long weeks pretending to be his adoring fiancée before participating in the traditional ceremony. It had been horrible.

After an awkward silence, Bebe finally responded, "I don't know what to say."

"We *must* marry, Bindu."

Akash's demand blasted from the computer speakers. She shook her head emphatically.

"No. That wasn't our agreement."

"I have changed my mind," he said flatly.

Bebe's breakfast of Greek yogurt and blueberries churned in her stomach, and she pressed her hand over it. Her pulse pounded in her ears, and she took several deep breaths in an effort to calm down.

For most of her life, she had tried to please her parents, but no matter how much academic success she'd achieved, it had never been enough. Her pathetic need for their approval was the sole reason she'd gone to medical school.

She had hoped that following in her parents' and brothers' footsteps would change the way they treated her. Her father was one of the foremost infectious disease experts in the world, and her mother was a well-known heart surgeon practicing at Johns Hopkins Hospital. Both of her brothers were physicians who boasted not only medical degrees but PhDs in their respective fields.

During Bebe's final year of medical school, she had realized she would never gain her parents' approval, no matter what she did. More important, she had realized they would never love her the way she wanted to be loved.

She'd had no real interest in being a physician, and a couple of months before she had graduated from Johns Hopkins, she had decided not to pursue her residency. Instead, she had applied to Harvard's joint JD/MBA program. She had missed the application deadline by a couple of weeks, and she had been surprised when she had been accepted.

Since pleasing her parents had been the only reason she'd agreed to marry Akash, she also decided to break off their engagement. When she'd called to tell him, he had been desperate and angry. He'd enjoyed having a fiancée who was more than seven thousand miles away because the engagement didn't interfere with his life, and his parents were content.

Akash had known Bebe's parents had cut her off financially, and he had proposed an alternate arrangement. He'd offered to pay her tuition and living expenses at Harvard if she would agree not to break their engagement.

At first, she hadn't been interested. She hadn't been willing to prostitute herself, not even for Harvard. But then Akash had explained that he didn't want to marry her, he just wanted to be engaged to her . . . a long-term engagement of convenience.

And then he'd sweetened the deal: she wouldn't have to pay back the money. She hadn't been able to walk away from his offer, especially since she hadn't been sure how she would pay for Harvard.

Outside of her family and Akash's family, no one knew about her engagement. She had kept it a secret from Teagan, as well as her colleagues. As far as they knew, she was single and unattached.

"You can't just change your mind," she protested, but Akash ignored her.

"I have told my parents that we must consult a swami to determine the most auspicious day for our wedding. That will buy us some time and allow you to make whatever arrangements necessary to move to Delhi."

"Akash, I am not going to marry you."

He slashed his hand in front of the screen. "We *will* marry. The only question is when."

"You can't make me marry you!"

Akash's eyes narrowed. "If you refuse, I must ask that you repay the money I loaned you."

Bebe's breakfast rose in her throat, and she swallowed to keep it down. Akash had been generous while she had attended Harvard. In total, he had deposited more than $600,000 into her bank account, and every single penny had been used to cover her tuition and living expenses while she attended school.

"It wasn't a loan. You gave me that money."

"I gave the money to my future wife." Akash smiled, and his large white teeth reminded her of a shark. "Either marry me or repay it."

"You know I don't have that kind of money."

Akash shook his head, clucking his tongue. "What a pity."

Fury rushed through Bebe, but she managed to control it. Akash had no leverage against her.

"I hate to repeat myself, but you can't force me to marry you *or* pay back the money. You would have a hard time proving it was a loan, since I never signed anything. And you definitely can't claim I stole it, since you deposited it directly into my bank account every month."

"You're right, of course. That law degree does come in handy, doesn't it?" He paused meaningfully. "Perhaps you'd be more comfortable if we handled this through legal channels. Perhaps a lawsuit for breach of contract?"

"Don't be ridiculous," she scoffed. "You don't want to be humiliated in an open court."

Akash cocked his head. "Are you aware that several members of your extended family are employed by Mehra or live in Mehra buildings? Your cousin Ashara, for example."

It took Bebe less than a second to understand exactly why he mentioned that fact, but she decided to play dumb. "Since Mehra is one of the biggest companies in India, that doesn't surprise me."

"Yes," he agreed, drawing out the word until it sounded like the hiss of a cobra. "Then it won't surprise you when they lose their jobs and their homes."

She wasn't close to anyone in her extended family, not even Ashara, but that didn't mean she didn't care about them. And she certainly didn't want to be responsible for ruining anyone's life—anyone's life except her own.

"Why should I care what happens to people I barely know?" she asked nonchalantly, hoping Akash wouldn't see through her bravado. "Are you forgetting that I grew up an ocean away from them? I wouldn't know them if they passed me on the street."

"Oh, come now, Bindu." He laughed boisterously. "I know you care about them simply because you're a decent person."

She stuck her face closer to the video camera. "You're blackmailing me into marrying you," she accused angrily.

"No, certainly not. You have a choice. Marry me or repay the money."

"Why are you doing this?" she asked desperately. "I know you don't really want to marry me."

"On the contrary. I *do* want to marry you. In fact, I can't wait for us to pledge our lives to one another."

Akash's voice was edged with just enough sarcasm to make his statement both insincere and condescending. His dark eyebrows were arched, his lips curled in a smirk.

Bebe's mind raced, trying to find a way out of her predicament. She needed time . . . time to either find the money or resign herself to marrying a man she barely knew.

"Okay. I will marry you on my thirty-fifth birthday *or* I will pay back all the money you gave me by that date. In exchange, you will agree not to fire, layoff, foreclose on, or evict anyone related to me by blood."

He laughed incredulously. "I cannot hold off my parents for another five years. We have already had an unusually long engagement."

"Three years."

He shook his head. "One year from today you will either marry me or pay back the money . . . with interest."

It was far more than she had hoped for, but she didn't let her relief show.

"I agree. And I want it in writing."

Akash narrowed his eyes. "No. This will be a verbal agreement."

"Like the agreement we made before—the one where you told me I never had to pay back the money? The one where you said we would never be husband and wife?" She laughed bitterly. "You're a liar, Akash."

He held up his hands in supplication. "I have been backed into a corner by my parents, and unfortunately, you are in that corner with me."

It was clearly his best effort at an apology. He clapped his hands, the action making a loud, cracking noise.

"I will notify my parents we have agreed on a date." She opened her mouth to protest, but he held up a hand. "We *have* agreed on a date, Bindu. They do not need to know the details."

She nodded in defeat, and he smiled brightly, obviously happy about the outcome of their chat. She, meanwhile, was fighting tears.

"I'm pleased we have come to an agreement. Have a pleasant day."

Akash's face disappeared from the screen, and Bebe slowly

closed her laptop before dropping her head onto the desk. The frosted glass was cool and smooth against her hot face, and she finally gave in to the overwhelming need to cry.

She had only three hundred and sixty-five days to come up with more than $600,000. Short of winning the lottery, robbing a bank, or dealing drugs, she could only think of one way to get that kind of money: Teagan. Her best friend was an heiress, and she had just married a multimillionaire.

Bebe gulped back tears. Maybe she was being stupid and prideful, but she hated the thought of asking Teagan for money. It wasn't as if she needed to borrow ten dollars to buy a Subway sandwich. She needed more than a half a million dollars, and it was doubtful she'd ever be able to pay it all back.

Yet the alternative was marrying Akash and being tied to him for the rest of her life.

Bebe squeezed her eyes shut, and tears trickled down her cheeks to pool on the desk. She didn't want to marry him. Even when she had initially agreed to the arranged marriage, she hadn't wanted to.

But she had wanted her parents to give her the same kind of love and attention they gave Pritam and Ranjit, and she had convinced herself that she could do a lot worse than Akash. There were probably a lot of women who would give anything to marry into the Mehra family. She just wasn't one of them.

Once she and Akash had agreed to their engagement of convenience, Bebe had pushed any and all thoughts of marriage out of her head. She had focused her energy on getting through Harvard, and once she had her diplomas in hand, she had dedicated herself to her career.

While other women worried about reaching the big 3-0 without finding a mate, Bebe had never been bothered by her lack of romantic relationships. Because her libido had been nonexistent, she hadn't been interested in dating or hooking up.

She could count on one hand the number of dates she'd been on. She had never gone shopping to find the perfect dress and shoes to dress up for a man, and she had never bought sexy lingerie with the intention of seducing one.

Not only was Bebe a virgin, but she had never even been kissed, and the thought of Akash being her first kiss—her first *everything*—made her want to fling herself off the Golden Gate Bridge.

Lifting her head from the desk, she wiped the tears from her eyes. She had three hundred and sixty-five days, and she was going to use every single one of them making sure Akash didn't get her firsts.

She would rather give them to someone else. *Anyone else.*

Chapter 3

THE MOUTHWATERING AROMA OF COFFEE AND FRESHLY BAKED pastries wafted to Cal the moment he opened the door to Sweet Nothings. It was his first visit to the new bakery, which was located a few blocks from his condo in the trendy Cow Hollow neighborhood.

An art gallery used to occupy the space, and while Cal appreciated art as much as the next guy, he appreciated baked goods a hell of a lot more. He had been excited when he'd heard about the bakery, and since he admired people who risked it all to open new businesses, he did his part to support them.

Cal eyed the recently renovated space. The shiny hardwood floors were the same, but the walls were painted a light, bright turquoise, and several black-and-white photos of historic San Francisco hung on the walls.

Glass display cases made an L-shape across the front and side of the room and overflowed with muffins, Danishes, and other assorted baked goods. White wrought-iron café tables and matching chairs filled the rest of the space, most of them occupied by customers.

Cal's gaze fell on a familiar face, and his chest got a little tight. His ex-girlfriend, Saika, sat at one of the tables enjoying a muffin, probably cranberry-orange since that was her favorite. He used to make them for her and her daughter for their weekly Sunday brunches.

He hadn't seen her since they'd broken up almost a year ago. He had gone out of his way not to run into her.

She looked up, and her dark, almond-shaped eyes widened when she saw him. Her lips, which were covered in light pink gloss, tipped up in a small smile.

"Cal," she exclaimed, surprise and pleasure evident in her voice.

Saika rose and moved toward him, giving Cal another shock. She was pregnant, several months, by the look of things. Her raspberry-colored dress clung to the swell of her belly and her breasts, which were fuller with pregnancy.

Reaching his side, Saika opened her arms and enveloped him in a big hug. With her heels, they were almost the same height, and her baby bump pressed into his stomach.

Almost by reflex, his arms closed around her and drew her close. He pulled in a lungful of her familiar fragrance, and for a brief moment, he was catapulted back to a time when he had been in love with her.

He and Saika had dated for a little more than a year. They'd met when he had taken a cooking class at her restaurant. She was one of the best chefs in the Bay Area, and he still wasn't sure what had caught his attention first, her sushi-making skills or her smile.

"Cal," she repeated softly before kissing his cheek.

She gave him a squeeze, and he let her go, just as he had a year ago. She laughed lightly.

"I'm so surprised to see you. Valerie is going to be heart-broken when I tell her that I ran into you. She misses you."

Cal's heart ached at the mention of Valerie. He had loved Saika's six-year-old daughter as if she had been his own flesh and blood, and it had hurt him to walk away from her. But it had been the right thing to do.

He cleared his throat. "I'm surprised to see you, too."

"We need to catch up. Why don't you grab a pastry and have breakfast with me," she suggested, tilting her head toward the display cases.

He nodded in agreement. He wanted to know how Valerie was doing . . . if she liked her new school, if Saika had gotten her the dog she had promised.

Cal quickly placed his order, and within moments, he had a chocolate croissant and a to-go coffee in his hands. He made his way to Saika's table and deposited his breakfast on top of it.

Pulling out one of the spindly chairs, he sat down, somehow managing to fold his long legs under the small table. Saika leaned forward and wrapped her hand around his.

"I'm so happy to see you, Cal. Valerie's not the only one who's missed you."

"It doesn't look like you missed me too much," he replied with a pointed look toward her belly.

Even though Saika was half-Japanese, she had fair skin, and just then, her cheeks flushed bright pink. She laughed self-consciously and smoothed her hand over her short, dark hair. A diamond-encrusted wedding band glinted on her ring finger. It was nice, but it wasn't as nice as the one he had planned to give her.

"You knew this would happen," she said.

He nodded and took a sip of his coffee, letting the rich flavor drench his taste buds. If he had to have this conversation, at least he had a strong Brazilian Arabica to get him through it.

The moment Saika's ex-husband had resigned his commission in the Navy, Cal had known his relationship with her had been doomed. Noble had been a SEAL, and his commitment to his job had been the main reason their marriage had failed. Saika hadn't been able to handle the soul-crushing fear of her husband's dangerous profession.

Noble had chosen the military over his family, and he and Saika had divorced when Valerie was a baby. It had taken him five years, but eventually he'd realized what an idiot he had been.

When Noble had moved to San Francisco to be closer to Valerie, Cal had seen the writing on the wall. Saika had never stopped loving her ex-husband, and Cal had known she never would stop loving him. More important, she hadn't loved Cal the way she had loved Noble.

"When's the baby due?"

She smiled and rubbed a hand over her bump. "He should be here around December seventeenth."

"So you're having a boy?"

"Yes. We're going to name him Judd after Noble's former commanding officer."

Cal took a big bite of his pastry. At one time, he had wanted to be the father of Saika's future children and to take care of her and Valerie.

"How's Valerie doing?"

Saika smiled. "She's great. She thinks she's a big girl now that she's in first grade and going to school all day instead of just a half day."

"And how is she with Noble?"

Noble had been an absent father for most of Valerie's life, and Cal wondered how the former SEAL had adapted to family life. He hoped the other man took her to the park, let her pick out his socks, and made pancakes with her—things she and Cal had done together.

"She adores him. He's really good with her. She's become a total daddy's girl."

He was relieved to hear that Noble had stepped up and become the father Valerie deserved. It was further proof that Cal had done the right thing.

Saika leaned her elbows on the table, and he studied her. Her eyes shone, and her skin glowed.

"You look happy, Saika."

"I am happy . . . happier than I've ever been. And I know you're partly responsible." She laid her hand on top of his. "Cal, I never thanked you for what you did . . . for ending things . . . for realizing that I . . ."

She stared at him for several moments before speaking again. "I'm sorry. I wanted to love you. I really did." She swallowed audibly. "I never would have broken up with you because you're a better man than he is." Her voice dropped to a whisper. "But he's the one. He always has been."

CAL'S MIND STILL BUZZED FROM HIS UNEXPECTED RUN-IN WITH Saika as he made his way to his office in Riley Plaza. Breaking up with her had been the hardest thing he had ever done, but he hadn't wanted to be with a woman who didn't love him as much as he loved her. It wouldn't have been fair to either one of them.

When he had stepped aside to clear the way for Noble, Cal had promised himself that he wouldn't waste time on what-ifs. He had accepted that he and Saika would never be together, and he had let time work its magic. He had moved on, although he obviously hadn't moved on as quickly or as completely as she had, since he wasn't married or expecting a child.

"Hey, Cal, come in here for a second."

Cal stopped abruptly at the sound of Quinn's voice. All the executive offices were grouped together, and he had to pass his brother's office to get to his. He backtracked a couple of steps to stand in the open doorway.

"What's up?" he asked.

Quinn was seated behind his big desk with his booted feet propped on the surface, and Priest was slouched in one of the leather chairs in front of the desk. His brother waved him into the office.

"Close the door."

Cal pulled the door shut behind him before sitting down in the chair next to Priest. He leaned back and crossed his ankle over his knee.

"What's up?" he repeated, raising his eyebrows and looking back and forth between them.

He and Quinn looked so much alike, it would be obvious to strangers that they were brothers. He was just a tad taller than Quinn, and his brother was a little broader in the shoulders. The big difference was the color of their eyes. Quinn's were dark blue, almost navy.

At thirty-four, Quinn was exactly eleven months and twenty-four days older than Cal. Since they were so close together in age, they had been practically inseparable growing up.

They were best friends by blood and by choice, and when Quinn had gone to college at the University of Southern California, Cal had followed a year later. During that year apart, Quinn had formed a close friendship with Priest.

Quinn and Priest had played football together at USC, and when Cal had arrived on campus, the three of them had become best friends. His mother called them The Three Musketeers, but Teagan said The Three Stooges was more apropos.

"Are you just now getting into work?" Quinn asked with a frown.

"Yeah."

It was only nine in the morning, but Cal usually started his workday before seven. He was a morning person, and he routinely rose well before dawn.

"Is everything okay?" Quinn asked.

"Yeah."

Priest shifted in his seat to look at Cal. "You missed our m-m-m-meeting this morning."

Shit. Running into Saika had messed with his head. It had totally slipped his mind that he was supposed to meet with Quinn and Priest to go over the museum project.

Before his Grandma Violet had died, she had set up an endowment to create a museum that celebrated the history of Riley O'Brien & Co. and the role it played during the California Gold Rush. Quinn had hired Priest to manage the project, and earlier this year his brother transferred supervisory responsibility from Teagan's group to Cal's department.

"I'm sorry. I forgot."

"You forgot?" Quinn echoed. "You never forget anything. What's going on, Cal?"

"I stopped by that new bakery I told you about, and I ran into Saika."

Quinn's dark blue eyes widened, and he dropped his feet to the floor. Leaning forward, he braced his elbows on the desk.

"And?" Quinn prodded.

"And just as I expected, she and Noble are back together. He liked it so he put a ring on it. And he did a little more than that . . . he knocked her up. She's due in December."

Quinn's mouth fell open, and Cal smiled at his brother's stunned expression. "Yeah, I was surprised, too. He didn't waste any time."

"Shit, Cal. I'm sorry," Quinn muttered.

Cal shrugged, and Priest nudged his knee into Cal's foot. "You n-n-n-need a distraction."

Shifting in his seat, Cal looked at Priest. "Is that how you got over Teagan?"

"I n-n-n-never got over your sister," Priest replied, shaking his tawny head. "I'll never *get* over her. That's w-w-w-why I married her."

"I know. But I'm over Saika."

"Really?" Quinn asked doubtfully.

"Yeah. I'm happy for her."

He wasn't lying. He was happy for Saika. But seeing her again had made him realize he hadn't filled the hole she and Valerie had left in his life.

Maybe Priest was right. Maybe he needed a distraction.

Quinn's phone buzzed, and he shot them an apologetic look. "Damn, I need to take this. Cal, we'll talk more later, okay?"

He shook his head. "I'm fine," he reiterated as he stood.

Priest rose and headed toward the door, and Cal followed him. Once they were in the hallway, he pulled out his phone and checked his schedule.

"I don't have time for our meeting right now. Do we need to reschedule or are we okay until the next one?"

"W-w-w-we're okay."

Cal nodded and held out his fist. Priest bumped it before slapping him on the back. "Distraction."

"Sex, sports, or spirits?"

"I'm a f-f-f-fan of all three," Priest replied before striding toward the double doors that separated the executive wing from the reception area.

Cal checked his phone again. He really needed to see if Teagan had reviewed the contracts he had sent over last week. He had a few minutes before his next meeting, so he headed toward her office. It was located at the end of the hall, and as he got closer, he could hear voices.

The door wasn't closed completely, and he was just about to knock when he heard Bebe's voice. He turned on his heel to head back to his office because he didn't think he had the emotional energy for a verbal duel but froze when one of her words floated to his ears.

"Virgin."

Flattening himself against the wall, he slid closer to the door and peeked through the crack. Bebe stood beside Teagan's desk, and his sister sat on top of it, her eyes intent on her best friend's face.

Cal edged closer and cocked his head so he could hear their conversation better. He ignored the angel on his shoulder warning him that he was going to hell for eavesdropping and gave in to the devil assuring him that this was worth hearing.

"It's unnatural!" Bebe exclaimed, throwing up her hands. "Do you know any other thirty-year-old virgins?"

Cal frowned. Who was a thirty-year-old virgin? And why was Bebe so upset about it?

"It's not unnatural," Teagan replied. "And it's probably more common than you think. A lot of women want their first time to be special, so they wait until they find the right guy."

"I don't care if my first time is special, and I don't care who the guy is! I just want to lose it! As soon as possible!"

Holy shit! Bebe is a virgin?

Cal shifted and used the tip of his finger to push open the door a little more. He didn't want to miss a word of what Bebe had to say.

"Why are you suddenly so determined to lose your virginity?" Teagan asked. "Did you just wake up and say to yourself, 'I don't want to belong to Club Virgin anymore'?"

Bebe made a growling noise, and damned if she didn't sound like a rabid dog. "Why am I even talking to you? You're having so much sex, I'm surprised you can even walk. And I'm never going to eat anything that's been made on your kitchen island, since you and Nick have sex there *all the time*!"

Cal winced. He definitely could have done without hearing that. And he agreed with Bebe. He wasn't going to eat anything prepared on Teagan's kitchen island, either.

"I always clean it with bleach afterwards," Teagan choked out between giggles.

"I've never even been kissed," Bebe wailed, and Teagan's laughter died in her throat.

"What?"

"I've never been kissed," Bebe repeated huskily.

Bebe had never been kissed? What the hell is wrong with all the guys on this planet?

Teagan stood and wrapped her arms around the shorter woman. "Oh, sweetie, it's okay."

"It's not okay," Bebe disagreed, her voice muffled against Teagan's shoulder.

Cal could tell she was crying, and he dropped his head back against the wall. Much to his surprise, he was overwhelmed with the urge to comfort her. He had no doubt he could have made her feel better.

Chapter 4

BEBE GAVE THE PUNCHING BAG ONE LAST KICK AND PULLED off her sparring gloves. Grabbing a towel, she wiped the sweat off her face before taking a long swallow from her water bottle.

Given how much she liked to punch and kick, you'd think she was a violent person. But she limited her aggression to training bags and sparring partners.

For the past ninety minutes, she had abused the bag in her building's fitness center. Usually she practiced her Muay Thai kickboxing at a facility a few blocks from her loft, but it was closed for renovations.

She had started training in the combat sport when she'd been an undergrad at Northwestern University, and after more than a dozen years of consistent practice, she was an expert. It was a good form of self-defense and cardio exercise, and it had the added benefit of calming her mind, too.

Her brain always seemed to be flipped to the "on" switch, and doing Muay Thai for an hour or two flipped the "off" switch. It definitely had been "on" since her discussions with Akash and Teagan yesterday morning.

She had been so upset after talking with her fiancé that she had rushed to Riley Plaza to see Teagan. She hadn't told her best friend about Akash's demands, and she had no plans to do so. It was her problem, not Teagan's. But she had wanted to enlist the other woman's help in crafting a strategy to lose her virginity.

As Bebe gathered her gloves, towel, and water bottle, she tried to think of ways to raise money to pay back Akash. Saving twenty bucks here and there by bringing her lunch to work wasn't going to get it done.

She replayed the conversation she'd had with her financial advisor earlier today. She had asked him to liquidate all her investments, including her 401(k). He'd been baffled by her request and had advised her against the move, pointing out the tax penalty she would incur. Of course, her advisor didn't know she'd suffer far worse than a tax penalty if she had to marry Akash.

Based on her estimates, she had enough money in savings and investments to pay back about thirty percent of what she owed him. She could make some extra money by taking on a few consulting gigs outside of work. Unfortunately, that wouldn't bring in more than a few thousand dollars. Still, it was worth a few phone calls, and she added that to her mental to-do list.

The amount she owed Akash was more than most people would make in a lifetime. And yet she had to come up with it in just twelve months.

What else could she do? She had to think of something.

Discouraged and disheartened, she headed to the elevator and stepped inside. Within seconds, she was on the twelfth floor, and she slowly made her way down the hall to her loft. Her legs and butt burned, and her arms were limp from her workout.

Once she was inside the loft, she deposited her equipment on the large recycled-glass bar that separated the huge living space from the kitchen. Leaning against it, she debated whether to shower or give in to her growling stomach and make a quick dinner.

Before she could decide, a sharp knock sounded at her door. She frowned, wondering who it could be. Her building had twenty-four-hour on-site concierge/security, and no one was allowed in unless they were on an approved visitor list or they called up.

Unfortunately, she was too short to use the peephole, so she had to hope the person on the other side of the door posed no threat. She opened it just a crack and stared in disbelief at the vision of hotness in front of her. She must have worked out too hard because now she was hallucinating.

"Hi," Cal said, his lips tipped up in a small smile.

When she didn't respond to his greeting, his smile widened. He leaned closer until his face filled the space between the door and the frame.

"May I come in?"

Gathering her wits, she opened the door and waved him in. As he passed her, his delicious scent wrapped around her, and she caught herself drooling.

She closed the door and followed Cal into the living area. He turned to face her, his gaze moving leisurely up and down her body. His light blue eyes narrowed, and she belatedly realized she still wore her workout clothes.

She never dressed in formfitting or tight clothes outside of the gym, and it made her uncomfortable to have so much of her body on display, especially to Cal. Her tight, red racerback tank top was soaked with sweat and plastered to her upper body, and her black exercise pants were equally tight and sweaty. A lame black sweatband around her forehead was the pièce de résistance.

She looked awful, and she probably smelled worse than she looked. She fervently wished she had showered and changed in the fitness center because it would have saved her a lot of embarrassment.

She casually walked toward the bar and moved behind it. Thankfully, her new position put about fifteen feet between them and shielded her from his assessing gaze.

Cal cocked his head before turning in a slow circle. When he had completed the turn, he met her eyes.

"I haven't been here for months. Not since Teagan moved out."

When Teagan had moved in with Nick, she'd suggested that Bebe lease her vacant condo. It'd worked out perfectly because Bebe's short-term lease had been ending.

Teagan had been nice enough to set the rent below market. Otherwise, Bebe never would be able to afford a place so spacious and luxurious, despite her generous salary.

Located in the trendy SoMa neighborhood in downtown, the loft was only a few years old. It mixed industrial with traditional, and original hardwood floors contrasted with brick walls and exposed ductwork.

"Do you like living here?"

"Yes," Bebe answered, wondering why Cal stood in her living room making small talk. "How did you get past security?"

He smiled, showing off his white teeth and kissable lips. "I'm on the list, Cookie. If you don't want me to be able to stop by anytime I feel like it, you need to put a big line through Callum James O'Brien."

"I'll take care of it tomorrow."

He laughed. "Maybe you'll leave me on the list once you know why I'm here."

"Why *are* you here?"

Instead of answering her, Cal propped his butt on the back of her putty-colored Pottery Barn twill sofa and crossed his arms over his chest. The movement pulled his button-down shirt tight over his biceps. He'd left it untucked and rolled up the sleeves, and she tried not to stare at his forearms, which were dusted with dark hair.

The muted blue-and-green-plaid pattern of his shirt coordinated with his dark indigo wash Rileys. He crossed his ankles, and she noticed he wore the same pair of brown leather boots he'd worn at the baseball game.

How could he look so sexy in such a normal, everyday outfit? She had no doubt he'd look even more gorgeous in a suit . . . his birthday suit.

"If we were at my place, I'd offer you a drink," Cal suggested without any subtlety.

She huffed in annoyance to hide how awkward she felt. *Why is he here?*

"I don't think unwelcome and unexpected guests should be treated the same as those who are welcome and expected."

His dark eyebrows arched, and his lips twitched. "So I'm not only unexpected, I'm also unwelcome?"

She sighed gustily. "Would you care for a drink, Cal?"

With a smile, he sauntered over to the bar. He was so tall, he didn't have to do more than move sideways to slide his butt onto the barstool. She needed a pole vault to get onto it.

"I'll take a beer if you have one."

"Sorry. I have some wine coolers, though."

He shuddered. "God, no. I'd rather drink anything but a wine cooler."

Turning toward the refrigerator, she pulled out two individual cartons of Horizon Organic chocolate milk and placed one on the bar in front of him. As she removed the straw from the side of her carton, he picked up his and read the front of it.

"You said anything," she reminded him.

He looked up, and his eyes made her think of water swirling under the polar ice caps—a light, pure blue with a ring of indigo around the edges. The combination of his glacier-blue eyes and his dark hair was striking.

"There's nothing better than a little chocolate milk to take the edge off," he said, raising his carton as if it were a bottle of beer.

She laughed and pushed the straw through the top of her carton. Taking a sip, she watched as he deftly unwrapped his straw and poked it through the carton. He had big hands and long fingers, and she briefly wondered how they would feel on her body.

"How's your week so far?" he inquired before taking a drink of his chocolate milk.

It had been one of the worst she could remember, but she wasn't going to tell him that. "Good."

He studied her for a moment, and she wondered what he was thinking. It was hard to tell because he always had a little smile playing around his lips and an amused glint in his eyes. His words were the only real clue, and even then, his delivery was often misleading.

"You had a bad day yesterday."

She frowned. "How do you know?"

"I overheard your conversation with Teagan."

It took her a moment to comprehend what he'd said, and when she did, all the blood rushed from her head and the floor seemed to tilt under her feet. Gripping the edge of the counter to steady herself, she pulled in a deep breath. There was no reason to overreact. Maybe he hadn't heard *everything*.

"How did you manage to 'overhear' our conversation?"

"The door wasn't closed all the way."

"It's not polite to eavesdrop. You should have walked away."

"If I had done that, I would have missed out on a *very* interesting conversation."

"It was a private conversation."

He smiled slowly. "I know . . . a private conversation about your privates."

Oh, my God.

She'd thought this week couldn't get any worse, but she had been wrong. She obviously had done something to anger the gods.

Pushing away from the counter, she pointed toward the front door. "Get out."

He ignored her, taking a big pull of chocolate milk. As he stared at her over the top of the carton, she gave him her meanest glare.

"Get out," she repeated.

"I've been thinking about your unique situation, and I'd like to participate in your de-virginization plan."

Mortification washed over her, and she decided to lock herself in the bathroom until he left. She rounded the bar, and he grabbed her forearm as she passed, pulling her to a stop. Since he was seated, they were almost eye level.

"You told Teagan you wanted to lose your virginity as soon as possible. I can help you with that."

Cal's offer was both intriguing and surprising. She had assumed he just wanted to make fun of her.

"Do you want to set me up with one of your friends?"

His fingers tightened on her arm. "*Hell, no*, I don't want to set you up with one of my friends."

"Then how can you help?"

He stared at her for a long moment before laughing softly. The deep sound thrummed through her body, and he pulled her closer until only a few inches separated them.

"Losing your virginity requires a penis, and I just happen to have one."

She digested his statement. Was he suggesting what she thought he was? Surely not.

"I don't understand."

"You're the smartest person I know, and you don't understand what I'm saying?" He sighed loudly, clearly exasperated. "I'm offering to relieve you of the heavy burden of your virginity."

She gasped. "Are you serious?"

He nodded, and she shook her head in disbelief. She jerked her arm, trying to loosen his grip, and he slowly let her go.

"That's crazy!" she burst out, barely resisting the urge to rub her hand over her forearm, where she still felt the imprint of his fingers. "Why would you do that?"

"What would you say if I told you that I've wanted you since the first moment I saw you?"

Cal's question surprised her so much, her mouth fell open. She tried to shut it, but it fell open again like a hungry guppy's. His lips quirked into a smile, and she knew he was teasing her.

"Yeah, right," she scoffed. "You saw me, and you were overcome with lust. You just had to have me."

The thought of Cal feeling anything but mild irritation toward her was so ludicrous, she started to giggle. Her giggles turned into guffaws, and she laughed until she was breathless and her stomach ached. Finally, she got herself under control and wiped tears of mirth from her eyes.

The whole time she had laughed like a loon, Cal had calmly sipped his chocolate milk. He arched an eyebrow when she took a deep breath.

"Thanks for the laugh. I needed that."

He nodded. "Laughter is good for releasing tension. You know what else works? Sex."

"That's what I've heard."

"Maybe you'd like a demonstration."

"I don't think so."

He cocked his head. "Why not?"

"Cal, why are you here?"

"I already told you. I want to participate in your de-virginization plan."

"Would you stop calling it that?"

"What should I call it? Cherry picking?"

Blood rushed to her face, and apparently her skin wasn't dark enough that Cal couldn't see her blush. He chuckled.

"We could have a lot of fun, Bebe."

"You could have a lot of fun with any woman," she shot back. "So why don't you tell me why you're really here."

He sighed. "I ran into my ex-girlfriend yesterday morning." He rubbed the top of his head, making his short hair stick up in a couple of spots. "Has Teagan mentioned anything about Saika?"

Bebe shook her head. She and Teagan rarely talked about Cal because Bebe always changed the subject. She didn't want to feed her obsession.

"This is the first time I've wished that my sister and her friends talked about me behind my back," he muttered, tapping his fingers on the bar. "Okay, I'm not going to go into details. You just need to know that I could use a little help moving on. I need a distraction. And I think you'd be a good one."

"A distraction? You think taking my virginity would be a good distraction?"

"No. I think *you* would be a good distraction."

He was serious. She couldn't believe it. And she didn't need a single second to think about her answer.

"I'm not interested, Cal."

He shifted on the barstool until his legs bracketed her body. She tried to step back, but he loosely wrapped his arms around her. She had never been this close to him before, and she wished he would respect her personal space. His skin was too warm, his arms too hard, his mouth too sexy . . .

"Why not?"

There were so many reasons, but she wasn't going to give him even one.

"I'm not interested," she repeated.

"You told Teagan you didn't care who the guy was," he reminded her.

She opened her mouth to reply, but he stopped her. "You don't have to like me to have sex with me." He smiled. "Sometimes that's the best kind."

"I'm not interested," she repeated more emphatically.

She liked him *too* much to have sex with him. *Way too much.*

His eyes narrowed before he flashed a smile. "Okay."

Cal loosened his arms, and she quickly stepped away from him. As he slid from the barstool, she hurried to the front door. She wanted to get him out of her loft *now*.

When she reached the door, she turned to face him. He was closer than she'd thought, and she backed up until she hit the hard surface.

"Thanks for coming by." She looked up into his face. "Don't do it again."

With a smile, he brushed his thumb over her lower lip. It was slightly rough, and she tried not to think about how his fingers would feel on her breasts and between her legs.

"Good-bye," she hinted.

He moved closer until they touched from chest to thigh, and she flattened her palms against the door to keep from grabbing his butt. She hoped he wouldn't notice her hard nipples pressing against the front of her tight tank top. Wrapping his hand around the back of her neck, he leaned down until they were face-to-face.

"Why aren't you leaving?" she asked breathlessly. "Is there something else you wanted to discuss?"

"Just this," he answered before settling his mouth on hers.

She froze at the touch of his lips. Her first kiss.

Finally.

She let her eyes drift closed so she could savor the feel of his lips. They were much softer than she had imagined. She sighed as warmth spread through her, just like a spring day after a long, hard winter.

Cupping her face in his hands, he tilted her head so he could cover her mouth more completely. He sucked lightly on her lower lip, and her blood started to rush through her veins, creating little pinpricks of sensation.

He flicked the corner of her mouth with his tongue before trailing it along her bottom lip. She let her lips fall open, and he eased his tongue inside, gently stroking the sides of her mouth before touching it to hers.

With each slide of his tongue, she got a little hint of chocolate and something else. Something rich and decadent. She had never tasted anything so scrumptious, and she wanted more.

More Cal.

He kissed her, slow and deep, and when she twined her tongue around his, he groaned against her mouth. He gripped her face tighter, and she slid her hands under his shirt and hooked her fingers into the waistband of his Rileys to anchor herself. He sucked her tongue into his mouth, and she felt the wet slide between her legs where her pulse throbbed.

Dropping his hands from her face, Cal palmed her behind. His big hands curved around her butt cheeks, and he pulled her up until the V of her thighs cradled his zipper. Lights sparked behind her eyelids as he ground his erection into her, and she jerked her mouth from his.

They were both breathing heavily, nearly panting, and they stared at each other for several moments before he loosened his hold. She slid down his body, her knees almost buckling when she touched the ground.

She clutched his waist, and he leaned his forehead against the door above her head. His body caged her in, but instead of feeling trapped, she wished she could crawl inside him.

After a few moments, Cal gripped her waist, lifting her away from the door. As he opened it, he looked over his shoulder.

"*That's* why I came here," he stated flatly before walking out and shutting the door with a loud snap.

Chapter 5

BAD DECISIONS TENDED TO LEAVE THEIR MARK ON BEBE. WHEN she had been six years old and learning to ride a bike, she had insisted that her nanny remove her training wheels after only a few trips down the sidewalk.

The nanny had given in to her bratty demands, and Bebe had ended up with a busted lip, a sprained wrist, and a skinned knee. The scar on her knee served as a constant reminder of what happened when she thought she was ready for something but really wasn't.

Everyone always said sex was like riding a bicycle, and if that was the case, Bebe didn't want to take off the training wheels too soon. She needed to start slowly.

A loud ding signaled the elevator's arrival, and Bebe shuffled toward it along with a dozen other people who had been waiting. They crammed themselves into the cab, and she ended up with her nose just inches away from some guy's armpit. Luckily, he was a fan of both bathing and deodorant.

GGB's global headquarters filled a seventy-five-story tower in downtown San Francisco. As a member of the company's executive team, Bebe had an office on the top floor of the building, and she probably would be the last person off the elevator.

As the elevator ascended, stopping on nearly every floor, she assured herself that declining Cal's offer was a good decision. If she was as smart as he thought she was, she should know he was too advanced for her.

Having sex with Cal would be like learning to ride a bike on a thirty-one speed. She didn't even want to think about the scars she would get if she rode him—figuratively speaking, of course. If she truly disliked him, she wouldn't be worried about getting hurt. That dislike would protect her, like a heavy-duty helmet and pads.

When Bebe had met Cal four years ago, she'd known instinctively that he was trouble. While she and Teagan had attended Harvard, Teagan talked about her family all the time, and Bebe had seen pictures of the hot O'Brien brothers.

But Bebe never could have guessed Cal would awaken her dormant libido. The first time she'd flown to Northern California to visit Teagan after they'd graduated from Harvard, her best friend had brought her to a family barbeque. Bebe had already met Teagan's parents when they'd visited their daughter in Boston, and she'd been excited to get to know Quinn and Cal.

When Quinn had arrived and Teagan had introduced them, he'd hugged Bebe. He had been even better-looking in person, and she suddenly understood why Teagan had said all her high school friends had drooled over her brothers.

And then Cal had walked in with a huge smile on his handsome face. He'd picked up his mom by the waist and spun her around before hugging his dad. Then he'd punched Quinn on the shoulder and tapped Teagan on the nose.

Finally, he'd turned his attention to Bebe. When he'd taken her hand in his, sexual energy had shot through her entire body. The feeling was so alien, so discomfiting, she'd scowled and tried to jerk her hand away. His icy blue eyes had narrowed, and his grip had tightened on her fingers before he'd let go.

He'd been too much for her to handle then, and he definitely was too much for her to handle now. She needed to find a guy who was the equivalent of a single-speed bicycle with training wheels.

Too bad the local sporting goods store stocks bikes instead of men.

Finally the elevator emptied enough for Bebe to punch the

button for her floor. When the doors opened, she made a bee-line for Pamela Piperato's office. The older woman headed up GGB's human resources department, and Bebe wanted to ask her about the company's employee fraternization policy.

Pam's assistant wasn't at her desk, but the door to Pam's office was open, so Bebe peeked in and knocked lightly on the door frame to get her attention. When Pam saw her, she smiled and waved her in.

"Good morning, SVP IR."

Bebe smiled at Pam's greeting. The older woman liked to refer to people by their job titles, and she often introduced herself as SVP HR.

"Do you have a few minutes to talk?"

Pam's auburn eyebrows rose a little. "Sure."

Bebe closed the door and dropped her bag on one of the upholstered chairs in front of Pam's desk before sitting in the other one. She linked her hands together in her lap to prevent herself from twisting her rings. It was a nervous habit, and she was trying to stop.

"Is this business or personal?" Pam asked.

Even though Pam was more than twenty-five years older than Bebe, they were friends. Pam wasn't as private as Bebe, so she knew Pam's husband suffered from erectile dysfunction, her son was dating a skanky waitress from Sacramento, and her daughter was flunking chemistry and philosophy at UC-Berkeley.

"A little bit of both."

Pam's brown eyes widened. "Did Lars grab your ass?"

Bebe laughed at Pam's ludicrous question. As GGB's CFO and Bebe's boss, Lars Endicott was so focused on business, he probably didn't even recognize she was female.

"Lars wouldn't grab my ass unless it was covered in one-hundred-dollar bills. I wanted to ask you about dating co-workers."

"Is someone in your department getting busy on the copy machine? Did someone in accounting subtract one from seventy?"

Bebe stared at Pam, completely baffled. "What?"

"You know," Pam said, waggling her eyebrows. "Sixty-nine."

"You're ridiculous," Bebe replied, shaking her head in exasperation.

Pam laughed. "What's your question?"

"I'd like to start dating now that I've been here a few months, and I wanted to know what you thought about me getting involved with someone from work."

"GGB's official position is that romantic relationships between co-workers are fine as long as they're not between managers and subordinates," Pam answered promptly. "That's the *official* position. The unofficial position is that anyone who wants to keep his or her job shouldn't double-dip."

Pam's answer was more or less what Bebe had expected. Big companies like GGB were never as progressive in real life as they looked on paper.

"The situation is even stickier for you since you're a member of the executive team," Pam continued with a grimace. "Any man you would date would not be of equal standing. You would have the ability to influence his career, positively or negatively."

Bebe was the youngest person on GGB's executive team by at least fifteen years, and she and Pam were the only women. When Lars had offered her the job, she'd been shocked. She had beaten out candidates who were twice her age—candidates who'd possessed far more experience.

But Lars was impressed with all the letters after her name: MD, MBA, JD. And her undergraduate degrees in biochemistry and molecular biology also helped, since they gave her a better understanding of GGB's research.

"Did someone ask you out?"

"No."

"Do you have your eye on someone?"

There were a couple of guys in the IT department who seemed like they'd be Bebe's speed—kind of geeky and awkward—and she had thought about asking one of them out for drinks. There was also a guy in payroll who had helped her when she'd had trouble with her direct deposit. He was really nice, and she had considered inviting him to lunch.

"No, it was just a thought," she fibbed.

Since she didn't want to endanger her job or anyone else's, she mentally crossed co-workers off her list. The only other place where she spent any significant time was her Muay Thai kickboxing facility. A lot of single guys exercised there, but it wouldn't reopen for three more weeks.

In the meantime, she could sign up for a couple of online dating sites. The thought filled her with dread because she doubted her profile would generate any attention. Even if it attracted hundreds of men, there was a big problem: she was bad on first dates.

Unbelievably bad.

In fact, she had never moved past a first date to enjoy a second. If her track record held, she'd have to sleep with her date within thirty minutes of meeting him to get any action.

Maybe she should save herself the effort and just go to a bar and pick up a man. That might be a better solution. It worked for other women, so why not her?

She wondered how difficult it would be to find a guy interested in a one-night stand. Wasn't every male interested in no-strings-attached sex?

They'd have to go to a hotel because there was no way she would bring a strange man back to her loft. What if he robbed her while she slept or turned into a creepy stalker?

Going to his place would be too dangerous. He might be a sadist or a serial killer. Bebe shuddered. She didn't want to end up on the eleven o'clock news. She could hear the promo teaser now: "Local woman murdered in quest to lose virginity."

And she had to worry not only about death, but also about disease. Since her dad was an infectious disease specialist, she'd heard way too many horror stories over the dining room table involving sexually transmitted infections. She had been subjected to graphic discussions about syphilis while eating spaghetti.

Losing her virginity might be more complicated than she had anticipated. She gave herself a mental slap. Of course it was going to be complicated. If it had been easy, she wouldn't still be a virgin.

"I could check with Nathan," Pam offered. "He might have some single friends. Maybe I could set you up on a blind date or two."

Pam was a sweetheart, but her son sounded like a lazy jerk. His friends were probably lazy jerks, too. Bebe didn't want to lose her virginity to a lazy jerk. He might expect her to do all the work.

She'd told Teagan that she didn't care if her first time was special, but she didn't want it to be a horrible experience, either. Was it too much to ask for a man who was disease-free, good in bed, and lacking murderous tendencies?

Bebe shook her head. "I appreciate the offer, but I'm going to pass." She rose. "I should let you get back to work."

"Let me know if you change your mind about the blind dates."

"I will," she promised as she grabbed her bag. "Thanks, Pam."

Bebe made her way to her office, waving to her assistant as she passed Tara's desk. The younger woman was on the phone, and she cupped her hand over the receiver to say, "Lars wanted to go over the third quarter numbers this morning, so I pushed back your eleven o'clock to fit him in."

Nodding her thanks, Bebe entered her office. After dropping her bag in her leather office chair, she took a moment to enjoy the view through the floor-to-ceiling windows.

She had lived in several big cities—Baltimore, Boston, Chicago—but she liked San Francisco the best. It felt more like home than anywhere else, and she knew a lot of it had to do with Teagan. Being close to her best friend was one of the main reasons she had taken the job at GGB.

Although she had been on the fast track to the CFO position at her previous company, she'd been all work and no play. When a recruiter had approached her about the investor relations position at GGB, she'd jumped at the chance to interview.

Joining GGB had been a good decision. She really liked her job, and she was much happier now that she lived in the same city as Teagan.

Leaning her head against the glass, Bebe studied the San Francisco skyline. More than seven million people lived in the Bay Area, and there had to be at least one guy out there who met her criteria—someone other than Cal.

Of course, she assumed he met her criteria. She was fairly confident he wasn't a serial killer, but she had no way of knowing if he was disease-free or good in bed.

She touched her fingers to her lips. If his kiss was an accurate representation of his skills in bed, he was more than good—he was exceptional.

He'd obviously had plenty of experience, and she had no doubt women threw themselves at him wherever he went. In fact, if sex were an Olympic sport, he wouldn't be allowed to compete because he wasn't an amateur. She, meanwhile, hadn't even started training.

Why would Cal want to have sex with her? She was baffled by the thought. He'd said he needed a distraction and thought she would be a good one. She wasn't sure if she considered that a compliment or an insult.

A bigger question was why he'd kissed her. Thanks to his big ears and lack of manners, he'd known that she had never been kissed. Had he felt sorry for her? She'd heard of pity fucks. Had Cal given her a pity kiss?

She cringed at the thought. She definitely preferred being a distraction rather than an object of pity. He'd had an erection, so he must have enjoyed their kiss, at least a little bit. Of course, the male body responded instinctively to sexual stimuli, so it might have had nothing to do with *her*, specifically.

He didn't even like her. Or did he?

For a moment, she considered the possibility that he might have actually meant what he'd said last night. His words echoed in her memory: *What would you say if I told you that I've wanted you since the first moment I saw you?*

She scoffed at herself. Cal wasn't an insecure guy who'd never been kissed. He had an abundance of confidence when it came to women. If he had been interested in her, he would have kissed her years ago.

Her heart fluttered a little when she thought about her first kiss. She had no basis for comparison, but she'd thought it was pretty amazing.

Would sex with Cal be just as amazing?

Chapter 6

IT WAS A PERFECT DAY FOR A COOKOUT. THE TEMPERATURE WAS in the low seventies, the sky was blue, and there was a light breeze. Cal leaned back in the deck chair and crossed his ankle over his knee before tilting back his baseball cap so he could feel the sun on his face.

A couple of times a month, his parents invited friends and family to their sprawling house in St. Francis Wood for food and fun. There was a pretty big crowd today, probably forty people or so, and the large, multilevel redwood deck was packed.

Most of the guests were grouped around the big patio table where the food was located. Today, they were having hamburgers and brats, and his dad was manning the grill with some help from Quinn.

Cal smiled when his older brother wrapped his arm around their dad's shoulders and gave him a hug. They were about the same height, and their smiles were almost duplicates.

The past several years had been tough on the O'Brien family, and Cal hoped the worst of it was behind them. A little over four years ago, James had been diagnosed with stage IIIB colon cancer. His prognosis hadn't been encouraging. The average five-year survival rate was only about fifty percent.

Cal still remembered how he'd felt when his dad had told

him about the diagnosis. He'd heard the word "cancer," and the sound of his own heartbeat had drowned out the rest of what his dad had said. He hadn't been able to pull in a deep breath until James had squeezed his shoulder in reassurance.

Despite the fact that his father had been grappling with his own mortality, he'd still put his son's feelings first. At that moment, Cal had decided he wasn't going to take comfort from his dad any longer, he was going to give it instead.

James had suffered through surgery, several months of radiation, and three rounds of chemo with his wife and children by his side. They'd tried to keep his spirits up and hide their own fear.

The treatment had worked, and a little over a year ago, the oncologist had said James's cancer was in remission. Every night, Cal took a moment to say a prayer, asking God to keep it that way.

James had decided not to return to work, and Quinn had officially taken over the president and CEO job in December. As the months had passed, his dad's energy level rebounded and he regained the weight he'd lost.

He was doing much better. He was enjoying retirement with his wife, and he also was relishing his new role of father-in-law. He adored Amelia, and he had been ecstatic when Priest had become an official member of the O'Brien family.

"Oops."

The softly spoken word was the only warning Cal got before icy water dribbled down his back. Vaulting to his feet, he spun around to find the source. He wasn't surprised to see Teagan standing behind his chair, wearing a white-and-navy-blue-checked dress, and calmly sipping out of a red plastic cup.

"You're such a brat," he growled. "You act like you're thirteen instead of thirty-one."

"It was an accident," she protested innocently, widening her blue eyes and blinking slowly. "I'm dreadfully sorry."

"Don't you have anything better to do than bother me?"

"Not really. Nick's watching the football game, and Bebe's not here yet."

Yet. So she *was* coming.

He had wondered if she would show up. At least he had some time to prepare for her arrival. He figured she'd take one look at him and slaughter him with her smart mouth. He wished she would use it for good instead of evil.

Teagan sat down in his chair, and he pulled another one over and dropped into it. He picked up his beer bottle, but it was bone dry. She passed her drink to him, and he emptied it in one gulp. Thinking about Bebe's hot mouth had made him thirsty.

And hungry.

"What did you make for dessert?" Teagan asked.

"Nothing for you."

She kicked him in the shin, just hard enough to get her point across.

"Lemon meringue pie," he replied with a laugh.

"Why don't you ever make my favorite dessert?"

"Because Letty spoils you enough as it is."

"Not just me. She spoils everyone equally. She makes a special dessert for Bebe every week, too."

Cal had always been curious about Bebe, but he had managed to keep his curiosity under control. He wasn't sure he could do that anymore.

"What's Bebe's favorite dessert?" he asked casually.

"Coconut cake. And she refuses to share. She eats the whole thing by herself. But she burns it all off kickboxing."

Not all of it. There's enough left over to create some mouth-watering curves.

When he had seen Bebe in her workout clothes, he'd almost stroked out. Her golden skin had glistened with sweat, and her tank top and pants had clung to every dip and curve of her little body.

His eyes had found that tiny sliver of skin peeking between her tank top and pants, and all the blood in his body had rushed straight to his cock. He was damn grateful his shirt had been untucked because his hard-on had pointed toward her like a compass seeking magnetic north.

"Do you like coconut cake? I can't remember."

"It's not my favorite," he answered before continuing his casually phrased interrogation. "So what are Bebe's other favorite things?"

Her forehead furrowed a little as she considered his question. Finally, she began to list off things.

"Lasagna. Shiraz wine from Australia. Cinnamon hard candy. Her favorite color is purple. She loves *The Fast and the Furious* movies."

"*The Fast and the Furious*? Vin Diesel and Paul Walker?"

Teagan nodded. "She's too impatient to sit still for serious, artsy movies." Her mouth tipped into a smile. "What's the problem?"

Confused, he asked, "What?"

She sighed loudly. "Why haven't you asked her out?"

Looking down, he rolled his empty beer bottle between his hands. He'd done a lot more than ask Bebe out, but she obviously hadn't told Teagan.

"Who?" he prevaricated.

"I've seen the way you look at her, Cal."

"I need a drink," he announced, rising abruptly from his chair.

She laughed softly. "I'm sure you do."

Cal escaped from his too-perceptive sister and ate his burger and brat standing in a corner to discourage any further conversation. Bebe still hadn't arrived by the time everyone had finished with their dinner, and he headed into the house to grab the lemon meringue pies he'd made.

The fridge in the kitchen had been too full for the pies, so he had been forced to stash them in the overflow fridge in the laundry room. Once he had the desserts in hand, he made his way back to the French doors.

He knocked on the door with his elbow, and seconds later, Amelia pulled it open. Her big brown eyes widened when she saw the pies.

"Oh, yum, Cal," she breathed before adding, "Quinn is going to be so excited."

Lemon meringue pie was his brother's favorite dessert. "I made an extra pie for him. It's in the laundry room fridge."

"Maybe I should have married you instead, since your skills in the kitchen far surpass your brother's."

He laughed at Amelia's quip. There had never been one spark of sexual attraction between the two of them.

Quinn had taken one look at Amelia and staked a claim, and she was so head-over-heels in love with his brother, she didn't even notice other men. The couple had married in March, so they were still technically newlyweds.

She held open the door for him, and he deposited the pies on the iron patio table. Pulling a couple of pie servers from his back pocket where he had stashed them, he got to work divvying up slices of dessert.

He'd just filled a plate for his dad when he heard Bebe's light laughter. Like always, a tingle of arousal shot through him.

He shook his head in frustration and continued to dish up pie. Her laugh was enough to turn him on, and she wanted nothing to do with him. Hell, he'd practically begged her to have sex with him, and she had made it clear he was the last guy she would choose.

He clenched his jaw at the memory. Even after Bebe had told him she wasn't interested, he'd tried to persuade her otherwise. He didn't know why he'd put the hard sell on her. He wasn't desperate. He didn't have to beg women to fuck him.

When all the pie-loving guests had been served, Cal filled two plates with dessert, grabbed a couple of plastic forks, and headed toward the lower level of the deck where Quinn and Amelia had gathered with Priest, Teagan, and Bebe.

Stopping next to Bebe, he held out a plate to her. She looked up, her golden eyes wide with surprise. He raised his eyebrows, and her cheeks flushed with color as she took the plate from him.

"Thank you," she said softly.

As she looked down at the dessert, he took a moment to study her. She'd pulled back her dark hair as usual, and small gold hoops adorned her ears.

She never wore much makeup, probably because she didn't have to. Even without the help of cosmetics, her skin was smooth and unblemished, and her eyelashes were long and curled up at the tips.

Lip gloss shimmered on her lips, and when he'd stared at her pink mouth long enough for his cock to notice, he forced himself to focus on his own plate. He'd prefer to have her for dessert, but right now it looked like lemon meringue pie was all he was going to get.

Taking a bite, he evaluated his creation. The lemon filling was smooth with just the right amount of tart and sweet, and the crust was flaky rather than soggy. He wasn't sure about the meringue, though. He never could seem to get the right consistency.

Apparently everyone else thought the dessert was delicious because they all smacked their lips and moaned in gastronomic bliss. He mentally gave himself a high-five.

When Bebe gave a little moan, his cock twitched eagerly, and he pushed down a moan of his own. He never should have kissed her because now all he could think about was the taste of her plump lips.

"Cal, this is best lemon meringue pie I've ever had," Quinn praised, his mouth full of dessert.

"I agree," Amelia added, nodding her curly red head. "I usually don't like meringue because it's either too gooey or too crunchy, but this is perfect."

"It's tricky to get it right," Cal noted. "The longer you beat it, the stiffer it gets."

Priest choked on his pie, his green eyes bright with amusement. When Cal realized his comment had been full of sexual innuendo, he chuckled. Teagan convulsed into giggles, and a split second later, Quinn and Amelia were in hysterics along with her.

"How long did you beat it?" Quinn gasped out around his guffaws.

His brother's question set off another round of hilarity. Laughter made everyone breathless.

Everyone but Bebe.

She wasn't laughing. Instead, she looked back and forth between them, a little frown of confusion etched between her eyebrows. She obviously didn't get the joke.

Her lack of understanding reinforced her sexual innocence, and he was overcome with a bewildering rush of tenderness toward her. He hoped the lucky guy who took her virginity was careful with her.

Finally, their laughter died down, and they finished the pie. Cal gathered the empty plates and left the group to dump them in the bin his mom had set out to gather recyclables. His hands were sticky, and he stepped into the kitchen to wash them.

As he lathered rosemary-scented soap into his hands, the French doors opened, and Bebe entered the kitchen. She immediately spotted him at the sink, and to his surprise, she walked toward him. Her light blue twinset and khaki capri pants were nothing special, but she looked good to him.

He rinsed his hands and turned off the commercial-style faucet with his forearm like a surgeon. Without a word, she passed him a paper towel from the rooster-shaped holder next to the sink. As he dried his hands and threw the paper towel in the trash, she studied him.

"Why did you kiss me?"

Because I couldn't stop myself.

He shifted to lean back against the granite counter, resting his palms on the cool surface. She tracked his motion, her gaze settling on his hands.

"You needed to be kissed."

Her eyes snapped to his, her dark eyebrows winging up her forehead. "I *needed* to be kissed?"

"Yeah. You should have been kissed a long time ago, so I decided to take care of it."

His decision to kiss her had been driven by a combination of frustration, desire, and the need to make her feel something—*anything*—for him. And he'd been determined to be her first kiss. For some unknown reason, it had been imperative to him.

"You decided to take care of it," she echoed.

He didn't bother to reply. She shook her head, and he wondered what was going on in that turbo-charged brain of hers.

"So you were just doing me a favor?"

He'd been doing himself a favor, finally taking what he had wanted for years. But the experience hadn't been anything like he'd expected.

He had kissed a lot of women, but he'd been shocked by how hot his and Bebe's kiss had been. She had practically inhaled him, and once he'd put his hands on her, he'd had a hard time stopping.

He certainly hadn't planned to dry hump her against the door, but that was exactly what he'd done. And if she hadn't pulled back, he probably would have done more than that.

Abruptly, she spun on her heel and walked toward the French doors. She stopped just as abruptly and turned to face him.

"I've changed my mind," she blurted out.

"About what?"

"If your offer is still on the table, I'd like to take you up on it."

A mix of feelings hit him at once. Surprise. Triumph.

Excitement. Lust. But the overwhelming one was relief. After all this time, he was going to have her exactly where he wanted her: in his bed.

He opened his mouth to let her know they had a deal, but then he hesitated. He'd felt like shit after she'd turned him down and kicked him out of her loft, and he had enough of the devil inside him to want to see her squirm a little.

"You'll have to be more specific, Cookie. I'm not sure I know which offer you're referring to."

"You've only made me one offer," she said curtly.

"Oh, I'm sure I've offered you a drink a time or two. Is that what you want now? You're thirsty?"

Her eyes narrowed, and she crossed her arms over her chest, tapping her fingers against her forearm and making her rings gleam in the bright sunshine filtering through the windows. If he got his way, those slender, be-ringed fingers were going to be very busy.

"I'm talking about your offer to participate in my . . ." She bit her lower lip as she very obviously struggled to think of the best word. "My deflowering."

He smiled. "I thought we agreed to call it cherry picking."

She growled under her breath, and he couldn't hold back a chuckle. Dropping her arms, she stalked toward him until she stood right in front of him. Her scent wafted over him, fresh and sweet, and he battled the urge to bury his nose in her glossy hair.

"You said you were serious," she reminded him, her gaze intent on his face. "Were you just making fun of me?"

Her eyes looked wet, as if she was holding back tears, and he immediately felt like a bastard. He knew her virginity was a sensitive subject, and he'd made her feel even worse than she already felt.

"I'm sorry. I shouldn't have teased you."

Cupping her hips, he pulled her between his legs. She dropped her forehead against his chest, and he bent down until his mouth was against her ear.

"I was serious. I *am* serious." He sucked her earlobe into his mouth, laving it gently with his tongue, and she trembled. "I want your sweet little cherry." She gasped softly, and he tightened his fingers on her hips. "Are you going to give it to me?"

After a long moment, she nodded. His heart thumped

heavily, and his blood heated until it felt as if lava flowed through him.

"Is that a yes?"

She raised her head and met his eyes. "Yes." She pulled in a deep breath. "But I have some conditions."

Of course she did. She was a lawyer, after all. And though he lacked a JD after his name, he had some conditions of his own.

"I'm listening," he said, trying to focus on her words instead of the feel of her body against his.

"I don't want this to be a one-time thing. I want a lover."

Chapter 7

"WINE OR BEER?" CAL ASKED. "OR DO YOU WANT SOMETHING nonalcoholic?"

"Wine," Bebe replied, surprised her voice actually sounded normal.

Her nerves were jangling, and she desperately hoped some wine would help her calm down. She probably would need a little—*a lot*—of liquid courage to get through this dinner.

After she had boldly announced she wanted a lover, Nick had walked in on her and Cal, making any further conversation impossible. Since Nick rarely spoke, it hadn't been a surprise that he hadn't commented on what he'd seen. He'd simply turned on his heel and left the room.

Cal had suggested that they discuss the conditions of their liaison over dinner at his place the following evening. He'd offered to pick her up, but she had declined.

"Merlot?"

She nodded, and within moments, Cal handed her a wine-glass full of ruby-colored liquid. She took a sip, trying to enjoy the fruity, peppery flavors of the Napa Valley vintage.

She could feel his gaze on her, and she barely resisted the urge to drain her glass, grab the bottle, and suck the rest of it down like a wino. Instead of looking at him, she let her eyes wander around his condo.

Located on the third floor of a well-preserved Victorian home, it was older, smaller, and cozier than her loft. The gleaming hardwood floors were the only real similarity.

It was very neat and very clean, much more so than her loft, and she didn't think she was a slob. Weren't bachelor pads supposed to be dirty and messy and smell like old gym socks? She had no way of knowing, since she'd never been inside a bachelor pad.

According to Teagan, Quinn and Cal had lived together for several years before Cal had decided he'd had enough of his older brother's mess. Bebe never would have guessed Cal was a neat freak, but it looked like he was.

From her position where she stood in the kitchen, she could see the dining room and living area. Although the rooms were separate, they flowed together through wide, arched doorways.

His kitchen looked as if it had recently been renovated, but it honored the age of the home with its white cabinets and black-and-white subway tile backsplash. It was spacious enough for an island, and a 1950s-era bar-height table was situated on one end of the room near the windows.

Suddenly, a buzzing sound echoed through the condo.

"Pizza's here," Cal announced and headed toward the front door.

While he took care of dinner, Bebe braced herself against the granite-topped island and practiced some deep breathing exercises she had learned for her Muay Thai kickboxing. She still wasn't sure this was a good idea, but she wasn't going to back out now.

This morning, Cal had texted his address and door code along with a message: Are you going to show up?

She didn't know if he had simply wanted to confirm their plans or if he had intended to make her mad. Given their antagonistic relationship, it probably was both.

She had replied with a short message: I'll be there. Almost immediately, he'd responded: Pizza okay? Toppings?

He obviously wasn't planning a romantic, intimate meal. She didn't know if she was relieved or disappointed.

Cal returned to the kitchen carrying two pizza boxes.

"Since you said you didn't care about toppings, I got my favorite: pineapple and anchovy."

Ugh. Was he *serious*?

Her stomach lurched at the revolting combination, the expensive merlot she'd imbibed churning unpleasantly. Her disgust must have been evident on her face because he chuckled.

"Let this be a lesson to you, Cookie. If you don't like something, you need to tell me."

She frowned. She got the feeling he was talking about more than pizza toppings.

Cal dumped the boxes on the island and pulled two black plates from the cabinets. Opening the boxes, he revealed the pizzas, one covered in crispy pepperoni and the other studded with a variety of vegetables.

He slid a mischievous glance toward her, his eyes glinting with amusement. "Better than pineapple and anchovy?"

She nodded emphatically, and he laughed softly. He put a slice of each on a plate and handed it to her along with a cloth napkin.

"Have you had a chance to try Rigghetti's pizza yet?"

"No."

Even though she had lived in San Francisco for seven months, she hadn't had a chance to frequent many restaurants or do much sightseeing. She'd been focused on work, and what little free time she had, she spent with Teagan.

"I think Rigghetti's is the best in the Bay Area," Cal said as he stacked pizza on his plate. "You're in for a treat."

He made his way to the high-top table and deposited his wine and pizza on top of it. He beckoned her over, and when she got close enough, he took her wine and plate from her and placed them on the table.

"Need a boost?" he asked, gesturing toward the tall chair.

Before she could answer, he gripped her waist and easily lifted her into it. She glared at him.

"I didn't need help."

He laughed. "You're welcome."

As he settled in his seat, she shrugged out of her suit jacket and twisted awkwardly to hang it over the back of her chair. When she turned back around, his eyes were focused on her chest.

Looking down, she was horrified to see two buttons on her white shirt had popped open from her contortions. Her girls and the beige cotton bra that covered them were on display for the world to see, and she fastened the buttons as quickly as her trembling fingers would allow.

"I liked it better the other way," he murmured. "Maybe we should eat dinner without our shirts."

She blanched at the suggestion, and he chuckled. She met his eyes, which were full of laughter and something else she couldn't identify.

"Maybe another time," he added, his lips turned up slightly.

Maybe never!

Making an effort to ignore him, she picked up her pizza and took a big bite. All at once, the acidic tang of tomato sauce, the smoky smoothness of mozzarella, and the spicy kick of pepperoni overwhelmed her taste buds.

"Oh, this *is* good," she agreed, trying not to talk with her mouth full.

He smiled. "I'm glad you like it."

They ate in silence for a few minutes until Cal spoke. "So what did you do today?"

His tone was relaxed and friendly, and not for the first time, she wondered why he was being so nice. His antagonistic attitude toward her had completely disappeared, and she was having a hard time adjusting to the absence of witty barbs and clever insults.

"We're getting ready to report third-quarter earnings, so I'm spending a lot of time preparing for that," she answered. "And one of the big investment banks is hosting a biotech conference in a couple of weeks. We've been asked to present, so I'm trying to get everyone ready."

"I'm not sure I could deal with Lars on a daily basis."

"You know Lars?"

A chuckle rustled in his throat. "Unfortunately."

"How do you know him?"

"He was a guest lecturer for my MBA program."

Earlier in the year, Cal had received his MBA from the University of Pennsylvania's Wharton School of Business, which had an executive program in San Francisco. In addition to his graduate degree, he also had a bachelor's degree from USC in marketing. He didn't possess as many degrees as she did, but what he lacked in quantity, he made up for in quality.

"He's also a member at the same golf club where I play," he continued. "No one wants to be paired with him because his golf etiquette sucks."

Bebe had never played golf, and she knew next to nothing about the game. She'd thought about taking lessons, though, since so much business was conducted on the golf course, and most of the men she worked with were avid golfers.

"What do you mean?"

Cal grimaced. "Well, Lars has a tendency to beat the ground with his golf club when he makes a bad shot. He's been kicked off the course a few times by the marshal."

Laughing, she shook her head. She had no trouble imagining her boss throwing a tantrum like a toddler.

"What did you do today?" she asked, changing the subject. She'd already spent too much time and energy on her boss, and she would rather learn more about what Cal did on a daily basis.

"A little of this, a little of that," he answered lightly.

From what she had heard from Teagan, Cal was pretty amazing at his job. He was in charge of protecting and managing one of the most iconic brands in the world, and he supervised a huge team of people who were responsible for everything from market research and media outreach to special events and social media.

Publicly, she was rude and bitchy to Cal. Privately, she had a lot of respect for him. Despite his big job, he never seemed to be overwhelmed or unsure. She wished she had that special something that made him so cool and unruffled.

"We have so much stuff going on at Riley O'Brien, and my group is heavily involved with all of it," he explained. "We've got Amelia's new line of accessories, the relaunch of the women's division, and Grandma Vi's museum, plus all the outreach to retailers and vendors."

Cal rose from the chair. "Do you want another slice?"

"No, I'm good."

After gathering their plates, he placed them in the sink. He grabbed the wine and gestured to the arched doorway.

"Let's take this into the living room."

She hopped from the chair, nabbed her wineglass, and followed him into the living room, which was a soothing green color, somewhere between sage and olive. An espresso-colored leather sectional filled it, along with a Mission-style coffee table and end table.

Two floor lamps with stained-glass shades bathed the room with a mellow glow, and a big bay window at one end of the room let in some light from the street below. One of the walls featured a large fireplace with an antique mantel. A huge flat-screen TV hung over it along with two vertical speakers that looked sleek and super-high-tech.

Built-in bookcases covered the remaining wall, overflowing with books, knickknacks, and photos of the O'Brien family. In every single image, Cal's smile conveyed his love for his parents and siblings. She had been around him enough to know he wasn't one of those guys who was ashamed to show his love for someone.

A set of French doors separated the living area from the foyer, which led into a hallway where the bathroom and bedrooms were located. He hadn't given her a tour, but he had succinctly explained the layout of his condo. Now, she couldn't stop thinking about what his bedroom looked like and when she was going to see it.

Cal dropped down onto the sofa, and he was so extraordinarily handsome, she couldn't help but stare. He always looked good. Better than good, in fact. Tonight he wore a pair of worn Rileys and a fitted, long-sleeved black T-shirt. He obviously hadn't dressed up for her, which was good, since she hadn't dressed up for him, either.

In all the time she had known him, she had seen Cal wear something other than jeans on only two occasions: Teagan and Nick's rehearsal dinner and their wedding. He'd worn a suit for the first and a tux for the second.

Both instances were burned into her brain. Cal in a tux was not something you could forget. It was, however, something you used as the basis for your dirtiest fantasies.

"Have a seat," he invited.

Leaning back, he propped his feet on the coffee table. She hadn't noticed before, but he was shoeless, his feet covered in a pair of black socks printed with bright orange jack-o'-lanterns.

The sight was so unexpected, so incongruous, a surprised giggle escaped her. At the sound, he jerked his head toward her, his eyes narrowed on her face. The dark color of his T-shirt made them seem even lighter, almost translucent.

"What?"

"I just noticed your socks."

He looked at his feet and then looked up at her, a huge grin on his face. His eyes crinkled a little at the corners, and a tiny dimple peeked out in his left cheek.

"One of my favorite seasonal selections. What do you think?"

"Umm . . . well, they're . . ."

He laughed as she groped for words. "They were a gift from Valerie. She gave me socks to celebrate every holiday."

She didn't know what to think about the fact that he wore a pair of socks his ex-girlfriend's daughter had given him. She wondered if he missed the little girl.

"Even Presidents' Day?" she asked.

"Even Presidents' Day. They're green and printed with the faces of our first presidents—Washington, Adams, Jefferson. I always feel a little guilty when I walk all over our Founding Fathers."

She laughed. "You're so disrespectful."

She kicked off her shoes before curling up in the corner of the sectional. For some reason, Cal's Halloween-themed socks made her feel more comfortable with him than the two glasses of wine she'd consumed.

"We should probably get some things nailed down before I nail you," he said, a little smile playing around his lips.

Her mouth fell open in surprise, and he chuckled. "Oh, Bebe, I'm so glad you changed your mind. We're going to have some serious fun."

Serious fun.

She'd never thought about sex as being fun. Before Cal, she'd never really thought about sex much at all.

"Serious fun is an oxymoron," she pointed out.

"So is adult male," he noted, giving her a big wink.

She couldn't help but laugh. He always had a snappy comeback. He smiled roguishly before sobering. Tilting his head, he studied her thoughtfully.

"What conditions do you have?" he asked.

She had made a list on her phone, but it wasn't difficult to remember the most important one. Explaining it to him was a little bit of a challenge, though.

"I'm making an assumption here, I know, but you've probably been with a lot of beautiful women. I'm sure they all complained that people didn't take them seriously—that no one paid any attention to their brain, only their body. They probably whined about men objectifying them."

She took a sip of wine to ease the dryness in her throat, licking her bottom lip to catch a rogue droplet. His eyes dropped to her mouth, his gaze tracking the movement of her tongue. Warmth spread through her stomach, and she swiftly deposited the goblet on the coffee table, trying to hide the tremble in her fingers.

"All my life, people have taken me seriously," she continued. "No one has ever paid attention to anything but my brain."

He brought his gaze back to hers. He was motionless, his striking blue eyes narrowed on her face.

"I want you to *not* take me seriously. I want you to ignore my brain and pay attention to my body. I *want* you to objectify me."

He blinked slowly, looking remarkably like an owl. "You want me to objectify you," he repeated.

She nodded, and he ran his hand across his mouth, his fingers making a rasping sound against his dark stubble. He pressed his lips together as if he was trying to hold back laughter.

"I'm a little out of practice. I stopped objectifying women about the same time I graduated from high school."

"It's probably like riding a bike. It'll come back to you."

He laughed softly. "I'm sure you're right." He cocked his head. "What else?"

Chapter 8

THE LIGHT FILTERING FROM THE LAMPS IN CAL'S LIVING ROOM made Bebe's eyes gleam like antique gold. He didn't know anyone else with eyes so gorgeous, and just like always, he had a hard time looking away from them.

The first time he had met Bebe, he'd looked into her eyes and felt a spark deep inside. He'd never experienced anything like it, and he had still been reeling from it when she'd leveled a hateful glare on him.

Her immediate, obvious dislike had prevented him from making a move on her, but learning about her plan to lose her virginity gave him the opportunity he'd longed for. She probably wondered why he wasn't throwing insults at her any longer, but he wasn't a complicated guy. Once she'd agreed to give her cherry to him, all his anger and aggression had evaporated.

No, he wasn't complicated at all. He was only a step above a caveman on the evolutionary chain.

"Do you have any conditions?" she asked.

He had a couple, but he wanted to hear the rest of hers before he shared. He didn't want to ask for something she wasn't willing to give and end up with nothing.

"You first."

She rose gracefully from the sofa. She'd picked a spot several feet away from him, and he was okay with that . . . for now.

"I made a list on my phone. Let me get it."

He laughed under his breath as she moved into the foyer where she'd left her bag. Of course she had made a list.

Bebe was unlike any other female he'd ever known. Without a doubt, she was the smartest woman he had come across, and he didn't make a habit of surrounding himself with stupid women. The women he'd dated in the past had been both beautiful and bright. And they'd all been one hundred percent aware of how attractive they were.

Interestingly, Bebe seemed completely oblivious to her sex appeal. Her clothing choices practically screamed it. Tonight she wore an unadorned navy suit and a white button-down shirt that were the very definition of plain.

It was the first time a woman had shown up at his house for dinner looking as if she were going to a business meeting. He couldn't remember the last time he had invited someone over, but he had no trouble recalling that female visitors usually showed up in revealing dresses and fuck-me heels.

Somehow Bebe managed to look good in her androgynous business attire, though. The stark color of the shirt contrasted with her dark hair and golden skin, and the suit pants accentuated her subtle curves.

If she ever wised up and realized how gorgeous she really was, the men in the Bay Area would be in a shitload of trouble. *He* would be in a shitload of trouble because she made him hard without even trying.

She returned to the living room, phone in hand, and resumed her seat. She looked as if she'd had a long day. Whatever makeup she'd had on had worn off, and faint shadows darkened the skin under her eyes. Her hair was in its customary bun, but it wasn't as neat and smooth as it usually was.

She studied the phone for a moment, her lower lip caught between her teeth. He'd noticed she had a habit of doing that when she was thinking, and it always made him wonder how her mouth would feel as she sucked him off. He hoped he wouldn't have to wonder for much longer.

"Okay, first of all, I want to do things outside the bedroom."

Outside the bedroom? Did Bebe have an exhibitionist streak?

He'd had sex in a lot of interesting places, but he definitely preferred locations where he could take his time. When he got Bebe naked, he didn't want any interruptions.

"Do you want to have sex in public places or in other rooms—kitchen, bathroom, laundry room?"

Her eyes widened. "Cal, I wasn't talking about sex. I was talking about going places and doing things together. Dinner, movies, things like that."

Now that was a shock. He hadn't expected her to want to spend time with him with their clothes on. She didn't even like him.

"You want us to go on dates?" he asked incredulously.

She flushed, and he swore under his breath. He needed to be more careful with his responses or he was going to fuck this up before he got a chance to fuck her.

"Yes." She dropped her phone into her lap and started to fiddle with her rings. "Is that a problem?"

He didn't know if it was a problem or not. Choosing to ignore that question, he prompted her, "What are your other conditions?"

Exhaling loudly, she picked up her phone. "I'll just read them off. I want to go out at least three times a week. Anytime either one of us wants sex, the other person has to agree, no excuses."

He could have her anytime, and as much as he wanted? A twenty-four/seven, all-you-can-eat buffet?

Fuck, yeah.

"Sleepovers are negotiable. While we're having sex, neither one of us can be with anyone else."

"Exclusive." He rolled the word around in his mouth, tasting it like fine Irish whiskey. "That sounds like a relationship, Bebe."

"No." She shook her head vigorously. "*No.* I meant no sex with anyone else. We can *see* other people . . . go out on dates." Before he could reply, she continued, "You have to be tested for STDs because I'd really prefer to not use condoms. Even with proper usage, they have a very high failure rate. I don't want to worry if one breaks or slips off or if we . . . umm . . . get caught up in the moment."

His cock twitched at the thought of sinking into Bebe's tight pussy without a rubber. He'd always used condoms, even with Saika. She hadn't wanted to go on the pill or any other kind of hormone-based birth control, and she hadn't trusted sponges or diaphragms.

"Are you using something for birth control?"

"Yes, of course," she replied without hesitation. "I wouldn't have requested no condoms otherwise. I'm on the pill."

"Do you take it like you're supposed to?"

"Yes. I don't want to get pregnant. I'm not trying to trick you into fathering a child, Cal."

He wanted children—someday—with the right woman. And he was traditional enough to want that woman to be his wife. He definitely didn't want an unplanned pregnancy from a fling with his sister's best friend.

"If you're worried about me taking the pill properly, I'll talk to my gynecologist about the birth control shot. It lasts for three months, I think."

He shook his head. "I just want to be clear. You need to be vigilant about taking the pill."

"I will. I *am*."

"What else is on your list?"

"I want our arrangement to be a secret. I don't want to tell anyone what we're doing, especially anyone in your family. I don't think Teagan would understand."

Cal snorted. His sister would understand, but she might not be very happy about it.

"And finally, this isn't a relationship. You're not my boyfriend. I'm not your girlfriend. And it can't last longer than twelve months."

"What happens in twelve months?"

"Nothing," she answered softly. "I just thought twelve months was a good time limit. I doubt it will last longer than a few weeks anyway."

He didn't know how long he needed to work her out of his system, but he doubted it would take a year. Nonetheless, he wasn't thrilled to put an expiration date on their arrangement.

"Is that it?"

She nodded. "What do you think?"

They sat in silence while he considered her conditions. He'd been expecting some no-strings-attached sex, and that wasn't exactly what she had suggested. She wanted more from him than sex; she wanted his time.

Unfortunately, that was something he didn't have in abundance. He worked sixty hours a week, usually more. When he'd dated Saika, he had cut back on his work hours to spend time with her and Valerie. They'd seen each other at least three times during the week, and he'd spent all weekend with them. Saika and Valerie had been regulars at O'Brien family gatherings.

Once they'd broken up, he'd resumed his normal work schedule. Actually, he'd worked more hours to take his mind off the breakup.

If he agreed to Bebe's terms, he'd have to adjust his schedule. He tried to hang out with Quinn and Priest at least once a week, along with squeezing in a visit to his parents, especially since his dad had been diagnosed with cancer.

Did he want Bebe enough to make time for her outside the bedroom?

"I'm fine with most of your conditions," he finally answered. "We need to limit the dates to twice a week, though, one during the week and one on the weekend."

"Okay. I don't really have time for more anyway."

"There's no way we're going to be able to keep this a secret, especially from Teagan. I'm not going to sneak around. It's too much effort, and I don't want to lie to my family."

"You're right. Teagan would figure it out eventually, and I don't like to lie to her, either."

Cal found that statement very interesting. "When have you lied to her?"

"Oh, just girl stuff. No, your butt doesn't look big in those pants. No, you don't look like a hooker in that dress." She waved her hand. "Nothing really important."

He got a fleeting mental image of Bebe and Teagan shopping together, and he chuckled. They were so different, yet they adored each other.

When Teagan had announced that she was moving across the country to attend Harvard, he'd been worried about her. Yes, she was an adult, and yes, she was able to take care of herself, but he hadn't wanted her to be alone or lonely in a strange, new city.

The first time he had talked to Teagan after she had settled in Cambridge, she'd spent thirty minutes telling him about Bebe, and his worry had drained away. His sister described her new friend as smart, sweet, and funny.

Bebe was all those things, although she'd never been sweet to him. Maybe that would change once he got her naked.

"What are your conditions?" she asked.

"I get to decide what we do for our dates."

Once he'd adjusted to the idea that she wanted to spend time with him outside the bedroom, he'd started imagining all the things they could do and the places they could visit. To his surprise, he realized he was looking forward to their dates.

"Why do you get to decide?" she asked, her surprise and confusion evident.

Because he liked being the one who made the decisions. Because he liked being in control. Because he wanted to wow her, in and out of bed.

But he sure as hell wasn't going to admit any of that out loud.

Instead, he said, "Because San Francisco is my hometown, and I know all the best places to go and things to do."

She smiled, one of those wide, gorgeous smiles she regularly bestowed upon everyone but him. He usually got her frowns, her glares, and her evil stares.

But this smile—this one *was* for him.

"Do I get veto power at least?" she questioned with a teasing lilt in her voice.

He shook his head. "No way."

"I don't want to do anything that could damage me for life."

"Such as?"

"Swimming with sharks. Base jumping. Movies with subtitles."

He laughed. "If we go to the movies, I'll let you pick what we see."

"Okay, you get to decide what we do for our dates. Is that your only condition?"

"No. I have one more, and this is a deal breaker: I'm in charge of your de-virginization plan."

"Cal!" she screeched. "Stop calling it that!"

He chortled, feeling happier than he had in months, maybe even years. "My apologies, Cookie. Your cherry-picking program."

She growled, but he continued as if he hadn't heard her. "After we have sex, your condition kicks in. But before that, I make all the decisions." He paused to let that sink in. "Do you understand what I'm saying?"

"Not really."

"I get to decide how far we go when we're together. And I get to decide when and where we have sex for the first time."

She stared at him, shaking her head slowly. "No. Absolutely not."

"It's a deal breaker, Bebe."

She huffed out a breath, clearly annoyed. "Why? Are you worried I'm going to make you wait too long?"

Her question was so surprising, he barked out a laugh. "Actually, I was thinking you'd be too eager, and we'd end up having sex before you're ready."

"Oh, really?" Her eyebrows shot up. "You think I'm going to be insane with lust the moment you touch me?"

Her tone made it clear how unlikely that scenario was, and it pissed him off, especially since *he* remembered being insane with lust the moment he touched her. He didn't want to be the only one who felt that way.

"Yeah, that's exactly what I think," he shot back.

She jumped up from the sofa. "I cannot believe how conceited you are!"

Dropping his feet to the floor, he slowly rose to face her. She propped her hands on her hips, a belligerent stance if he'd ever seen one.

"Is your penis as big as your ego?" she asked sarcastically.

He reached out, hooked two fingers in the waistband of her suit pants, and pulled her against him. She stumbled, and he snaked his arm around her waist to hold her tight.

"If you want to know the answer to that question, you have to agree to my conditions."

"Why are you being such an ass?" she snapped, pushing against his chest with her palms.

"Because you bring out the best in me."

After a beat of stunned silence, she started to laugh. "You bring out the best in me, too."

"I've noticed that."

He cupped her smooth cheek in his free hand, tilting her head back. Her mouth was bare, a delicate light pink with a sweet little bow at the top. Ever since he'd had his first taste of it, he had wanted another.

He bent down and let his lips hover over hers. She pulled in a surprised breath, sucking the air from his lungs.

"Do we have an agreement?"

He waited patiently, knowing he was *this* close to getting exactly what he wanted: the right to touch her whenever he felt the urge. Finally, she nodded.

"Yes, we have an agreement. I'm going to defer to your judgment. But you shouldn't get used to it."

He responded by covering her mouth with his. It was flavored with merlot, but underneath the vintage he could taste *her*.

She was so fucking delicious, better than anything, or anyone, he'd ever tasted. If her mouth tasted this good, her pussy was going to be sweeter than honey, more intoxicating than wine.

He nibbled and licked her luscious lips until they fell apart. He kept things slow and easy, feeding her several wet kisses until she fisted her hands in his shirt and rose on her tiptoes to suck on his bottom lip.

He gave his mouth to Bebe, and she licked inside, touching her tongue to his before timidly moving deeper. He let her set the pace, licking and stroking until his cock pressed painfully against his zipper.

He broke their kiss, pulling back until he could look into her eyes. They were hazy with desire, the pupils huge and dark against the vivid gold of her irises. By his count, that was her second kiss. He planned to give her so many they couldn't keep track.

"You need to get used to this . . ." he warned.

He knew his words surprised her because her eyes flared. But she recovered pretty fast, looping her arms around his neck and pressing her hot little body even closer to his. His hard-on poked into her stomach, and he clenched his teeth when his balls twinged.

"Because I'm going to put my mouth on you every chance I get," he finished, his voice hoarse with arousal.

"Good."

Chapter 9

BEBE WAS ONLY A COUPLE OF MINUTES LATE WHEN SHE DROVE up in front of Teagan's house, but her best friend was outside waiting for her. The brunette jogged down the steps, and when she reached the curb, Bebe handed the extra helmet to her.

"Sorry I'm late, *kanya*."

"Not a big deal," Teagan assured her with a wide smile.

Bebe and Teagan had a standing date on Wednesday nights. Their evenings together always included dinner and a girly activity, such as shopping or spa treatments.

Teagan placed the helmet over her wavy hair and deftly fastened the chin strap. Knowing the drill, she bent down a little so Bebe could test how tight it was. Satisfied with the fit, she patted the top of Teagan's helmet, and the other woman straightened.

"Where are we going?" Bebe asked.

"Fillmore and Broadway. Vanessa told me about this new lingerie shop called The Black Orchid. She said it's fabulous." Teagan patted her girls with both hands. "Supposedly they carry expanded sizes for my double D's."

"Lingerie," Bebe groaned, rolling her eyes. "Again?"

Teagan laughed. "I'm a newlywed," she reminded Bebe. "What do you expect?"

Bebe shook her head in exasperation. "Climb on, *kanya*, so we can spend an hour or two perusing cheeky panties and bustiers."

Teagan hopped on the back of the scooter, and Bebe accelerated away from the curb. She headed down Sacramento Street, cautiously navigating the hilly thoroughfare so Teagan wouldn't scream in her ears.

When Bebe had moved to San Francisco, she had traded in her old Vespa scooter and upgraded to a new model. The city had a great public transit system, but she tended to work odd hours, arriving in the office very early and leaving late. Taking a bus or the trolley at eleven o'clock at night wasn't ideal, and the scooter was a good compromise between public transportation and a car.

A work van pulled out in front of her, and she swerved slightly to avoid it. Teagan squealed, clutching her waist.

"You're such a weenie," Bebe teased over her shoulder.

In response, Teagan pinched her lightly under her rib cage. Bebe laughed as she made a left on Fillmore Street.

Minutes later, she stopped the scooter and squeezed it into a small space in front of a storefront with a black-and-white-striped awning. The windows were frosted with large opaque stripes, and "The Black Orchid" was stenciled in black cursive across them.

She and Teagan dismounted from the scooter and removed their helmets. Bebe took a moment to stash them under the seat before grabbing her purse.

"Ready?"

Teagan nodded. "I'm so excited to see this place."

Pulling open the door, Teagan ushered Bebe through it before following behind her. The shop was much, much larger than it appeared from the outside. In fact, the space was both deep and wide, and it was filled with hundreds of silky unmentionables.

"Oh," Teagan breathed. "This *is* fabulous. I'm going to have to thank Vanessa."

Bebe nodded in agreement, impressed despite herself. The shop was both elegant and sexy.

Black-and-white marble tiles covered the floors, arranged in a checkerboard pattern, and the walls were papered in a tonal black-on-black damask pattern. Several high-backed black velvet chaises were scattered around the room, and large crystal chandeliers hung from the ceiling, which was covered in mirrors.

Most of the lingerie was displayed on black iron tables with white marble tops, but a large selection of bras, camisoles, and nightgowns hung from wrought-iron rods that dropped from the ceiling. Several mannequins were situated around the shop, dressed in a wide variety of styles from reserved to risqué, and black floor-to-ceiling drawers covered the longest wall of the shop.

The shop not only looked good, but smelled good, too. Although Bebe couldn't identify all the scents, she was able to pick out jasmine and bergamot, two of her favorites.

A curvy woman about Bebe's age made her way toward them. Her black sleeveless sheath set off her creamy skin and blond pixie-styled hair. She'd paired the dress with a thin black snakeskin belt and black snakeskin heels, and Bebe winced a little as she imagined the pain of standing all day wearing those shoes.

Even though she could use the extra height heels provided, she preferred flats. And from a health perspective, flats were much better for the lower body, especially the back and hips.

"Welcome to The Black Orchid. I'm Jillian. Is there anything in particular you're looking for?"

Teagan shook her head. "Not really. A friend told me about your shop, so I decided to check it out."

Jillian smiled. "Please, check us out," she invited. "We carry a wide range of brands for every budget and body type."

Jillian eyed Teagan's chest, which was clad in a silky, raspberry-colored shirt. "Are you a D or a double D? Unfortunately, most brands stop at D. That's why we carry Curvy Kate's full line, which ranges from D to K."

Teagan smiled. "I would have side boobs and muffin tops if I wore anything smaller than a double D."

Jillian nodded and turned toward Bebe. "And you?"

"I'm a B."

Jillian cocked her head. "Have you ever been professionally fitted? I'm quite confident you're a C cup, and you've been squeezing the girls into a B. They're suffering."

Bebe looked down. How could Jillian tell? They looked fine to her.

"Once you make your selections, you can try on B's and C's to see the best fit."

"Oh, I'm not buying. I'm just here with her," Bebe said, pointing toward Teagan.

Jillian nodded before gesturing toward a round table in the middle of the store. A half mannequin sat on top, dressed in a sheer red bra with small black dots and matching panties.

"You might want to start there," she told Teagan.

"Thank you," Teagan replied before grabbing Bebe's arm and dragging her toward the table.

It was covered in colorful bras and matching bottoms in a variety of styles, including thongs, bikinis, cheeky panties, hipsters, and boy shorts. Bebe picked up one of the thongs. It had a panel of silky teal material in the middle and sheer black fabric on the sides and back. It was pretty, but she wondered how it could be comfortable.

She was a full brief kind of gal. She didn't even do bikinis or boy shorts. And she liked cotton. Most of her panties came in a value pack of beige and white.

Teagan held up a bra for Bebe's review. "What do you think?"

The bottom half of the cup was made of smooth, mocha-colored fabric, and the top half was sheer fabric of the same color. An aqua-colored ribbon was woven through the tops of the cups.

"I really like it," Teagan said with a naughty grin. "And I know Nick would."

Bebe snorted. Nick would find Teagan attractive even if she dressed in a nun's habit and wore granny panties underneath it. In fact, it might even have a perverse appeal.

Teagan held up another bra. The entire cup was made of black fabric and overlaid with gold lace. It was kind of gaudy and reminded Bebe of baroque furniture.

"What about this one?"

Bebe shrugged. She was already bored, and Teagan was just getting started. She let her gaze wander around the shop. None of the bras on display looked anything like the ones she had in her drawer at home. Her bras were nothing special.

Most of them were plain cotton like her panties and either beige or white.

Comfort and function were her priorities. She didn't really care what her underwear looked like as long as it felt good. It wasn't as if someone was going to see it . . .

Oh, my God.

It hit her in a blinding flash. Someone *was* going to see her underwear.

Cal was going to see it.

Oh, my God.

She stumbled to the closest chaise, dropping heavily onto it. She didn't want Cal to see her underwear. It wasn't pretty or sexy or interesting.

If her underwear was an extension of her, then she was boring, plain, and unappealing. She didn't want to be any of those things, and she definitely didn't want Cal to see her that way. He probably was used to women wearing leather bustiers and crotchless panties or, at the very least, sheer thongs and lacy bras.

She needed new underwear.

Now. Right this minute.

Jumping up from the chaise, she rushed toward the back of the store, where Jillian had disappeared. Bebe met her just as she came out of a narrow corridor.

"Jillian!" she exclaimed, grabbing her hand. "I need your help."

The other woman's eyebrows shot up. "What's wrong?"

"I need new underwear. Underwear that makes a man . . ."

"Hot and bothered?" Jillian suggested.

"Yes! Exactly."

Jillian studied her for a moment. "Right. Let's get you measured, and then we'll pick out some sets."

Jillian ushered Bebe toward the dressing rooms, stepping into one with her. She shut the door behind them and pulled a measuring tape from a basket in the corner.

"Since I'm about to get fresh with you, I suppose I should know your name," she quipped.

"Bebe."

"Bebe, please take off your shirt."

Bebe quickly unbuttoned her blue long-sleeved shirt and

pulled it off. Jillian wrapped the measuring tape around her torso and then around her breasts.

"Just as I thought . . . 30C," she announced. "You have fairly sizable breasts for your frame."

Looking down at her chest, Bebe reviewed her breasts with interest. They were encased in a white cotton bra with no decoration or ornamentation. The bra flattened them rather than pushed them up. It did *nothing* to enhance them.

Bebe's parents had taught her to maximize her most valuable asset: her brain. That was why she had applied herself to her studies and worked so hard to obtain her degrees. On a professional basis, it didn't matter what she looked like. Her brain was on display, not her boobs.

But Cal wasn't interested in her brain. In fact, she'd told him to ignore it. But she hadn't really thought about what that meant. If her brain wasn't getting all the attention, she needed to make the most of her other assets, starting with her "fairly sizable breasts."

"With the correct bra, your girls will perk right up," Jillian promised as she unwound the tape measure and dropped it back into the basket. "Wait here. I'll be back soon with some things for you to try on."

"Nothing white or beige," Bebe requested.

"No white or beige," Jillian agreed. "What's your favorite color?"

"Purple. I like lavender, too. And coral. And hot pink."

She liked all those colors, but she rarely wore them. Maybe she should start.

Jillian nodded and left the room. With nothing left to do except wait, Bebe perched on the velvet bench situated along one of the walls. Running her fingers across the soft nap of the material, she let herself think about *being* with Cal.

She still couldn't fathom why he wanted to have sex with her, but apparently he did. When she'd been at his condo, he had kissed her until she was light-headed and her panties were soaked. Almost from the moment he touched her, he'd had an erection. It had been so hard, she'd felt it through his jeans and her shirt when he'd pressed it into her stomach.

Just the thought of it turned her on, eliciting a trickle of arousal, and she squirmed a little on the bench. By the time he had finished kissing her, she'd been ready to rip off his clothes.

She was embarrassed to admit he'd been right about making her insane with lust. He was very talented.

"Bebe, where are you?" Teagan called.

"Here," she answered, opening the door and sticking out her head.

Teagan turned toward Bebe's voice. Piles and piles of bras and panties filled her arms, along with a corset-like contraption with hooks hanging from the bottom.

"What are you doing?"

"I decided to buy some new underwear," Bebe explained, trying to be casual.

Apparently she failed because Teagan's eyes got all squinty. Her best friend could read between the lines better than anyone Bebe knew. Teagan moved closer, pushing her way into the dressing room. Fortunately, it was spacious.

"Why did you suddenly decide you needed new underwear?" Teagan asked, tossing her armful of lacy and racy undergarments onto the bench.

When Bebe didn't answer, Teagan drew her own conclusions. "Is this about your virginity? Have you already found the guy?" She gasped. "You haven't already done it, have you?"

"No," Bebe said, hoping Teagan would accept that as an answer to all of her questions.

Unfortunately, Teagan was too smart and too much of a lawyer to accept that answer. Sitting down on the bench, she crossed her legs.

"No to which question?"

Bebe sighed. "No, I haven't done it yet," she clarified.

Teagan leaned forward. "But the new underwear is about your virginity?"

"Yes."

"I have some prospects for you," Teagan assured her. "I just want to vet them a little more."

Cal had made it clear that Bebe needed to tell Teagan about their arrangement as soon as possible. He'd been equally clear that he wouldn't make any explanations to his sister, either. That was Bebe's job.

"I've already found someone, *kanya*."

Teagan's mouth dropped open. "You have? Who?"

Bebe leaned back against the door and took a deep breath. "Cal."

After a second or two of silence, Teagan blinked slowly. "Cal who?"

"Cal O'Brien."

"My *brother*?"

"Yes."

Teagan frowned. "Wait a second. When you say you've already found someone, and that someone is Cal, what does that mean?"

"It means Cal offered to take care of my virginity. He's going to . . ." She trailed off, unsure how to explain it. Finally, she settled on a suitable phrase. "He's going to show me the ropes."

"*Are you serious?*" Teagan asked, her voice so high, it sounded as if she'd sucked on helium. "You're going to have sex with Cal?"

"Yes."

Teagan gasped, her eyes wide with disbelief. "How did this even happen?" She shook her head. "There's no way you would have approached him."

"He overheard us talking that day in your office."

Teagan vaulted to her feet. "Cal eavesdropped on our conversation?" she shrieked. "Oh, my God! I'm going to kill him!"

Bebe ignored her outburst. "The next night, he stopped by the loft and offered his services. I turned him down at first, but then I reconsidered."

Teagan collapsed onto the bench like a rag doll. "What did he say exactly?"

"He said he'd thought about my situation, and he could help me with it. At first I didn't understand, but then he explained that he was offering to relieve me of the burden of my virginity."

Teagan looked down and mumbled something beneath her breath.

"What?"

"Nothing," she answered, waving her hand. "Did you ask him why he offered?"

"Yes. He made some ridiculous joke about wanting me from the first moment he saw me. Then he got real and explained that he needed a distraction to take his mind off Saika. I guess he's still hung up on her."

Teagan cocked her head. "How do you know he was joking?"

Bebe shrugged. "Because he doesn't like me. And I cannot imagine a guy who looks like Cal would lust after someone like me for even a few seconds, let alone a few years."

Teagan stared at her for a long moment, her bright blue eyes assessing. "Why did you turn him down?"

"I just thought it would be better to find someone else. But then I realized he was my least worst option."

"Your least worst option? What does that mean?"

"It means that I don't really have any good options. I can't hook up with anyone from work without jeopardizing my job. I thought about online dating, but that takes time, and you know how bad I am on dates. I thought about going to a bar and picking up a guy, but then I realized that might be too dangerous because he might be a serial killer or have a terrible disease."

Teagan pressed her fingertips to her forehead as if she was in pain and closed her eyes. "I told you I would help you. You just needed to be patient."

"I've been patient for thirty years," she shot back.

With a big sigh, Teagan met her gaze. "Did you tell Cal that he was your least worst option?"

"No. He didn't seem to care why I changed my mind."

"I'm sure he didn't," Teagan muttered. "He was too busy thinking about how fast he could get you naked."

"I had dinner at his condo on Monday night, and we negotiated the terms of our arrangement."

"Negotiated the terms of your arrangement, huh? I wish I'd been a fly on the wall for that conversation." She snickered. "What did you have to negotiate? Who gets to be on top?"

Bebe flushed. She and Cal hadn't been that specific, but she had agreed to let him be the decision maker when it came to sex.

"Well, are you willing to generously share the details of your conversation, or do I have to beg for them?"

"You know I've never really dated or done any fun couple stuff, so I asked Cal to take me out a couple of times a week, and he agreed."

"So you're dating then?"

"Not exactly."

"Then what exactly?"

She blew out a breath in frustration. "Is it so wrong for me to want to experience all the things I've never experienced?"

Teagan eyed her thoughtfully. "Tell me something. Do you really dislike Cal?"

"I don't have to like him to have sex with him," she said instead of answering the question.

"That's true."

"*Kanya*, if it upsets you, I won't do it."

"I'm not upset," Teagan countered, shaking her head emphatically. "In fact, I agree with you. Cal is your least worst option."

Her gaze dropped to Bebe's chest. She studied the no-frills bra, her rosy lips curling in distaste.

"You definitely need some new underwear." She laughed softly. "Though you probably won't have it on for very long once Cal sees you in it."

Chapter 10

CAL PULLED BACK HIS RIGHT ARM AND LET THE DART FLY, BURY-
ing it in the center of the board. Quinn and Priest groaned
dramatically, and Cal raised his arms high above his head.

"I am the King of Darts," he proclaimed. "And you are
my pitiable subjects."

Quinn shook his head. "I don't understand how you can
be so good at darts when we only play every few months.
Are you practicing in secret?"

Cal gave his brother a look that clearly said, *Are you fucking
kidding me?* before taking a swallow of his Blue Moon. Priest
removed the darts from the board and handed them to Quinn.

"You're down almost two hundred points," Cal reminded
his brother. "You should just give up."

"You should just kiss my ass," Quinn suggested.

The three of them usually hung out at least once a week,
most often on Wednesday nights when Teagan and Bebe had
their regular date. Amelia was busy with her accessories and
the relaunch of the women's division, so she didn't mind having some time to herself. In fact, she'd happily kicked Quinn
out of the house.

Sometimes they invited Beck, one of the guys Quinn had

met while working on his MBA at Stanford, or Deda, the head of business development for Riley O'Brien & Co. They went to bars, sporting events, the driving range—whatever sounded good at the time.

More often than not, they ended up playing basketball. It was the only sport where their athletic skill was evenly matched. Quinn and Priest were much better football players than Cal, while he was a scratch golfer and a damn fine baseball player.

Over the past fifteen years, Cal had enjoyed hundreds of nights out with Quinn and Priest. Tonight they'd elected to go to Murray's, a little hole-in-the-wall bar near Quinn's house in Laurel Heights. It was within walking distance, so they didn't have to worry about a designated driver.

With its dark hardwood floors, long mahogany bar, and stained-glass windows, it was a piece of a bygone era. Dark green leather booths lined the wall, and small circular tables and sturdy wooden chairs filled the rest of the space.

The dart boards were located in a little alcove toward the back of the long, narrow space. Right now, the three of them were the only ones playing, so they had the space to themselves.

Priest leaned against the wall and pulled his phone from his Rileys. He tapped the screen, and whatever he saw on it made his eyes bug out and his mouth go slack.

"What's wrong?" Cal asked Priest, slightly alarmed by the man's expression.

"Nothing," he answered slowly.

"Are you sure?"

Priest nodded. "Just a text from T."

Quinn assumed his stance, lined up the dart, and threw it. The sharp tip hit one of the large black spaces toward the outer edge.

"*Shit.* I suck at this game." Quinn looked at Priest, who continued to stare at his phone with a bemused expression. "Priest, is T okay?"

Priest looked up. "Yeah. She's fine."

When Priest had a couple of drinks, his stutter improved significantly. Cal found that fact more than a little ironic, since most people slurred their words when they had too much to drink. Priest, meanwhile, could throw back a couple of shots, and his speech became crisper, although he still had trouble with *w*'s.

"She's shopping w-w-w-with Bebe," Priest added.

Before Cal could stop himself, he blurted out the question that had rattled around his head all evening. "Where did they go?"

Priest smiled, his white teeth flashing in the dim light. "A new lingerie shop on Fillmore Street."

Suddenly, Cal's cock was interested in the conversation. Right this moment, Bebe was standing in a lingerie shop, surrounded by silk and satin? Maybe she was sliding a tiny thong up her slender legs or palming her tits to arrange them in a lacy bra . . .

His cock thickened, and he casually pressed his cold beer bottle against his zipper. Hopefully the chilled glass would cool him down.

Quinn sighed. "Too bad Amelia didn't go with them."

Priest chuckled at Quinn's woebegone expression. "T says they bought so much stuff, it w-w-w-won't fit in Bebe's scooter."

Cal wondered if Bebe had thought about him when she'd made her selections—if she had bought anything specifically for him. He really liked those lacy panties that cupped the ass and showed just a hint of cheeks.

Maybe he could convince her to model her new things. He would love to have his own private lingerie show with Bebe as the starring attraction. Sweat broke out on his forehead when he thought about seeing her in nothing but a tiny pair of panties . . . and then stripping her out of them.

He had already taken the first step to making that happen. Earlier today, he'd made the short trip from Riley Plaza to California Pacific Medical Center for an appointment with his primary care physician. His doctor had given him a full physical and complete sexual health screen. It had been relatively quick and painless, requiring him to pee in a cup and give some blood.

Since he hadn't been with anyone in more than three months, all the tests would be conclusive. The results were supposed to be back by early next week, which was fine because he wasn't planning to move that fast anyway. Even though he was eager to get into Bebe's pants, he didn't want to rush things.

In the meantime, he needed to come up with something

fun for them to do this weekend. The weather was supposed to be nice, so maybe they should do something outside—maybe a picnic.

He could whip up some finger foods for a nice afternoon snack. And if he picked a secluded spot, he could lay her down on a blanket after they'd eaten and kiss her for a few hours.

"It's your turn, Cal."

He forcefully redirected his thoughts back to the dart game. "Did Priest already go?"

Priest nodded. "W-w-w-while you were staring into space." He took a deep pull on his Anchor Steam, his green eyes assessing. "W-w-w-were you thinking about Bebe?"

Priest obviously knew something was going on between Cal and Bebe. After all, he had seen them in a slightly compromising position at the cookout. But Cal hadn't expected him to ask about it.

Quinn looked back and forth between them. "What? Why would you be thinking about Bebe?"

Priest pulled his phone from his front pocket, tapped it a couple of times, and handed it to Quinn. He read the screen before passing the phone back to Priest.

"So, Bebe's a virgin, and you've taken it upon yourself to get rid of her pesky hymen," Quinn noted dryly. "You're such a martyr to sacrifice yourself like that. Maybe you'll be canonized as Callum, the Patron Saint of Cherry Popping."

Cal scowled, angry with Teagan for sharing such personal details about Bebe. He was sure she wouldn't want Priest and Quinn to know her intimate business.

"I'm not going to talk about this. It's between me and Bebe."

He wondered how Teagan had responded to the news that he and Bebe were going to be frenemies with benefits. Was she supportive of their de-virginization plan, or had she tried to talk her best friend out of it? His sister knew he was hot for Bebe, and he wondered if she'd told Bebe that he liked her.

He shook his head, annoyed and disgusted with himself. Were they in middle school? Maybe he should pass Bebe a note in homeroom that said, *Do you want to fuck me? Check the box below. Yes or no.*

"I'm confused," Quinn admitted. "I thought you and Bebe hated each other. Every word you say to her is an insult. Since when do you have a thing for her?"

Cal laughed, but the sound lacked any real amusement. "Since always. Why do you think I act like such an ass whenever she's around?"

"I had no idea." Quinn shook his head. "You usually have more finesse with the ladies, brother. *A lot more.*" He grimaced. "You're like the little boy who pulls the little girl's pigtails because he likes her. You've regressed."

No shit.

"Are you sure you know w-w-w-what you're doing?" Priest asked.

"Are you questioning my sexual prowess or my judgment?" Cal shot back, more than a little irritated. "You don't need to worry. I've done it a few times, although maybe not as many as you have since I'm not a dog like you are."

Quinn sucked in a surprised breath at his testy response. Cal rarely lost his temper, and he definitely didn't lose it with his older brother or his best friend.

Pressing his lips together, Priest shook his head. "You're pissing me off," he informed Cal, his mild tone a total contrast to his harsh words. "You're not a choir boy, and I haven't been w-w-w-with anyone w-w-w-with anyone w-w-w-with T for years." He made a little humming noise. "You and Bebe . . . it could be messy."

Cal eyed Priest with a fair amount of rancor. "I guess you're not talking about the pleasurable exchange of bodily fluids."

Quinn gave a muffled laugh, and Priest shook his head in exasperation. "Messy," he repeated darkly.

"Jesus Christ, Priest, you're the one who told me I needed a distraction."

Priest's dark blond eyebrows arched. "Bebe's not a distraction."

"I disagree," he countered. "I think she's a damn good distraction." He pointed at the former football player. "Tell me . . . how is this any of your business?"

"Bebe is T's best friend," Priest reminded Cal. "Hurt Bebe, hurt your sister. And *she* is my b-b-b-business."

Cal took a moment to digest what Priest had said. Frankly, Cal didn't know how the other man handled Teagan, but the guy made her so happy, she almost glowed. And Priest walked around with a goofy smile on his face all the fucking time.

Priest sighed loudly. "Bebe w-w-w-was there for T when

I should have b-b-b-been. I owe her. She's a good person. D-d-d-don't hurt her, okay?"

Forget irritated. Anger suddenly sizzled through Cal's veins.

"I don't believe this bullshit! When you told me and Quinn that you'd fucked up with Teagan, I had your back. I could have been an asshole about it, but I wasn't."

Priest nodded. "I know. But the situation is d-d-d-different."

"How is it different?"

"I w-w-w-was in love with T."

Quinn threw his arm around Cal's shoulders, oblivious to the anger swirling inside him. "I agree with Priest. If things go sideways with Bebe, it would make everything really awkward when we get together. Bebe can find another guy and—"

"No fucking way."

There was no fucking way Cal was going to let another guy have Bebe. He wasn't going to give her up, and he didn't give a good goddamn what his brother and Priest thought.

Shoving Quinn's arm away, Cal turned to face his brother. "Do you remember when you told me you wanted Amelia? I told you to take what you wanted. I gave you my blessing to put yourself above Riley O'Brien. I had your back."

He looked back and forth between them. "Whatever you wanted, I wanted for you. I wanted you to be happy, and I sure as hell didn't stand in the way. Do you hear how selfish you're being? You should have my back instead of giving me shit. You should want me to get what I want." He paused to suck in a lungful of air. "You should want me to be happy, damn it."

"Are you saying Bebe would make you happy?" Quinn asked doubtfully.

"Fucking her would make me happy. Extremely happy. It's just sex. As much as I want, and as often as I want it."

"Holy shit," Quinn breathed. "She agreed to that?"

Cal laughed. "It was her idea. She had an entire goddamn list of conditions. She doesn't want a relationship. She doesn't even like me. She's just using me for my body."

"And you're okay with that?" Quinn asked.

"Hell, yeah, I'm okay with it. Wouldn't you be okay with a beautiful woman using your body?"

Quinn cocked his head. "You think Bebe's beautiful?"

Her big luminous eyes. Her glossy dark hair. Her smooth golden skin. Her pretty pink lips. Her sweet little body.

Beautiful.

He nodded emphatically. "Don't you?"

"Umm . . . well . . . no, I really don't," Quinn answered somewhat apologetically. "I guess she's kind of cute."

Cute? Puppies are cute.

"You're not only blind," Cal told his brother, "you're stupid."

Priest sighed loudly. "You don't know w-w-w-what you're doing," he warned direly. "This is going to b-b-b-backfire on you."

"I don't see how it could backfire, since Bebe and I want the same thing. If it does, though, I'll deal with it, and you can be a supportive friend by throwing it in my face. How does that sound?"

Priest snorted in disgust. "Messy."

Chapter 11

"WHEN WAS THE LAST TIME YOU WENT ON A PICNIC?" CAL asked as he unfolded the faded patchwork quilt.

"I've never been on a picnic," Bebe answered, trying not to stare at his muscular forearms and big hands.

He frowned. "Never? Not even when you were a little girl?"

"No." She shook her head. "Not even then."

He studied her for a moment before raising his arms to snap the quilt. It settled gracefully onto the grass, and she bent over to smooth the edges.

As she straightened, she glanced at Cal. His gaze was glued to her backside.

"Are you checking out my butt?" she demanded baldly.

"I'm just following your directive to objectify you," he said solemnly before giving her a wide grin. "I forgot how much fun it is."

She couldn't help but laugh. He was just so rascally.

"When was the last time you went on a picnic?" she asked, purposely redirecting the conversation away from her posterior.

"Hmm . . . sometime last summer." He grabbed the leather straps of the wicker picnic basket, moving it to the edge of the quilt. "Saika and I took Valerie to Strawberry Hill."

She was extremely curious about Saika. How they had met. What Cal had liked about her. Why they had broken up. Whether he still loved her.

But she didn't ask any of those questions.

"What's Strawberry Hill?"

"It's a small island in the middle of Stow Lake. You can get there by rowboat or walking trails connected by bridges."

"Why didn't we go there today?"

"You don't like this spot?"

She looked around. They were situated on a hill overlooking a picturesque lake. Although it wasn't totally secluded, it seemed a little off the beaten path, and the view was amazing.

"I was just curious. It wasn't a criticism of this locale."

"Stow Lake and Strawberry Hill are two of the most well-known spots in Golden Gate Park. Metson Lake is just as pretty, but it's not overrun with people. I wanted us to have some privacy."

She opened her mouth to ask, *Privacy for what?* But as she met his icy blue gaze, she realized that was a very, very stupid question. Suddenly, she felt compelled to study her feet.

Out of the corner of her eye, she saw him toe off his sneakers, uncovering a pair of plain white athletic socks. She had expected a pair like the ones he'd worn at his condo.

"Why aren't you wearing a pair of Valerie socks?"

"I only wear them with boots and dress shoes. I don't like to wear them with tennis shoes."

"I'm kind of disappointed. I wanted to see your entire collection."

He looked down into her face, and she was reminded once again of how good-looking he was. His dark hair gleamed almost blue-black in the sun. Teagan's hair was the exact same shade, as was Quinn's.

Cal's hair was cut close to his head, the top slightly longer than the sides and back. It looked thick and silky, and she wondered if she'd ever have the opportunity to touch it.

"I'll show you my sock collection if you'll show me the lingerie you bought when you went shopping with Teagan."

"How do you know about that?"

"Priest mentioned it." He smiled slowly, not a full-fledged smile but more of a sexy smirk. "Did you buy anything I might like?"

She hoped so. After all, she had bought it all for him. Piles and piles of panties, bras, camisoles, corsets, garter belts, and thigh-high stockings.

Her face heated at the thought of him seeing her in her sexy new underthings, and she felt the need to press her palms to her hot cheeks. She hoped he had packed something cold to drink in that basket because she needed to cool off.

Dropping down onto the quilt, he stretched out his long legs. Like always, he wore Rileys, but this pair was even more disreputable than all the other pairs she'd seen him in.

The cuffs were frayed, and there was a hole in one of the knees and a tiny worn spot next to his fly. She had a hard time tearing her eyes away from it.

He leaned back on his elbows, the motion making his USC T-shirt tighten against his arms and chest. The red cotton was faded and worn, and it clung to his muscular torso.

"How long have you had that T-shirt?" she asked, since it looked like it was just a tad too small.

He looked down, almost as if he had forgotten which T-shirt he'd picked. He shrugged.

"Probably since college. Why?"

Because you look so good in it, I want to rip it off you.

"Just curious."

Cal patted the quilt. "I saved a spot for you."

As she stared down at him, she was swamped with misgivings, not about having sex with him, but about spending time with him outside the bedroom. She had forced him into these outings, and it had been evident he wasn't exactly thrilled about them. She, meanwhile, had looked forward to this picnic ever since she had received his text earlier in the week.

Kicking off her gray Sketchers sneakers, Bebe stepped onto the quilt. She sat down near his hips, facing him with her legs crisscrossed. The position put her socks on display, and his lips twitched.

"I like your socks."

She wiggled her toes, making the colorful octopuses printed on the socks look as if they were waving their tentacles.

"Thanks. Teagan bought them for me after I refused to eat squid when we went out for sushi."

He chuckled. "Why did you refuse to eat it? What was wrong with it?"

"Nothing. I just kept thinking about its big eyes, and I couldn't eat it."

He studied her intently. "So no sushi restaurants for our dates?"

"It's not my favorite," she admitted, knowing she was among the minority. It seemed everyone except for her loved sushi. "Do you like sushi?"

"Love it. I've taken a couple of sushi-making classes, and I usually make my own."

Bebe knew Cal was a good cook, almost gourmet chef level. She'd eaten his food at various family gatherings, and she had always wondered where he came by his skills.

"Do you take a lot of cooking classes?"

"I've taken a few. I'd like to take more but I don't have a lot of extra time."

"Which one was your favorite?"

"One taught by the head chef of Fig."

Fig was a popular Moroccan restaurant in the Mission District. Bebe had always wanted to try it.

"I've never been there, but I've driven by it. It's always packed."

"It's one of the best in the city. The head chef is a guy named Omar. He taught a series of cooking classes a few months ago, and I took one." Cal smiled a little. "Omar is taller than I am but probably weighs less than you do. He looks like an optical illusion."

Bebe laughed, clearly envisioning Omar in her mind.

"He has some kind of metabolic disorder that keeps him from gaining weight," he continued. "Maybe it's a blessing, though, because I've never met anyone who loves food more than Omar. He's passionate about making food *and* eating it. You know, a lot of chefs love to cook, but they don't like to eat."

"You're more like Omar."

She had been around Cal enough to know that he liked to eat as much as he liked to feed people.

"Yeah. That's probably why I enjoyed the class so much."

"Maybe you can make me one of the dishes you learned from Omar."

"You want me to cook for you?" he asked, his voice shaded with surprise.

She suddenly felt the need to backpedal as quickly as her

mouth would allow. "Only if you want to. It was just a thought."
She told herself to stop talking, but her mouth continued to
spew out words. "I've never had Moroccan food, and I'm sure
I'd love whatever you would make. You're a really good cook.
Everything you make is delicious."

He sat up. "I must be imagining things because that sounded
like you just gave me a compliment . . . actually, two compliments."

No wonder he was surprised. She had never complimented
him before. She kept all her nice thoughts to herself, along
with her naughty ones. Maybe it was time to start sharing
them.

"You're definitely imagining things," she confirmed. "I
would never, *ever* compliment you. I would never, *ever* tell you
that you're a really good cook or that everything you make is
delicious." She paused meaningfully. "And I never, *ever* want
you to make Moroccan food for me."

He leaned forward until their faces were only inches apart.
"I would never, *ever* compliment you, either. I would never,
ever tell you that your smile lights up a room or that your eyes
remind me of antique gold. And I never, *ever* want you to take
your hair down so I can run my fingers through it."

She sucked in a surprised breath. With the exception of
Teagan, no one had ever remarked on her appearance, positively or negatively. She was stunned by his compliments. It
sounded as if he really meant them.

"I would never, *ever* thank you for your compliments
with a kiss," she said, shocking both of them.

And then she leaned forward and did exactly what she
had just claimed she would never, *ever* do.

IT WAS JUST A LIGHT BRUSH OF HER MOUTH AGAINST HIS—A
brief press of soft, smooth lips—but it was enough to make
his blood sizzle. Bebe drew back, and Cal licked his lips,
getting just a hint of coconut. He'd never liked coconut all
that much, but suddenly it was one of his favorite flavors.

He was just about to pull her onto his lap so he could kiss
her until all that coconut-flavored gloss was gone, but she
leaned away from him to tug the picnic basket closer. The
action made her black T-shirt twist a little, and he saw a flash

of golden skin between it and the waistband of her slate-colored cargo pants. He wondered if she wore her new lingerie under them.

"What kind of goodies did you bring?" she asked as she unhooked the latch.

It took him a moment to answer, since all the blood in his body had rushed from his head to his crotch. He cleared his throat roughly.

"Italian subs and caprese kabobs. Cream cheese swirl brownies for dessert."

"Mmm. That sounds delectable." She opened the basket's lid and brought her golden gaze back to him. "Did you make everything?"

He nodded, and her lips tipped up at the corners. "Thank you," she said softly.

He shrugged. It wasn't a big deal to throw together a couple of sandwiches and shove some cherry tomatoes and fresh mozzarella balls onto a wooden skewer. It hadn't taken more than thirty minutes. The brownies had required a little bit more effort, but they were always a hit.

Edging closer to the basket, he gently shouldered Bebe out of the way so he could serve her. He pulled out a bottle of sparkling lemonade and handed it to her along with two plastic cups.

"I brought some bottled water, too, if you'd prefer that instead."

"This is fine."

He quickly unloaded the basket, plated their food, and poured some lemonade. He passed a plate and cup to her before sitting down. He chose a spot so they were facing each other, both of them with their legs crisscrossed so the plates could balance on their knees.

"This looks so good," she observed. "Thank you."

He held up his plastic glass. "To firsts."

Her lips quirked, and she shook her head in exasperation before raising her glass and tapping it against his. "To women with bad judgment."

He laughed. "You think you have bad judgment?"

"It's definitely questionable at this point," she answered wryly.

He didn't like the sound of that. Was she having second thoughts?

Shit.

"I think you should give yourself more credit," he advised, doing his best to keep her from bailing on their arrangement. "It takes a lot of courage to go after what you want."

She shook her head. "I should have done something about it a long, long time ago," she admitted before taking a big drink of lemonade.

Cal pondered her comment while they ate their sandwiches and kabobs. He had wondered why Bebe was a virgin . . . why she had never even been kissed before he'd stepped in.

He didn't know the average age when females usually lost their virginity, but if he had to guess, he'd say late teens. He doubted many girls got past their high school graduation with their hymens intact.

"This was really good, but I don't think I can eat any more," Bebe announced. "I need to save room for dessert."

"Why are you still a virgin?" he blurted out.

She jerked her head back as if he'd slapped her, her eyes wide with surprise. He winced, both annoyed and embarrassed by his tactless delivery.

She opened her mouth, and he leaned forward, eager to hear her answer. But she pressed her lips together and looked down without answering. He took her plate from her, stacked it on top of his, and set them aside. He'd clean up later.

"Bebe, why are you still a virgin?"

She took a deep breath. "I think it's partly because of lack of opportunity and partly because I was never attracted to anyone enough to want to have sex."

That was definitely *not* what he had expected to hear. He had assumed her virginity was the result of her high-powered career, or perhaps a product of her religious beliefs or social mores.

His surprise must have been evident on his face because Bebe giggled. "Better close your mouth, Cal, or you'll swallow a bug."

He snapped it closed, and she flashed him a big smile. His heart stuttered before giving a huge thump. He liked her smiles *so* much better than her scowls.

"Can I have a brownie now?" she requested.

"Sure, you can have a brownie. But don't think that just because your mouth is full, I won't expect you to answer my question."

She frowned. "I already answered your question."

"I have more."

She shrugged. "Cream cheese swirl brownies in exchange for answers to your questions. I'm getting the better deal."

He was sure he was getting the better deal because he was intensely curious about her. He had been forced to keep his curiosity under wraps for years, but now he didn't have to.

He dug around in the picnic basket until he found the plastic container filled with dessert. Popping off the top, he held it out to her so she could grab a brownie. The moment she had one in hand, she took a big bite.

"Mmm," she moaned, closing her eyes. "I love these brownies. I could eat them every day and never get tired of them."

Taking another bite, she let out another long moan. He shifted uncomfortably on the quilt when his cock pressed into his zipper. It was downright painful to be semi-erect while sitting with your legs crisscrossed.

"What did you mean when you said you were a virgin partly because of lack of opportunity?"

She opened her eyes, and the brilliant gold of her gaze sucked him in like a riptide. After a long moment, she blinked slowly, breaking the hold so he could breathe again.

"My parents enrolled me in a math and science magnet high school when I was twelve, and I graduated when I was fifteen. I was too young to date. And I was younger than everyone else, even though all the other students were academically advanced like me."

"How did you jump so far ahead?"

She shrugged. "Before high school, I was in a private school that believed students should advance at their own pace."

"We were in high school at the same time, even though you're three years younger than I am," he noted.

"Yes, although I'm sure your experience was different than mine," she said dryly.

"What was your high school experience like?"

"Isolating," she answered succinctly.

Cal was sure "isolating" was exactly the right word. He doubted she'd had any friends, let alone boyfriends.

"Did you immediately go to college after you graduated from high school?"

"Yes. I left for Northwestern when I was fifteen. Again, I

was younger than everyone else, and even if a guy had been interested, it would have been illegal for him to mess around with me."

"I don't think I could send my fifteen-year-old daughter away to college, no matter how smart she was," he admitted.

"My parents had no trouble with that. They were happy to see me go. In fact, they didn't even take time to drive me. They put me on a plane to Chicago and gave me money so I could take a taxi from the airport to campus. They shipped all my stuff to me."

"*Are you fucking kidding me?*" he burst out, horrified by the thought of a teenage Bebe being forced to navigate a huge city like Chicago by herself.

"No, I'm not fucking kidding you," she parroted with a small smile.

He didn't know how she could smile about something so awful. Her parents should have been charged with child abuse. Neglect at the very least.

"After I graduated from Northwestern, I moved back to Baltimore and started medical school at Johns Hopkins," she continued as if she were narrating a film. "I was old enough to date but still younger than all the other students. The guys either hated me—medical school is super competitive, you know—or they wanted to be my study partner."

"Explain something to me. You graduated from medical school, and you have a medical degree, but you can't practice medicine because you never completed your residency."

"Right."

"Why would you work so hard to get your medical degree and then just walk away?"

"Because I didn't want to be a doctor," she replied flatly.

"You wanted to be a lawyer?"

She bit her lip. "No, not really. I had turned down my residency, and . . ."

"And what?" he prompted her.

She fiddled with her rings, twisting them around and around her slender fingers. He had realized that was her tell. She did it when she was upset, nervous, or uncomfortable. He waited patiently, and after a long moment, she finally answered him.

"I was a little lost. I'd never done anything but go to school.

Education was my comfort zone, I guess. I thought more schooling sounded like a good idea. It seemed like a safe choice."

"And there were no guys at Harvard who interested you?"

"No," she answered curtly. "Cal, I don't want to talk about this anymore."

He instinctively knew that if he pushed her right now, she would walk away—from the picnic, from him, from their arrangement—so he let the subject drop.

"I just want to let you know that I would never, *ever* tell you that your brain is like a race car with NOS," he said.

Her eyes lit up when she got his reference to *The Fast and the Furious* movies and the nitrous oxide systems that street racers used to give their cars an extra burst of speed.

"That's good to know. I would never, *ever* tell you that your kisses are better than cream cheese swirl brownies."

Chapter 12

BEBE SMILED WHEN SHE SAW HIM, A TINY TILT OF HER PINK LIPS, and warmth filled Cal's chest. She had given him more smiles in the past two weeks than she had in the past four years, and he hoarded them like a starving man saved breadcrumbs.

"Good morning, Cookie," he greeted her when she reached him.

Her smile widened, giving him a little glimpse of her even white teeth. "Good morning."

He straightened from his slouch against the side of his car, which he'd parked in front of her building. They were heading to an orchard north of the city to pick apples, and he had made the short drive from his place to pick her up.

This was date number three, and so far they hadn't done anything more than kiss. Despite the fact that he'd already waited years to get into her pants, he didn't want to rush things.

He had realized that Bebe wasn't just inexperienced; she was *innocent*. Because of her medical degree, she was informed and knowledgeable about intercourse. But she was completely unaware of the pleasure that sex offered—like someone who knew the ingredients in chocolate but had never savored a gourmet truffle.

Given how innocent she was, he didn't want to scare her.

Nor did he want to give her any reason to back out of their agreement. He wanted her to experience all the excitement and exhilaration that led up to sex . . . the tension, the anticipation, the foreplay, both verbal and physical.

That was why he'd decided they needed to go on at least a dozen dates before he revoked her V-card. He would probably be frothing at the mouth like Cujo by the time they got to number twelve.

"I want to amend our arrangement," he announced abruptly as he passed a to-go cup of chai tea to her.

Her smile disappeared. "Fewer dates?" she guessed.

That thought hadn't even crossed his mind. He enjoyed their dates, and he would enjoy them even more when they ended with him snug inside her virginal body.

"No, I want to add a new condition."

"What?" she asked warily before taking a sip of tea.

"When you greet me, you have to say hello with a kiss."

She studied him over the plastic lid of the to-go cup, her eyes a kaleidoscope of amber and gold. They shimmered vibrantly in the late-morning sunlight.

He bent down until their noses almost touched. "Is that acceptable?"

She nodded but still didn't give him what he wanted. "The new condition is effective immediately," he hinted.

Leaning forward, she gave him a quick peck. Her lips barely grazed his before she drew back, her dark eyebrows arched inquiringly.

"No," he said, answering her unspoken question. "I want a real kiss."

"That was a real kiss."

"It wasn't," he countered.

"I'm sorry," she replied contritely, but her eyes held a glimmer of amusement. "I'm not an expert like you are. Maybe you should show me how to give a real kiss."

"Good idea." He took the tea from her and placed it on the roof of his car. "First, you should put your hands here," he instructed, drawing her arms up around his neck. "Or on my chest. That works, too."

He cupped her hips in his palms. "And you should get as close as possible so I can feel you," he continued, tugging her closer until his belt buckle brushed her stomach.

Bending down until their mouths almost touched, he murmured, "And you should definitely open your mouth so I can taste you."

He lightly settled his mouth over hers, and her lips parted easily. He eased his tongue inside her mouth, which was spiced with chai tea, and licked deeply.

He hadn't seen her . . . hadn't kissed her . . . in four days, not since he'd taken her to a pub in his neighborhood to listen to an Irish band and drink Guinness. After their date, he had limited himself to a brief good-night kiss because it was so late.

Since then, he'd looked forward to kissing her again. And now that he had his mouth on hers, she tasted even better than he remembered. Her tongue slid against his, and he barely held back a moan when she licked inside his mouth.

He was starting to think that kissing Bebe was better than getting naked with other women. And if kissing her was this good, having sex with her was going to blow his mind.

He played with her mouth until a horn honked nearby. She jerked away from him, her eyes a little glazed and her lips rosy from his kiss.

"You want me to kiss you like *that* to say hello?" she asked doubtfully, pressing her fingers against her lower lip.

"Yes. Exactly like that. Every time you see me."

"What if we're in front of people?"

"I don't care if the Pope is standing next to us."

She laughed softly. "Okay. If you insist."

He nodded in satisfaction before stepping away from her and opening the car door. "Hop in," he ordered, grabbing her drink from the roof and gesturing toward the car's interior. "We've got apples to pick."

Minutes later, they were headed out of the city across the Golden Gate Bridge. The fog had burned off the Bay, and the sky was a deep, pure blue.

"Where are we going?" Bebe asked.

"Sebastopol. It's a tiny farming town in Sonoma County about an hour away."

Squinting a little against the bright sunshine filtering through the windshield, she grabbed her big purse from the floorboard and placed it on the bench seat between them. She situated her chai tea between her thighs, and for one fleeting moment, he actually was jealous of a paper cup.

After rummaging around in her leather bag, she pulled out a pair of sunglasses and set them on her nose. With their big tortoiseshell frames, they reminded him of the sunglasses movie stars wore to conceal their identities. She looked sexy and mysterious in them.

"Have I told you how much I love your car?" She shifted slightly so she could look at him. "It's like riding on a cloud."

His vintage Cadillac Coupe De Ville was very comfortable. It also was a gas-guzzler and almost impossible to parallel park, but he couldn't give it up. His Grandma Violet had given the powder-blue car to him, and he liked feeling connected to her, even if it was through a piece of machinery.

Bebe stroked her hand over the dark blue leather seat, her rings glimmering in the sunlight, and for one fleeting moment, he was insanely jealous of a bench seat.

"When Teagan and I were at Harvard, she told me that you called your car Belva. I thought it was kind of weird, but once I saw her, I understood. She's too cool for a boring name."

"Yeah, Belva's pretty cool."

"Where did you come up with the name?"

"From my Grandpa Patrick. He said the Caddy was the same color as the dress Grandma Vi was wearing when he met her. She introduced herself as Belva instead of Violet."

"Why did she do that?"

Cal shook his head. "I have no idea. When I asked my Grandpa Patrick about it, he said she was playing hard to get."

Bebe laughed, a light, happy sound that made him smile. "Teagan says your grandma was a unique woman . . . kind of eccentric."

"I don't think she was eccentric. She just didn't care much about what people thought of her. She had enough confidence to be herself."

"It's hard not to care about what other people think of you, especially the people who are supposed to love you," Bebe noted softly.

Cal briefly took his eyes from the road to look at Bebe. Her lips were turned down in a little frown, and she was twisting her rings.

"Yeah, sometimes they can be the harshest critics," he agreed.

It didn't take a genius to realize Bebe lacked love and

acceptance from her family. From what she'd shared during their picnic, her mom and dad weren't going to win any parent-of-the-year awards. In fact, he got the feeling they had messed her up pretty badly.

His situation was completely different. The people who loved him were not his harshest critics. Instead, they were his biggest fans, and he had never been forced to prove himself to them. They didn't want him to be anyone except the person he was.

Bebe tilted her head. "Why did she leave her Caddy to you?"

Cal tapped his fingers on the steering wheel. No one had ever asked why Grandma Vi had left the car to him. They always wanted to know why he drove the Caddy instead of putting it in storage and buying a new car.

"Because she wanted to remind me of what's important," he finally answered.

"What's important?"

"Being myself. Having the confidence to be myself."

"I don't see lack of confidence as a problem for you." Bebe laughed softly. "In fact, I'd say it's the opposite."

He didn't lack the confidence to be himself. But he hadn't always been so sure of who he was. Although he didn't really care what people thought about him now, there had been a time when he had.

"Grandma Vi wanted to make sure that I knew I was my own person, not just Quinn's younger brother. She worried about me feeling that I had to compete with him—to do everything that he did."

Bebe didn't reply, but he could tell she was listening intently. "She always told me that I was Cal first and Quinn's brother second. That I was Cal first and an heir to Riley O'Brien & Co. second. She told me that as long as I was myself, things would turn out okay."

"Your grandmother was a *very* smart woman. I wish I had known her."

Cal had no doubt Grandma Vi would have loved Bebe. She would have appreciated her intellect, enjoyed her sense of humor, and admired her steadfast friendship with Teagan.

"I wish she were still here."

"Is that why you drive Belva? Because you want to feel close to her?"

"That's the main reason," he admitted. "But there are other reasons, too."

"What other reasons?" Bebe asked before taking a swallow of chai tea.

"Practical reasons. I'm a big guy, and I don't have to squeeze myself into her."

ALTHOUGH CAL'S STATEMENT HAD BEEN COMPLETELY FREE OF sexual innuendo, the only thing Bebe could think about was how "big" he was and how he was going to squeeze into *her* instead of Belva. Her naughty thoughts made her choke on her tea.

As she gurgled and fell into a coughing fit, he shot a concerned look toward her and patted her back vigorously—so vigorously she started to laugh in between her gasps.

"Are you okay?" he asked, continuing to pound her on the back.

"Cal, stop," she ordered breathlessly. "I'm good."

Somewhat reluctantly, he removed his hand and brought his eyes back to the road. Deciding that she needed to redirect his attention before he realized why she had gotten all choked up, she pointed to the iPhone anchored to the dashboard. It synced with the car's speakers.

"Can we listen to some music?"

"Go ahead."

She nabbed the phone and quickly opened the music app. She didn't bother to scroll through the songs; she just hit Play. Almost immediately, weird background noise filled the car. Then a sudden drumbeat blared out of the speakers, and a guy shouted out "Ey" several times before launching into song.

She glanced at Cal. "What is this?"

"It's an indie band from Southern California called the Cayucas." He smiled, tapping his fingers against the steering wheel. "Give it a chance. You might like it."

She listened for a while. He was right. She did like it. The song had a funky, fun beat, and she liked the lead singer's voice.

"What's the name of this song?"

"'High School Lover.'"

"I'm sure you had plenty of those," she noted dryly.

He laughed. "That's pure speculation."

"Teagan is a reliable source."

He jerked his head toward her, his mirrored aviator sunglasses reflecting her image. "What did she tell you?" he demanded, turning down the volume on the radio.

For years, Teagan had filled Bebe's ears about Quinn's and Cal's sexual exploits. In fact, Teagan had claimed that she'd held on to her virginity until college because of the bad example her older brothers had set.

"Teagan said you and Quinn tapped a lot of ass when you were in high school. She also said you were a manwhore in college. I'm quoting her, by the way."

"Jesus Christ on a pogo stick," he muttered. "I'm going to kill her."

Bebe watched with fascination as Cal's face flushed with color. "Your face is red, Cal. Are you embarrassed about something?"

"No." He pursed his lips. "Maybe."

She snickered, enjoying his embarrassment. He frowned darkly.

"If you have a question about my sexual past, you need to ask me instead of Teagan," he snapped.

She gasped in affront. "I *did not* ask your sister about your sex life! She volunteered the information years ago, before you and I even met. Now I wish I had paid more attention, though."

Cal huffed out a breath. "She's not a reliable source. If you want to know something, now is the time to bring it up because after this conversation, the subject is closed."

"So you'll answer any questions I have?"

"Yes."

Bebe narrowed her eyes. "What's the catch?"

"You *are* a smart cookie," he praised, his lips turned up in a small smile.

"Well?" she prompted him when he didn't answer her question.

"For every answer I give you, you have to go down on me."

Her mouth fell open in shock. *Is he serious?*

Needing clarification, she asked, "You want blow jobs in exchange for answering my questions?"

"Yeah, that sounds like a fair trade to me."

The idea was a little intriguing, she had to admit. And she was willing to perform fellatio on him. More than willing, in fact. She was downright eager to do it.

Cal burst out laughing. "You should see your face."

"You were joking?"

"Yes, I was just teasing you," he confirmed with a deep chuckle.

He never let an opportunity to embarrass her go by. He teased her unmercifully, deriving far too much pleasure from her discomfiture. Maybe it was time for her to turn the tables.

"I thought it sounded like a fair trade, too."

Cal's laughter died in his throat. "*What?*"

"I was going to agree to your terms. Blow jobs in exchange for answers."

"*Holy shit*," he whispered, looking back and forth between her and the road.

She shrugged. "But since you were just teasing me . . ."

"No!" he exclaimed loudly, his deep voice echoing throughout the car. "I was serious. Serious as an economic crisis. Serious as a bomb threat. Serious as an outbreak of Ebola virus."

"Those things are pretty serious," she noted, amused by how quickly he was backtracking.

"Do we have a deal?"

Ignoring his question, she asked one of her own. "When did you lose your virginity?"

"When I was fifteen."

"That's young."

"Too young. I wouldn't want my son to be sexually active at that age. I might have held on to it longer if Quinn hadn't lost his, but once he was doing it, I didn't want to be left out."

"The average male loses his virginity at sixteen point nine years."

Cal glanced at her suspiciously. "Did you memorize that statistic?"

"I remember most things I read."

He shook his head in disbelief. "Bebe, your brain is already turbocharged. Please tell me you don't have a photographic memory."

"There is no scientific proof that eidetic memory really exists."

He laughed. "Did you read that, too?"

"Maybe. Probably."

"What's the average age that females lose their virginity?"

"Seventeen point four years."

"That sounds about right." He sighed gustily. "I hope I don't end up with daughters. I'll be a hypocrite when I tell them to wait for the right guy. I sure as hell didn't wait for the right girl."

"Do you remember the first girl you had sex with?"

He nodded. "You always remember your first." He flashed a big smile. "You know what that means, right? I'm not going to be a footnote in your history. I'm going to be an entire section."

Bebe took a deep breath. She had never really thought about it that way, but she was glad that Cal would be the one she remembered years from now instead of a stranger she had picked up in a bar.

"Who was your first?"

"Belinda McAllen," he answered promptly. "Everybody called her Lindy."

"What was she like?"

"Tall. Nice ass. Great rack. Long blond hair. Blue eyes. Kind of quiet. Played the drums in the school band. I'd had a crush on her since seventh grade."

Bebe was dying of curiosity. Had he and Lindy dated? Where had they done the deed? Had it been a good experience?

Cal laughed softly. "Don't stop now, Cookie. I can almost hear the gears grinding in your head."

She hadn't really expected him to answer her questions, but a lot of things about Cal surprised her. His openness was just one of them. He wasn't nearly as guarded and private as his siblings.

"How did it happen?"

"One day after football practice, I went back into the main building to get a book from my locker. *To Kill a Mockingbird*, I think. The shortest route was past the music hall, and I ran into Lindy. I was so nervous and tongue-tied, I couldn't even talk to her. She didn't say anything, either, just grabbed my hand and pulled me into one of the practice rooms. I did her against the wall. The whole thing only lasted ten minutes. Actually, it probably was more like five minutes."

"Was she a virgin?"

"Not even close," he replied wryly. "She went to drumline camp the summer before our sophomore year, and she played with more than one kind of stick."

Bebe couldn't help but giggle at his joke. Now that he no

longer used his quick wit to insult her, Cal made her laugh more than anyone else, even Teagan.

"I was lucky she'd done it before because I wasn't even thinking about diseases or pregnancy. I probably would have been stupid enough to have sex without a condom, but she had some in her bag."

Before Bebe could think about it, she blurted out, "Was it good for you?"

Cal barked out a sharp laugh. "Jesus, Bebe. Of course it was good for me. Any kind of sex is good for a teenage boy with no experience." He rolled his lips inward. "It wasn't good for her, though."

"How do you know?"

He grimaced. "When it was over, she said, 'You need some practice.'"

"*Oh, my God.* She did not!"

He laughed with a fair amount of self-deprecation. "Unfortunately, she did."

Bebe was incensed at the thought of a gangly, insecure Cal being dissed by a slutty mean girl. She felt strangely protective of his teenage self, even though the experience obviously hadn't scarred him in any way.

"That's so horrible! What a little bitch."

He shook his head. "Nah, she softened the blow by letting me practice on her." He smiled crookedly. "I'm a fast learner. By the time we got to her last rubber, she was screaming 'Thank you!'"

Bebe placed her palms against her hot face. Was it normal to be turned on by the recounting of his teenage sexcapades? Normal or not, she *was* turned on. Soaked-panties turned on.

"So, Lindy was your first."

"Yep."

"And how many since?"

Picking up her left hand, he brought it to his mouth. He kissed it softly before linking his long fingers through hers and settling their hands on the thick muscles of his thigh.

"Let's just say you'd have a hard time catching up."

Chapter 13

EVERYWHERE BEBE LOOKED, SHE SAW APPLES. THEY WERE ON the ground, hanging from tree limbs, and piled in big wooden baskets. The air was scented with them, a crisp, sweet fragrance that filled her lungs.

Surprisingly, the orchard wasn't crowded. In fact, there were only a few couples and families wandering around. She had expected a lot of people to be here because it was Saturday and the weather was perfect for outdoor activities. The temperature was in the low seventies, and the sun shone against a cloudless blue sky.

Cal walked beside her, one hand holding a couple of stacked wooden baskets by their metal handles and the other entwined with hers. The tall trees created a leafy canopy above them, filtering the bright sunlight so it dappled them with a golden glow. They were heavy with ripe fruit, and a wooden ladder was situated under each one.

"This is one of the biggest orchards in the state," he said.

The orchard was at least several hundred acres. Row upon row of mature apple trees dotted the countryside, and the ground beneath was lush with ankle-high grass. She was glad she'd worn hiking boots instead of tennis shoes.

"The owners have added a lot of land and trees over the

years. The first time I visited, it was only a few acres, and the trees were short and small-limbed." He slanted a teasing glance toward her. "Kind of like you."

She rolled her eyes. He loved to point out the disparity between their physiques.

"Every fall my parents would load us into the car, and we'd take a day trip up here to pick apples," he continued. "We would always stop and have dinner on the way home, and when we woke up the next morning, we'd have cinnamon apple waffles made from the fruit we'd picked the day before."

Bebe didn't have any childhood memories like the one Cal had just shared. She'd never done anything fun like apple picking with her parents and brothers. She was eighteen years younger than Pritam and fifteen years younger than Ranjit.

When she had been born, Pritam was already in college and Ranjit was attending a college-prep boarding school in Pennsylvania. Growing up, she'd spent time with them during the holidays, and those occasions had been tense and uncomfortable. Now she only saw them once every couple of years, if that.

Cal gently squeezed her hand. "This is another first for you, isn't it?"

"Yes, it's another first. I've never been apple picking." She nudged him with her shoulder. "Are you purposely choosing activities that I've never done so you can have all my firsts?"

He chuckled. "How could I possibly know all the things you have and haven't done, Cookie?"

"I don't know. But everything we've done together, I've never done before. The picnic, the Irish band, and now apple picking. What's next?"

"Hmm, I don't know yet. What do you want to do?"

I want to do you. As soon as possible.

"Maybe a musical."

"A musical?" he repeated, groaning dramatically. "That's just another word for torture."

She laughed at his typical guy response. "At least I didn't say the ballet."

"A musical sounds like a great idea," he backtracked hastily. "Thanks for the suggestion." He frowned thoughtfully. "Priest and T's Halloween party is next weekend, so we'll have to go during the week."

"Oh! I forgot to tell you. I have to be in New York all week for work. I'm leaving tomorrow night."

"Do you want to have dinner before you leave? I can take you to the airport afterward."

His offer surprised her. Did he *want* to spend time with her? Their antagonistic relationship of the past had transformed into a teasing camaraderie, and he seemed to enjoy their outings. But she never forgot that she had forced him into them.

"I don't think I have time," she replied. "I have a lot of work to do to get ready for the investor meetings, plus I have to pack."

They passed another tree with plenty of apples on it, but Cal continued on. She wondered if he had a specific destination in mind.

"We've passed dozens of trees. Why haven't we stopped?"

He looked down at her. "I'm looking for the right tree."

"The right tree? What's the right tree?"

"The one that says, 'How do you like them apples?'" he answered with a grin.

They had reached the end of the row, and he tugged her toward a huge tree that sat on the edge of a hilly pasture. It had a thick trunk and long branches covered with dark green leaves. Dozens of fallen apples surrounded the base, and sweet-smelling fruit dotted the limbs.

"This is the one," he announced as he placed the baskets on the ground next to the ladder.

Propping his hands on his hips, he eyed the tree. While he was busy formulating his apple-picking strategy, Bebe took a moment to appreciate the sight of him in such a scenic setting.

His long-sleeved waffle-knit shirt was almost the same shade of red as the apples hanging from the trees. It emphasized his broad shoulders and muscular arms, and the bold color made his hair look darker and his eyes lighter.

As usual, his lower half was clad in Rileys. They were obviously a newer pair, since they were dark instead of faded. With his long, muscular legs, lean waist, and tight butt, he had a perfect body for jeans, and they fit as if they had been made for him.

"You can use the ladder," he suggested, tapping the toe of his brown hiking boot against one of the steps. "I'm tall enough to reach some of the low-hanging fruit."

She looked up at the lower branches. They seemed really far away.

"Are you sure you can reach?"

In response, Cal lifted his arms straight up to touch a thick limb. His shirt rose with the movement, baring his stomach, and she couldn't help but stare at his cut abs and the silky-looking dark hair that trailed toward his waistband. She wanted to touch him so badly, to trace those sculpted muscles, first with her hands and then with her tongue.

"These are Braeburn apples," Cal explained, oblivious to her lustful gaze. "They're bicolored, which means they're not uniformly red."

Plucking an apple from the tree, he held it out to her. Her hand shook a little bit when she took it from him, but he didn't seem to notice.

"They're really good for baking, and I'm going to use the fruit we pick today to make a few pies."

"What kind of pies?" she asked, doing her best to stop thinking about his incredible body.

"Apple pies," he answered with a smirk.

She shook her head in exasperation. "You're such a smart-ass. There are different types of apple pie, you know."

He laughed. "I know. I was thinking about apple-cranberry or maybe apple-caramel. Which one sounds better to you?"

"They both sound delicious. But I'm not going to be here to eat them."

He shook his head. "I'll freeze one for you." He tilted his head toward the ladder. "If you want a pie, you need to get busy."

As she climbed the ladder, he stood beside it to hold it steady. "Don't climb too high, Cookie."

"I'm not," she protested. "Geez, you're so bossy."

"Get used to it," he shot back, passing a basket to her. "I'm even bossier in bed."

Before she could think better of it, she asked, "Really?"

He looked up at her. His full lips tilted in a small smile, and his light blue eyes glinted with amusement.

"Yes, really." He patted her on the butt. "Don't worry, you'll like it."

As Cal turned away from her and began to pluck apples,

she absentmindedly placed her basket on top of the ladder. Her mind buzzed with all the ways he was going to boss her around when they were in bed together.

Touch me there. Open your legs wider. Suck me deeper.

She couldn't wait.

An apple dropped from the branch next to her, pulling her from her X-rated thoughts. She grasped a piece of fruit still attached to the tree, and it took her a moment to realize the apple was easier to remove if you twisted and pulled at the same time.

The monotonous action gave her plenty of time to think about her arrangement with Cal. So far, they hadn't done anything more than kiss, and she was getting impatient with his snail-like pace.

He hadn't even tried to touch her boobs or put his hands in her pants, and she was starting to think her new underwear was a waste of money. Sure, it was pretty, but it wasn't nearly as comfortable as her cotton briefs and soft-cup bras.

Right now, in fact, her cheeky panties were more crack-y than cheeky. She wished she could pull them loose, but she didn't want Cal to see her adjusting her underwear.

"I really like apples," he said before dropping a couple of pieces of fruit into his basket and moving closer to the ladder.

Even though she thought his comment was somewhat inane, she replied, "Me, too."

Hooking an arm through one of the rungs of the ladder, he gazed up at her. "Spread some peanut butter on them, and you've got a tasty snack."

She nodded. She often ate an apple with peanut butter for her afternoon snack at work. It was healthy, and it gave her a boost to get through the rest of the day.

Cal added, "Apples aren't my favorite fruit, though."

"What's your favorite?" she asked as she picked another apple.

"I'm partial to the cherry."

It took her way too long to get his innuendo. When she finally did, she glanced down into his face. His eyes sparkled with devilment.

"Yeah, there's nothing like a sweet, ripe cherry." He smacked his lips. "So juicy and delicious."

BEBE'S FACE WAS NEARLY AS RED AS THE APPLE SHE HELD IN HER hand. "You are so bad," she murmured. "*So bad.*"

He ignored her. "I recently came across a new variety of cherry called the Bebe."

She turned slightly on the step and looked down at him. Her new position put his face even with her crotch, and he didn't even bother to pretend he wasn't staring straight at her zipper and talking about what was behind it.

After a long moment, he leisurely moved his gaze up her body to meet her eyes. He smiled.

"This new variety is very rare, and it takes a little longer to ripen, but I have no doubt it's going to be the sweetest of them all."

Her face turned even redder, and he couldn't hold back a chuckle. It was so damn fun to tease her—to make her golden skin turn dusky with a fierce blush.

She shook her head slightly as she shifted on the ladder to drop the apple in her basket. She stretched up to pull another one from the tree, and her oatmeal-colored sweater rose with the movement. He got a brief flash of smooth skin above the waistband of her pants, and the lust that had churned in his gut all day moved lower.

"My basket is full," she announced. "Can you help me with it?"

Reaching up, he easily hefted the basket from the ladder and placed it on the ground. He turned back to her just as she bent forward to descend the steps. The action pushed out her ass, and he took a good long look, knowing it was much too late to avert a full-fledged erection.

He was pretty sure he'd never seen an ass as mouthwatering as Bebe's. Her cocoa-colored corduroy pants were tight enough to show the high, tight curve of her cheeks and the roundness of her hips.

He wanted to run his fingers down the crevice of that ass until he reached her slick folds. He wanted to clench his hands on those hips as he pumped into her from behind.

Before he could even think about what he was doing, he grabbed her around the waist and plucked her from the ladder. She squealed in surprise, and somehow he managed to turn her in his arms until she faced him.

"Cal!" She clutched his biceps. "What are you doing?"

As he hooked an arm under her ass, he looked around. They were alone, not another person in sight.

"Put your legs around me," he ordered, his voice nearly a growl.

Her eyes widened, and she opened her mouth, but he cut her off. "Now," he demanded.

She immediately spread her legs and wrapped them around his hips. Cupping her ass in both hands, he circled the tree so they were shielded from view by its thick trunk. He backed her against it until his cock was snug between her legs.

Dropping his head, he found her lips. He eagerly licked at them before thrusting his tongue aggressively into her mouth. She welcomed him, wrapping her arms tightly around his neck and sucking on his tongue. He felt that deep suction throughout his body, radiating from his mouth to his cock.

He eased away from her lips to trail kisses across her cheekbone and down her neck. She tilted her head to give him better access, and he licked circles on the fragile skin below her ear before sucking the lobe into his mouth. She gasped and turned her mouth back to his.

"Touch me," she whispered against his lips. "Everywhere. Anywhere. Just touch me."

Reaching between them, she unbuttoned her sweater. He barely had a moment to appreciate the sight of her breasts in their pastel pink bra before she snapped open the hook between the pale gold mounds.

She pulled the lace cups apart, and her breasts bounced out of them, full and firm. They were bigger than he'd imagined and tipped with large, perfect nipples the color of his favorite chocolate truffles.

"*Fuck, yeah,*" he breathed.

He hastily shifted her higher so her breasts were right in his face. "Give me one of those nipples."

She pressed her hands against her nipples. "What?"

He reminded himself he was dealing with a virgin. "Bring it to my mouth, baby, so I can taste you."

Biting her lip, she slowly cupped her hand around her breast.

She raised it to his mouth, and he quickly covered her nipple with his lips. He sucked gently on the tight little bud, rolling his tongue over it, and she moaned.

"Is it normal for me to feel that everywhere?" she asked breathlessly.

He released her nipple. "Where?"

"Everywhere."

"Here?" he guessed, rocking his erection into her.

She gasped. "Yes. *Yes.*" Her head fell back against the tree. "Do that again."

She tightened her legs around him and did a little shimmy that made his eyes cross. He was so hard it was painful, and for one fleeting moment, he wished she weren't a virgin. If she weren't, he could have fucked her fast and hard in the shade of the apple tree.

He balanced her on his thigh and reached between them to unsnap her pants. Finding the tab of her zipper, he pulled it down before sliding his hand across her stomach. She nervously grasped it, and he flattened his palm against her warm skin.

"Let me in," he whispered against her ear. "Let me touch you." He rubbed a circle on her belly. "Let me touch your sweet pussy. It's all I think about. How wet and hot and soft you'll be. The sounds you'll make when you come."

She jerked against him, and her grip loosened before falling away. He eased his hand into her panties, smoothing over the hair covering her pussy. It was damp and tangled, and the evidence of her arousal sent a surge of satisfaction through him.

She might not like me, but I turn her on.

She shifted, and the movement nudged his fingers into her wet slit. Her juice drenched his fingers, and he stroked deeper into the hot folds of her pussy.

"Oh, baby, you are *soaked*," he murmured against her mouth. "You must like the way I touch you."

"You don't even have to touch me. Just looking at you makes me wet."

"Just looking at you makes me hard."

He stroked higher until he reached her clit, and she shivered when he rubbed the tip of his finger over it. "Oh!" she exclaimed. "That's a zinger."

He laughed breathlessly. "Did you like that?"

She nodded.

"Want me to do it again?"

Another nod, this one more emphatic. He smiled against her mouth as he shifted his fingers to lightly graze the sensitive nub with his fingernail. She let out a breathy moan that made his cock pulse against his zipper.

He took a deep breath, and the delicious tang of her arousal flooded him. Wedging his hand deeper into her panties, he found the opening to her body. She was so fucking wet, his entire hand was slippery with her juice.

She might not like me, but I make her wet.

He dipped the tip of his finger inside her, and she sucked in a breath. "It's okay," he crooned, slowly working the rest of it into her. "It's going to be good. I promise I'll give you what you need."

She exhaled loudly. "It feels weird, Cal."

God, she was tight. Her hot flesh gripped his finger like a vise.

"Weird bad?"

She took her time, obviously considering his question. Finally she answered, "No."

He pulled out slightly and then pressed deeper. She clutched his shoulders.

"Okay?"

"Oh, yeah. I *really* liked that."

He pulled out again, and this time when he pushed back inside, he added another finger. Her pussy sucked them in, the muscles tight and supple.

"Oohh," she moaned, and a droplet of sweat dribbled down the middle of his back.

This was *killing* him. His pulse thundered in his ears, and he told himself to stop because he was too close to the edge. His fingers were too busy to listen, though, withdrawing and plunging deeply. She tensed against him.

"Am I hurting you?"

"No."

"Then you need to relax. The more relaxed you are, the harder you'll come."

"What if I'm one of those women who can't have an orgasm?"

He laughed croakily. "Baby, you're almost there right now. You just don't know it."

"I am?"

"Yeah," he answered hoarsely.

He stroked her clit rhythmically with his thumb as he pumped his fingers in and out of her pussy. She whimpered.

"I can't feel my fingers or my toes," she admitted. "Is that normal?"

He smiled against her cheek. *Damn, she's sweet.*

He slowly increased the rhythm until she was panting in his ear. Her pussy clamped down on his fingers, the muscles quivering with her orgasm.

"Oh, my God, Cal!" she cried out.

He covered her mouth with his, swallowing her pleasure. He was pretty sure this was her first orgasm, and he felt a rush of satisfaction that *he* was the man who had given it to her.

She might not like me, but I make her come.

The feel of her against his fingers, the taste of her in his mouth . . . it was too much. His balls tightened, and he clenched his jaw as sensation surged into his cock. Black spots danced in his vision, and he closed his eyes as he shot off in his boxer briefs. His orgasm seemed to go on forever, and he had a hard time catching his breath.

That had never happened to him before. *Never.*

He knew he should be appalled by his lack of control, and he would castigate himself later. But right now he was too wrung out to care. As he dropped his forehead against the rough bark of the apple tree, a single word echoed in his head.

Messy.

Chapter 14

THE MOON WAS A SILVER SLIVER IN THE INKY SKY WHEN CAL drove up to Priest and Teagan's house. It was nearly ten o'clock, and the party had started about an hour ago.

The entire street was packed with cars, and he assumed most of the owners were at the party. Since he was family, he got to park in the driveway instead of fighting for a space on the street.

The house was located in Pacific Heights, one of the most expensive neighborhoods in San Francisco. It was filled with historic homes in a variety of styles, although the neighborhood was known for its Victorians. Priest and Teagan's Italianate-Victorian home had been built in the early 1910s, and it was so large, it really deserved to be called a mansion.

Cal let himself into the mudroom, which was located toward the back of the house next to the laundry room. Even though the door to the rest of the house was closed, he could hear the sounds of a raucous, well-attended party. As he opened the interior door and entered the kitchen, the upbeat melody of Atlas Genius's "If So" filtered to him.

The entire house had recently been renovated from top to bottom, and the kitchen was a masterpiece. It had a huge granite island—the same island where Priest and T got busy, according to Bebe—and cream-colored cabinets with leaded glass fronts. Since Letty was a gourmet chef, all the appliances were commercial grade, and Cal wasn't ashamed to admit that he lusted after the Viking cooktop and warming drawers.

The kitchen was jammed with people, all of them in costume. Apparently, they had taken Teagan's "costumes mandatory" directive seriously. In one quick glance, he saw a mummy, two vampires, a bum, a football player, a naughty nurse, and a nun.

He had the cynical thought that the costumes represented a cross section of humanity. They all waved to him, and the mummy, whoever the hell he was, gave him a high-five.

The tall French doors that connected the kitchen to the formal dining room were open, and he noticed several large metal buckets beside the entryway. A variety of cold beer filled them, and he snagged a Sam Adams Harvest Pumpkin Ale.

Unscrewing the cap on his beer bottle, he headed into the dining room. Like the kitchen, it was overrun with costumed revelers. They spilled into the hallway and formal living room, which was connected to the dining room.

The lighting was dim, and a wooden casket sat on top of the dining room table, filled with Halloween-themed food. He knew Letty had made all the food instead of hiring a caterer, and he took a moment to appreciate her efforts.

Along with deviled eggs that resembled bloodshot eyeballs, Letty had wrapped cocktail franks in piecrust to make them look like severed toes in bandages. She had garnished them with a sliced almond as the toenail.

She'd molded Parmesan breadsticks into the shape of bones and served them with marinara sauce to mimic blood, and she had created a witch's cauldron out of a big brown bread bowl and filled it with spinach dip. The most amazing element was a huge graveyard made out of different cheeses with the fence constructed from crackers.

He let his gaze roam the dining room, unsurprised to see Quinn and Priest in a far corner of the room. They were smart guys and always staked out the best locations to access food and drink.

They stood next to a huge display with a cast-iron cauldron filled with red punch. A sign hung from the dipper with

"WITCHES' BREW" printed on it, and he wondered how much liquor was in the punch.

As he made his way toward Quinn and Priest, he tried to tuck the bottle cap into his pocket. He quickly realized his pirate costume didn't have any, and when he reached Quinn's side, he handed the cap to him.

"What am I supposed to do with this?" Quinn asked.

"Put it in your pocket. I don't have any."

"You could just find a trash can, idiot," his brother groused, shoving the cap into his pocket.

Quinn was dressed as a Prohibition-era gangster. With his dark hair, blue eyes, and thick stubble, he looked surprisingly realistic as a lawless hooligan.

His black pinstriped suit included a double-breasted jacket, baggy trousers, and a bright red dress shirt and handkerchief. He'd completed the ensemble with a skinny black tie, black hat, and black-and-white dress shoes.

"Where's your Tommy gun?" Cal asked over the music.

"Right here," Quinn answered, reaching behind him to pull out a huge plastic machine gun. It was at least three feet long.

Priest laughed. "You're compensating."

Obviously, Priest had sucked down a few Jell-O shots because his stutter was conspicuously absent.

"I'm not the one carrying around a fucking sword," Quinn pointed out as he shoved the end of his oversized gun into Priest's gut.

Priest had ignored his wife's suggestion to be a Greek god. Instead he was dressed as a Viking. Personally, Cal wasn't sure a Viking was any better than a Greek god, since Priest wore a horned helmet and fur legwarmers instead of a bedsheet.

The broadsword was pretty cool, though. His pirate costume only had a jeweled dagger.

"Did T force you to wear that costume?" Cal speculated before taking a pull on his beer.

Priest shook his head. "I agreed to be a Viking if she'd be my slave girl."

Cal choked on his beer. "What?"

Priest laughed. "Her costume. It's a slave girl."

Teagan was a ball buster, and there was no costume that was less suited to her personality than a slave girl.

"Where is she?" Cal asked, eager to taunt her about her demeaning costume.

"Somewhere," Priest answered, waving his hand. "She's showing off the house. She's hoping it will generate some new b-b-b-business for Vanessa."

Vanessa was the architect who had created the new floor plan for the house and supervised the renovations. She was also Letty's daughter, and Teagan had welcomed the younger woman into her circle of friends.

"The renovations turned out great," Cal noted. "Vanessa did a really good job."

Priest nodded. "Her d-d-d-design focus isn't residential, though. It's commercial. She only does residential on the side."

"Beck is looking for a designer for Trinity's new headquarters," Quinn said. "Maybe you should introduce them."

Beck owned a micro-distillery that produced high-quality bourbon whiskey. He and his two college friends, Ren and Gabe, had launched the company a few years ago using start-up capital provided by Quinn, and they had just moved into a larger facility.

"Why are you so late?" Quinn asked abruptly, directing his question toward Cal.

"Mom asked me to make a couple of breakfast casseroles for brunch tomorrow, and I didn't want to get up at the ass crack of dawn to make them when I'll probably be hung over."

Priest laughed. "They probably taste better if you make them sober. W-w-w-what kind?"

"French toast casserole and ham, Gruyère, and asparagus."

Priest nodded. "Your food is almost as good as Letty's."

Although it sounded like faint praise, it wasn't. Letty was an amazing chef. She was good enough to work in the world's best restaurants, but she was happy taking care of Nick and Teagan.

"Letty really went wild with the Halloween-themed food," Cal noted.

"She's the second-best thing that's ever happened to m-m-m-me." Priest smiled. "She and T spent hours planning the menu and w-w-w-working on decorations."

The house definitely had a spooky vibe. Fake spiderwebs hung in the corners of the doors and windows, and large black bats swooped down from the ceiling. Real jack-o'-

lanterns filled the house, along with other fright-inducing decorations.

"So they did all the work, and you just stand around and look good?" Cal asked. "That's typical. You've coasted on your looks your whole life."

Priest laughed, knowing that Cal was joking. "I d-d-d-did the playlist."

Priest had good taste in music, although he didn't appreciate alternative and indie rock as much as Cal did. Right now, the Divine Fits were belting out "Would That Not Be Nice."

While Cal and Priest talked, Quinn lost interest in their conversation. As he gazed over Cal's shoulder, a frown came over his face, and his dark blue eyes narrowed with menace.

Cal turned to see what had caused Quinn's glower and immediately realized why his older brother looked ready to hurt someone with his fake gun. Amelia stood across the room wearing a tight, red sequined dress with a thigh-high slit, and a guy dressed as a bullfighter had crowded close to her, his hand on her bare shoulder and his mouth against her ear.

"Your wife looks just like Jessica Rabbit," Cal noted.

Quinn ignored him, the frown on his face growing darker. Priest glanced toward Amelia, and his dark blond eyebrows arched when he saw the bullfighter's arm around her waist.

"I'd rip his arms from his b-b-b-body," Priest claimed, throwing fuel on Quinn's jealous fire.

Cal sighed. "Don't you guys recognize the bullfighter? It's Harris, Deda's partner."

"I didn't recognize him with that mustache," Quinn admitted. "But I don't care if he's gay or not. He needs to get his hands off her."

Cal had a hard time understanding Quinn's behavior. Unlike his brother, Cal wasn't a possessive guy. He never had been, not even with Saika.

"You're acting like a pathetic loser," he told Quinn.

Quinn eyed him. "One day you're going to act like a pathetic loser, and when that day comes, I'm going to give you all kinds of shit."

He shrugged. "You keep telling me 'one day,' yet it never happens."

"It w-w-w-will," Priest promised with a chuckle. "Trust me on that."

Quinn turned his attention back to his wife. She must have felt his gaze because she looked toward them. Her bright red lips tipped up in a smile, and she turned to say something to Harris. The man immediately dropped his arm, and she quickly made her way over to them.

When she reached Cal's side, she gave him a big hug. "Ahoy, matey," she said.

"Argh," he replied, giving her a squeeze.

She giggled. "I don't think you could have picked a more perfect costume, Cal."

"I could say the same about you, Mrs. Rabbit."

She cocked her head. "I'm not Jessica Rabbit," she countered, recognizing his movie reference. "I'm a gangster's moll."

Quinn wrapped his arm around her waist. "My moll, to be specific."

"Yes, your moll." Amelia leaned up and kissed Quinn's cheek, leaving a big red lip print. "I'm going to get a drink. Do you want anything?"

Priest raised his bottle in a silent request, and she nodded. "What about you, Al Capone?" she asked, looking toward her husband.

"I'm good," Quinn answered with a smile.

Quinn patted her butt as she walked away, and once she was out of sight, he turned to Cal. "Have you seen Bebe?"

"No."

"Oh," Quinn replied, and Cal wondered why that one word seemed so loaded with meaning.

He hadn't seen her since he had dropped her off after visiting the apple orchard. The trip back from Sebastopol had been completely different from the trip there. Instead of talking, they had traveled in awkward silence until Bebe had cued up some music. He had been lost in his own thoughts, trying to wrap his head around what had happened in the orchard.

His behavior had been so out of character, he'd barely recognized himself. Never before had he lost control the way he had with her, and he didn't know what had happened.

Although he had purposely picked a tree toward the back of the farm so they could exchange a few kisses, he hadn't planned to finger fuck her and come in his jeans. It was something a teenage boy did, and he hadn't acted like a teenage boy even when he'd been one.

Mercifully, she had been oblivious to his sticky humiliation. He had been able to clean up in the bathroom at the orchard's visitor center, but the whole experience had shaken him like 007's martini.

He'd been with a lot of women—too many, if he were honest with himself—yet none of them had made him feel the way Bebe did. He didn't understand what it was about her that made him so hot. It was as if he were a nuclear reactor, and she had flipped his switch from normal core operations to meltdown.

Of course, he hadn't been the only one who'd overheated. He had barely touched her, and she had come apart. He wanted to believe it was because of *him*—that he made her so hot, she almost combusted. He wanted to believe she wouldn't respond that way to just any guy.

"How are things going with her?" Quinn asked.

"Fine," Cal answered curtly, hoping Amelia would come back soon so his brother would stop talking about Bebe.

He hated to admit how much he wanted her, especially since he wasn't sure she really wanted him. Teagan had let it slip that Bebe had described him as her "least worst option," which pissed him off.

When they'd been at the orchard, and his fingers had been wedged inside her wet pussy, it definitely had felt like she wanted him. But maybe he was just convenient.

He had told Quinn that he was okay with Bebe using his body, but now he wasn't so sure. He wanted her to want *him*. Hell, he wanted her to like him. He'd always wanted that.

Quinn continued with his interrogation. "Why didn't you and Bebe come to the party together?"

Cal shrugged, taking a swig of his beer. He had texted her with an offer to pick her up at the loft, but she had declined. He also had suggested that he meet her at the airport last night, but she had texted, No thanks. He had really wanted to see her, but obviously she hadn't been as eager to see him.

Halfway through the week, he'd realized that he missed her. He usually got to see her at his parents' house for Sunday brunch or dinner, but of course she hadn't been there because of her trip.

Even though they'd been on only a few dates, he had missed spending time with her. He had missed talking to her.

In fact, he had been bored without her smart mouth to entertain him.

He'd even texted her a couple of times to see how her trip was going and had received one-word answers. He didn't know if she was too busy to reply with lengthy texts or if she just didn't want to text with him.

Priest nudged his shoulder to get his attention. "She's over there," he informed Cal, gesturing toward the living room.

Cal turned to look for her, and it took him a minute to spot her because she didn't look like his Bebe. He blinked a couple of times, sure he was seeing things.

It *was* Bebe.

"*Holy shit!*" he gasped, feeling as if someone had punched him in the solar plexus.

She hadn't taken his suggestion to come as an encyclopedia. Instead, she was dressed as a belly dancer, and her costume looked authentic. It was a light aqua color and consisted of a beaded bra and a transparent skirt that sat low on her hips.

The bra was so minuscule, her breasts almost spilled out of it, her nipples barely covered. Thin gold chains dangled from the bottom of it, drawing attention to her smooth skin, and gold bangles covered her slender arms.

The skirt had a beaded waistband and fell in sheer aqua folds to her ankles, which were highlighted by more gold bangles. Her toned stomach was completely bare, and the shape of her legs was visible through the filmy material.

He brought his gaze from her small, bare feet to her thick hair, which was piled on top of her head in glossy ringlets that fell down around her neck and shoulders. Sparkly pins glinted in the dark strands, and big gold hoops swung from her ears.

She's gorgeous.

She laughed, and he jerked his eyes toward the person beside her. Beck. He was touching Bebe just like Harris had touched Amelia, only there was one huge fucking difference.

Beck wasn't gay.

Cal clenched his hand around his beer bottle when Beck's eyes dropped to Bebe's chest and stayed there for several heartbeats. Cal could feel the lust rolling off the other man like a storm coming in from the Pacific.

Beck moved closer to Bebe, leaning down to say something in her ear. His mouth grazed her cheek, and Cal had a sudden and overwhelming urge to ram Beck's head into the wall.

Beck had no right to touch her. Cal was the only man who did, and Beck needed to be made aware of that fact.

Depositing his beer bottle on the table next to him with a loud thud, he started toward Bebe and Beck. He'd only taken a single step when Priest grabbed his forearm and stopped him.

"You said it w-w-w-was just sex," he reminded Cal, his green eyes serious.

Cal had a hard time digesting Priest's words because his ears buzzed and a red haze filled his vision. Quinn flanked his other side.

"Brother," he said quietly, "you need to be careful."

Cal jerked his arm away from Priest. "Fuck off," he snarled, directing his comment to both of them.

As he headed for the living room, he heard Quinn mutter behind him, "This can't be good. You need to find Teagan."

Pivoting on his heel, Cal pointed his forefinger toward his brother and his best friend. "Stay the fuck out of this. I mean it. This is *my* business."

Bebe is my business.

Chapter 15

BEBE LOVED CHEMISTRY, AND SHE FOUND THE DISTILLING PRO-
cess to create bourbon whiskey very interesting. When Beck
had realized she understood the basics of fermentation, his
brown eyes had lit up, and he told her about the recent
improvements he had made to his micro-distillery.

Although she had run into Beck at various O'Brien gatherings, she hadn't had an opportunity to talk with him very
much before tonight's party. He had a strong Southern drawl,
and his voice was so deep, it sounded like it came from the
farthest reaches of his body.

Beck was actually his last name. His first name was
Jonah, but he said no one called him that because every male
in his family was named Jonah, and it was confusing to have
so many of them running around.

"I'd love to show you around the distillery," Beck invited.
"You could be a guinea pig. We're thinking about starting
tours to generate some buzz about Trinity, but we're not sure
what we need to do to make them interesting."

"I'd love to see it," Bebe replied. "I like wine more than hard
liquor, but I find the whole distilling process fascinating."

He smiled slowly, flashing his straight white teeth. "Maybe

I can change your mind. Maybe when I'm done with you, you'll like Trinity more than watered-down grape juice."

She laughed. "I'm willing to try it."

As he took a swallow of beer, he studied her over the neck of the bottle. His eyes reminded her of dark chocolate, the kind that melted on your tongue the moment you put it in your mouth.

His thick hair was the same color as his eyes, and though it was cut short, she could tell it was wavy. It probably would be nothing but curls if he let it grow out.

Beck was *really* good-looking. In fact, he would probably be the most handsome man at the party if not for Nick and Quinn. If Cal were here, though, Beck would drop to a distant fourth place in the hot-guy rankings, and Cal would be in first place.

She wondered where hot guy number one was. The party had started well over an hour ago, and he should have been here by now. She was excited to see him, and she was excited for him to see her in her belly dancer costume.

She had agonized over the perfect costume, especially after his rude comment a few weeks ago suggesting that she dress as a dictionary or an encyclopedia. She had wanted something sexy—something that would encourage him to put his hands and mouth all over her.

She had arrived at Nick and Teagan's house several hours early to help with the party preparations and also to solicit her best friend's assistance with hair and makeup. Teagan had been thrilled to help, and when she'd finished, Bebe had been stunned by her transformation from brainiac to belly dancer.

Her eyes were smoky with dark eye shadow, and thick black eyeliner emphasized their shape. A triple coating of mascara made her eyelashes so long and lush, they looked fake. Teagan had been insistent that smoky eyes called for light-colored lips, so Bebe had used her new peach-colored gloss.

"We're also thinking about opening a restaurant and bar so we can spotlight Trinity," Beck added, pulling her thoughts away from lip gloss and back to liquor. "Gabe's really pushing for it, but I'm not sure."

He shifted toward her, and his leather jacket made a crackly noise. He was dressed as an old-fashioned aviator in a brown flight jacket with a sheepskin collar, khaki pants, and brown leather knee boots. The bomber hat and goggles tucked under his arm added an element of authenticity.

The music abruptly increased in volume, and he leaned closer to her ear. "Maybe you'd like to do a little research with me . . . go out to dinner and check out a restaurant or two."

His mouth glanced off her cheek as he straightened, and she stared up at him. Was he asking her out on a date? It sounded like he was, but she had so little experience with guys asking her out, she couldn't really tell. It was possible he just wanted to pick her brain.

"Tuesday night?" he suggested, his dark eyebrows arched in question.

As she opened her mouth to answer, she saw a flash of white in her peripheral vision. Glancing toward it, she realized it was a billowy cotton shirt. The tall, muscular body under it stopped beside Beck, and she looked up into Cal's gorgeous face.

She didn't know if it was the lighting in the room or something else, but his eyes had never looked so intensely blue. His gaze dropped to her chest, reminding her of the feel of his mouth on her nipples, and heat flashed over her.

Cal glanced toward Beck. "Having a good time, chief?" he asked, offering his right hand.

With a smile, Beck shifted his beer so he could shake Cal's hand. "Good food, free alcohol, and beautiful women in barely there costumes," he drawled. "I'd say it's better than good."

Bebe looked back and forth between Cal and Beck, a little overwhelmed by the abundance of masculine beauty in front of her. Beck was just a tad shorter than Cal, but other than that, they had very similar physiques. They were both blessed with broad shoulders, lean waists, and long legs.

Cal's pirate costume showed off more of his body than Beck's aviator costume, though. His white shirt was loose, but the material was so thin, you could see the muscular shape of his arms and chest. The drawstring was undone halfway down his chest, showing a sprinkling of dark hair over well-defined pecs.

His cropped black leather vest stretched over his shoulders, and his tight black pants showed off his strong thighs. A wide black leather belt highlighted the V-shape of his torso, and his black knee boots made him look even taller.

He's the hottest pirate I've ever seen, and I want him to plunder my booty.

"I was telling Bebe about the upgrades we're making at the distillery," Beck explained with a grin. "I offered to give her a tour."

Cal tilted his dark head toward Beck. "How thoughtful," he said flatly.

Beck stared at Cal for a moment, his smile fading. An awkward silence fell over their small group, and she felt compelled to fill it.

"Beck thinks he can turn me on to bourbon."

"Turn you on," Cal echoed.

She frowned. Why was he acting so strangely? Was he intoxicated?

"Yes. I told him I was willing to give it a try."

"It's an acquired taste," Beck chimed in. "Most people don't like it the first time they try it."

"Is that right?" Cal asked, staring into her eyes. "I guess it depends on how good it is the first time."

She knew Cal wasn't talking about bourbon, and Beck quickly realized it, too. He looked back and forth between her and Cal, his gaze frankly assessing, and she flushed.

"Beck, there's not going to be any tour," Cal announced abruptly without looking away from her. "Bebe is going to be too busy. She's going to have her hands full."

Frowning at Cal's rude and autocratic comment, she glanced toward Beck. "I want to see your distillery," she assured him. "I am busy, but I'll make time."

Beck's lips twitched. "I'd love to give you a tour, Bebe, but I think you and Cal might need to discuss it."

She shook her head. She didn't need to talk to Cal about it. She didn't tell him how to spend his time.

"No, we don't—"

"There's not going to be any tour," Cal repeated, his voice hard. *"Ever."*

Beck nodded. "I hear you." He inclined his head toward her. "It was a pleasure talking with you, Bebe." He raised his bottle to Cal. "I'll see you on the court," he added before turning on his booted heel to saunter away.

Bebe tracked Beck's progress out of the room before bringing her gaze back to Cal. "I thought you and Beck were friends."

"We are friends."

"Then why do you have a problem with me touring his distillery? I thought it sounded fun. I find the fermentation process extremely fascinating, and we had an interesting conversation about achieving the right pH balance to create the ideal sour mash."

He huffed out a laugh. "Jesus Christ on a pogo stick," he muttered. "Are you really that blind? Beck doesn't want to give you a tour of his distillery."

"He's the one who suggested it. I didn't ask for one."

"He doesn't want to give you a tour. He wants to fuck you."

"What?"

"He could barely keep his eyes off your tits. He was almost drooling." He looked down at her chest. "I can't really blame him, though. They're on display for the whole goddamn world to see."

She sucked in a surprised breath at his harsh words. The top of her costume was revealing, but it wasn't *that* revealing. Plus, she had worn it for *him*. And she didn't like the word "tits," either.

"We were just talking," she explained, unsure why she defended herself.

Wrapping an arm around her waist, he pulled her against him. He was hot and hard everywhere he touched her.

"Trust me, he didn't hear a word you said. The whole time you were talking, he was thinking about fucking you."

"You don't know what he was thinking," she shot back, a little angry and a lot insulted.

He leaned down until he was in her face. He must not have shaved all week in preparation for his pirate persona because his cheeks and chin were scruffy. His lips looked even sexier surrounded by all that dark stubble.

"I know exactly what he was thinking because it's what I'm thinking now." He stared into her eyes. "The whole time you were running your mouth about fermentation, I was thinking about how tight and wet your pussy would be. While you were blathering on and on about sour mash, I was thinking about you going down on me, and when you moved

on to pH balance, I was thinking about making you come
with my mouth."

She gasped, embarrassed and offended. "Cal! People can
hear you!"

He jerked his head up, looking around as if he had forgotten where they were. He grasped her upper arm.

"You're right. We need privacy for this conversation."

He tugged her along with him as he stalked out of the living
room and into the wide hallway. It was crowded with people,
but when they saw him coming with her in tow, they just
stepped aside and let them pass. She tried to shake off his hand,
but he tightened his grip and pulled her through the kitchen.

"Release me," she demanded. "I am an adult, not an
unruly child, and I don't appreciate you manhandling me."

He ignored her, continuing until they reached the laundry
room. He gently pushed her into it before flipping the light
switch and slamming the door behind them. Leaning back
against it, he crossed his arms over his chest and glowered at her.

Extremely annoyed, she turned away from him, and with
nothing else to look at, she let her gaze roam around the room.
As far as laundry rooms went, it was quite nice. It was a large
space with grayish-blue walls accented with cream-colored
wainscoting.

"You violated our agreement," he accused from behind her.

She spun around. "How exactly did I violate our agreement? Beck and I were talking. That's it."

Pushing away from the door, he prowled toward her. She
didn't know why, but she felt compelled to back away from him.

"You're acting like a . . ." She fumbled for a word that would
accurately describe his boorish behavior. "Like a swine."

He closed the space between them until she was backed
against the dryer and her breasts were flattened against his
cotton-covered chest. "You violated our agreement," he repeated. "You agreed to kiss me hello, but you didn't."

She let out a shaky breath. "That's what you were talking
about?"

He settled his hands on her hips just above the waistband
of her skirt. His palms were hot against her skin, and she
broke out in goose bumps.

"Yes."

"I thought you were talking about me and Beck."

"There is no you and Beck."

Gripping her hips, Cal boosted her onto the dryer. He stepped between her legs, bringing them face-to-face.

"I haven't seen you in a week. Kiss me hello."

Torn between the desire to kiss him and kick him, she just sat there, staring into his eyes. She didn't understand what had just happened. Was it possible that he was jealous of Beck?

Cal had exclusive access to her body, but he didn't have exclusive access to *her*. They weren't a couple. Yet his behavior had been unmistakably possessive.

She relished the idea of a guy being jealous over her, especially if that guy was Cal. But she definitely didn't relish it when he acted like a swine.

Before she could talk herself out of it, she asked, "Are you jealous, Cal?"

His jaw tightened. She waited for him to reply, and when he didn't, she asked again. In response, he dropped his head until his mouth hovered above hers.

"Kiss me hello," he repeated, his voice cajoling rather than demanding.

Since she wanted to kiss him more than she wanted to argue, she did what he asked. She touched her lips to his, opening her mouth a little because she knew he liked it that way.

He slid his hands into her hair, his palms cupping the base of her skull, and slanted his mouth over hers. He licked the corner of her mouth before running his tongue over her lower lip. Suddenly he pulled away from her.

"You taste like pumpkin pie." He licked his lips. "Why do you taste like pumpkin pie?"

"It's my new lip gloss. Do you like it?"

Cal dropped his forehead against hers. "*God, you're killing me.*"

"What? Why?"

He raised his head to look into her eyes. "I love the way you taste, and I love pumpkin pie. And now I get to have both at once."

He loves the way I taste?

Dropping his head, he settled his mouth over hers and nudged her lips open with his tongue. He licked inside her mouth, tiny little darts that barely gave her a taste of him.

She locked her hands around his neck, hungry for more. She was glad he loved the way she tasted because she felt the same about him. His mouth was flavored with the yeasty tang of beer, along with a hint of cinnamon and ginger. Underneath it, she could taste his unique essence, and she sucked aggressively on his tongue.

Moaning against her mouth, he pulled her hips forward until she could feel his erection between her legs. It was hard and long, and she pushed against it. She was wet, even wetter than she had been at the orchard, probably because she now knew how good it felt to have him touch her between her legs.

All week, the memory of his long, talented fingers had flashed into her mind at inappropriate times. While she'd been in a meeting with one of the largest hedge funds in the world, she had been soaked because she'd been daydreaming about her first orgasm.

As Cal's tongue swiped along her bottom lip, she dropped her hands to his chest and slid them into the open V of his pirate shirt. His chest hair was silky yet springy against her fingers, and she stroked the hard planes of his chest.

"Take off your shirt. I want to touch you."

He stared at her, his eyes glazed and his cheekbones flushed with color. This, *this* was what Cal O'Brien looked like when he was turned on. And it was because of her: boring, geeky Bebe Banerjee.

"I don't think that's a good idea," he countered hoarsely.

"Okay. I'll just take off my top, then."

She quickly reached behind her and unhooked the beaded bra. Shrugging it from her shoulders, she pulled it away from her breasts.

He sucked in a breath, his eyes widening as he stared at her chest. Her nipples were hard, the dark skin pebbled tightly. Bringing his hands to her breasts, she held them against her, savoring the feel of his hot palms on her nipples.

He shaped her breasts, squeezing gently and brushing his thumbs against her nipples. His fingers were slightly rough, and they sent a spark up and down her spine.

"I love your nipples." He plucked at them with his long fingers. "They're so big and dark."

Sliding his hands around her, he pressed his palms against

her back until her breasts thrust forward. He dropped his head and wrapped his firm lips around one of her nipples.

His stubble abraded the skin of her breasts as he sucked deeply. She felt it between her legs, almost as if there were a direct line of communication between her nipple and her clitoris.

He switched his attention to her other nipple, and while his mouth and tongue were busy with that one, his hand continued to stroke the other. He rolled his tongue over her nipple, using his teeth to scrape it lightly.

Sensation bombarded her. The hot pull of his mouth. The roughness of his fingers. The wet pulse between her legs. She hooked her legs around his hips and wriggled against his erection, trying to ease the pressure that had built between her thighs.

He drew back, panting heavily. "We need to stop."

"I don't want to stop."

She had waited thirty years for this. And she had wanted Cal for four long years.

Four. Long. Years.

He eased away from her, stepping back a couple of feet. He roughly scrubbed his hands over his face, his fingers making a loud rasping noise against his thick stubble. With his hands covering his face, he took several deep breaths.

Grasping the fabric of her skirt in her hands, she raised her hips and pulled it out from under her. Once it was free, she hooked her fingers in her panties and pulled them off. She dropped down her skirt to cover her lap but kept it high enough to give him the access he needed to get the job done.

"Here," she said.

He dropped his hands, and she tossed her panties to him. He caught them automatically against his chest, clenching them in his hand.

Opening his fingers, he looked down at the aqua-colored scrap of material. He obviously didn't realize what he held at first, and when he did, his head snapped up and he speared her with his light blue gaze.

"No," he protested, his voice shaded with disbelief. "You did *not* just take off your panties and throw them at me."

She couldn't help but laugh at the expression on his face. It was a mixture of shock and awe.

"Yes, I did."

He was close enough for her to lean forward and grasp the drawstrings on his billowy shirt. She tugged him toward her, and he tripped a little and fell against her. He steadied himself by grabbing her hips.

"That works," she murmured, wrapping her legs around him.

Leaning forward, she licked his throat and nuzzled her nose into the spot where his shoulder met his neck. He smelled so good, a tantalizing blend of his own unique fragrance and the spicy, citrusy scent of his cologne.

Nothing smells better than Cal.

He drew back, and she loosened her legs just enough to create some space between them. Reaching down, she cupped her hand over his erection. She really liked these pirate pants. They were tight, the material was fairly thin, and best of all, they had only three buttons holding them together.

He hissed and pressed her hand flat against his hard-on. "We need to stop."

She didn't want to stop. She was tired of being a virgin. She was tired of not having what she wanted. The amazing experience in the orchard had given her a hint of what she'd missed all these years, and she didn't care how shamelessly she was behaving.

Before he could stop her, she popped his buttons and pushed the dark fabric apart. Reaching inside his boxer briefs, she palmed his penis. It was smooth and silky, and she worked to wrap her hand around it. Shockingly, it was so thick, her fingers barely encircled it.

She lightly squeezed his erection, uncertain how much pressure she should use. She had never touched a live penis, only those on cadavers in medical school. His was different, that was for sure.

Moaning, Cal jerked against her. He encircled her wrist with his fingers, gently stilling it.

"We need to stop," he repeated, his voice barely audible.

I don't want to stop, and I'm not going to.

She pulled against his hold, and he let go reluctantly. Hooking her fingers in the waistband of his underwear, she pushed it down until his erection sprang free. She gasped in surprise, appreciation, and a fair amount of wonder.

Oohhh.

So that was what an erection looked like.

Wow. *Wow.*

She had never seen one before. She had never watched porn or looked at dirty magazines, so this was her first view.

From what she had read, the average length of an erect penis was 5.6 inches. Cal's was longer. *A lot longer.*

Wow. *Wow.*

She ran the tip of her finger up his hard-on until she reached the plump head. Creamy fluid oozed from the tiny slit, and she rubbed a circle in it, fascinated by the consistency.

Isn't the human body so interesting?

"*Fuck,*" he groaned, squeezing his eyes shut and dropping his head back. "Why is it like this with you?"

She didn't know what he meant, and frankly, she didn't care. She only cared about getting him inside her. His test results had come back clean, and she was on the pill, so there was nothing stopping them.

She was so wet, the top of the dryer was slick with her arousal, making it easy for her to scoot forward toward the edge. As she widened her legs, she palmed his erection and placed it against her damp flesh. She hoped he would take over from here because she had run out of courage.

He opened his eyes, and she met his intense gaze. His pupils were huge, almost obliterating the pale blue irises. His fingers dug into her hips, and he shifted just enough for his erection to slide deeper between her folds.

"*Goddamn,*" he growled. "You are so fucking wet."

He was hot against her, so hot, and she tilted her pelvis in encouragement. He shifted again, and she felt him at the entrance to her body.

This is it.

Taking a deep breath, she stared into his eyes as he breeched her flesh. He slowly pushed forward, and at first, she didn't feel anything but heat and hardness. But then there was pressure, her muscles twinging as he stretched her. She tensed a little against the discomfort, and he froze, a muscle jumping in his clenched jaw.

Just then, a huge thump sounded from the hallway, and something hit the laundry door. Loud laughter filtered through it, the revelry just a few feet away.

His eyes widened, the haze of lust disappearing like fog

burning off the Bay. "*Jesus Christ*," he whispered, carefully withdrawing from her body. "What the fuck is *wrong* with me? You're a virgin, and I'm doing you during a party. In a laundry room. On top of a dryer."

Bebe sighed in disappointment. Unfortunately, Cal had stopped the tumble cycle while she was still damp.

Chapter 16

"BINDU, MY DARLING!" AKASH EXCLAIMED WITH A HUGE SMILE. "My heart sighs with pleasure at the sight of you."

Akash's affectionate greeting warned Bebe that this video chat wasn't going to be like their other chats. He had never been so effusive or pleasant, and she wondered what had compelled the change.

"Good evening, Akash," she replied neutrally.

"Bindu, you will be delighted to know that my mother and father have joined me for our chat."

Oh, no.

Akash's parents suddenly flanked him. Both of them were smiling widely.

Ishani and Tushar Mehra were in their late sixties, but their wealth had provided the resources they needed to stay healthy, active, and youthful-looking. They had an extensive staff of private chefs and personal trainers.

Despite her age, Ishani was one of the most beautiful women Bebe had ever seen. Although silver streaked her dark hair, her face was relatively unlined. She looked better than most women half her age.

Tushar, meanwhile, was one of the most unattractive men Bebe had ever seen. His face was narrow, his nose large and hooked, and his eyes beady and close set. His gray hair was wiry and cut close to his head.

Akash definitely got his looks from his mother. Unfortunately, he got his ruthlessness from his father.

"Bindu, I hope you will forgive our intrusion, but Tushar and I wanted to express how pleased we are that you and Akash have finally agreed on a wedding date," Ishani said in her lightly accented English. "We are eager to welcome you into our family."

Bebe knew Ishani's words were sincere. Akash's mother had always been kind to her. She thought Bebe was the ideal wife for her beloved youngest child.

"Yes, we are very pleased," Tushar added. "We have been waiting for far too long."

Bebe had no doubt that Tushar was the reason Akash felt pressure to marry. She knew Akash's relationship with his father was strained. Tushar thought Ishani had spoiled Akash, and he viewed Bebe and Akash's long engagement as yet another example of his son's immaturity.

Ishani and Tushar had arranged marriages for all seven of their children. As the youngest, Akash was the only one still unmarried. His four older brothers and two older sisters had been married for years, and all of them had children.

Like Akash, his brothers were involved in the family business. His sisters, meanwhile, had married wealthy men and focused on their families.

"It is unfortunate that we still must wait another eleven months for the marriage, however," Tushar noted.

"I explained to *Pitaa* and *Maataa* that we are simply following the swami's recommendation," Akash said, his smile a little strained.

Tushar shot an annoyed glance toward Akash. "Perhaps we should consult another swami," he suggested.

Oh, no.

Ishani laughed. "Do you see, Bindu? Tushar is eager to be your *sasur*."

"Yes, I am very eager to be your father-in-law," Tushar agreed with an emphatic nod.

Bebe smiled weakly. She didn't know how to respond to their excitement when she wanted to forget she had ever agreed to marry their son.

"When are you planning your next trip to Delhi?" Ishani asked with a bright smile. "We have so much to do to prepare for the wedding. And we also need to talk about the *Sangeet* ceremony."

Oh, no.

"Bindu and I have already discussed her next trip," Akash said, lying through his straight white teeth. "Unfortunately, she has several important projects at work that she must complete. The soonest she can visit is March."

Ishani's smile disappeared. "Are you sure you cannot visit before then?"

"Bindu cannot disappoint her superiors," Akash declared. "What kind of person would she be if she did not honor her commitments?"

Nausea churned in Bebe's stomach. Akash's statement had been a private message to her: *You will honor your commitment to me or suffer the consequences.*

Ishani sighed gustily. "Of course you must honor your commitments, Bindu."

"Perhaps we can visit Bindu instead," Tushar suggested.

"What a wonderful idea!" Ishani exclaimed.

Oh, no.

"Bindu is far too busy, *Mataji*," Akash broke in hastily. "And March is only a few months away. You can do some of the planning via video chat and email."

Ishani nodded. "We will find a way to make everything perfect." She smiled brightly and gestured to the camera. "Please, Bindu, tell us how you have been."

Before this morning's chat, Bebe had been happy. Really happy. But now she felt like throwing up.

"I'm doing well, thank you."

"And tell us how you've been keeping busy," Ishani requested.

Bebe wet her dry lips, trying to gather her thoughts. She had been keeping busy with Cal, but she couldn't tell Ishani that.

He had asked her to come to brunch at his parents' house the morning after the Halloween party, and she'd spent the day with him and the rest of the O'Briens. They'd enjoyed Cal's delicious breakfast casseroles and mimosas made with fresh-squeezed orange juice before settling in the family room to watch football.

A full stomach plus a stressful week of work travel and only a few hours of sleep the night before had added up to Bebe falling asleep in the middle of the game. When she'd woken up, she'd been curled up on the sofa with her head resting on Cal's thigh. A light cashmere throw had covered her, and his arm had been draped across her waist.

She had been horribly embarrassed that she had fallen asleep on him. Somehow that had seemed more intimate than allowing him into her body.

He must have sensed her mortification because he'd gone out of his way to tease her about her nap. He'd proclaimed loudly that she snored, drooled, and talked in her sleep.

Even worse, he'd insisted that she must have been dreaming about him because she'd called his name. She hadn't been able to tell if he was joking about that or not.

When Cal had dropped her off at her loft that evening, he'd barely kissed her. She had hoped he would come up so they could finish what they'd started the night before, but she hadn't been brave enough to say so. She had used up all her courage in that laundry room at the party.

She had been so disappointed they had been interrupted. He might have been horrified he'd almost taken her virginity while she sat on a dryer, but she didn't care about the where, only the who.

"Tell us about these work projects that Akash mentioned," Ishani prompted, pulling Bebe back into the conversation.

"I recently returned from New York, where I met with a number of large institutional investors. Several plan to visit GGB's headquarters in early December, and I'm responsible for coordinating their trips and their meetings with our executives."

Tushar nodded. "We are considering the creation of a venture capital fund through Mehra that would invest in biotechnology," he disclosed. "Perhaps we can discuss that when you visit in March."

His request stunned her. While Ishani previously had expressed interest in Bebe's career, Tushar had been noticeably silent. Bebe had always assumed he was opposed to females focusing on anything but their husbands and children, despite the fact that Mehra employed thousands of women.

Did Tushar simply want to solicit her opinion, or was he

suggesting that she be involved in the management of the fund? The idea of launching a new biotech fund was intriguing, but it wasn't intriguing enough for Bebe to want to marry Akash.

"I am sure Bindu would be happy to discuss biotechnology with you, *Pitaji*," Akash said. "Right, Bindu?"

"Yes, of course," she murmured.

"And have you seen your mother and father recently?" Ishani asked.

"Not since our engagement ceremony."

Noor and Charak had attended the ceremony, but she knew they had done so only because they hadn't wanted to offend the Mehras. If she had been engaged to anyone else, her parents would not have made the effort.

"It was such a pleasure to see them," Ishani added. "I just wish they had been able to spend more time with us. But I know they have many demands for their time and expertise. When Akash told us you had set a wedding date, I called Noor to express my pleasure that our families would finally be united. She mentioned she would be visiting San Francisco next week for an awards dinner. Are you attending it with her?"

"I'm not sure," Bebe prevaricated.

In truth, Bebe wasn't aware of her mother's plans, but that wasn't a surprise. She rarely talked with Noor, and if she wanted to see her mother while she was in town, Bebe would have to make the effort to contact her.

"We have occupied too much of Bindu's time," Akash broke in. "We don't want her to be late for work."

Ishani sighed. "I wish we had more time. We have so much to discuss."

Akash laughed heartily. "*Mataji*, in just a few months, Bindu will be a Mehra, and we will have all her time."

Oh, no.

CAL TOOK ONE LOOK AT AMELIA AND KNEW SOMETHING WAS wrong. Her face was whiter than rice, and her freckles looked like freshly ground cinnamon on her smooth skin.

"What's wrong?" he asked.

She smiled wanly. "Is it that obvious?"

He nodded. "What's wrong?" he repeated.

"I'm not feeling that great."

As she scooted onto a metal stool in front of a large table in her workshop, she pressed a hand to her lower abdomen. He cocked his head.

"Is there a little O'Brien on the way?"

Cal knew Amelia and Quinn wanted children, but he hadn't thought they would have them so soon. They'd been married for only eight months, and even though Quinn said he was ready, Amelia wanted to make sure the women's division was healthy before they added to their family.

"I'm not pregnant," she denied with a shake of her head, her long red hair swinging around her face in a tangle of kinks and curls.

When he had first met Amelia, she had reminded him of the Scottish princess in the Disney movie *Brave*, but with brown eyes and a Texas accent. He had taken Valerie to see the animated film while Saika taught a cooking class.

"Then what's wrong?"

She huffed out a breath. "Cal, it's woman stuff. I have cramps. How's that for too much information?"

He laughed at her chagrin. "You're not the first woman to tell me she has cramps."

He studied her for a moment. She *definitely* did not look like she was up to doing a lunch and a lengthy interview with a seasoned reporter.

"I'm thinking you need to take some ibuprofen and go lie down on the sofa in my office. I'll take Carrie to lunch, and you can do the interview when we get back."

She looked so relieved by the suggestion, he knew he had made the right call. He had given Amelia enough media training that she was able to handle interviews like a pro, but she needed to bring her A game to every single one.

Usually he didn't get involved in media interviews, allowing his public relations managers to handle them. But this interview with the leading fashion trade magazine was a great opportunity to let retailers know about all the new and exciting things going on with the company.

It was important to generate buzz with retailers, since they were such a critical part of Riley O'Brien & Co.'s success. If consumers couldn't find Rileys at their favorite stores, they would just buy another brand.

"Are you sure you don't mind doing lunch alone?"

"It's not a problem," he assured her. "After all, you *are* my favorite sister-in-law."

"I'm your only sister-in-law," she pointed out with a smile.

"Even if I had a million, you'd still be my favorite." Pulling her to her feet, he wrapped his arm around her shoulders. "Come on. I have some ibuprofen and bottled water in my office. I keep it on hand for when your irritating husband gives me a headache."

She laughed softly. "He makes my headaches go away."

"Did you just make a dirty joke?" he asked with a fair amount of surprise.

Amelia didn't curse, and she was fairly reserved, in public, at least. But he had the sense that Quinn was more than satisfied with her behavior in private.

"No, it wasn't a dirty joke," she answered wryly. "You just have a dirty mind."

"Amelia, I didn't know you thought so highly of me."

He shepherded her out of the workshop and to the elevators. Within seconds, they were in the second-floor reception area. The double doors to the executive offices were unmanned, so Cal used his key card to unlock the door and pulled it open for Amelia.

"I'll come and get you when it's time for the interview. I want to find you stretched out on my sofa and feeling better. Okay?" he asked, tugging on one of the curls hanging over her forehead.

She nodded. "Thanks, Cal."

The door swung shut behind her, and he stopped by the reception desk to let Liza know she should text him when Carrie arrived. He had a little less than an hour before the reporter's appointment, and he decided to spend that time in Riley Plaza's rooftop garden. Now that November was here, they'd probably have only a few more days of nice weather before the seasonal rains started.

As he stepped off the elevator, he sucked in a deep breath scented with the sweet smell of rosemary and the pungent odor of basil. He caught a hint of citrus from the potted lemon and key lime trees, along with the familiar aroma of roses and other floral fragrances.

Cal meandered along one of the stone walking paths that crisscrossed the garden until he found his favorite cedar bench. He sat down and propped his foot on his knee before leaning back and closing his eyes.

He let his mind wander, and it immediately found its way to Bebe. She was always there on the periphery, no matter what he did. Over the years, he had spent way too much time thinking about her, even when he'd been with other women.

When he had dated Saika, he'd gone out of his way to avoid Bebe whenever she visited. Although he had been in love with Saika, his desire for Bebe had still been there, lurking in the background, and he'd felt guilty about it.

No matter how hard he had tried not to think about her, she'd shown up in his dreams every once in a while. And now that he'd had a taste of her, he dreamed about her every night.

He wanted Bebe more than he'd ever wanted a woman, and he had wanted a few quite badly. He didn't know why she made him so senseless with lust, but she did.

Thanks to Bebe, he had an almost perpetual hard-on, and he had masturbated more in the last month than he had over the past five years. He figured it was a good thing he took the edge off with a little self-pleasure, since he couldn't seem to control himself around her.

He was still struggling to come to terms with the fact that he'd almost taken her in Priest and Teagan's laundry room while she had perched on top of the dryer. He had pulled her into the small space with the intention of doing nothing more than kissing her, but things had quickly escalated when she'd stripped out of her panties and thrown them at him.

He had never been so shocked in his entire life, but that shock had quickly melted into mind-numbing lust. When she'd wrapped her slender fingers around his hard-on and placed it against her pussy, his mind had emptied of everything except the feel of her.

Great. Now I have an erection while sitting in the garden at work.

Blowing out a harsh breath, he casually glanced around. This part of the garden was deserted, so he pressed his hand against his hard-on to give himself some relief.

There was no way he was going to make it to twelve dates before taking her virginity. In fact, he doubted he would make it past their date tonight.

He had bought tickets for *The Wizard of Oz* because she

wanted to go to a musical and because it would be another first for her. After sitting next to her for three hours in the Orpheum Theater, he would be revved up and ready to go.

He had wanted to take things slowly with Bebe, never anticipating he would have trouble holding back. He hadn't wanted to rush her, but there was no reason to wait. After what had happened in the laundry room, it was obvious that she was ready.

More than ready.

She seemed to have no hesitation about losing her virginity, and that surprised him. Actually, a lot of things about Bebe surprised him.

Her sense of humor, which ranged from sarcastic to off-the-wall. Her curiosity about everyone and everything. The softness that hid beneath her practical, logical exterior.

Yeah, a lot of things about Bebe surprised him. But the most surprising thing of all was the way she made him feel.

Chapter 17

"GRIP THE SHAFT TIGHTER, COOKIE, AND MOVE YOUR HANDS lower," Cal directed.

"Like this?" Bebe asked, shifting her fingers on the golf club.

"No. Let me show you."

Moving behind her, Cal wrapped his arms around her and settled his fingers over hers. His body surrounded her, hot and hard, and her stomach trembled with arousal. Too bad she couldn't do anything about it.

She wanted to curse Mother Nature for her bad timing. She'd gotten her period the day she and Cal had gone to see *The Wizard of Oz*, and when he had asked if he could come up for dessert, she had been forced to tell him it was a bad time for sweets. No one had warned her about that awkward conversation.

He had stared at her for a long moment before his eyes had widened in understanding. He had dropped a quick kiss on her lips and told her to keep Saturday free for their golf lesson.

"Make sure your palms are facing each other and your thumb is just slightly to the side of the center of the shaft," he instructed.

She and Cal were on the driving range at Cal's favorite golf course, The Olympic Club's Lake Course. It was situated in the southwestern corner of San Francisco and offered incredible views of Golden Gate Park and the Golden Gate Bridge.

"How long have you been a member here?" she asked, trying to take her mind off how good he felt pressed against her.

"My great-grandfather Joseph was one of the first members of The Olympic Club," he answered as he stepped away from her.

She looked up from her hands. "Your *great-grandfather*? How old is this course?"

"It opened in 1917, but the Club itself opened in 1860. It's the oldest athletic club in the United States. It started out as a club for boxing, and in 1918, the Club bought the Lake Course. It's one of the oldest golf courses in the nation."

She straightened and turned to face him. "Cal, don't you think it's amazing that you play on the same course that your great-grandfather played? And your grandfather and your father?"

He smiled slowly. "Yeah, I think it's amazing. And I hope one day my own kids will play here with me."

Cal was such a fascinating mix of bad boy and family man. He was hotter than the earth's inner core, yet he loved his family and made no secret of the fact that he eventually wanted a wife and children.

He leaned on his golf club, and she took a moment to appreciate the best view in the city, which just happened to be him. He'd chosen a pair of flat-front khaki trousers and topped them with a long-sleeved navy-blue polo shirt and a matching sweater vest with a thin white stripe around the V-neck.

While her personal style was questionable, Bebe thought sweater vests were the nerdiest piece of clothing a man *or* a woman could wear. But somehow Cal managed to look sexy in his.

The dark color of the shirt and vest made his eyes look almost periwinkle. They sparkled in the late morning sunlight, almost mesmerizing in their beauty, and she couldn't help but stare.

He smiled quizzically. "Are you okay?"

She swallowed thickly, trying to get rid of the saliva that had pooled in her mouth. "Yes, I'm fine."

What else could she say? *You are the most gorgeous man on the planet, and scientists should find a way to clone you so all women can enjoy you in the privacy of their own homes?*

She gathered her thoughts and managed to formulate a question. "Did your dad teach you how to play?"

"Yeah. He brought me and Quinn out here when we were in grade school. He tried to teach T, too, but she kept twirling the clubs like a baton. She lost control of one and hit Quinn in the head. He needed stitches, and my mom refused to let her back on the course. My dad tried to tell her it wasn't a big deal, but she wouldn't give in."

"I love your sister," Bebe said with a laugh.

He smiled. "I know you do, Cookie. She's lucky to have you."

"I'm lucky to have her."

She had told Cal that her high school experience had been isolating, but what she'd really meant was that she had been friendless for most of her life. Before Teagan, she'd never had a best friend, someone she could count on and trust with her whole heart.

Thanks to Teagan, her circle of friends had widened. Now she could count Amelia and Vanessa as friends, along with Amelia's best friend, Ava Grace Landy.

Bebe also felt lucky to know Teagan's family. James and Kate were so friendly and loving, and they had welcomed her into their fold. It was nice to spend time with the O'Briens—more than nice. It felt like she belonged.

"And what about me? Are you lucky to have me?" he teased.

Yes, she was lucky to have Cal. He was smart and interesting, and his dirty mind and juvenile sense of humor made her laugh. And she couldn't overlook the fact that he made her so hot, she tore off her clothes in apple orchards and laundry rooms.

They'd always had a hostile relationship, but strangely enough, when she was with him, she was free to be herself. Maybe she was free to be herself *because* they'd always had a hostile relationship. He was never intimidated by her intelligence or put off by her sarcasm, and he had no problem with her annoying habit of asking too many questions.

Of course, she couldn't let him know how lucky she felt. She couldn't tell him how much she liked him—how much she'd always liked him. That wasn't their deal.

"Am I lucky to have you?" she echoed, arching her eyebrows. "I haven't *had* you yet."

"Believe me, I am well aware of that fact," he replied dryly before nodding toward her club. "Show me your stance."

"Have you ever taught anyone to play golf?"

"No. Why? Do you think I'm doing a bad job?"

Quite the opposite. He was patient, thorough, and most important, encouraging. He wasn't one of those guys who expected you to get it right on the first try. She was having a lot of fun, and it was all because of him.

"No, you're a good teacher."

"There are a lot of things I can teach you, Cookie," he said, giving an exaggerated wink.

She decided to ignore him. He had tossed around sexual innuendos all morning like a juggler at a kid's birthday party.

She positioned her feet and body like he'd shown her, and he smiled in approval. "Good. Show me your grip."

She carefully placed her hands on the club's shaft, making sure to line up her palms and overlap her fingers. She looked up and met his gaze.

"Am I doing it right?"

His eyes dropped to her hands, and when he looked back up, they held an amused glint. "Make sure you're using the right amount of pressure on the shaft. You don't want it to slip out of your hands at a critical moment."

Golf had to be *the* most sexually charged sport played today. How could anyone focus on the game with all the talk of shafts, balls, holes, and strokes?

She straightened. "Why don't you show me again?"

Depositing his club in the bag next to him, he stepped behind her. He placed his hands on her hips, bending down until his lips were against her ear.

"Spread your legs a little more and bend your knees just a bit."

She did as he instructed, trying *really* hard not to think about spreading her legs and bending her knees so he could push into her body. He tweaked her stance, and when he finished, he sucked her earlobe into his mouth. The wet suction made her nipples harden, and she pulled in a breath that was saturated with Cal's intoxicating scent.

"Okay, look down at the ball."

She bent her head, and he kissed the nape of her neck before giving it a swipe with his tongue. He was killing her one lick at a time.

Shifting closer, Cal aligned his arms over hers. As he adjusted her grip, his erection pressed against her, and heat pooled in her stomach.

"This is called a Vardon grip," he noted huskily. "It's not the classic grip, but it's what all the great players use."

When he had arranged her fingers to his satisfaction, he caressed them gently. "Ben Hogan said golf begins with a good grip," he spoke close to her ear. "He was one of the greatest golfers of all time."

She looked over her shoulder, and her lips hit his nose. "How good are you?"

"Very," he answered without hesitation. "I'm very good." He pursed his lips. "Oh, were you talking about golf? I'm good at that, too."

She snorted. "Very few people are fair judges of their own talent."

He chuckled. "I have a zero handicap, and I've won the club championship five out of the last seven years."

"So you lost twice?" she asked archly.

He loosened his hold on her, and she turned in the circle of his arms. The golf club was wedged between them.

"I missed the tournament last year because Valerie had a dance recital, and the other year I had to attend a wedding in Houston."

She looked up at him. "How did you get so good?"

His lips twitched. "I'm naturally talented."

She lightly jabbed him in the stomach with the top of the club. "Are you sure you want to tease me when I'm holding a long piece of metal that could be used as a lethal weapon?"

"The reward is far greater than the risk," he replied with a big grin. "Teasing you is one of the greatest pleasures of my life."

Spending time with him was *the* greatest pleasure of her life.

BEBE TOOK A SWING AND MADE CONTACT WITH THE GOLF BALL with a loud crack. It flew up into the air, passing the 180-yard marker before dropping to the ground out of sight.

Cal shook his head in disbelief. She had never even held a golf club before today, yet she was hitting the ball like she'd been playing for years. She was a goddamn natural.

"Cookie, you are incredible. Absolutely incredible."

She looked toward him, a huge smile on her face. It was so gorgeous, his breath whooshed out, and he pressed a hand to his chest, where his lungs worked hard to pull in some oxygen.

"Maybe I just had an incredible teacher."

And maybe she's just incredible.

A wisp of shiny dark hair had escaped from her bun, and he tucked it behind her ear. Looking down into her face, he ran his gaze from her arched eyebrows, feathery eyelashes, and big golden eyes to her delicate nose, glossy mouth, and rounded chin.

He couldn't stop himself from touching his thumb to her lower lip and giving her a kiss. She tasted like pumpkin pie again, and he pushed down the urge to gobble her up like his favorite holiday dessert.

"I'm having such a good time," she announced.

Suddenly, she leaned forward and hugged him. The action surprised the hell out of him and not just because her golf club hit him on the back of his thigh. She had never hugged him before, and his heart thumped heavily as he looped his arms around her slender waist.

"This is your first golf lesson," he pointed out, squeezing her tightly against him.

"Yes, *pahale*, it's another first. You can add it to your tally."

He drew back to eye her. "What's *pa-hah-lee*?"

"It's my nickname for you. You call me Cookie all the time, so I thought you should have one."

"What does it mean?"

She smiled impishly. "Are you worried?"

Yeah, he was a little worried. It probably meant jackass in Hindi.

"Why would I be worried? I'm sure it means outrageously handsome."

She giggled and shook her head. "No. *Sundara* is the word for handsome."

"Then it must mean genius."

"*Pratibha* is the word for genius."

He decided he was better off not knowing what *pa-hah-lee* meant. He dropped a kiss on her nose.

"How many languages do you speak, Cookie?"

"Only five," she answered somewhat apologetically.

Only five.

Jesus.

"Which ones?"

"English, Spanish, French, Hindi, and Bengali. I'd like to learn Mandarin Chinese, but I haven't had time."

"Did you learn Hindi and Bengali from your parents?"

Frowning a little, she stepped away from him. "No." She grabbed a ball from the bucket and placed it on the tee. "We were an English-speaking household. I learned them from my grandparents."

"Do they live here or in India?"

"India."

He was curious about her family and her Indian ethnicity. She rarely mentioned either.

"How often do you visit them?"

She leaned against her club. "Every summer until I went to college. When I was six years old, my parents started sending me to camp for the first half of summer, and I spent the rest of it with my grandparents in Delhi."

Their childhoods could not have been more different. While her parents had shipped her off to camp and far-flung relatives, his parents had loaded him and his siblings into an RV or onto a plane to spend several weeks together exploring new places.

When he was a young child, it had seemed like an adventure. When he was an adolescent, it had seemed like torture, and he'd whined and complained about it along with Quinn and Teagan. Their grumbles had fallen on deaf ears. His parents had been determined to spend their vacations together.

As an adult, he had a much greater appreciation for the way his parents had raised them. Despite the fact that his dad had run one of the largest apparel companies in the nation, he'd still made his family a priority. And his mom had made the choice to focus on her children instead of her career.

He felt a fair amount of sympathy for Bebe. Her parents sounded like real assholes, and he hoped her trips to India had been good experiences.

"What's India like? I've never been there."

Cal had visited a lot of places outside the United States, but he'd never had any interest in India. Once he had met Bebe, however, he had done a little research on the country. Just to educate himself, of course. His near obsession with a smart, sexy Indian chick had nothing to do with it.

She tilted her head, clearly giving his question serious thought. "Crowded. Noisy. Hot. Dirty."

Well, that doesn't sound pleasant.

"Colorful. Alive. Welcoming. Exhilarating."

Now that sounds better.

"When was the last time you visited?"

She looked down and inspected the rubber material that covered the top of the golf club. "January," she murmured.

Bebe dropped her club to the ground and assumed her stance. Clearly she was done talking about India.

He moved back several feet to evaluate her position. It was the perfect excuse to stare at her ass, and he sent a silent prayer of thanks to the sports gods for creating the game of golf.

Her pants were similar to his khakis, only they were black. They weren't tight, but her ass looked awesome in them. He looked forward to palming her bare cheeks while he fucked her against the wall.

A long-sleeved, cream-colored cardigan sweater with big red and black flowers topped her red polo shirt. The bright colors highlighted the richness of her dark hair and the burnished tones of her skin.

She looked dainty and feminine, but he knew she could whip someone's ass with little effort thanks to her kickboxing skills. And her sharp tongue could castrate the entire male population.

"Where did you go on your last trip outside the U.S.?" she asked, her attention focused on her grip.

"France."

"Paris?" she guessed.

"Provence."

"I've never been there. Did you go with Saika?"

"Yes."

He had taken his ex-girlfriend to Provence for her birthday. The region was a foodie paradise, and they had wandered through farmers' markets all day and made love all night. The trip seemed like a lifetime ago.

"How romantic," Bebe observed, her voice completely devoid of emotion.

Her face was turned away from him so he couldn't see her expression, but the tone of her voice made him wonder if she was jealous. He hoped she was. He hoped the thought of him with Saika made her burn with jealousy.

He hoped she was possessive of him because he sure as hell was possessive of her. And that possessiveness made him think and behave irrationally. If Beck hadn't backed off at the Halloween party, Cal probably would have slammed his fist into the man's face.

He knew his deal with Bebe was supposed to be just sex, but he wasn't sure it *was* just sex. Well, sex was a huge part of it, but it had started to feel like more than that. He liked spending time with her. He looked forward to it like he looked forward to dessert after dinner.

Bebe brought the club back and took her swing. Just like before, the head connected with the ball, and this time it flew past the 200-yard mark.

"Holy shit!" he blurted out. "You may be the next Inbee Park."

"Who's that?"

"She's the best female golfer in the world."

She laughed lightly. "I'm sure it's just beginner's luck."

"All of us have our own special talents. Maybe you're just really good with balls and shafts." He paused for emphasis. "I'm really good at getting it in the hole and scoring."

She spun around, her face etched with a mix of amusement and chagrin. "Cal O'Brien, you are shameless!" she admonished.

"What?" He pushed down the laughter that welled in his chest and widened his eyes to look as innocent as possible. "I *am* good. I don't waste time with false modesty."

She snorted. "You don't waste time with any kind of modesty."

"You're the one who ripped off your panties in the laundry room and threw them at me."

He had expected the reminder to make her blush, but it didn't. Instead, her luscious lips quirked, and her eyes glinted with amusement.

"I can't be the only woman who has thrown her panties at you."

He shook his head in exasperation. "Actually, you're the first."

He still couldn't believe Bebe had thrown her panties at him. At the same time, he had realized it was *exactly* something she would do. She was unpredictable.

"Finally! I get to be one of *your* firsts."

She didn't know it, but she was going to be another first. He'd never been with a virgin.

Chapter 18

IN BEBE'S OPINION, THE FAIRMONT SAN FRANCISCO WAS ONE
of the most luxurious hotels in the world. Located atop Nob
Hill, the historic hotel offered panoramic views of the Bay
and the city. It was known for unparalleled accommodations
and service.

When investors came to town to meet with GGB, the company reserved rooms for them at the Fairmont and hosted dinners at the hotel's Laurel Court Restaurant, as well as the Tonga
Room & Hurricane Bar, which featured live entertainment,
dancing, and a unique water feature that mimicked a rainstorm.

This evening, however, Bebe's visit to the Fairmont was
personal instead of business. She was meeting her mother
prior to the awards dinner where Noor would be honored for
her contributions to the medical community.

Cal had asked her to come over after she had visited with
Noor, and she had told him she would think about it. She
didn't know how she would feel after seeing her mother. Usually she felt like fruit after a spin in a high-powered blender.

As Bebe drove up to the hotel, she took in its Beaux-Arts
architecture. It was a beautiful, massive structure with nearly
six hundred guest rooms. She came to a stop at the hotel's

covered entrance, and a uniformed valet waved her toward a small parking area toward the right.

After parking her Vespa, she hurriedly stowed her helmet and grabbed her bag. She wasn't late, but her mother did not wait for anyone, and she certainly wouldn't wait for her daughter.

The Laurel Court Restaurant & Bar was located on the hotel's lobby level. It was a lovely setting with its pristine marble floors, Corinthian columns trimmed in gold, and three huge domes.

Stopping just inside the entrance to Laurel Court, Bebe scanned the bar area for her mother. Her heart sank when she spotted Noor seated in a tall-backed chair in front of a small circular wooden table. She had hoped to get here first.

Bebe made her way over to her mother, and when she stopped beside her, Noor looked up from her tablet. Her face showed no warmth or excitement at the sight of her only daughter, which wasn't surprising to Bebe.

Noor hadn't requested this meeting; Bebe had.

"Hello, Mother."

Noor frowned. "Bindu, I've asked you several times to address me by my given name."

"I'm sorry. I won't forget again."

Noor took a moment to place her tablet inside her leather bag before gesturing toward the empty chair in front of her. As Bebe sat down, she studied her mother, cataloging any changes since they had last seen each other ten months ago.

Noor was a beautiful woman—not as beautiful as Akash's *maataa*, but pretty close. Bebe could only see a faint resemblance between herself and her mother.

The most obvious similarity was their eyes. Bebe had inherited her strangely colored eyes from her mother. Most Indians had coffee-colored eyes, but Noor's and Bebe's eye color was the result of their ancestors mixing their DNA with invading Persians.

Despite her age and the demands of her career, Noor's face showed only a hint of wrinkles, just a few fine lines around her eyes. Her skin was still fairly smooth and young-looking, and Bebe had a fleeting thought that she hoped she had inherited her mother's agelessness.

Noor's dark hair was streaked with silver and gray, and she wore it pulled back from her face in a low bun. It was another thing Bebe and her mother shared, and she abruptly decided to change her hairstyle.

"Congratulations on the award, Noor. It's quite an honor to be recognized by the Society of Thoracic Surgeons."

Noor nodded. "It is an honor."

Noor had been the first female to be born into her family in nearly two hundred years. Her birth had stunned and delighted relatives near and far, and she had been pampered and spoiled from her first breath. When she'd expressed an interest in healing like her ancestors, her parents had sent her to Great Britain to obtain her medical training.

"Have you been well?" Bebe asked when it became apparent Noor had nothing else to say.

Again, Noor nodded. "Yes."

Bebe sighed internally. She always told herself that her interactions with Noor couldn't be as horrible and awkward as she remembered them. But every time she met with her mother, she realized they were *worse* than she remembered.

Bebe's relationship with her mother had always been strained. When she had been a little girl, she hadn't understood why her mother didn't treat her as she treated Pritam and Ranjit. Eventually she realized that Noor resented her.

Noor had been thirty-nine when she'd gotten pregnant with Bebe. She had been an accident, a big pothole in the fast lane of Noor's medical career.

"And how is Father?"

Bebe hadn't been in touch with her father since the engagement ceremony. She didn't know where he was or what he was doing. He probably hadn't read her email that let him know she'd moved to San Francisco.

Noor gave an almost imperceptible shrug. "I believe he is in Africa. I haven't heard from him in several months."

Bebe never had understood how her parents had managed to come together to create three children. They showed no affection to each other. In fact, they seemed to be colleagues more than spouses.

Surprisingly, Noor and Charak's marriage had not been arranged. They had met while attending medical school in Great Britain and had married halfway through their training.

Bebe always had suspected they had married because Noor had been pregnant with Pritam. He had been born eight months after Noor and Charak had wed, and Ranjit had followed three years later.

Noor had managed to get through medical school with a baby and toddler at home by outsourcing all her parental responsibilities to nannies and housekeepers. It was the same way Bebe had been raised.

"And Pritam and Ranjit?"

As far as Bebe knew, Pritam continued to work on mapping the human genome at Duke University in North Carolina. Ranjit, meanwhile, was in Atlanta at the Centers for Disease Control. Like their father, he specialized in infectious diseases, and he worked in a biosafety level four lab with some of the planet's deadliest pathogens.

Finally, Noor smiled. "They are doing well. I am proud to call them my sons."

A wave of anger rushed over Bebe. She was *so* tired of being compared to her brothers and coming up short simply because Noor and Charak hadn't been careful enough to prevent her conception.

"And is your daughter doing well?" Bebe asked sarcastically.

Noor's eyes narrowed. "I assume so."

"But you don't know since you haven't asked. In fact, you haven't talked to her in more than eight months."

Noor didn't blink an eyelash at her criticism, and Bebe swallowed back her tears. Why did she continue to hold on to the ridiculous hope that Noor would one day be the mother she needed?

Finally, Noor said, "Ishani notified me that you and Akash plan to marry next October."

She shifted slightly and crossed her legs. The expensive fabric of her black pantsuit made a swishing sound.

Noor's personal style was understated and businesslike, and her Armani suit, red silk blouse, and black pumps reflected it. Bebe had never seen her mother in a dress or anything casual like jeans or yoga pants.

Taking a deep breath, Bebe clenched her hands together in her lap to prevent herself from twisting her rings. She had come here tonight to beg her mother for the money she needed to release her from Akash.

Noor's family was exceptionally wealthy, and when her parents had died, they left her a substantial inheritance. Bebe wasn't sure how much, but she knew it was a lot. She knew her mother could help her if she wanted to do so.

"Noor, I came here tonight to ask for your assistance."

Noor's dark eyebrows rose. "My assistance?" she echoed, her voice tinged with surprise.

Bebe had not asked for anything from either of her parents since she'd graduated from medical school more than eight years ago, but she was beyond desperate. She had to find a way out of the deal she had made with Akash.

"I need six hundred thousand dollars," she stated baldly. "Will you loan it to me?"

Noor blinked, her lashes fluttering rapidly. "Why do you need so much money? Are you involved with drugs? Gambling?"

"Seriously, Mother? Your first thought is that I owe money to a drug dealer or have a gambling debt?" She laughed mirthlessly. "What have I ever done to make you have such a poor opinion of me?" She held up her hands. "Wait. I already know the answer: I exist."

"Why are you so dramatic, Bindu?" her mother sighed.

Bebe ignored her. "Akash gave me six hundred thousand dollars to pay for Harvard, and he wants it back."

Noor stared at her for a long moment. "Why would your future husband want you to repay the money he gave you, especially when six hundred thousand dollars is a mere fraction of the Mehra wealth?"

She did not want to explain all the details regarding her arrangement with Akash. She knew she had made a mistake, and she didn't want to hear Noor's castigations.

"I don't want to marry Akash. I want to break off the engagement, and in order to do so, I need to repay him."

Noor shook her head emphatically. "No, I will not give you the money."

"I asked for a loan."

"No, I will not loan you the money. You will honor your commitment to the Mehras. You should not have agreed to marry Akash or taken his money if you did not plan to honor your commitment."

"I agreed to marry him because I wanted your approval! That's the only reason! I thought it would make you proud of me."

Two months before Bebe had graduated from medical school, Noor had notified her that she and Charak had decided not to attend her graduation ceremony. The news had devastated Bebe, but it had served as the wake-up call she'd needed to realize that her parents didn't care about her.

They had never cared about her. They hadn't attended her graduation from Northwestern, either, and she hadn't even bothered to walk the stage at Harvard because there'd been no one in the audience to cheer for her.

"Why should I be proud of you?" Noor shot back. "What have you done to deserve my admiration and esteem? You have done *nothing*." Her voice was full of vitriol, her eyes flashing with loathing. "You threw away your medical career, the only opportunity you had to contribute to this world in *any* way. You shamed me amongst my colleagues when you refused to fulfill your residency, and now you want to dishonor me again by breaking off your marriage with the Mehras. *You disgust me*."

"Why do you hate me so much?"

"It is impossible to love you." Noor stood abruptly. "You were a selfish, useless child, and now you're a selfish, useless woman. I am ashamed you are my daughter. I do not want to hear from you again."

Bebe watched with dry eyes as Noor gathered her bag. Her mother tossed one final hateful look toward her before skirting the tables in the bar area and leaving the restaurant.

That hadn't gone well.

She fell back against the chair. She hadn't expected Noor to help her. She had known it was unlikely, but she'd had to try.

A tall waitress with long, honey-colored hair walked by, and Bebe flagged her down to order a double vodka martini. She rarely drank, but right now, when her heart was shredded, was a great time to indulge.

Meetings with her mother were never pleasant, and over the years, she had become accustomed to Noor's disapproval. But this meeting had been the worst by far.

When the pretty waitress delivered the martini, Bebe threw it back in one gulp. She had never done that before, and she wasn't prepared for her body's response.

The alcohol burned the back of her throat, and fire spread to her chest. Her eyes watered, and she coughed as she tried to catch her breath. Within moments, her lips were numb, and she couldn't feel her extremities. Soon, her muscles relaxed, and her breathing slowed.

Leaning her head back, she stared up at the dome overhead. She wondered how many other women had looked up at this exact dome.

How many had mothers who hated them? How many had fathers who didn't even know where they lived? How many had brothers who never called them or visited them?

Her vision was a little blurry, and she blinked to try to clear it. Something tickled her lips, and when she licked them, she tasted salt.

Why are my lips salty?

"Are you okay?"

Bebe looked up. After a moment she was able to focus on the blond waitress, who passed a white cloth napkin to her.

"Are you okay?" the waitress asked again.

Bebe had a hard time getting her lips to move, but finally she was able to answer. "Fine."

Her phone rang in her pocket, and she fumbled to remove it. As she pulled it out, she dropped it on the floral-patterned carpet. The nice waitress picked it up and held it out to her, but Bebe didn't want to talk to anyone.

"You," Bebe directed, trying to tell the waitress to answer the phone.

She heard the waitress talking, but she couldn't make out what the woman said. Pulling her legs up, she turned sideways in the chair, tucking her head against her knees and closing her eyes.

She hoped Noor was wrong. She hoped she wasn't impossible to love.

"BEBE."

Someone was calling her name, but she was having a hard time opening her eyes. Warm fingers cupped her cheek and turned her face.

"Come on, baby, wake up."

Finally, she got her eyes open. She was in the bar of Laurel

Court, curled up in a high-backed chair, and Cal was crouched in front of her, his face close to hers.

"There you are," he said softly.

Reaching out, she touched his cheek. "Oh, Cal. I'm so glad to see you."

I'm always glad to see you.

He grasped her hand and kissed her palm before turning to look at the waitress. "How much did she have?"

"A double martini, but our bartender is generous, so it probably had close to five shots of vodka," the chatty waitress answered. "I've never seen anybody slam one back so fast. It hit her hard, and then she started crying."

"Fuck."

Bebe put her fingers to his lips. "You have such a potty mouth."

"Yeah," he agreed, staring into her eyes. "I'll work on it."

Wrapping his arm around her waist, he gently pulled her to her feet. Her head felt funny, and she pressed her hand to it.

"Why do people drink hard liquor, Cal? The physical effects are horrible."

He nodded to the waitress. "What's your name again?"

"Shelly."

"Thank you, Shelly."

He grabbed Bebe's bag and navy pea coat, and they slowly made their way out of the hotel. Belva was parked right in front with a valet holding open the passenger door, and Cal helped her into the car, buckling the seat belt over her lap.

Just before Cal closed the door, she heard him tell the valet that they would return tomorrow to retrieve her Vespa. She leaned her head against the cool glass of the window, and seconds later, Cal slid into the car. They accelerated away from the hotel, the lights of the city flashing by the window, and she closed her eyes against the brightness.

"What happened?" he asked quietly.

Somewhere inside her foggy mind, she knew she should keep her mouth shut, but it started to move anyway. "She said I was a selfish, useless child who had grown up to be a selfish, useless woman. She said I didn't deserve her admiration or esteem. She said I disgusted her."

Her nose was itchy, so she rubbed it on the sleeve of her gray suit jacket. "I knew she resented me. She's told me before that I was a mistake. An accident. But I didn't know she hated me."

Her rings felt as if they were cutting off the circulation in her fingers, and she started to pull them off. "Do you know what, Cal? I'm going to need more rings."

"Why do you need more rings?"

She glanced at him, wondering why his voice sounded so strange. He was staring straight ahead.

"Because."

"Because why?" he prodded.

"Because I add a ring for every mean thing she or my father or my brothers say—every time they tell me what a disappointment I am. She said a lot of mean things tonight." She laughed, and even in her inebriated state, she could hear the hysteria underneath it. "I'm going to run out of room on my fingers. I'll have to put rings on my toes!"

He said something under his breath, but she couldn't hear what it was.

"What?"

"Nothing, baby. It wasn't important."

She shifted toward him. "She said it's impossible to love me."

"*Fucking bitch*," Cal muttered.

She realized she was crying, and she wiped her face with her sleeve. "Do you think it's impossible to love me? I don't want to be unlovable."

Stopping at a red light, he turned to look at her. The dashboard lights limned the planes of his face, all sharp angles and smooth curves.

"You don't need to worry," he replied softly. "You're lovable."

Chapter 19

BEBE SHIFTED UNCOMFORTABLY, TRYING TO STRETCH OUT.
Something heavy pressed on her side, holding her down and
making it hard for her to breathe. Running her hand over her
body, she was horrified to realize the weight holding her
down was a man's arm.

Oh, my God!

Her eyes flew open, and she realized she was in a bed . . .
whose bed she didn't know. She knew immediately she
wasn't in her loft because her bedroom was much brighter.

Panic flooded her, making her heartbeat thunder in her
ears and her breath seize in her chest. She pushed off the male
arm and scrambled from bed, moaning as her head pounded
with pain.

What's wrong with me? Where am I?

The sheets rustled, and seconds later, a light flicked on,
almost blinding her. Spinning around, she closed her eyes
and grabbed her head when it felt like her brain split in two.

"Bebe, take a deep breath. You're safe."

It sounded like Cal's voice. Softer than she'd ever heard it
but still Cal's voice. She cautiously raised her eyelids, hoping
she wasn't just imagining things.

Oh, thank God. It was Cal.

He was sitting up in the bed, his chest bare. Throwing back the covers, he got up and came around the bed to her. He clasped her elbow, steadying her and calming her at the same time.

"Do you need to throw up?"

"No," she gasped. "I was just scared. And my head hurts."

"You're okay. It's just a hangover."

The last thing she remembered was ordering a martini. *Oh, that explains it.*

Glancing down, she took an inventory of herself. She wore one of Cal's USC T-shirts. The worn gray cotton hung off her shoulder, reaching to her knees. He'd left her bra and panties underneath it.

"Climb back in, baby," he invited, pulling back the covers and helping her into the bed. "I'll get you some aspirin."

"Acetaminophen. It's better for hangovers."

His eyebrows arched. "How do you know?"

"I went to medical school, remember?"

He nodded. "I remember. Sit tight. I'll go get some Tylenol."

Calmer now, she snuggled down into the soft sheets and fluffy comforter. She had no idea how she'd ended up in Cal's king-size bed, but she was happy enough to be there.

While he was gone, she let her gaze roam around his bedroom. She had been curious about it, and now she had an opportunity to indulge her curiosity.

It was about the same size as her bedroom in her loft, large but not overly large. Neat and clean. Nothing out of place.

Toward her right, big windows covered the entire wall and a comfortable-looking navy-blue leather club chair sat in the corner. In the dim glow of the lamp, the walls looked as if they were the same color as the chair. The white trim around the windows and the matching crown molding were a stark contrast to the walls.

The wood furniture, a dark honey color, was simple and straight-lined. A long dresser faced the bed, along with a tall armoire.

Brushed nickel lamps with navy-blue shades occupied matching nightstands. A down comforter with a striped duvet in various shades of blue covered the bed. The light blue cotton sheets were obviously expensive because they were so smooth they felt like silk.

"How's your stomach?" Cal asked as he entered the room.

She arranged the pillows against the headboard and sat up. "Okay. It's just my head."

He passed her a bottle of water before popping the cap on the Tylenol and dumping two tablets into his hand. He gave them to her, and she swallowed them down with a big gulp of the cold liquid.

"Drink it all," he directed, nodding toward the water bottle.

Obediently, she took another drink. He absently scratched his chest, and even though her head was killing her, it didn't stop her from staring.

A light dusting of dark hair covered his muscular torso, his nipples flat brown disks on his sculpted pecs. His stomach was tight with a six-pack, and his plaid flannel pajama pants showed his V-cut in mouthwatering detail.

She gulped down more water, hoping it would ease her dry throat. She wanted to think she was parched because of the alcohol, but she knew it was because Cal's gorgeous, seminaked body was less than a foot away.

"How did I get here?"

He cocked his head. "You don't remember?"

"If I'm asking, I obviously don't."

He grinned at her snarky reply. "I called your phone, and Shelly the waitress answered. She told me you were passed out in the bar of the fanciest hotel in the city like a frat boy at a keg party, so I came to get you. I loaded you into Belva, and I easily carried you up three flights of stairs because I'm strong and manly. Once we were here, I stripped off your clothes with my eyes closed to preserve your modesty and tucked you in." He gave an exaggerated wink. "From now on, I expect you to refer to me as your knight in shining armor."

Bending her head, she covered her eyes with her free hand. She was so embarrassed. She rarely drank hard liquor, and when she did, it was always mixed with some type of fruit juice.

"Cal, I'm sorry," she mumbled. "*So* sorry."

He laughed softly before kissing the top of her head. "Not a problem, Cookie."

She dropped her hand and met his gaze. This went well beyond their sex-only arrangement.

"Thank you for coming to get me."

He stared at her for a long moment. "You needed me."

Yes, she had needed him. But more alarming was how much she had wanted him.

Gesturing to the water bottle, he said, "One last swig, and then we're going back to sleep. It's three in the morning, and I'm only up at this time of night for one reason."

Is he talking about sex?

"No, I'm not talking about sex," he denied, keenly reading her mind. "I'm talking about the British Open."

"You get up in the middle of the night for golf?"

"Yes." He smiled slowly. "And I get up in the middle of the night for you."

"I'm sorry."

"You can make it up to me later."

"Whatever you want," she promised.

His eyes widened a little bit, and she quickly changed the subject. "Where are my rings? They're missing."

Clenching his jaw, Cal rolled his lips inward. He didn't reply for a long moment, and she wondered why he suddenly seemed upset. She immediately felt guilty for all the trouble she had caused him.

"Your rings are in Belva. You took them off on the way home."

"I did?"

He nodded curtly. She had no recollection of removing her rings. Actually, she had no memory of the ride to Cal's place at all. She abandoned the subject of her rings. She could get them in the morning.

"Do you have an extra toothbrush?"

With a nod, he headed toward a door in the corner of the room. As he opened the door, he beckoned her to him, and she joined him in the en suite bathroom. Rummaging through a drawer in the vanity, he found a spare toothbrush and handed it to her.

"Toothpaste and floss are in the top drawer." He patted her on the butt. "See you in bed."

He closed the door behind him, and she leaned against the

sink to look around. His bathroom was spotless, confirming her suspicions that he was a neat freak.

Like his kitchen, the bathroom reflected the age of the condo with its white subway tile and tiny hexagon-shaped tiles on the floor. The vintage bathtub was free-standing, and a circular shower rod hung around it. When she saw the shower curtain, she laughed softly; it was solid white except for two words in black print: GET NAKED.

Pulling open the top drawer, she found everything she needed to get ready for bed, including hand lotion and a hairbrush. She spent a few minutes on the typical nighttime rituals before turning off the light and opening the door.

Cal had left on the lamp on his nightstand, and he was propped up against a mound of pillows. His eyes widened as she got closer to the bed.

"Your hair . . . it's so long," he noted, his voice shaded with surprise.

She touched the braid hanging over her shoulder. When her hair was loose, it fell to her waist. As soon as she had the opportunity, though, she was going to get it cut and styled. She wasn't going to wear her hair in a bun any longer.

Climbing into bed, she turned toward him. The fact that she was here, in Cal's bed, seemed completely surreal. A fantasy.

He ran the tip of his finger down the tail of her braid before looking into her eyes. The dim lighting in the room made his pale blue eyes seem darker than usual.

"I want to see it loose."

Somehow, he made that sentence sound like both a demand and a request.

"Okay."

He didn't wait for her to do it. Instead, he pulled the elastic band from her braid and unwound it. When her hair was completely free, he eased his hand into it and ran his fingers through it. With his gaze wholly focused on her hair, he clenched and unclenched his fingers in the strands, testing the weight and texture.

"It's beautiful." He brought his eyes to hers. "This is another first, isn't it? I'm the only man who's seen it this way."

Her breath stalled in her throat, and she couldn't do anything but nod. He slid his fingers through her hair until his palm cupped the base of her skull and brought her head toward him.

He kissed her gently, just a chaste peck of his lips, and drew back. Pulling his fingers from her hair, he turned off the light and settled on his back.

His voice whispered into the dark silence. "Come here."

She shifted closer, and he wrapped his arm around her. She dropped her head onto his chest, and he adjusted her like a rag doll, placing her hand over his heart and pulling her leg over him until her crotch nestled against his hip.

"You feel good here." He sighed loudly. "Good night, Cookie."

Almost immediately, his breathing evened out, and he slid into sleep. She tried to stay awake so she could savor the feel of his body against hers, but she was too warm and comfortable, and she quickly followed her *pahale* into the land of nod.

AS USUAL, CAL'S INTERNAL ALARM CLOCK WENT OFF AT SIX o'clock. No matter how late he was up the night before or where he was in the world, his body woke up at six fucking a.m. Pacific time.

Rolling over, he aligned his front against Bebe's back and threw his arm over her waist. He buried his face in her hair and pressed his hard-on against her until it nestled into the space between her thighs and the curve of her ass.

Ahh. Much better.

He closed his eyes and dozed until the sunlight peeked through the slats on the wooden blinds covering his windows. When he couldn't ignore the brightness any longer, he carefully eased away from her and got out of bed. She'd had a shitty night, and he didn't want to wake her.

He quickly threw on a long-sleeve thermal tee and closed himself in the en suite to take care of his morning business. When he exited the bathroom, he checked the alarm clock by the side of his bed. It was just after seven, and he should probably wake Bebe soon.

Minutes later, he returned to his bedroom with a mug of coffee—lots of cream, no sugar, just the way she liked it—and her cell phone. He placed her phone on the nightstand and took a moment to study her.

She was completely zonked out, her dark hair a wild tangle around her head. The early morning light made her skin look faintly metallic, and he marveled at the smoothness of it.

"Time to wake up, Cookie," he said as he gently shook her awake.

Her eyelids rose, and he stared into the sleepiest, most gorgeous eyes he'd ever seen. She blinked slowly and gave him a small smile.

"Hi," she greeted him huskily.

For some reason, his voice wasn't working, so he just held out the mug. Scooting up the bed, she pushed her hair out of her face before taking it from him. He barely controlled the urge to shove his hands into those glossy strands and cover her mouth with his.

"How are you feeling?"

She took a sip of coffee before answering. "I think the Tylenol worked because I feel completely normal."

"Do you have a lot on your schedule today?"

She shrugged. "I *always* have a lot on my schedule."

He placed her phone with its hot pink protective cover on top of the navy-striped comforter. "Call in sick. We can play hooky and spend the day together."

After passing her coffee back to him, she picked up her phone. She tapped the screen a couple of times, bit her lip, and then tapped it a few more times before placing the phone on the nightstand.

"I've never played hooky before."

"Another first."

She smiled. "Another first."

"Have you ever had breakfast in bed?"

Her golden eyes widened. "That would be so messy."

He laughed at the combination of curiosity and horror on her face. "Last time I checked, sheets are washable."

She smiled ruefully. "I've never had breakfast in bed. Another first."

"Okay, here's what I propose: you lounge in bed for the next hour or so, and I'll clear my schedule and make you breakfast."

"Are you taking requests?"

"What do you have in mind?"

"French toast?" she asked hopefully.

Bending down, he dropped a kiss on her pink lips. "You got it."

He was already out the door when Bebe called out to him. He backed up and stuck his head into his bedroom.

"Is it okay if I take a shower?"

"Cookie, you can do whatever you want. Towels are in the cabinet above the toilet."

He headed back to the kitchen, stopping in the living room to grab his tablet from the coffee table. He sent an email to his assistant to let her know he wouldn't be coming in today and asked her to clear his schedule.

Picking up his coffee cup, he leaned against the island. He preferred to use challah bread to make French toast, but he didn't have any. He had a sourdough baguette and fresh hazelnuts, though, so he could make baked French toast, which was even better than the original.

Cal turned on the oven and put a pan of hazelnuts in to roast before quickly slicing several thick cuts of baguette. He whipped up the egg batter, sprinkled in some cinnamon and orange zest, and let the bread soak in it while he answered emails. By the time the bread was fully saturated, he'd addressed the most critical messages and was ready to grind the hazelnuts.

Once he had ground them to the right consistency, he poured them into a dish and dipped the soaked bread into them. He let the slices sit in the hazelnuts for a while to make sure they adhered to the bread before placing them in a dark rectangular pan and sprinkling them with cinnamon.

While the French toast baked in the oven, he made a mixed-berry coulis and heated up the maple syrup. He pulled two plates from the cabinet, along with the syrup dispenser and a small cream pitcher for the coulis.

When then timer sounded, he removed the French toast from the oven. It was baked to perfection, a nice golden brown.

He quickly plated several slices for himself and Bebe, garnishing them with fresh blueberries, strawberries, and raspberries. He loaded the plates, syrup, and coulis onto a large tray along with some Amish butter, his coffee cup, and two glasses of orange juice, and carefully made his way to his bedroom. It was empty, and he placed the tray on the dresser before knocking lightly on the closed bathroom door.

"Breakfast is ready."

The door opened immediately, and fragrant steam spilled into the room. Bebe smiled at him from the doorway, her face dewy from her shower and her hair hanging in wet tendrils around her face.

She had pulled on the USC T-shirt she'd slept in, but he was pretty sure she had left off her bra because there were no straps visible where the shirt had slipped off her shoulder. He wondered if she wore any panties underneath, and the hard-on he'd woken up with made a sudden reappearance.

"How does breakfast in bed work?" she asked.

He knew how he'd like for it to work—him licking syrup off her naked body.

"It can be like a picnic, or we can lean against the headboard. Whatever you want to do."

She cocked her head. "Picnic, I think, so we can face each other."

She dove for the bed, and his eyes almost crossed with the effort to see beneath the long T-shirt. Maybe she would sit with her legs wide open and give him a flash of her pretty pussy.

He watched as she settled on the bed with her back toward the headboard. She crisscrossed her legs, but unfortunately, she tucked the T-shirt between them for modesty.

Damn.

After placing the tray in the middle of the bed, he climbed onto the bed with his back toward the footboard. He let one of his legs hang toward the floor because he was semi-erect, and he remembered the pain of sitting cross-legged with a hard-on during their picnic at Metson Lake.

Bebe studied the tray, and when she looked up, her eyes shone brightly. "You're the first man who has ever cooked me breakfast."

"To firsts," he toasted, raising his orange juice.

"To firsts," she echoed with a smile. She took a sip before returning the glass to the tray. "This looks so good."

He doused her French toast with syrup and a dollop of coulis and passed the plate to her along with a napkin and silverware. She immediately dug in, dribbling syrup down her chin.

"Oops!"

She tried to catch the droplet on her napkin, but it fell onto her T-shirt near the tip of her breast. He could see her nipple budded against the thin cotton, the syrup just a lick away.

Looking down at his plate, he shoveled French toast into his mouth to keep from attacking her like a rabid dog. After their enlightening discussion last night while she'd been drunk and sleeping with her all night, he had very little self-control this morning.

They ate in silence for several minutes until Bebe deposited her plate back onto the tray. She sighed gustily.

"This was so good. I wish I had four stomachs so I could eat it all."

He laughed at her gluttony. "Or I could just make it for you again."

She nodded. "Or I could just eat it for lunch and dinner."

Dropping his plate on top of hers, he stood and removed the tray from the bed. He placed it on his dresser and turned back to Bebe.

"Cal, I want to thank you again for coming to get me last night. I rarely drink hard liquor, but the meeting with my mother didn't go well, and I was upset."

Didn't go well?

That was the understatement of the century. He pressed his lips together, doing his best to keep from shouting that her mother was a bitch who didn't deserve an amazing daughter like Bebe.

"My mother and I have a difficult relationship."

Difficult?

What *bullshit*! They had an abusive relationship.

What kind of mother told her daughter she was unlovable? If he ever ran across Noor Banerjee, he was going to have a hard time abiding by his personal rule never to harm a woman.

"Thank you for letting me stay over last night."

Cal leaned back against his dresser, resting his ass on the top and bracing his hands on the edge. He'd waited for years to have Bebe in his bed, and while it hadn't been exactly what he had imagined, since she had been either passed out or hung over, it still had been pretty damn awesome. And now that she was there, he didn't want her to leave anytime soon.

"And thank you again for an amazing breakfast. I know I've already told you, but you're a fabulous cook."

Pushing away from the dresser, he crawled onto the bed on his hands and knees until he leaned over her. She propped herself on her elbows, raising her face to his, and he dropped a kiss on the corner of her mouth. She smiled, and he felt the movement against his lips before he drew back to look into her eyes.

"So, *pahale,* what are we going to do today?" she asked with a big smile.

"Each other."

Chapter 20

BEBE'S EYES WIDENED, AND SHE SUCKED IN A SURPRISED breath. Cal chuckled at the look on her face, a conflicting mix of dread and anticipation.

"What did you say?"

"I said 'each other.' We're going to do each other today."

She stared up at him before letting herself fall back onto the bed. "I was thinking something fun like Alcatraz or a museum so I could learn something new."

"This is going to be fun, and you are going to learn something new."

He stretched out on his side so he could look at her. She turned her head, and they eyed each other in silence for several heartbeats.

"I think I'm afraid to do this," she admitted quietly.

"That's a big change from the woman who threw her panties at me in a laundry room," he noted as he played with the wispy tendrils along her hairline.

She frowned. "If you hadn't stopped in the laundry room, we wouldn't be having this conversation at all."

He ignored her complaint. "Why are you afraid? You went to medical school, so you already know the mechanics. You know it might hurt the first time. But there's a reason why people have sex. It feels good. *Really good.* You just have to get past the pain to enjoy the pleasure."

"That's not why I'm afraid, Cal."

He traced one of her dark eyebrows with his forefinger. "Tell me why you're afraid, baby."

She took a deep breath and exhaled loudly. "I'm worried that I'm not going to be good at this, and you won't want to continue our arrangement."

He thought about telling her there was no way it wasn't going to be good between them. He thought about telling her it was going to be *so* good, he wouldn't get enough of her for a long, long time. But he knew she wouldn't believe him, so he didn't bother.

"I'm worried, too. If I mess this up, you're going to be scarred for life."

He said it jokingly, but honestly he *was* a little worried. He wanted her first time to be memorable because it had been good, not because it had been a disaster.

She smiled. "That's a little dramatic."

"I'm serious," he insisted, widening his eyes for emphasis. "You may need therapy after today."

She giggled, and the happy sound made his chest feel as if it were filled with bubbles. He rubbed his thumb over her bottom lip.

"It's going to be fine," he promised. "In fact, it's going to be better than fine."

She stared at him for a moment before smoothing her hand over his hair. "I told Teagan you were my least worst option, but you're not. You're my best option." She smiled, a tiny upward tilt of her full lips. "I wouldn't want anyone else to be my first. Only you."

Something unraveled inside him—a knot of hurt he hadn't even known was there. He had needed to hear that he was her best option—that she wanted him.

Because he wanted her more than he'd ever wanted anyone or anything.

Dropping his head, he settled his mouth over hers. It was sticky with maple syrup, and he sucked lightly on her bottom lip before giving it a little nip. Her lips fell open, and he stroked his tongue along the seam of her mouth, dipping inside to get a little taste of her.

Bebe wrapped her arms around his neck, pulling him toward her, and he shifted until his torso covered hers. They both had on too many clothes, but he wasn't in a hurry—they had all day.

He spent some time licking and nibbling her lips until her tongue darted into his mouth. She swirled it along the interior of his upper lip, and he got a hint of mixed-berry coulis along with Bebe's sweet flavor.

As he sucked her tongue deeper into his mouth, he thought about doing the same thing to her dark nipples and her sweet clit, and his cock thickened. Her tongue slid against his, and he thought about her wet pussy. He couldn't wait to taste it.

She moaned against his mouth, and he started to sweat. He was fully, painfully erect, and he wondered how long he could wait before he *had* to be inside her.

With previous lovers, he'd been able to last for a good long time, both for foreplay and fucking. But things were different with Bebe, and he started to think he should have jacked off while she had been sleeping so he wasn't so close to the edge.

He let go of her mouth and tugged her arms from his neck so he could sit up. Pulling his T-shirt over his head, he threw it on the floor and immediately reached for the hem of her shirt. She stopped him by trailing her fingers across his chest and down to his stomach.

"You are the most gorgeous man," she breathed as she lightly scraped her fingernails through the hair that pointed south.

"I'm glad you think so."

She met his eyes. "All women think so."

He didn't care about other women. He only cared about her.

"Sit up. I want that shirt off so I can see you."

She rose to her knees in front of him, and he slowly lifted the T-shirt, baring the smooth golden skin of her thighs and the dark hair of her pussy. It was trimmed in a neat triangle, neither bushy nor bare. It was just right.

Grasping the hem, she pulled the shirt over her head, and he got his first view of her nude body. She was small, but she had curves exactly where they were supposed to be.

He had wanted her for so long, and now that she was here in his bed, he didn't know where to start. He felt like a starving man at an all-you-can-eat buffet, overwhelmed with options and hungry for everything.

He wanted to palm her breasts and suck on her nipples until she moaned. He wanted to spread her legs and rub his face against her pussy before licking those juicy pink lips and tonguing her clit. He wanted to turn her over, drop kisses along the delicate bumps of her spine, and nibble the cheeks of her ass.

There were a million things he wanted to do to her and with her, and he wasn't going to waste one more second thinking about them. He was going to *do* them.

Bending toward her, he traced the curves of her breasts with his hands. "These are so much larger than I thought they'd be." He shaped the plump mounds with his fingers. "You're so petite, I expected them to be little bites. But they're cupcakes."

She laughed softly. "Cupcakes?"

"Yeah. You can't fit a whole cupcake into your mouth. You have to eat it in little bites. Or you can suck off the icing."

He wrapped his lips around her hard nipple, circling it with his tongue and sucking deeply. She moaned, and he lightly bit the tip before letting go.

"Better than icing," he rasped before tonguing her other nipple.

It was a tight little bud, and he hummed a little in his throat when she arched her back to push it more deeply into his mouth. He laved it with small strokes, his pulse pounding in his ears with every lick.

"Cal," she gasped, "I need you to touch me."

"Show me where you want me to touch you."

Staring into his eyes, she took his hand and placed it over her pussy. She widened her legs and pressed his hand against her.

"Did you know that I can multitask?" he asked as he petted the tiny triangle of hair. It was silky against his fingers.

"No man can multitask," she countered breathlessly. "Why don't you prove it to me?"

In response, he pulled her dusky nipple into his mouth and slid his fingers between her slick folds. Just like before, she was drenched, and she jerked against him when his finger grazed her clit. He circled it while he sucked her nipple, and she started to pant.

"That feels so good. More. Please."

His cock agreed, and he pressed it against her hip to silence its demands. Sliding his fingers lower, he eased one inside her as he switched his attention to her other nipple. Her hot flesh welcomed him more easily than last time, and he withdrew to add a second finger.

"Oh, yeah," she moaned. "This is the good part."

He laughed breathlessly against her nipple, and she shivered. He worked his fingers into her in a slow, steady rhythm while rubbing her clit with his thumb. When she started to whimper, he increased the pace and the pressure.

"Move with my fingers, baby," he coached her. "Take what you want."

"Cal," she gasped. "I don't know how."

"Raise your hips so my fingers go as deep as you want them." He gritted his teeth as his balls twinged. "Roll them so my thumb presses the sweet spot on your clit."

She tentatively raised her hips, and his fingers sank deeper into her. She gasped and wiggled against his thumb until she tensed against him. He pulled his eyes from her breasts to meet her eyes. They were a clear, vivid gold, and they shimmered with desire.

"*Oohh*," she whispered. "Now I get it."

She caught the rhythm of his hand, moving her hips as he plunged in and out of her. She cupped her hand over his, and he watched her as she came.

The supple muscles of her pussy clenched tightly on his fingers, and she closed her eyes, arching her back in pleasure. He stayed with her as she came down from her orgasm, and once the last vibrations had faded, he pulled his fingers from her body.

His head felt as if it were about to explode, but he reminded himself that he had only one chance to do this right. That thought cooled his eager body, and he scooted down the bed until he was even with her hips.

Lifting her leg, he wedged his shoulders between her thighs and licked a circle around her belly button. Her stomach was tight and defined with tiny muscles, and it trembled under his tongue as he licked lower and lower.

He took a deep breath. The smell of her arousal infused the air around him, musky and intoxicating. He arranged her legs so they draped over his shoulders, and using both hands, he opened her pussy to his gaze.

Her pink flesh glistened with juice, and he swiped his fingers through the wetness and licked it off. The taste of her filled his mouth, and saliva pooled there like he was about to feast on a particularly delicious meal.

"*Goddamn*." He couldn't hold back a groan. "You're delicious. I could lick you all day."

She settled her hand on his head and let her thighs fall open while keeping her knees hooked over his shoulders. Shoving his face against her, he palmed the cheeks of her ass to pull her closer and wrapped his lips around her clit.

She cried out, clenching her fingers in his hair, and he sucked tenderly on the hard little nub before sliding his tongue through her folds to the entrance of her body. He eagerly licked through the abundant wetness, moaning as her juice flooded his mouth.

He thrust his tongue inside her, and she cried out again. In the back of his mind, he realized this might be too much for her first time, but he couldn't bring himself to stop. He replaced his tongue with his fingers, thrusting slowly as he tongued her clit with long strokes and tiny swipes.

Suddenly, she stiffened against him and let out a low moan that thrummed through his entire body. He pushed deeper and felt the rapid flutter of her pussy against his fingers as she came. His balls drew up, and he slid his free hand into his pajama bottoms to squeeze his cock so he wouldn't shoot off.

Bebe's legs trembled on his shoulders, and she whimpered softly as she recovered from her orgasm. He reluctantly removed his fingers from her body and raised his face from her juicy pussy.

His vision was a little hazy, and he was breathing hard. Lust boiled in his veins, and he knew he couldn't wait any longer to be inside her.

Lifting her legs from his shoulders, he rolled to the side and quickly shucked his pajama pants. He crawled over her, and she opened her legs so he could settle between them.

Bracing himself on his forearms, he stared down into her face. Her eyes were glazed, her cheeks were flushed, and her lips were red from his kisses. She looked just like a woman who had enjoyed two orgasms. He planned to give her a third, and probably a couple more before the day was over.

"Now?" she asked huskily.

"Now."

"Thank you for doing this . . . for doing me."

He laughed croakily. "Thank *you*. I've wanted this for a long fucking time."

Her eyes flared, but before she could say anything, he ran his hand down her hip to grasp her thigh. "Wrap your legs around my hips, baby."

She did as he requested, and he reached between them to gather some of her slippery wetness with his fingers. He coated his cock with her juice and guided it to the entrance of her body.

He had never taken anyone's virginity, and he'd never had sex without a condom. He probably was going to implode the moment he popped her cherry.

"It's going to hurt, but don't tense up, okay? Once I'm in, the pain will fade, and I'll make it good for you."

"You've already made it good for me, *pahale*," she replied softly. "Now you need to make it good for you."

Taking a deep breath, he slowly pushed forward until the head of his cock was wedged inside. Her hot flesh sucked him in, and his vision blurred from the heat and pressure. He had to stop and count to twenty before he could go deeper.

Sweat rolled down his face, and a fine film of perspiration covered his body. Nothing, *nothing*, had ever felt this good, and he couldn't imagine anything would *ever* feel this good again.

She shifted under him, gripping his lower back and raising her hips. He slid in a little farther, and blood roared in his ears.

"*Oh, fuck, fuck, fuck*," he groaned, squeezing his eyes shut as his cock pulsed. "Don't move."

He stayed like that for an eternity until he could open his eyes and meet Bebe's gaze. Her chest moved in steady, deep breaths, and even though she was soft and relaxed beneath him, he could tell by the look in her eyes he was hurting her.

"Do you want me to keep going?" he asked, his voice sounding like he had swallowed gravel.

"No, I want you to stop. I've changed my mind."

Cal, you fucking idiot! his cock shouted. *Why did you have to be a nice guy and ask if she wanted to keep going?*

"Okay. Don't move. I'm going to pull out."

"Are you *crazy*?" She squeezed her legs around his hips. "I was joking. Of course I want you to keep going."

"*Jesus Christ, Bebe.*" He dropped his forehead against hers. "I'm hanging by a thread here, and you're making jokes?"

She raised her head until their mouths were barely touching. "Do it, Cal," she said against his lips. "*Take it.*"

He thrust forward, burying his cock fully inside her. She gasped, inhaling the breath from his lungs, and he covered her mouth with his. He licked at her lips and sucked on her tongue as she adjusted to his presence.

He had fantasized about this moment a million times. He had pleasured himself by thinking about what it would feel like to be balls deep inside her, and the reality of it was so much better than he ever had imagined.

He remained motionless, her body gripping him tightly, and she pulled her mouth from his with a little gasp. He stroked the smooth skin of her cheek, hoping he hadn't hurt her too badly.

"I know that hurt, baby. Are you okay?"

"I'm better than okay. You executed the de-virginization plan with skill and patience."

Her comment shocked a laugh out of him, and the action nudged him deeper inside her. She gave a little shimmy, and heat flashed through him.

"We're not finished," he said hoarsely.

She shook her head. "No, we're not. You still have some work to do."

Holy shit, she's amazing. And she's all mine.

"Remember what I told you before. Move with me and take what you need."

She nodded, and he carefully withdrew before slowly pushing back in. His climax was building already, but he didn't want this to be over too quickly, especially not before he gave her another orgasm. He needed a distraction, so he started to talk.

"How does it feel?" he asked as he pulled out and slowly pressed forward.

"Good." She moaned when he nudged deeper. "*So good.*"

Pumping his hips, he sank into her, little by little. "Tell me how good."

"I don't know how to describe it." She raised her hips. "I can feel you everywhere. Stretching me. Filling me. You're big. A lot bigger than the average guy."

"How do you know?" he asked breathlessly.

She answered, equally breathless, "I read a research study."

"They say size doesn't matter, it's how you use it."

"You have size *and* skill."

He surged into her with slow, deep strokes until she tightened her legs around his hips. She let out a breathy moan that sent little shocks down his spine.

Squeezing his eyes shut, he withdrew and then plunged hard into her. Lights sparked behind his eyelids as she met his thrust, digging her nails into his ass and forcing him so deep he bottomed out inside her.

Desperate now, he slid his arm under her waist and pulled her up with him as he knelt with his legs spread. He draped her thighs over his hips and palmed her ass so he could work her over his cock.

By sheer willpower, he kept things slow and steady until they were panting. Then he increased the pace, each downward stroke rubbing her clit over his cock.

He was so fucking close, his balls burned with his orgasm. He didn't know how much longer he could last. Seconds, if he was lucky.

She whimpered, and he recognized the sound. She was there with him, and he adjusted the angle of her hips so his cock hit her clit more directly. One more thrust, and she flew apart, screaming his name.

Bebe's a screamer, and I fucking love it.

Her pussy clenched around his length, and he held her tightly against him when his climax crashed over him. He shouted hoarsely, his cock jerking over and over as he flooded her with his release.

She wrapped her arms around his shoulders, and he dropped his head to her chest, nestling his face into the valley between her breasts. He could feel the furious beat of her heart against his lips, but he couldn't feel the rest of his body. He was numb from pleasure. All his senses were so overwhelmed, they barely worked.

He'd *never* had sex like that before, and he wasn't sure he should do it again. It might kill him.

Bebe pressed little kisses over the parts of his face she could reach. He looped his arms around her waist, and she brought her lips to his ear.

"You wanted to know what *pahale* means," she whispered. "It means first."

Chapter 21

THE LABRADOR PUPPY WAS ADORABLE. HIS PALE GOLD FUR WAS soft and fuzzy, his belly was round, and his paws were oversized.

Bebe held the dog close to her chest and let him lick her face even though she knew it was unsanitary. He was just so cute, and she could always disinfect later.

"You're such a sweet boy, aren't you?" she crooned in a high-pitched, singsong voice she had never used before.

Teagan laughed as she shifted from her crisscrossed position on the floor to lean back against the brown leather sofa. Stretching out her legs, she crossed them at the ankles before taking a sip of her chardonnay.

"I had no idea you were such a dog lover, Beebs."

Bebe and Teagan had decided to stay in for their weekly date night, and they were hanging out in Teagan's spacious family room. Her best friend had wanted to introduce her to the newest member of the O'Brien-Priest household, and once Bebe had met the puppy, she hadn't wanted to leave him.

"I didn't know I was," she admitted as she stroked the puppy's silky fur.

She hadn't grown up with pets, and the only time she had

ever been around a dog was when she'd been in the park and one ran by with its owner. She had been missing out.

"What did you decide to name him?"

"Rip Van Tinkle. It seemed appropriate since he pees everywhere and passes gas every two seconds."

Bebe raised the puppy in front of her face. His pink tongue lolled out of his mouth, and she swore he smiled at her.

"Is that true, Rip? Do you potty all over the house?"

"I wanted to name him Fred," Teagan confided.

"Why Fred?"

"I've always wanted a yellow dog named Fred. I don't know why." Teagan flipped her long ponytail over her shoulders with a little shrug. "But Nick liked Rip. And since he doesn't have any trouble pronouncing *r*'s and *f*'s are a little iffy, it seemed like Rip was a better choice."

Bebe gently placed Rip in her lap, and the puppy rolled onto the floor and grabbed one of the chew toys strewn across the area rug. Clasping it in his mouth, he shook his head back and forth.

"He's a chewer, too," Teagan noted wryly.

Bebe uncrossed her legs and scooted across the rug until she could lean back against the club chair. Blond dog hair covered her blue silk shirt and black suit pants, but she didn't care a bit.

"Did you have pets growing up?" Bebe asked.

It was something they had never discussed in all the years they'd known each other.

"Yes. We had a black Lab and a golden retriever, Indiana and Jones. My parents let us draw straws to name them, and I lost. Quinn and Cal were obsessed with Indiana Jones."

Just the mention of Cal made Bebe's panties damp. Because of him, she thought about sex constantly—the last time they'd done it, how good it had felt, and how soon she could get him inside her again. She greatly feared she was turning into a sex addict.

"I've missed having a dog, but it just wasn't practical before now. Letty's here all day, so Rip won't have to be crated during the day."

Bebe took a sip of her wine, trying to focus on the conversation. It had been exactly eight days since she had lost her virginity. She and Cal had spent V-Day, as he called it, in bed, but they'd only had sex twice.

She'd wanted to do it all day, but Cal had refused. He had worried that she would be sore, so they'd watched movies and played Scrabble for part of the day.

He had won the board game, but she was convinced it was only because she'd been distracted by the way his biceps flexed when he moved the tiles around. They'd also made out like teenagers whenever the urge came over them.

The next day she'd been tremendously grateful for Cal's restraint because she had been *sore*. Fortunately, the human body was resilient, and once she'd recovered, they had spent every spare moment with their hands and mouths on each other's bodies.

Remembering what she and Cal had done last night in his big bed, she squirmed a little, acutely aware of the seam of her pants where it pressed against her center. Who knew she'd be such a fan of the reverse cowgirl position? She'd come so many times she was nearly comatose when he finished with her.

Teagan continued to talk, and Bebe replied at various intervals with noncommittal murmurs. She looked down into her wineglass, studying the sweet vintage.

It reminded her of the bottle she and Cal had shared before he'd laid her down on his sectional and put his mouth between her legs. She didn't know if every woman loved oral sex, but she sure did. She really loved it when he sucked on her clit and put his fingers—

"Bebe!"

Bebe jerked her eyes to Teagan. Her best friend studied her with a mix of exasperation and amusement.

"You seem a little distracted," Teagan noted with a knowing smile.

She smiled ruefully. "A little."

"You and Cal have obviously done the deed."

Her cheeks heated. "Yes," she muttered.

"I'm dying of curiosity. How was it?"

She shot Teagan a surprised look. "You want me to tell you what it's like to have sex with your *brother*?"

"Don't look at me like that," Teagan replied with a laugh. "I swear I'm not a pervert. You're my best friend, and I love you. I'm concerned. I want to hear how your first time was—if you liked it, and if you're okay. I'm trying not to think about the fact that you're doing my brother."

Teagan cocked her head. "And it's not the first time I've heard about Cal's sexual exploits. He took one of my friends to his junior prom, and she talked about their after-prom activities for weeks."

A sour taste flooded Bebe's mouth, and she swallowed thickly. She knew Cal had been with a lot of women, but it bothered her to think about it. She knew she had no right to be jealous, but she hated to think about him touching other women the way he touched her.

"So . . ." Teagan said, drawing out the word. "Are you going to tell me how it was?"

Rip clambered onto Bebe's lap, curling up with his little paws over his eyes. She pointed down at the puppy.

"Even Rip is embarrassed by this conversation."

Teagan laughed. "I know you want to talk about it."

Unfortunately, her best friend was right. Bebe did want to talk about sex with Cal. She had so many things swirling around in her head, and she needed to share them.

"Tell me," Teagan cajoled.

"I know Jason was your first," Bebe said, referring to Teagan's college boyfriend. "But we never talked about what it was like with him the first time. Was it good?"

Teagan considered Bebe's question for several moments before speaking. "He was a virgin, too. It was like the blind leading the blind. I was nervous. He was nervous. It hurt. *A lot.* It didn't last very long." She snickered. "Let me rephrase. *He* didn't last very long. I didn't have an orgasm." Her nose wrinkled. "It took Jason a long time to figure out how to give me an orgasm without my help."

Bebe's eyebrows shot up. "Really?"

"Yes," Teagan confirmed with a grimace. "I read some books and masturbated to figure out what I liked, and then I showed him."

"You showed him?" she asked faintly. "You masturbated in front of him?"

Bebe was quickly realizing she had been an über virgin. She knew it was hard to believe, but she'd never masturbated.

Teagan nodded. "Yes. He had to learn somehow." She

smiled impishly. "All the lovers he had after me should have sent me flowers."

Bebe laughed. "Definitely," she agreed emphatically. "After you showed him what you liked, was it good?"

"It was good *enough*." She shrugged. "It wasn't mind-blowing. It wasn't incredible. I didn't think about it when I was doing something else."

Bebe smoothed her hand over Rip's side. He was passed out, and little snores escaped from his open mouth with every breath.

"I remember the first time you had sex with Nick. It wrecked you."

A wistful smile curved Teagan's mouth. "That's a perfect way to describe how I felt."

Bebe was worried that having sex with Cal had wrecked her. It was more than she had expected, and she was afraid it was more than she could handle.

She rubbed Rip's floppy ear between her thumb and forefinger. "What's it like with him now?"

"Fun. Serious. Sexy. Sweet. Rough. Tender. Fast. Slow. Messy. Perfect." Teagan's rosy lips tipped up in a small smile. "It's everything. And every single time, it's love."

Bebe blew out a breath. "Wow."

Having sex with Cal was everything Teagan had described. Everything except love.

"Yeah, wow."

Rip twitched in his sleep, and Bebe soothed him by making circles on his round tummy. It was so warm and velvety.

"Tell me about your first time," Teagan requested.

"It was indescribable," she admitted softly, looking down at Rip. "I never imagined it would be that way."

Having sex with Cal for the first time had been the most amazing experience of her life. She had expected it to be awkward and embarrassing, but it hadn't been. It had felt *right*.

And every time they had sex, it was even better than the last time. Was that normal?

"Did he take care of you?"

Bebe looked up. "What do you mean?"

"Was he careful with you?" Teagan elaborated.

"He was careful, but it hurt quite a bit. He's big. Really big."

Teagan groaned and covered her eyes with both hands. "Unfortunately, I've heard that before."

She couldn't help but laugh at Teagan's disgust. "You asked, *kanya*."

Teagan dropped her hands. "I know, but I'm going to have to give myself a concussion after you leave so I forget this conversation."

Bebe giggled. "I can help you with that. I know exactly how hard to hit you without causing permanent damage."

Teagan rolled her eyes. "Did you come?"

"Yes."

Teagan nodded. "I think first times fall into two categories: orgasm and no-orgasm. Orgasms equal a good first time and no-orgasms equal a bad first time."

"Then I had an amazing first time. I had three orgasms."

Cal had been such a generous, considerate lover. She was lucky he had wanted to participate in her de-virginization plan.

"Wow," Teagan uttered, her dark eyebrows winging up her forehead.

"I had four the second time."

Four mind-blowing, screaming-at-the-top-of-my-lungs orgasms.

Teagan's mouth fell open. "You're kidding, right?"

"No, I'm not kidding. He's very skilled."

Teagan studied her for a long moment. She rolled her lips inward, and Bebe could tell she was trying to figure out what she wanted to say.

"It's obvious you and Cal have some serious chemistry. But I think you need to realize sex usually isn't that good unless there are feelings involved. And I'm not talking about dislike."

"YOU'RE ONE OF THE SEXIEST MEN ALIVE," CAL CALLED OUT TO Priest. "Show us what you've got."

Priest shot Cal the bird behind his back while Sienna Thornton continued to snap pictures of him for Riley O'Brien & Co.'s newest marketing campaign. They were in a photography studio near the Yerba Buena Center for the Arts, where Sienna did most of her shoots.

The young photographer did a lot of work for fashion magazines, and she had been highly recommended. The photos she took today would be used online, as well as in print and outdoor advertising such as billboards, public transit, and benches.

"Nick, raise your arm and lean your elbow against the wall," Sienna directed.

This was Priest's second campaign with the company. A little over two years ago, Cal had approached his best friend with the idea of Priest becoming the face of Rileys for men. Fortunately, Priest had agreed, and his first marketing campaign had been a huge success.

Men wanted to be Priest, so they bought Rileys to be like their idol. Women wanted to fuck Priest, so they bought Rileys for the men in their lives with the hope that they would look like the former NFL player.

Objectively speaking, Cal had no trouble admitting Priest was a good-looking guy. With his height, fit physique, and handsome face, he was a perfect spokesperson for Rileys. The only challenge was figuring out how to work around his stutter.

Photography wasn't a problem because Priest didn't have to talk, but video presented some difficulties. For the first campaign, they'd used a voice-over so Priest hadn't needed to speak.

This campaign was even better. It paid homage to the popular musical *West Side Story*, but with a twist. Cal had come up with the idea after talking with Ava Grace.

Ava Grace had won *American Star*, the popular national singing competition, more than four years ago. Since then, she'd vaulted into stardom with several number one songs. She was a household name akin to Miranda Lambert and Carrie Underwood, except she was more talented.

She also was hotter than hell. She was tall, thin, and blond, and her uniquely raspy voice embodied sex.

After Amelia had joined Riley O'Brien & Co. to revamp the women's division, Ava Grace had signed on to promote the new jeans and other apparel. Cal had figured that they should take advantage of Ava Grace's voice and her looks, so the two of them had brainstormed until they'd come up with an awesome idea.

The new campaign, which was called Backside Story, would replicate the musical's rumble scene between the two rival gangs, the Sharks and the Jets. Ava Grace was working on an original song for the commercial, which was scheduled to shoot in March.

Ava Grace and Priest would share the spotlight in the commercial, which would involve lots of singing and dancing. As a former pro football player, Priest was light on his feet and had dance moves to rival Justin Timberlake. His stutter would be a nonissue because he'd either be singing or lip-syncing.

The photos from today's shoot would be used to create campaign art that had a similar look and feel to Broadway musical posters. Ava Grace would fly in later this month for Thanksgiving at his parents' house, and her photo shoot was scheduled for the following week.

"Okay, Nick, I think we've got it," Sienna called out.

Priest relaxed from his posed stance, and Sienna pulled the thick strap of her camera over her head and deposited the expensive equipment on the table beside her. She headed over to Priest, and they were close enough for Cal to hear their conversation.

"You're a natural in front of the camera, Nick," Sienna praised, placing her hand on Priest's chest. "And the jeans and leather jacket are a very good look for you."

Along with Rileys, Priest wore a black leather motorcycle jacket and black motorcycle boots. Sienna obviously thought he looked good.

"It was a pleasure to shoot you," Sienna continued as she smiled up into Priest's face.

Sienna was giving off "do me" vibes, and Cal was interested to see how Priest would react. She was attractive, and Cal knew Priest would have fucked her in a dark corner of the photography studio in the old days. He hoped his friend would remember he was married to Cal's sister because he didn't think he could beat the shit out of him without some help.

Priest returned Sienna's smile before reaching into the pocket of his jacket. He pulled out his platinum wedding band and casually slid it onto his finger. Sienna had suggested that he remove it for the shoot, and Priest was sending a very clear, yet subtle message that he was married *and* faithful to his wife.

Cal laughed under his breath when Sienna frowned and dropped her hand. *Message received.*

Priest nodded to Sienna before striding toward the exit. He had a lunch date with T, while Cal had plans to meet Quinn at their favorite burger place nearby.

Sienna returned to the table where her equipment was located. She began to pack up, and Cal headed toward her. She looked up when he reached her side and gave him a big smile.

"I think we got some good shots, Cal."

"I think so, too," he replied with a nod.

"I want to thank you again for the opportunity to be involved in this campaign. I think you're doing something really fun and unique."

"We're happy to have you, Sienna. I have no doubt you're going to blow us away."

She tilted her head, and he recognized the look in her eyes. Apparently he was a nice consolation prize if she couldn't have Priest.

"Would you like to go out for a drink after work? We can discuss all the ways I can blow you away."

She obviously wasn't talking about work anymore, and he briefly considered her invitation. He could have drinks with Sienna if he wanted to. It wouldn't violate his arrangement with Bebe. But he *didn't* want to, and before he could even think about it, words came out of his mouth.

"I'm seeing someone."

His statement wasn't entirely true, but he wanted it to be. He wanted to scrap the arrangement he'd made with Bebe and start over. He wanted more than sex. Unfortunately, he had no idea how she felt about him, and he didn't know if she would consider something more than what they had.

With a coquettish smile, Sienna stroked his forearm. "That's not a problem for me if it's not a problem for you."

"It is a problem for me."

It was a problem for two reasons. One, he didn't cheat, and two, Bebe was the only person he wanted to blow him away. And she was doing a damn fine job of it. In fact, the sex between them was so fucking hot, he was always surprised he was still breathing when she finished with him.

Sienna stepped closer. "Are you sure you're not interested?"

"Three months ago, I would have taken you up on your offer," he replied honestly. "But not now."

She dropped her hand with a loud sigh. "I'll have these proofs ready by Monday."

"We're still on your schedule for Ava Grace's photo shoot, right?"

She nodded. "There is no way I'd forget that. I *love* Ava Grace Landy."

"She is talented." He held out his hand. "Thank you again."

She clasped his hand. "My pleasure."

He nodded his appreciation before exiting the building. Once he was outside, he hooked a right and made the short walk to Zombie Burger.

His stomach was growling in anticipation of juicy beef patties and freshly baked pretzel buns, and he was happy to see that Quinn had already snagged a booth. As he slid into the seat opposite his older brother, he accidentally rammed his knee into Quinn's leg.

"I should have asked for a table. Now that you're here, my legs are cramped," Quinn complained.

"You're such a goddamn whiner."

Quinn didn't reply, but when he picked up a menu from the holder on the side of the table, he only used two fingers, his thumb and his middle finger.

"How did the photo shoot go?" Quinn asked as he opened the menu.

"I think it went well. Sienna thought Rileys and leather were a good look for Priest. She came on to him."

Quinn looked up from the menu. "And?"

"Priest made it clear he was taken, and then he rushed off to have lunch with T."

His brother nodded thoughtfully. "Did you ever think Priest would be so . . ."

"Pussy-whipped?" Cal supplied.

Quinn smiled ruefully. "Yeah, that's exactly what I was thinking."

Cal laughed. "Have you looked in the mirror lately?"

"Every morning."

"And what do you see?"

"I see a lucky man."

Cal took a moment to study his older brother. Quinn was different since he'd met and married Amelia. At first the change hadn't been that noticeable, but as months had passed, it had become more obvious.

Cal had always thought of Quinn as a dormant volcano. On the surface, everything seemed fine, but underneath, things were shifting constantly, and pressure was building.

Amelia had that special something that reduced Quinn's pressure. She was his release valve.

"You're pussy-whipped," Cal informed his brother. "Accept the reality. *Own it.*"

Quinn laughed, but didn't dispute Cal's claim. "What do you see when you look in the mirror?"

That was a damn good question.

"I see the same thing you do. A lucky man."

He *was* lucky. The people he loved were happy and healthy (fingers crossed). He had a wonderful, supportive family; an interesting, fulfilling job; and great friends he could count on.

He also had all the money he would ever need (thanks to Grandma Violet, who'd left him and his siblings significant inheritances). And thanks to Bebe, he had as much sex as he wanted.

Incredible, brain-melting, forget-my-name sex.

"I have everything I could possibly want," Cal added.

But even as the words came out of his mouth, he knew he lied. He didn't have what Quinn had with Amelia or what Priest had with Teagan.

He didn't have the love of an amazing woman.

Chapter 22

BEBE FLUNG OPEN THE DOOR TO HER LOFT THE MOMENT CAL knocked on it. After not seeing him for nearly two weeks because of an overseas business trip, she couldn't wait to get her hands and mouth on him.

Her speedy response to his knock clearly shocked him because he froze with his fist up in the air and his eyes wide with surprise. Before he could open his mouth to greet her, she hooked her fingers in the waistband of his Rileys and pulled him into her loft.

He outweighed her by more than a hundred pounds, but she was strong from kickboxing, and she had the element of surprise on her side. He stumbled inside, and she slammed the door before pushing him back against it.

She shoved her hands under his brown leather jacket, jerking it off his shoulders and down his arms. Once it was off, she tossed it on the ground and dropped to her knees in front of him.

Lifting the hem of his forest-green Henley, she quickly unbuckled his belt, popped the button on his Rileys, and pulled down the tab of his zipper. She pushed her hands inside the waistband of his boxer briefs, yanking them down along with his jeans until they hung around his hips. Lucky for her, he was already erect, and saliva pooled in her mouth when she saw creamy fluid oozing from the slit in the plump head.

"*Yes,*" she whispered. "That's what I want."

Much to her surprise, she loved going down on Cal. She loved the way his scent wrapped around her, the way his penis filled her mouth, and the way he tasted.

She had no basis for comparison, but she thought his penis was beautiful. Its sinuous shape as it curved upward toward his navel from its nest of dark hair. The thick tracing of veins along the length. The smooth skin that stretched tightly over hardness.

Beautiful.

She gently ran the tip of her finger from the base to the purplish head before digging her fingers into the cheeks of his tight butt. Swiping her tongue along the tiny slit, she gathered his cream, moaning with appreciation at the taste of him. She couldn't get enough of him, an intense salt and yeast flavor with a dash of something that was uniquely Cal.

Groaning harshly, he fumbled with her hair. She knew he liked it loose when she went down on him, so she quickly released it from its anchors and let the heavy strands fall around her face. He shoved his fingers into her hair, and she grabbed his butt again before wrapping her lips around the head of his cock.

"Your mouth feels so fucking good."

His voice was nothing more than a guttural rumble. She sucked deeply on the head before slowly moving her lips down his length. Relaxing her throat, she took as much of him as possible.

He had taught her what he liked, and she put those lessons to good use right now. She hummed a little in the back of her throat as she licked the head and pushed her tongue into the tiny slit.

He had a particularly sensitive area on the underside of his cock just below the head, and she pressed her tongue against it. He groaned harshly, clenching his fingers in her hair and pulling her face closer to him. She pressed against his sweet spot again before swirling her tongue around the head, and his cock grew larger and harder in her mouth.

"Yes," he hissed. "Just like that."

Pulling her hands from his butt, she cupped his testicles.

They were heavy and tight in her hands, and she squeezed them gently as she moved her mouth back and forth along his length.

She kept things slow and easy, enjoying the taste of him in her mouth and the texture of his cock against her tongue. He helped her, gently moving her head with his big hands and thrusting into her mouth with small movements. He began to pant, and she knew his orgasm was close.

"Faster," he growled.

Going down on him always excited her, and as she increased the tempo of her mouth and the strength of her suction, she slid her hand past the waistband of her yoga pants and into her lacy panties. She had never touched herself while performing fellatio, but the ache between her legs was too strong to ignore.

Cal had not only shown her what he liked, but shown her what *she* liked, and while she had been in London, she had masturbated for the first time. It had taken her a while to get the hang of it, but when she had imagined him touching her, she'd enjoyed a very satisfying orgasm.

Dipping her fingers between her slick folds, she rubbed her clit while she sucked strongly on his big cock. Her orgasm was tantalizingly close, so she pushed two fingers inside her body and massaged her thumb against her nub.

When she squeezed his testicles and pressed her tongue against his favorite spot again, he stiffened and made a growling noise deep in his throat. Semen jetted into her mouth, and she closed her eyes and swallowed deeply as her vaginal muscles pulsed with a powerful orgasm.

Cal slumped against the door, and she fell heavily against him. She was stunned by the intensity of what had just happened. There was something incredibly erotic about coming at the same time he came in her mouth.

His fingers loosened from her hair, and she removed her hand from her body before pulling her mouth from his spent penis. As she licked the excess semen from her lips and wiped her wet fingers on her pants, he stroked the wispy hairs on her forehead.

He cleared his throat roughly. "That's one way to kiss me hello."

She looked up, over his ridged stomach and broad chest, to his gorgeous face. "Hello."

He smiled slowly. "Hello, Cookie. Nice to see you again."

She returned his smile. "Nice to see you, too."

Grasping her hands, he pulled her to her feet before dropping a kiss on her nose. "Thank you," he said as he pulled up his underwear and jeans.

"It was my pleasure."

He laughed softly. "You mean it was *my* pleasure."

She picked up his jacket from the floor and hung it on one of the pegs near the door while he fastened his Rileys and buckled his belt. She headed into the kitchen, and he followed her.

Opening the stainless steel fridge, she pulled out two bottles of water and passed one to Cal as he settled on the barstool. She twisted off the cap on her bottle and took a drink while he gave her an appraising glance. She fought the desire to fidget with her hair, which was tangled around her face.

Finally, he asked, "How was your trip?"

"Good."

She had spent ten days in Europe meeting with several institutional investors, including two of the largest German pension funds. She had purposely planned the trip to coincide with the Thanksgiving holiday.

After what had happened with Noor at the Fairmont, she had known she wouldn't be welcome in Baltimore. Although she had tried to push that night from her mind, she couldn't stop thinking about it.

Her mother's words haunted her. *It is impossible to love you.*

Those six words had created a wound that was so deep, Bebe doubted it would ever heal. And even if it eventually scarred over, she would never be able to forget.

But to her surprise, she felt more relief than pain. That last conversation with Noor had freed Bebe. She could no longer fool herself into believing that her mother would ever love her. And she was slowly accepting the fact that she would never have a meaningful relationship with her parents or her brothers.

But at least she had Teagan. And she had Cal . . . for now.

They had invited Bebe to spend Thanksgiving with the O'Briens. And even though she'd wanted to spend the holiday with them, she had declined.

Enjoying the holiday with Cal and his family made it feel like they were a real couple instead of just lovers, and she already had a hard time keeping things completely sexual. In fact, that was why she had set up meetings across Europe.

"How was Thanksgiving?" she asked.

"Good." He studied her for a moment, his light blue eyes intent on her face. "It would have been better if you had been there."

Even though she tried to ignore it, his words sent a tingle of pleasure through her. He said things like that a lot. Things that made her think he wanted to spend time with her . . . that he wanted to *be* with her.

But that wasn't their deal.

She would never regret giving her virginity to Cal, but her initial concerns about liking him too much to have sex with him hadn't been unfounded. She had suspected that she wouldn't be able to separate her emotions from her actions, and her suspicions were confirmed every time they were together.

Changing the subject, she said, "The company I hired to paint my bedroom didn't finish the job while I was in Europe. When I got home last night, all my furniture was shoved into my study, and my bedroom was covered in drop cloths."

She had decided to paint her bedroom months ago, and even though she might not be living in the loft for much longer if she couldn't get out of her deal with Akash, she had gone ahead with her plans.

"They said they can't finish for two more weeks," she continued. "I have no idea why they started and stopped. It's very unprofessional."

"You can stay with me."

She stayed over at Cal's condo at least a couple of nights a week. Sometimes he stayed with her, but not very often because her bed was only a queen and he was too big for it. She wanted to spend every night with him, and she knew that was a huge problem. Moving in with him, even for a couple of weeks, was the absolute last thing she should do.

"I was hoping you would help me paint my bedroom."

"I can do that," he agreed with a nod.

"Right now?" she asked hopefully. "We have everything we need. They left rollers and brushes behind."

"Sure. Your bedroom isn't that big. It probably won't take long." He tilted his head. "Did they already tape it?"

She nodded, and he slid from the stool. He toed off his

tennis shoes before pulling his shirt over his head and tossing it over the bar.

Despite the fact that she'd just had an orgasm, desire welled inside her, and she cursed herself silently. Why was she wasting time painting when she could be doing him instead?

"Do you need to change or are you ready now?"

I'm ready now—ready to do you.

On the way to her bedroom, Cal snagged the portable speaker from the living room. She followed morosely, and once they were inside the bedroom, he placed the speaker in the corner and took a moment to cue up some music. She recognized the alt rock sound of Nothing But Thieves, one of Cal's favorite bands.

As the lyrics for "Trip Switch" filled the room, Cal picked up the paint can and inspected the label. "If this is darker than the color you have now, we don't need to use primer."

"It's darker."

Currently, her bedroom was a creamy light yellow. It had been Teagan's choice, and while it was pretty, Bebe preferred darker colors. She had picked a deep, intense purple called "Soul Mate."

The name had made her smile when she'd seen it. Paint manufacturers were so creative in their name choices.

Grabbing the paint can, Cal shook it vigorously, his arm and shoulder muscles flexing with the movement. Bebe worried her tongue might loll out of her mouth like Rip's when she rubbed his belly.

Once he had mixed the paint to his satisfaction, Cal popped off the top of the can with his pocketknife and poured paint into the tray in the middle of the room. He handed the longer roller to her before taking the shorter one for himself.

"Do you know how to paint?"

"It's not rocket science, is it?" she snapped, angry that she had been stupid enough to ask him to paint her bedroom instead of lick her body.

His eyebrows shot up at her bitchy tone, and she was immediately ashamed she was taking her anger out on Cal. At the same time, she was powerless to stop the emotions roiling inside her.

"It's not rocket science, but there is a right way and a wrong way."

"Okay, Picasso," she jeered with an exaggerated roll of her eyes. "What is the right way?"

He stared at her for a tense moment before answering her question. "Don't saturate your roller with too much paint," he instructed as he ran his roller through the paint. "Make long strokes with the roller in a V-shaped pattern and overlap them so you don't get lines." He demonstrated what he meant before turning to face her. "Okay?"

"Yes," she answered curtly, and he frowned darkly.

After dipping her roller in paint, she began to cover the wall in front of her while he applied his roller to the wall to her left. With music in the background, they worked silently for a long time before he spoke.

"I like this color. I never would have considered purple, but it looks really good. Of course, the color isn't purple, it's 'Soul Mate.'" He snorted. "Lame."

"I take it you don't believe in soul mates."

Cal jerked his head toward her, his eyes wide with surprise. "Of course I believe in soul mates." He shook his head slightly. "I was talking about the names paint manufacturers come up with."

"Since you're in marketing, I would have thought you'd have a greater appreciation for their creativity."

Ignoring her comment, he added, "I see soul mates every day. My mom and dad. Quinn and Amelia. Priest and T. Hell, even my Grandma Vi and my Grandpa Patrick."

"Was Saika your soul mate?"

The question slipped past Bebe's lips before she could stop it. He continued to paint in smooth strokes, and she wondered if he would answer her.

Finally, he replied, "No, Saika wasn't my soul mate."

His deep voice held no inflection, and Bebe wondered if the flat tone hid residual pain. She had been curious about Saika for months. Actually, she'd been curious about the other woman for years. She still remembered the first time Teagan had mentioned Cal's ex-girlfriend during one of their phone calls.

She had been living in Boston, and Teagan had offhandedly remarked that Cal had brought his new girlfriend and her daughter to the O'Briens' Sunday dinner. It had been a shock to hear that he was serious enough about someone to introduce her to his family, and even more of a shock to realize his girlfriend was a single mother.

The news had upset Bebe, but she'd told herself there was no reason to be upset. No reason at all.

And she had no reason to be upset now. Cal wasn't *hers*.

"What happened between you and Saika?"

He sighed, and she glanced at him out of the corner of her eye. The muscles in his back and shoulders flexed as he rolled paint onto the wall, and she promised herself that she wouldn't rip off his jeans until he finished the job.

"It's pretty simple, Cookie. Saika's ex-husband was her soul mate. Not me."

"If he's her ex-husband, he must not be the one."

Cal turned toward her. "After we broke up, they remarried. She's going to have a baby later this month."

"Oh."

"Yeah, oh," he mocked.

"Were you in love with her?"

He dropped his roller down to his side. "Yes. I was going to ask her to marry me, but her ex-husband came back like a bad case of jock itch."

Jock itch? Eeew.

Wait . . . marriage?

For some reason, hearing Cal admit that he'd wanted to marry Saika sent a spear of pain through Bebe. She sucked in a surprised breath and turned to face him.

"I was in love with her, but it also was the right time for me to be in love. And Valerie was a huge part of it."

Bebe swallowed thickly, trying to ease the tightness in her throat. "What do you mean?"

"I was ready for a relationship. It was easy to be with Saika." He shrugged. "Right time, wrong woman. Deep down, I knew she couldn't give me what I wanted because she was still in love with her ex-husband. Marrying her would have been a huge mistake."

"And what about Valerie?"

"I loved Valerie, maybe even more than I loved Saika. She needed a father, and it was easy for me to be what she needed. I didn't realize how much I wanted kids until I spent time with her."

"I'm sorry." Despite her jealousy, she really meant it. She

hated the thought of a brokenhearted Cal. "I'm sorry you loved someone who wanted to be with someone else."

Cal studied her for a long moment, his normally expressive face completely blank. "I'm not in love with Saika anymore, Bebe." He shook his head. "I haven't been for a long, *long* time. I thought you knew that."

She didn't know why it mattered so much that he wasn't still in love with Saika. She didn't know why it mattered that he wasn't touching her when he loved someone else. It shouldn't have mattered, but it did.

He dipped the roller in paint and turned back to the wall. "Do you believe in soul mates?"

Yes, she believed in soul mates. She believed in "the one."

She believed some people were lucky enough to find exactly the right person for them, the person who made the difference between a satisfactory life and a satisfying life. But she didn't believe she would have a chance to find her soul mate, not as long as Akash hung over her head like a guillotine.

While she'd been in Europe, she had suffered through yet another monthly video chat with her unwanted fiancé. He'd made it clear he was unwilling to budge on their agreement, and she was no closer to a solution today than she had been two months ago.

Despite the freelance financial consulting projects she'd taken on to supplement the "Free Bebe" fund, she had managed to accumulate only about forty percent of the money she owed him. With every day that went by, she felt more and more like a rabbit trapped in a snare.

The hopelessness of her situation made her angry, and she furiously rolled paint onto the wall. Her ire increased when she thought about the fact that she would probably be living in Delhi this time next year as Mrs. Akash Mehra.

"Do you believe in soul mates?" Cal repeated, clearly under the impression she hadn't heard him the first time.

She wanted to stop talking about soul mates. She wanted to stop *thinking* about them before she started to cry.

"How are things going at work?" she asked, trying to change the subject.

Cal stopped painting and came to stand beside her. "Do you believe in soul mates, Bebe?"

"I don't want to talk about soul mates anymore," she responded without glancing in his direction.

Gently grasping her left arm, he pulled her around to face him. He stared down at her, his eyes glinting with an emotion she didn't recognize.

"Too bad," he replied lightly. "I do."

"Too bad," she countered rudely. "I *don't*. In fact, I don't want to paint, either."

She jerked away from him and threw her roller into the tray, splashing purple paint all over his white athletic socks and the bottom of his faded Rileys. He looked down at the mess she'd made, and when he lifted his eyes, they blazed with anger.

"What the hell is your problem?" he asked quietly, his lips barely moving.

She had seen him irritated and pissed off, but she had never seen him truly angry. He must be one of those people who didn't shout when he was mad.

"You asked me to help, and that's what I'm doing. If you don't want to paint, why are we painting? What do you want to do?"

As she stood there in her half-painted bedroom, she could only think of one thing she wanted to do: *him*.

She didn't say it out loud, but he heard her anyway. He dropped his roller in the tray next to hers, cupped his hands around the back of her head, and slammed his mouth down on hers.

His kiss was selfish. It took everything from her. She could barely breathe, and when she opened her mouth, he shoved his tongue inside. He twined it around hers, and she moaned against his lips.

Cal pulled back abruptly, and before she could even blink, he jerked her yoga pants and underwear to her feet. He stepped on her clothes, easily lifting her out of them, before clumsily unbuckling his belt and opening his Rileys.

"What are you doing?" she asked faintly, covering her exposed privates with her hands.

"I'm doing what *I* want to do," he answered tersely. "You think I wanted to spend one fucking second painting your goddamn bedroom? I haven't seen you in ten miserable fucking days. I don't want to paint. I want to be inside you."

He pushed his jeans and underwear past his hips, and his

cock sprang free. He was hugely erect, and just the sight of him made her wet.

He reached for her, palming her butt and lifting her against him. She automatically spread her legs, squeezing them around his waist, and he took three steps until her back hit the wall she had been painting.

It crossed her mind that she was getting paint in her hair and all over her clothes, but then Cal roughly dipped his fingers between her legs, and she decided she didn't care. When he felt how wet she was, he grunted in satisfaction.

Wrapping one hand around the back of her neck, he met her gaze as he plunged into her. They both groaned as her body welcomed him, clasping him tightly, and neither one of them looked away as he began to move in deep, hard thrusts.

"I thought about you every fucking minute you were gone. *Every fucking minute.*"

She had thought about him, too, no matter what she'd been doing or who she'd been with. She had tried not to think about him, but she hadn't been able to stop.

He continued to pound into her. Harder, faster, rougher. Ribbons of sensation unraveled inside her as he gripped her tighter, his pelvis rocking against hers.

"I missed you, damn it."

He surged into her, and she couldn't see anything or feel anything but Cal. Her orgasm rushed over her, and she came so hard, the spiraling pleasure held a sharp edge of pain.

He was there with her, and she held his gaze as his cock pulsed and he emptied himself inside her with a harsh groan. He leaned his forehead against hers, and she closed her eyes.

The sex between them was always hot. Always intense. Always incredible.

But it had never been like that. *He* had never been like that.

"Tell me you missed me."

She had missed him while she had been gone. She had missed the sound of his deep voice. The sight of his smile. The feel of him inside her.

"I missed you."

Chapter 23

"BOWLING IS MORE FUN THAN I THOUGHT IT WOULD BE," BEBE said. "And I know you like it because it gives you an opportunity to make jokes about fingers and holes."

Cal chuckled and pulled her down onto his lap. "You know me too well, Cookie."

Looping her arms around his neck, she gave him a kiss that would have led to sex if they'd been in private. Unfortunately, they were surrounded by people at Spare Time Bowling Club, so he reluctantly pulled his mouth from hers. He didn't want to stand up in front of his friends and family and bowl with a full-fledged hard-on.

"This place is so cool. Are all bowling alleys like this?"

He shook his head. "No, this one is a little nicer."

Spare Time Bowling Club was part of the popular trend of twenty-one-and-over bowling alleys that served food and alcohol in an upscale environment. Located in the Mission District just a few blocks from Bebe's loft, the venue had six lanes, two levels of dining space, and an outdoor covered patio.

Instead of typical plastic seats grouped around a built-in computer, Spare Time Bowling Club had long, deep sofas and cocktail tables with metal bowling pins for legs. The lighting was dim, and music poured from the overhead speakers. The tunes were too mainstream for Cal's taste, but everything else was pretty damn cool.

"Bebe, it's your turn," Teagan called out.

Bebe wiggled from his lap, and he swore his eyes crossed from the pressure of her round ass against his zipper. He snagged his Fat Tire from the table next to him and took a big swallow, hoping the cold beer would cool him down.

Teagan had reserved three lanes and a private room for an impromptu party. Christmas was only three days away, and they had a pretty big crowd. In addition to his sister and Priest, Quinn and Amelia were here along with Ava Grace, who had flown in from Nashville to spend the holiday with them.

Deda and his partner, Harris, had accepted Teagan's invitation, and they occupied the adjacent lane with Vanessa and her younger sister, Kyla. Quinn had invited Beck, who had brought his business partners and buddies, Ren and Gabe.

Cal watched as Bebe carefully selected a ball, a hot pink one that would fit her slender fingers. Her rings—the rings he now hated with a deep, intense passion because of what they represented—were in his pockets so they wouldn't get stuck in the ball when she bowled. He was tempted to throw the damn things in the garbage every time he saw them, but he knew that wouldn't accomplish anything.

Bebe approached the lane, pausing long enough to push back the sleeve of her sweater. He'd bought it for her when they'd gone Christmas shopping together a couple of weeks ago. Nearly the same color as her bowling ball, it was considerably tighter than her other clothes. He loved the way it showed off her rack.

He dropped his gaze to her ass, which was covered in slim-fitting black pants. He knew she wore a lacy red thong under them because he'd watched her slip it on after they had spent an hour in his bathtub with her bouncing on top of him.

Assuming her stance, Bebe threw the ball. It thundered down the lane, hitting the center pins before wiping out all ten. She had bowled a strike, her sixth in a row. She was a natural not only on the golf course, but at the bowling alley.

She also happened to be a natural in the bedroom.

"Good job, Cookie," he called out, raising his beer bottle. "There's your six-pack."

She tossed him a wide smile as Teagan gave her a high-five. She regularly bestowed smiles on him nowadays, but no matter how many he received, they always made him lose his breath.

She immediately made her way back to him and scooted onto his lap. Wrapping his arm around her waist, he nuzzled his nose into her neck. She smelled like cinnamon, and he swiped his tongue against her smooth skin. She shivered a little, squirming against his zipper, and he groaned under his breath when his cock twitched. Maybe they should make their excuses and head home.

"I think I'm good at bowling, *pahale*."

He loved it when she called him *pahale*. Every time the word came out of her mouth, he got a rush.

"Since this is your first time, it's probably beginner's luck," he teased.

Beginner's luck had become a private joke between them. So many things were new for Bebe, and he was lucky to be able to experience them with her.

"I'm a quick learner. That's what you said last night."

Jesus Christ. He didn't want to think about what they'd done last night, not when he was in a room full of people. She laughed softly, obviously reading his mind.

"When we made chocolate pecan pie," she clarified.

He pressed a hard kiss to her soft lips. "Maybe I'll teach you something new when we get home."

"Something good?"

He smiled against her mouth. "Yeah, it'll be good."

"It's always good."

He didn't know if she was talking about sex or not. She didn't have enough experience with dating and relationships to realize they were good together, in and out of the bedroom. He had plenty of experience, and he knew the truth: what they had was special.

Bebe started to pull back, and he cupped his hand around her head and kissed her again. He never could get enough of her kisses.

"Cal, your turn," Quinn bellowed. "Stop making out with Bebe and bowl."

Cal ignored his older brother, especially since Quinn had no room to talk. Earlier this evening, they'd eaten dinner in the reserved dining area, and when they'd finished, everyone had lined up to bowl—everyone but Quinn and Amelia. When his brother and sister-in-law finally emerged from the private room, a French fry was stuck in Amelia's curly red hair and Quinn's shirt was buttoned wrong.

"Get your ass over here," Quinn demanded.

Bebe slid from his lap, and he stood. He took his time getting to the balls, knowing it would irritate Quinn. Once he was there, he picked his bowling ball, lined up, and let it fly. The ball shot down the lane, but it veered to the left at the last minute and only knocked down eight pins. He quickly bowled his second turn, wiping out the remaining pins.

It was the last frame, and the scores flashed on the screen above the lane. Bebe had won this game along with the previous one.

Teagan cheered. "Bebe won again!"

"I think we need to create two teams, men against women, and have a showdown," Quinn suggested. "But first, we need more beer."

Priest stood, and the two of them followed Quinn into the bar area. Quinn placed their order for a few beer buckets, and they leaned against the long wooden bar while the bartender put the buckets together.

"Are you still telling yourself this thing between you and Bebe is just sex?" Quinn asked abruptly.

Cal wasn't surprised by Quinn's question, but he was surprised his older brother had managed to hold it in for so long. It probably had been burning in his throat like acid reflux from a chili dog.

"I stopped telling myself that before we even had sex."

"So what's the deal with you two then? Are you a couple?"

"No. Yes." He rubbed his hand over his hair. "I don't know what the fuck we are."

He no longer wondered if Bebe wanted him sexually. She was a screamer, and only a deaf man would have any lingering doubts. And he was pretty sure she enjoyed the time they spent together. She was busy with work, but they spent almost all their free time together, and she slept over at his place more often than not.

"You seem like a couple to me—a couple of idiots," Quinn quipped.

Priest pointed at Cal. "Told you it w-w-w-would be messy."

"I know you tried to warn me," Cal acknowledged. "Maybe you should set up shop as a fortune-teller."

A mind-reader would have more value to Cal than a fortune-teller, though, because Bebe confused the hell out of him. She seemed perfectly content with their arrangement, which was why he hadn't suggested they modify it. There was always the risk she would say no, and then he'd be forced to backpedal because he wasn't ready to say good-bye to her.

Yet he just couldn't stop himself from pushing for more. Thanksgiving was a perfect example.

He had known she'd had no place to go thanks to her bitch of a mother. He'd invited her to spend Thanksgiving with him and his family because he hadn't wanted her to be alone *and* because he had wanted her to be there.

Although he had tried to be persuasive instead of demanding, she'd rebuffed him and left the country. It had been difficult to enjoy his turkey and pumpkin pie with Bebe nearly six thousand miles away.

He had been determined she would spend Christmas with him even if he had to steal her passport and handcuff her to his bed. He knew her reluctance had nothing to do with the religious nature of the holiday, but he couldn't figure out why she was so against spending Christmas with him and his family. When he asked, she changed the subject.

After much cajoling and a little bullying on his part, she'd finally agreed. He was looking forward to kissing her under the mistletoe on Christmas Day.

"I don't know the details of your relationship with Bebe, so I can't offer any good advice," Quinn said.

"You n-n-n-never offer good advice," Priest noted dryly.

Quinn tilted his head. "Are you aware I'm the reason Teagan gave you another chance?"

Priest's green eyes widened. "W-w-w-what are you talking about?"

"I let her cry on my shoulder, told her to take a risk on you, and now you're married. What do you think about my advice now?"

"Thank you," Priest responded sincerely before turning to Cal. "M-m-m-maybe you *should* listen to him."

Before Quinn could offer any advice, good or otherwise, Beck strolled up. His gaze landed on Cal, and he smiled.

"How are things going with the belly dancer?" Beck asked.

It was the same question he had posed to Cal every time they'd seen each other since the Halloween party. He never referred to Bebe by name, probably because he instinctively knew it bothered Cal for her to be objectified—by anyone except him, that is.

"I sure liked that costume," Beck added, his smile widening.

Cal frowned. Beck was goading him on purpose, but he had no doubt that if he weren't in the picture, the other man would be all over Bebe. She clearly had made an impression on him.

"The only thing I liked better was her—"

Cal moved closer to Beck. "You need to stop talking now," he advised quietly.

Beck's eyebrows arched. "*Brain*," he continued. "She has an amazing grasp of the fermentation process. She had a couple of really good ideas that I passed on to my operations manager."

Cal stared at him in disbelief. "I told her that you didn't hear a word she said because you were thinking about fucking her."

Beck grinned. "I heard at least forty percent of what she said."

Priest gave a muffled laugh, and Cal smiled wryly. "That's what I thought."

Their conversation about Bebe ended when Ava Grace joined them. The tall blonde stopped next to Quinn, and he passed a beer to her from the bucket the bartender had just placed on the bar. She thanked him with a smile, her white teeth flashing against her shiny lips.

"Are you guys ready to play?" she asked.

Quinn nodded before tilting his head toward Beck. "Ava Grace, have you met Beck?"

Ava Grace looked briefly at Beck before returning her gaze to Quinn. "Yes. Amelia introduced us earlier."

"Beck and I have been talking about the best ways to entice women to try bourbon, and I thought that might be something you could help with," Quinn said. "You and Beck should talk. Maybe there are some opportunities for you to work with Trinity."

"I don't really like Trinity all that much, or any kind of

bourbon," she admitted with a shrug, glancing toward Beck. "I just don't have a taste for it."

"That's okay," Beck drawled. "I don't really like your music all that much. I just don't have a taste for it."

Ava Grace's hazel eyes widened at the casual insult, and Quinn waded into the awkward silence. "Maybe you two can continue this conversation later. Much, much later." He turned away, and Cal heard him mutter under his breath, "Or not."

Ava Grace eyed Beck for a moment before trailing her gaze over their little group. "We're ready to play when you are. Women against men. Brains against brawn."

Cal laughed. "You're not giving us enough credit."

"I actually prefer brawn over brains," she confessed with a small smile. "That's much more fun for me."

With that intriguing statement ringing in their ears, Ava Grace left them in the bar. They watched her as she walked away, enjoying the sight of her ass swaying in her tight Rileys.

"*Goddamn*," Beck swore. "That woman is so fucking hot, she could melt the polar ice caps." He shook his head, a conflicting mix of lust and disgust on his face. "And she knows it, too."

Quinn shot Beck an amused glance. "She'd chew you up and spit you out."

A frown darkened Beck's face. "I wouldn't give her the chance. I'm not that stupid."

After a beat of uncomfortable silence, they grabbed the beer buckets and headed back to the bowling lanes. As they gathered in front of the sofas, Amelia announced, "Deda and Harris had to leave so they could pack for their flight tomorrow morning. That leaves us with an even number of men and women."

Dropping the bucket on one of the cocktail tables, Cal looked around for Bebe. He found her standing a few feet away with Teagan, their heads close together. He wondered what they were talking about. Maybe Bebe was telling his sister how much she liked being with him.

Cal shook his head, annoyed with himself. He needed to stop being a pussy and just tell Bebe what he wanted: a real relationship without a time limit or conditions. And if she didn't immediately agree, he'd just have to convince her to give him what he wanted.

Bebe looked up, and a spark of energy coursed through him when their eyes met. He had never felt this way about another woman. She was a fascinating mix of pragmatic and whimsical, shy and audacious, sweet and sarcastic.

She challenged him at every turn, and her smart mouth was a constant source of entertainment. He had never had so much fun with anyone, and no other woman turned him on the way she did.

Teagan and Bebe finished their conversation, and Bebe made her way to his side. He snaked his arm around her waist, settling his hand just under the swell of her breast.

"Okay, people, listen up," Teagan called out. "It's going to be men versus women, three games, the team with the highest score wins. Make your bets now."

Bebe looked up at him with a little frown notched between her dark eyebrows. "This is why I rarely play games with your sister. She is crazy competitive."

Her accurate assessment made him laugh. T was downright cutthroat when it came to winning, probably because she'd grown up playing games with him and Quinn.

"Are you going to make any bets?" Bebe asked.

He considered her question. He'd love to make a wager with her that involved a sexual favor or two, but given the winning streak she was on tonight, he would probably lose.

"What did you have in mind?"

Her eyes widened. "I wasn't talking about a bet between you and me."

"Why not?"

She shook her head. "It would be like gambling with the devil. You're too crafty."

He chuckled. "It's one of my best qualities."

She rolled her eyes, and he gave her a little squeeze. "If my team wins, you have to give me a striptease in that bustier and garter belt set that matches your eyes."

"That's all you want?"

He wanted a lot more than that. Unfortunately, what he really desired couldn't be obtained through a wager.

"Yes."

"Okay."

She agreed so quickly, he knew he had made a tactical error. "You have to start the striptease with clothes on, and it has to last at least ten minutes," he added. "And I get to pick the music. And I want you to use body glitter."

She smiled. "Too late to negotiate the terms now, *pahale*. We've already come to an agreement."

He sighed in disappointment but then perked up when he realized that the shorter the striptease, the sooner he could be inside her.

"What do you want if your team wins?" he asked, brushing his thumb against the underside of her breast.

"I want you to cook for me."

He was slightly deflated by her answer. He had hoped she would want something sexual, and if not that, at least something a little interesting.

"I cook for you all the time," he pointed out. "I make dinner for you almost every night, in fact."

"I know, and I appreciate it." Her lips twitched. "I want you to cook for me without any clothes."

A shocked laugh escaped him. "You want me to cook naked?"

She nodded as she held out her right hand. "Do we have a bet?"

Clasping her hand, he shook it vigorously. "I'm going to make damn sure my team wins," he warned her.

Three games later, the women were crowing with victory, and the men were drooping dejectedly on the long sofas.

"We lost," Beck lamented, his voice shaded with disgust. "And we're supposed to be the ones with the upper body strength."

"We weren't even close," Ren muttered. "We don't deserve to be called men."

Cal didn't know Ren well, but the guy seemed decent enough. He and Beck had attended the University of Kentucky together, and now he handled all the marketing for Trinity. Earlier in the evening, Ren had picked Cal's brain about Riley O'Brien's new social media efforts.

"They had a strategy," Quinn said. "A very effective strategy."

Priest nodded. "Distract. Disarm. Defeat."

"I've never seen so much hip shaking and ass wiggling in my whole life," Cal noted.

Beck chuckled deeply. "It was awesome."

"I lost the bet I made with Amelia," Quinn added before smiling suddenly. "Lucky me."

They were distracted again when the women invaded their seating area. Bebe had a big grin on her face, obviously pleased with the outcome of the bowling showdown. He patted his thigh, and she obediently sat on his lap.

"I guess I'm going to make breakfast bare-assed," he grumbled, making sure to keep his voice low so other people didn't hear about his humiliation.

"I'm looking forward to it." She wiggled against his zipper. "I love sausage for breakfast."

Chapter 24

CAL CHECKED THE TIME ON HIS PHONE, AND WHEN HE SAW IT was after 9 p.m., he used the remote to turn off Bebe's flat-screen TV. He headed to her bedroom but leaned his shoulder against the doorjamb instead of entering the room. If he stepped over the threshold, his cock would see that as a green light for naked fun, and they'd never leave the loft.

"What's the holdup, Cookie? You never take this long to get ready."

Bebe emerged from the walk-in closet still clad in her long lavender robe, her glossy hair piled messily on top of her head and her face bare. It looked like it was going to be a while before she was ready to go.

"Since you won't tell me where we're going, I don't know what to wear."

"I told you to dress warmly. You don't need to know anything else. It's a surprise."

She scowled. "I cannot make an informed decision with so little knowledge. There are too many variables."

Straightening from his slouch, he made his way over to her and hooked his finger in the belt of her robe. "That's fine. I prefer you naked anyway. We can stay in for New Year's Eve and make our own fireworks."

He doubted she'd be impressed with his clichéd comment, and he was right. She snorted in disgust.

"That line lacks originality," she shot back. "I'm sure millions of guys say that to avoid going out with their girlfriends on New Year's Eve."

"Are you my girlfriend, Cookie?"

Her smooth skin immediately darkened with a blush. He knew she didn't think of herself as his girlfriend, but he hoped she would by the time the clock struck midnight.

"That's not what I meant," she replied sharply.

He tugged on the knot of her belt, and the robe gaped open to reveal her sweet little body. His cock twitched when he saw the royal blue satin bra and matching bikini panties he'd bought her. He had given the underwear to her after they celebrated Christmas at his parents' house. She'd thanked him with a private lingerie show. It was one of his fondest memories.

Sliding his hands over her hips, he palmed her ass and squeezed gently. "Throw on some jeans and a sweater or I'm going to throw you on the bed."

"Thank you! Now I know what to wear." She patted his chest. "Give me five minutes, and I'll be ready."

He reluctantly removed his hands, and she headed into the en suite bathroom, presumably to put on her makeup and fix her hair. She wore it down only when they were alone.

While Bebe primped in the bathroom, he stretched out on her bed. The dark purple velvet quilt was soft underneath him, and he shoved a fluffy pillow under his head to get more comfortable. The lavender pillowcase smelled like her, and he sucked in a lungful of scented air. Nothing smelled better than Bebe, not even his favorite Ethiopian Yirgacheffe coffee.

He let his gaze wander around her bedroom, taking in the dark purple walls. The day they had painted them was burned into his memory, and not only because she'd torn open his jeans and gone down on him in the foyer.

No, it was burned into his memory because of their discussion about soul mates and the way she'd shut down when he'd asked her whether she believed in them. That hadn't been the only time she had shut down, either. There had been a few occasions when their conversation had touched on marriage and children, and her face had gone blank and her eyes had gone flat as if she weren't even there with him.

He had no idea what was going on in her head, but he was going to find out tonight.

Bebe emerged from the bathroom, her hair neatly pinned in a bun and her golden eyes emphasized with subtle makeup. As she made her way to the long espresso-colored dresser, he rolled onto his side and propped his head on his palm. He didn't know why, but he loved to watch her dress.

"What's the plan for tomorrow?" she asked, bending to pull a pair of jeans from the bottom drawer.

"Sex. Food. Sex. Football. Sex. Sleep."

She giggled. "There's not a lot of variation in your plan."

"We can switch up the positions. That would provide some variation."

For as long as he could remember, his parents had opened their home on New Year's Day to kick off the calendar's clean slate and watch college bowl games. Friends and family stopped by throughout the day to enjoy food and football.

It was one of his favorite days of the year, and this year it would be even better because Bebe would be with him. Everything was better when she was with him.

She tossed a red sweater on the bed along with the jeans. "I never thought football would be such a big part of my life," she observed wryly. "Or baseball. Or basketball. Or hockey. Or golf."

He laughed. "I never thought musicals would be such a big part of my life."

She had loved *The Wizard of Oz*, so he had taken her to see *Chicago* and *The Nutcracker*. They had tickets for *Grease* later this week, and he was thinking about surprising her with a weekend trip to New York City to see *Kinky Boots* and *An American in Paris*.

"I never thought *you* would be such a big part of my life," she blurted out.

Almost immediately, her eyes widened with dismay, and she spun back toward the dresser and jerked open a drawer. It was obvious she hadn't meant to say that out loud, but he was relieved to hear he was a big part of her life. She was a big part of his life, too.

"I never thought you'd be such an important part of my life," he admitted.

She froze, her hands clenched on the edge of the dresser. "I'm an important part of your life?" she asked without turning around.

"You know you are."

She turned to face him, and they stared at each other. Her gaze roamed over him, and he wondered what she was thinking. He wondered if he was as important to her as she was to him.

Shrugging the robe off her shoulders, she reached between her breasts, opened the clasp of her bra, and pulled it off. Her dark nipples were pebbled with arousal, and his lips tingled with anticipation. She took a step closer, stopping to shimmy out of her panties before crawling onto the bed until she knelt next to him.

"Show me, *pahale*. Show me how important I am."

BEBE COULDN'T BELIEVE CAL HAD GONE TO SO MUCH TROUBLE to surprise her. She had been intrigued when he had brought her to Riley Plaza, but she hadn't realized what he'd planned until they'd arrived on the roof.

"This is one of the best places to see the fireworks over the Bay," Cal said, his breath warm against her ear. "And I'm betting this is the first time you've been in a rooftop garden."

He would have won his bet. She had never been in a rooftop garden, and she had a feeling this one was more impressive than most.

"This is incredible." She leaned back against him and placed her arms over his. "I can't believe you did this for me."

She took another look at the round dining table, which was covered in a pristine white tablecloth and set with fine china, shiny silverware, and sparkling crystal stemware. A cobalt-blue vase of white flowers and an old-fashioned metal lantern occupied the middle of the table, and two white wooden chairs were positioned next to it.

The table was surrounded by several tall outdoor heaters like the ones used to keep restaurant patios comfortable in the winter. They emitted enough warmth to make her pea coat and knitted cap unnecessary.

"I hope you meant that as an expression of gratitude, Cookie, rather than a commentary on my general lack of thoughtfulness."

His wry tone made her laugh. "You're thoughtful."

Thoughtful was an understatement. Cal did nice things for her all the time, little things such as buying her favorite wine and big things such as surprising her with romantic dinners on rooftops. She wanted to think she was special, but he did nice things for a lot of people, not just her.

"We're going to enjoy the fireworks, kiss when the clock strikes twelve, and then we're going to have a midnight supper. And we have champagne, of course."

Dropping his arms from her waist, he turned toward the ice bucket and pulled out a green bottle. "In my humble opinion, this is the best champagne out there," he added as he tore off the foil covering the cork.

"There's nothing humble about you."

He smiled. "Humility is overrated."

She shook her head in amused exasperation. He never apologized for the person he was. It was one of the things she admired most about Cal, but sometimes he was just a little too sure of himself. He never seemed to suffer self-doubt like the rest of the human race.

He deftly popped the cork, quickly pouring two glasses of champagne and passing one to her. He held up the flute, the pale liquid fizzing inside it.

"To us."

She tilted her head, surprised by his words. Usually they toasted to "firsts." She hesitated, and he smiled slowly, his blue eyes glinting against the backdrop of the night sky.

"You don't like my toast?"

She liked it. She liked it a lot. But not nearly as much as she liked him.

"To us," she echoed as she tapped her flute against his.

They sipped their champagne, staring out over the San Francisco skyline. "This is an amazing view," she observed. "I have a pretty good one from my office, but it's nothing like this."

"It's just as amazing during the day, especially in the fall when the sky is so blue, it hurts your eyes and the sun feels like it's kissing your skin."

She shot him a teasing glance. "You're so poetic."

"I can be a lot more poetic, especially when it comes to you. Your laughter reminds me of music. Your skin feels like silk against my mouth. You walk with the grace of a dancer." He arched an eyebrow. "Should I go on?"

Her breath was trapped in her chest, so she was forced to just shake her head. She wasn't sure she could hear any more without throwing herself at him.

He tucked a strand of loose hair behind her ear. "You have no idea how gorgeous you are."

Fireworks exploded over the Bay, and they both jerked in surprise. "It must be midnight," he said.

Taking the flute from her hands, he deposited both of them on the table before turning back to her. He bent down until his mouth touched hers.

"Happy New Year, baby," he murmured against her lips before kissing her gently.

She wrapped her arms around his waist and leaned into him, loving the feel of his strong body. Everything in her seemed to sigh in relief when he hugged her tightly against him. There was no place she'd rather be than right here with him.

Drawing back, he ended their kiss way too soon for her liking. "I don't want you to miss the fireworks. This is your first fireworks show over the Bay."

She didn't care about fireworks, not when he was pressed against her. But before she could protest, he moved behind her and wrapped his arms around her so they could watch the pyrotechnics.

The colorful bursts illuminated the night sky, throwing the graceful shape of the Golden Gate Bridge into stark relief. The Bay reflected the fireworks, its glassy surface glowing with shades of electric blue, magenta, and bright green.

It was spectacular, and it was even more spectacular because Cal was with her.

When the fireworks show was over, she turned in the circle of his arms and looked up at him. She stroked her hands over his broad chest, which was covered in a soft cashmere sweater that matched his eyes.

"Thank you, *pahale*. This was a really special way to celebrate the New Year."

He smiled. "It's not over yet, Cookie. We still have our midnight supper." He waggled his eyebrows. "And dessert."

He fished his phone out of the front pocket of his dark-washed Rileys. "I need to let in Omar's team downstairs."

"Omar? Are we having food from Fig?"

"Since we haven't had a chance to eat in the restaurant, I thought this would be the next best thing."

She nodded enthusiastically. "I am so excited to try Moroccan food."

"You get excited about trying a lot of things." He chuckled. "Lucky me." He dropped a kiss on her nose. "I'll be back in a few minutes. Get ready for your taste buds to be amazed."

She watched him as he made his way to the elevator. She never got tired of staring at his butt. If it weren't totally unprofessional, she would take a picture of his backside and make it her screen saver at work.

As she turned to enjoy the view of the Bay, her phone rang. She pulled it out of her back pocket and answered it automatically.

"Did you forget something?" she asked, assuming it was Cal.

"Bindu!" Akash exclaimed jovially. "Happy New Year!"

It was such a shock to hear his voice, she couldn't get her mouth and brain to cooperate so she could reply. She tried to take a deep breath, but her chest was too tight.

"Bindu? Are you there?"

"Yes," she managed to gasp. "I'm here."

"I wanted to wish my beloved fiancée a Happy New Year."

She closed her eyes as nausea began to churn in her stomach. His parents must be nearby. There was no other reason he would have called.

"Happy New Year," she replied numbly.

"You and I will celebrate a new beginning this year. I am eager to start our life together."

Affection filled his voice, and surprisingly, it sounded genuine. Apparently, he was quite an actor. Good enough to work in Bollywood.

A light film of perspiration bloomed on her skin, and she shivered in the chilly air. Anxiety made her parched, so she picked up her champagne and drained it in one gulp. Unfortunately that made her nausea worse.

"*Maataa* wants me to tell you that she is very excited to see you. Have you made your travel arrangements?"

No. No. No. She wasn't going to India for any reason and definitely not to visit with Akash's parents.

Frantically she glanced around. Cal would be back any second, and she didn't want him to find her talking on the phone with Akash. How would she ever explain her unwanted fiancé to her much-wanted lover?

"I have to go," she said, disconnecting the call before he could respond.

She slipped her phone back into her pocket and leaned her elbows against the concrete wall that encircled the entire roof. She wasn't sure she could stand on her own, and she was grateful for its cold support.

With just a few words, Akash had ruined a wonderful night with Cal. Why hadn't she looked at the screen to see who was calling? She could have avoided the horrible conversation and enjoyed the first few hours of the New Year before reality crashed the party.

Voices sounded behind her, and she looked over her shoulder. Cal was back with three men, one dressed in chef whites and the other two clad in dark pants and white dress shirts. All three rolled large insulated bags behind them, and she wondered how much food Cal had ordered.

Akash's phone call had obliterated her appetite, and she added that to her mental list of grievances against him. She had been quite excited about sampling food from Fig.

Cal quickly made his way to her side. "They just need a few minutes to get everything ready." He cocked his head, studying her closely. "Are you okay, Cookie?"

She nodded. She refused to let Akash ruin Cal's evening, too.

"Let's go for a walk while they're setting up," Cal suggested. "I'll show you my favorite part of the garden."

Weaving his fingers through hers, he gently tugged her down the stone path. They walked for a while, the sounds of revelry floating up from the crowds of people in the streets below. The rooftop garden was much larger than she had imagined, and parts of it were designed in a way that made them feel secluded and private.

When they reached a fountain near the back of the garden, he stopped and turned to face her. Their hands were still linked, and he rubbed her rings with his thumb.

"We need to talk," he announced, his gaze intent on her face.

His expression was more serious than she'd ever seen it, and her stomach cramped with apprehension. Was he going to end things? Surely he wouldn't have gone to all this effort to give her a memorable New Year's Eve only to dump her?

No, "dump" was the wrong word. Arrangements were "terminated."

"I'm not satisfied with our arrangement anymore."

She tried to keep her face impassive, but his words sliced into her. She wasn't ready for this. She wasn't ready to give up Cal.

"Things have changed," he continued.

She wanted to shout, "What things?" but she didn't. Instead, she pressed her lips together and let him talk.

"When we entered into this arrangement, I was okay with your conditions because it was just sex."

She winced internally, dropping her eyes to her feet. It never had been just sex for her. That was the main reason she hadn't wanted to get involved with him in the first place.

"Bebe, I need you to look at me." He placed a finger under her chin and tilted her head until their eyes met. "It's not just sex. This hasn't been about sex for a long time. It was more than that before we even had sex."

He dropped his hand and pulled in a deep breath. "I care about you. I want to be with you—really be with you. I want to have a real relationship with you. One that doesn't have an expiration date like it's a fucking carton of milk. I don't want to see other people, and I sure as hell don't want you to, either. I don't want to limit the amount of time we spend together to two dates a week. And if you want to put a label on it, I want to be your boyfriend, and I want you to be my girlfriend."

What?

She was blindsided. That was not what she had expected to hear. In fact, it was the opposite of what she had expected to hear. It was too much for her to digest, and she didn't know how to respond.

She had never imagined he would want to be with her. Well, that wasn't exactly true. She had imagined it. In fact, she had fantasized about it for years. But she never, ever had thought it could or would happen.

It didn't seem possible. Was it? She wondered if maybe she was having an extreme reaction to the champagne or she had passed out after Akash's phone call and this was all just a dream.

Akash.

Oh, God. Cal wanted to be with her, and she wanted to be with him. She wanted it more than she had ever wanted anything.

But she was engaged.

Did it matter that the engagement didn't feel real to her? Did it matter that she was trying to find a way out of it? Did it matter that she didn't have any feelings for Akash other than dislike and disgust?

Did any of that matter?

Her engagement hadn't mattered when things between her and Cal had been limited to sex. But now there were feelings involved, just as Teagan had said.

He fell silent, giving her the opportunity to reply. When she didn't, he frowned.

"You don't look all that thrilled by what I just said."

Her chest felt funny, and she pressed her hand against her sternum. Maybe she was having a heart attack. Although heart attacks weren't common in young women, they happened. She didn't have any of the risk factors, but sometimes the heart just misfired.

Cal looked down, rubbing a hand over his dark hair. "Okay, back up, chief," he muttered to himself. "Back up."

Exhaling loudly, he brought his gaze back to hers. His eyes were darker than she'd ever seen them, and she didn't recognize the emotions swirling in their depths.

"I'm very satisfied with our arrangement," he stated firmly. "In fact, I'm more than satisfied. It's perfect. Nothing needs to change. We can keep doing exactly what we've been doing."

Would it be so wrong to give him what he wanted? To let herself have what she wanted?

Their relationship would probably be short-lived. Relationships ended all the time, for all kinds of reasons. By the time she had to make a decision about Akash, she and Cal would probably be over.

More than likely, they would be looking for ways to avoid each other. In fact, it was almost a certainty they would return to their former antagonistic ways.

"Just forget I said anything," he added quietly, tucking his hands into the front pockets of his jeans.

"I don't want to forget. I want to be with you, too. Effective immediately, our arrangement is terminated."

Chapter 25

CAL DARTED AROUND THE ASSHOLE IN FRONT OF HIM AND passed the basketball to Priest. The former pro athlete grabbed it out of the air, pivoted sharply, and shot the ball. It bounced on the rim, once, twice, before dropping through the net.

"Hell, yeah!" Quinn yelled, holding up both hands for Priest to slap before doing the same to Beck and Deda.

It was Wednesday night, and the five of them had gathered at the City Clubhouse to play basketball. After the game was over, they were going to grab some dinner.

"Fucker," the asshole muttered.

Cal laughed under his breath. Someone was a bad sport. It was just a pickup game, for Christ's sake, not the final NBA Championship match.

One of the asshole's teammates took possession of the ball and started the next play with a bounce pass. The other team was pretty good, but Cal's team was better, primarily because all his buddies were so tall. Deda was the shortest guy on the team, and he was six-one.

"Take it," Deda shouted.

They pounded down the court, tracking the dribble drive toward the basket. The asshole crowded Cal, shoving against his back.

"Watch the pass!" Cal called out, jabbing his elbow hard into the asshole's ribs.

The skinny guy with the ball tried to pass it, but Deda nabbed it out of the air. He threw a hard pass to Beck, who used his upper body to protect the ball before dropping it to the ground in a controlled dribble.

Beck was a damn good basketball player, and he hated to lose, especially to a team of dickheads. With a quick turn, he did a chest pass to Quinn, who was open at the three-point line.

Quinn had the option of taking the shot or dribbling closer to the basket, but Cal knew his brother would take the shot. With a hard bounce, he made a jump shot, and the ball banked in.

Game over!

Quinn raised his fist in victory, and Cal slapped his back. "Good job, brother."

Priest, Beck, and Deda joined them, and they spent a couple of minutes congratulating each other on their win. As they headed toward the sidelines to grab their water bottles and towels, the asshole walked past him, roughly shoving his shoulder into Cal's upper arm.

A laugh tickled his throat. That guy needed to get laid.

Fortunately, Cal didn't have the same problem. He was getting laid regularly by his girlfriend—the smartest, sexiest woman on the planet.

The thought of Bebe brought a smile to his face. They had terminated their sex-only arrangement more than a month ago, and they were in a committed, monogamous relationship.

She was his, and he was hers. And he'd never been happier.

Quinn tossed him a towel, and Cal wiped the sweat off his face. They played full-court basketball instead of half-court like most pickup games, and by the time their games were over, they all were soaked with sweat and barely able to move.

"I need a minute," Deda drawled, falling into one of the chairs on the sidelines.

They dropped down next to Deda, stretching out their legs and gulping water as if they had just walked through the Sahara. Cal grabbed his phone, smiling when he saw a text from Bebe.

The end of their arrangement had marked the beginning

of a new dynamic between them. She was much more affectionate and open with him. He no longer received one-word replies to his texts. In fact, she texted him throughout the day, and when he called, she answered, even if she was in the middle of a meeting.

"I'm an old man compared to you guys," Deda groused, wiping a towel over his dreadlocks.

Deda's Southern accent was stronger than Beck's, but not by much. He hailed from a small town in Mississippi and had been the first in his family to go to college.

He had joined Riley O'Brien & Co. out of law school, and he had headed up the business development group for nearly seven years. He didn't know it, but Quinn was going to promote him to COO next month.

Quinn had asked Cal if he wanted the job. He was qualified to do it, but he didn't want it. He didn't want to be in charge of everything in the company, from human resources and IT to logistics and real estate. He liked what he did, and he actually thought his job was more important than the COO gig.

"Maybe I'm too old to be a father," Deda added with a big sigh.

Quinn shook his head in exasperation. "You're being stupid. You're only forty-three. Clint Eastwood had a kid when he was sixty-six."

Earlier this evening, Deda had announced that he and Harris were expecting a baby with a surrogate. They had been together for nearly fifteen years, and they had wanted a child for a long time.

When Deda had told them about the baby, they'd all offered their congratulations, but Priest's smile looked more like a grimace. Cal wondered what had caused his brother-in-law to look like he'd taken a punch to the gut.

"Anyway, it's too late for second thoughts," Quinn added with a grin. "The bun is already in the oven."

Deda chuckled. "Way too late."

"My Grandpa Joe fathered a child when he was seventy-five," Beck chimed in.

"Holy shit!" Cal exclaimed. "That was before Viagra, too. I hope I can still get it up when I'm that old."

Beck laughed. "You can't get it up now."

"You don't even have a dick," Cal shot back.

"How does your belly dancer feel about your limp biscuit?" Beck asked with a smirk.

Before Cal could respond to Beck's insult, Deda slapped the back of Beck's head. "Shut it."

Quinn patted Deda on the back. "See, you're already acting like a father."

"Harris thinks we need a new place," Deda said, continuing with their previous conversation as if it hadn't been interrupted. "One that's more kid-friendly."

"Rayna can help you with that," Quinn suggested. "She helped me and Priest find our houses."

Rayna Sullivan was a longtime O'Brien family friend. Her husband, Sam, was in charge of Riley O'Brien & Co.'s real estate department, and Cal had grown up with their daughters. In fact, he and their middle daughter, Erica, had fucked each other on and off since high school. It was mutually satisfying and never meant anything to either one of them.

After he'd broken up with Saika, he hadn't been with anyone until he'd run into Erica at Quinn and Amelia's wedding. He'd gone back to her hotel room, and they'd spent a very enjoyable night getting reacquainted.

He hadn't seen her again until the Memorial Day barbeque at his parents' house, and later that night, he'd gone back to her place. She'd given him a blow job, they'd had sex, and then he'd left.

Erica was the last woman he'd been with before he and Bebe had gotten together, and when Erica had stopped by his parents' house on New Year's Day, he had been reluctant to introduce them. It wasn't the first time two of his lovers had come face-to-face, but it was the first time he was ashamed of his indiscriminate sexual past, especially compared to Bebe's innocence.

When he had seen Bebe and Erica standing side by side, another hard truth had slapped him in the face: sex with Bebe wasn't anything like sex with other women. It meant something when he put his hands on her. It meant something when he was deep inside her.

She meant something.

"I like Pacific Heights," Deda noted. "But I'm not sure we can afford a place there. Harris wants to cut back on his hours once the baby is here."

Harris was an oral surgeon, and he brought in some serious bank. Together, he and Deda had a combined household income higher than ninety-nine percent of the U.S. population. Cal seriously doubted they wouldn't be able to afford a house in Pacific Heights, even though it was an expensive neighborhood.

Deda turned to Quinn. "Have you talked with Amelia about how you would handle a child and two demanding careers?" He glanced at Priest. "Have you talked with Teagan about it?"

Both Amelia and Teagan had extremely high-pressure jobs with a lot of responsibility. Bebe's job was even more intense, and Cal wondered how she felt about careers and babies and the juggling act that two working parents had to perform every single day.

When he had dated Saika, he had pitched in to take care of Valerie. Being a parent was hard enough with two people around to share the load, and Saika had needed his help.

He had no idea how many times he'd made breakfast for Valerie, packed her lunch, dropped her off at school, and brought her home from daycare. He had even picked her up a couple of times when she was sick and Saika was tied up at the restaurant.

When he had children, he wanted a spouse who would share child-rearing responsibilities with him. He would never expect his wife to give up her career, although he would support her if she wanted to. His job was flexible enough where he could tele-commute, and that would help when the kids were young.

"Aren't you worried about being able to handle kids?" Deda asked.

Priest shook his head emphatically, and Deda laughed incredulously. "How can you not be worried?"

Priest shrugged. "I can h-h-h-handle anything as long as T's w-w-w-with me."

"I feel the same way about Amelia," Quinn admitted quietly. "And, Deda, you feel the same way about Harris. You guys can handle anything as long as you're together."

"You're right." Deda exhaled roughly. "Even my bad days are good because of Harris."

Cal knew exactly what Deda meant. He felt the same way about Bebe.

BEBE KNEW SHE WASN'T A NORMAL WOMAN. THE BIG CLUE WAS her aversion to shopping. Browsing through racks and racks of clothing was not fun for her. It was the opposite of fun. It was torture.

Today, however, she approached the activity with a fair amount of excitement. She was searching for a special outfit for Cal's birthday, and she was determined to find the perfect dress and shoes, along with jewelry and underwear.

Teagan was always willing to shop, so Bebe had enlisted her best friend's help. Bebe had little patience with snobby designer boutiques, and Teagan was well aware of that fact, so she had suggested they head to Saks Fifth Avenue in Union Square.

"You have no idea how excited I am," Teagan exclaimed. "I am so happy we're shopping for something other than work clothes."

On a daily basis, Bebe wore trouser suits she purchased on sale from department stores. She stuck with conservative colors—black, navy, and gray—and most of her suits had designer labels simply because she met with investment bankers and institutional investors who wore six-thousand-dollar suits.

She let sales associates pick out her shirts, and most of them had designer labels, too, for the same reason her suits did. She usually wore flats, and when she really got wild, she put on a pair of dress shoes with a one-inch heel.

All in all, her work wardrobe was boring with a capital *B*. That wasn't a problem because she didn't need to be exciting at work.

Her nonwork wardrobe wasn't much better. She bought most of her clothes from Banana Republic or J.Crew because it was easy to mix-and-match pieces and they carried petite sizes. She tended to pick neutral colors, and Teagan was the only reason she had any color in her wardrobe. Her best friend was also the only reason she had some reasonably cute clothes.

All in all, her nonwork wardrobe was boring with a capital *B*.

Cal never seemed to notice her clothes, unless he was removing them. He paid attention to her underwear, but mostly he just noticed *her*.

He complimented her all the time, telling her how

gorgeous she was and how much she turned him on. Sometimes his comments were sweet, and sometimes they were naughty. But they always made her feel good about herself.

He made her feel special, and she wanted to do something for him that made him feel special. She wanted to dress up for him and take him someplace nice for his birthday.

"So you decided to take Cal to The Ellington Club for dinner and dancing," Teagan said as she stroked her fingers over a teal silk dress. "Did you book a room in the hotel? If you haven't, you should."

Named after jazz great Duke Ellington, The Ellington Club was an old-fashioned supper club. It was located on the top floor of the Hudson San Francisco hotel and offered panoramic views of the Bay. From what Bebe had heard, it was supposed to be sexy and romantic.

"Why? Cal's condo isn't that far away. We can take a taxi if we drink too much."

Teagan shot an amused glance toward her. "Haven't you been sleeping with my brother long enough to know exactly why you should get a hotel room?" She shook her head in exasperation. "Let me spell it out for you. You'll be slow dancing. Your bodies will be touching. Your hands will be all over each other. You won't be able to wait until you're home to get naked. If you don't get a room, Cal will probably do you in the elevator or in Belva."

A wave of heat flashed over Bebe, both from embarrassment and arousal. Having sex in Belva was one of her secret desires.

"I'll book a room when I get home tonight."

Teagan smiled. "Home as in Cal's condo, you mean?"

Yes, that was what she had meant. She had fallen into the bad habit of spending almost every night with Cal at his place. Right then and there, she made a mental promise that she would stay every Thursday night at her loft, no matter how much he tried to persuade her otherwise.

Teagan held up a strapless coral-colored dress. "What about this one?"

Except for the color and the length, the dress reminded Bebe a little bit of the bridesmaid dress Teagan had worn for Quinn and Amelia's wedding. Although that dress had been silvery-gray, it also had been made of chiffon, and the bodice had criss-crossed just like this one.

"I'm not sure about the length," Teagan mused. "You need to show some leg, and this one might be too long. It would be hard to alter because of the layers."

"I like it," Bebe said. "It's bright, and Cal likes it when I wear bright colors."

Teagan nodded. "The color would look gorgeous with your skin and hair," she noted. "You could pull your hair into a loose bun and add some sparkly pins for flair."

"I don't want to put my hair up."

Teagan's eyes widened. "What?"

"I want to cut my hair and get it styled so I can leave it down. I want you to come with me when I get it done."

"*Oh, my God!*" Teagan squealed. "I'll make an appointment with Jasmine."

Bebe laughed at her enthusiasm. "I'm not sure you need to be so excited. It's just a haircut."

"Just a haircut?" Teagan repeated. "I've been waiting for an opportunity to give you a makeover, and my patience has been rewarded."

Bebe held up her hand like a traffic cop. "I said nothing about a makeover."

"You can't get a new hairstyle and a fancy dress without getting new makeup and doing your nails." Teagan paused. "How's your bikini line?"

"Teagan O'Brien-Priest! It's fine. Geez."

Her best friend snickered. "No complaints?"

"Stop talking about my bikini line, or I won't let you come with me to get my hair cut."

Teagan immediately pressed her lips together. She obviously wanted to be involved in Bebe's new hairstyle.

Bebe perused the dresses on the rack in front of her. A pale pink one caught her eye, a simple sheath dress with spaghetti straps.

"What do you think of this one?" she asked, holding the dress up for Teagan's approval.

Teagan frowned. "No. Absolutely not."

"Why not? I like it."

"That dress will do nothing to show off your body. If you

want a form-fitting dress, you need one that has definition at the waist. And the color is so bland."

Bebe shrugged before hanging the dress back on the rack. Teagan definitely had more experience in this department than she did.

They moved to the next rack, and Teagan began to flip through the dresses. "Are you going to get him anything for his birthday other than yourself?"

"Yes, of course," she replied with a laugh.

Teagan pulled a mint-green dress from the rack and held it up near Bebe's face. "Ugh. I think I just found a color you should never wear. It makes you look like you're about to vomit."

"That's good to know," Bebe replied dryly. "I'll make a note of it."

"What are you going to get him?"

"I'm not sure."

Teagan pursed her lips. "Definitely not clothes. Every woman he's ever dated has given him clothes. They wanted to dress him up like a mannequin."

Bebe's stomach cramped at the mention of Cal's other women, and she moved to the other side of the rack to distract herself. A raspberry-colored dress caught her attention, and she pulled it from the rack. The top was perfect, but the bottom was made out of lime green and white squares. It was hideous.

"When I was a senior in college, my parents planned a surprise birthday dinner for Cal. They didn't bother to talk to each other about the guest list, and my mom invited the woman she thought Cal was dating, and my dad did the same thing. And then Cal showed up with another one."

Bebe shook her head. She had no trouble imagining the jealous glances and snarky comments.

"Cal wasn't even upset. He thought it was funny. And then he spent the next three hours surrounded by women like a sultan with a harem. I was sure one of them would pull a bunch of grapes from her purse and start feeding them to him."

Bebe winced. "*Kanya*, I'm a member of his harem now."

Teagan met her eyes over the top of the rack. "Does it bother you that he's been with so many women?"

"Yes," she admitted with a sigh. "It bothers me a lot, especially since I'm nothing like the other women he's been with."

Teagan cocked her head. "How do you know that?"

"I'm making an assumption." She smiled wryly. "Although I did meet Erica."

Meeting one of Cal's former lovers had not been at the top of Bebe's to-do list. And now that she had, it was at the top of her not-to-do list.

When she had come face-to-face with Erica, it had been very difficult for her to be civil to the tall strawberry blonde. Her emotions had ranged from embarrassment to jealousy. Cal, meanwhile, had been oblivious to her discomfort and had seemed completely at ease when he'd made the introduction.

"How do you know he's been with Erica? Did he tell you?"

"No. But I could tell by the way she looked at him."

"Erica," Teagan muttered, her voice shaded with disgust. "She's been ridden more times than the carousel at PIER 39."

Bebe couldn't help but laugh at Teagan's analogy. "That was my impression."

"She doesn't mean anything to him," Teagan assured her. "And that's what you have to remind yourself." She shrugged. "Even if he wanted to, he can't go back and erase his past. You just have to find a way to accept it. That's what I had to do with Nick."

Bebe didn't want to talk about Cal's roster of past lovers anymore, so she changed the subject. "Do you have any ideas of what I can get him? I don't think I'm a suitable birthday present."

Teagan looked up from the ruffled red dress she had pulled from the rack. "Bebe, you are exactly what he has wanted for *years*."

"What are you talking about, *kanya*?"

Teagan sighed. "You thought he was joking when he said he's wanted you from the first moment he saw you, but he was telling the truth."

Bebe snorted. "You're ridiculous."

"He's wanted you for years," Teagan reiterated.

"It's *so* obvious he's been pining for me . . . in between screwing every hot woman who smiles at him and falling in love with Saika," she said sarcastically.

Teagan shook her head. "If you had given him just one little sign you were interested, he would have been all over you years ago, Bebe. *All over you*. He probably would have asked you out within seconds of meeting you."

"He didn't even like me."

"He liked you as much as you liked him," Teagan shot back. "And this is where I call you on your bullshit. You've always had a thing for him. Admit it!"

"Fine! I've always had a thing for him."

"I knew it! I'm so mad at myself for not noticing sooner. I was just too wrapped up in my own misery to wonder why you acted like such a bitch to him."

Bebe sucked in a breath at Teagan's harsh words. "Don't you understand? I liked him, and I didn't want him to know. I didn't want to be the pathetic girl who had a crush on the hot guy."

Teagan eyed her with sympathy. "Oh, Beebs, you know I understand. I felt the same way about Nick. The only difference is you acted like a bitch, and I acted like Nick's little sister." She grinned suddenly. "None of that matters now. I'm not Nick's little sister, I'm his wife. And you're not a pathetic girl with a crush. You're Cal's girlfriend."

Teagan's words sent a thrill through Bebe. She still had trouble believing she and Cal were a couple. Things between them were too good—too good to last. Every day she reminded herself to enjoy her time with him because she knew it wouldn't last much longer.

If she believed they had a future together, she would tell Cal about Akash. But she didn't believe that, so she didn't bother to share.

There was no reason for him ever to know.

Chapter 26

BEBE TOOK A FINAL LOOK IN THE FULL-LENGTH MIRROR THAT hung on the back of the hotel room door. She was already late for dinner with Cal, and a few more seconds wouldn't make much of a difference. Fortunately, she was only an elevator ride away from The Ellington Club.

She nervously smoothed the front of her coral-colored strapless dress. It was the one Teagan had liked best, and Bebe had agreed with her. The chiffon material was delicate and feminine, and the crisscrossed bodice made her breasts look full, yet perky.

The wide piece of material separating the bodice from the floaty skirt accentuated her waist, and the hem of the dress hit mid-thigh. She couldn't imagine how short it would be on a tall woman.

She had never dressed up like this before, not even for business cocktail parties. She always wore a black sheath dress for those events and matching flats so she'd be able to stand for long periods.

Tonight, she wore a pair of gold sandals that wrapped around her foot and ankle with delicate straps. With their four-inch heels, they were the tallest, sexiest shoes she had ever owned.

She hadn't been able to walk in them when she had first tried them on, and Teagan had explained that Bebe would have to practice walking, standing, and dancing in them. Over the past week, she'd spent the time she usually dedicated to her kickboxing to strolling around the executive floor in her new high-heeled sandals.

She was pleased with the results of her efforts. She couldn't run in them, but she could definitely walk without tripping and sway to a slow song.

Grabbing her beaded gold clutch, she pulled out a tube of lip gloss and took a moment to apply another layer. It was a peachy-pink color that complemented her dress and her skin tone, and it tasted like peaches.

She'd bought the lip gloss at Teagan's salon, where she had spent most of the afternoon. The stylist there had trimmed Bebe's hair by almost twelve inches until it hit just above her bra strap. She had cut in some long layers to create body, and she'd given Bebe long side-swept bangs.

Bebe thought her new haircut was fabulous. It was youthful and sexy, and she couldn't wait to see Cal's face when he saw her.

While she had been at the salon, she'd also had her makeup and nails done. The makeup artist had used shimmery gold shadow on Bebe's eyes, along with smoky eyeliner and several coats of mascara. Her fingernails and toenails were a shimmery beige color, and they were set off by her gold rings and gold sandals.

For the first time in her life, she actually felt pretty. Not smart—pretty.

She double-checked to make sure the hotel key card was in her clutch, and she quickly made her way out of the room and to the elevator. Seconds later, she stepped out into a dim marble foyer with a cobalt-blue glass reception stand. A tall redhead greeted her with a smile.

"Can I help you?"

"Yes. I'm meeting someone. He's probably already here."

The hostess nodded. "Name?"

"Banerjee."

The woman blinked. "Wow. Lucky you."

Usually when women admired Cal, Bebe felt insecure. Tonight, however, she had enough confidence to respond differently.

"Very lucky," she replied with a smile.

The hostess's answering smile was tinged with envy. "This way," she invited, leading Bebe through a set of frosted double doors.

The Ellington was laid out in a half-moon shape. Two rows of high-backed velvet booths encircled a spacious hardwood dance floor, and a live jazz band played on a stage at the front of the room. The lighting around the stage was fairly bright, but it was soft and mellow around the dark blue booths and dance floor.

The hostess took Bebe to the second row toward the end of the half-moon. Although the booths were full, they all seemed very private and very intimate.

Cal was seated in the last booth. He was looking toward the band and didn't notice her until she was almost in front of the table.

"Have a nice night," the hostess murmured from behind her.

The noise drew Cal's attention, and he turned his head toward her. When he saw her, his blue eyes widened, and his mouth fell open slightly. He stared at her, his gaze trailing from her face to her feet and back up again.

"Hi," she said.

He tried to stand, but the table stopped him. His thighs hit the edge, shaking the table and the votive candles on top of it. He abruptly sat down before awkwardly scooting out of the booth. He rose in front of her, and she tried not to drool when she got a good look at him.

She hadn't seen him in a suit since Teagan's rehearsal dinner last August. When they went to musicals or nice restaurants, he usually wore trousers and a sports jacket, and that was enough to make her mouth water.

She had never seen him in this light gray suit, but she was familiar enough with high-end designers to recognize it as an Ermenegildo Zegna. The jacket hugged his shoulders and arms perfectly, and the pants emphasized his long legs and lean waist.

His light blue striped dress shirt matched his pale eyes and made the contrast between them and his dark hair even more striking. His gray-and-blue-patterned tie brought everything together, and she had a fleeting fantasy of him wearing it and nothing else.

"You look nice," she said, almost laughing at the inaccuracy of that statement. He didn't look nice. He looked amazing . . . incredible . . . *delicious.*

She waited for him to respond, but he just stood there staring down at her. She shifted awkwardly on her heels, clutching her little purse in front of her.

"Happy birthday, *pahale.*"

"You . . ." His voice cracked a little, and he cleared his throat. "You . . . umm . . ."

He shook his head slightly before tracing the edge of her bangs with his fingers until they slid into her hair. Wrapping them around the back of her neck, he bent down and covered her mouth with his.

His kiss wasn't gentle or soft. It was ravenous. He devoured her mouth, pushing his tongue past her lips, and she pressed her palms against his chest. They needed privacy for this kind of kiss.

"Cal," she gasped against his mouth. "Not here."

His hand loosened, and she drew back. He stared into her face, his eyes hazy with desire.

"You overwhelm me," he said hoarsely.

"Is that a good thing?"

He laughed huskily. "Usually."

Dropping his hand to the middle of her back, he ushered her into the booth. He slid in behind her, his suit-covered legs brushing against her bare ones.

"You look beautiful."

She smiled. "I'm glad you think so. I wanted to look good for you."

He reached for her hand, weaving his long fingers through hers. "You always look good to me, baby. Don't you know that?"

She shook her head, and he kissed her knuckles. "I like your hair." He smiled. "Your dress almost gave me a heart attack, though. And your shoes spoke to me."

"Oh, really? What did they say?"

"They said, 'We look even better when she's wearing us and nothing else.'"

She giggled. "Hmm . . . why didn't they speak to me?"

"Only a few people know their language."

"Maybe something was lost in translation. Are you sure that's what they said?"

He nodded solemnly. "Completely sure."

"Did they say anything else?"

"Yes."

"Tell me."

"They said, 'We're lucky she picked us.' And I said, 'I feel the same way.'"

THE FABRIC OF BEBE'S DRESS WAS SOFT AGAINST HIS FINGERS, and Cal pulled her closer until there was no space between their bodies. This was the first time he had ever danced with her, and he made a mental note to take her dancing more often.

"Thank you for taking me out for my birthday."

She looked up. "I wanted to do something special for you."

He was flattered she had gone to all this effort. He was a pretty simple guy, and he would have been happy with pizza and a movie at home as long as she sat next to him—or on his lap.

"Are you having a good time?"

"Yes."

He always had a good time when he was with her, no matter what they did. But he had to admit, The Ellington Club was pretty cool.

The food had been superb, and the service had been flawless. The music added to the sexy, intimate vibe, and anyplace that allowed him to hold Bebe close got an A+ in his book.

"Have you ever been here before?"

"No."

"I'm surprised."

"Why are you surprised? I haven't been *everywhere*," he joked.

She shrugged a little. "This is one of the most romantic restaurants in the city, and I just thought . . ."

He knew what she thought, but she was wrong. He had gone on hundreds of dates, but he hadn't put a lot of thought or effort into them.

He'd never gone out of his way to be romantic, not even with Saika. But he went out of his way for Bebe. In fact, he had scheduled a ride in a hot air balloon for their first Valentine's Day together. It was a little clichéd, but he hoped she would like it anyway.

As she leaned her head against his chest, he nuzzled his face into her hair. It smelled different than it normally did, and he assumed it was because she'd had her hair done before their date.

Her new haircut was so fucking sexy, he'd almost swallowed his tongue when he saw her. He loved the way her bangs played peek-a-boo with her eyes and the way the glossy strands framed her face before falling around her shoulders.

He hadn't been exaggerating when he'd said her dress had almost given him a heart attack. Bebe made him hard when she wore flannel pajama pants and a T-shirt. Seeing her in a short, strapless dress that showed off her smooth shoulders, full tits, and gorgeous legs had made his heart stop. He was shocked he hadn't needed CPR.

"You're a good dancer," she murmured. "I'm not surprised, though. Research shows that men who are good lovers usually are good dancers."

He chuckled. She routinely quoted research studies, and they were an endless source of amusement for him.

"Is that your way of telling me I'm a good lover?" he teased.

"No. I do that by screaming at the top of my lungs when I come," she answered wryly.

He dropped a kiss on her luscious mouth. "Baby, I love that you're a screamer."

A wave of red washed over her face, and she dropped her head back to his chest. He also loved how easily he could make her blush.

"I had a hard time deciding what to get you for your birthday," she said, obviously making an effort to change the subject.

"This is the perfect present."

She was the perfect present. She was all his birthday and Christmas gifts rolled into one sweet, sexy package.

"This isn't your birthday present."

"It's not?"

"No. I got you five private cooking classes with Andre Shiroc."

Her answer stunned him so much, he stopped dancing. "Are you shitting me? Andre Shiroc is the best chef on the entire West Coast."

Looking up into his face, she smiled widely. "I know. You

can use them anytime, all at once or spread them out. You can do them at any of his restaurants, your choice."

Shiroc owned several highly rated restaurants in San Francisco, Seattle, and Los Angeles. It was nearly impossible to get reservations, even for someone whose last name was O'Brien.

"Keep moving," she directed, nudging his knee with her leg.

He found the band's rhythm again and began to dance. "He never offers classes. How the hell did you convince him to give me *five* classes?"

"I'm naturally talented," she quipped, using one of his favorite smart-ass sayings. "And the classes didn't cost me a penny. We bartered."

"I hope you didn't agree to have sex with him in exchange for cooking classes," he joked.

She gave him a look of mock reproach. "I only have sex with one man, and it's not Andre Shiroc." Smoothing the lapel of his jacket, she added, "Tara's boyfriend is one of his sous chefs, and she made the introduction."

"Your assistant is more well connected than anyone I know." He stroked the silky skin of her back. "What did you barter?"

"He's launching a new cooking show, and he wants Ava Grace to be one of his guests."

Nodding his head in understanding, he said, "So you pimped out Ava Grace."

Throaty laughter spilled from her. "I wouldn't have described it that way, but yes, that's essentially what I did." She arched her eyebrows. "What do you think of your birthday present?"

"It's fucking awesome. Thank you."

She rolled her eyes. "Maybe you could try that without the F-word."

"It's awesome," he repeated. "Thank you, Cookie."

"You're welcome."

She licked her lips, and he tracked the movement of her pink tongue. "I have something else for you, too."

"What?"

"Me. Anything you want, any way you want me."

Oh, Jesus.

He'd been semi-hard all evening, and that was all it took

to give him a full-fledged erection. His suit pants did nothing to hide it, and she noticed.

"I have a room here in the hotel." She smiled slowly. "Do you want to unwrap your present?"

Fuck, yeah, I do. Right fucking now.

Dropping his hand from her waist, he tugged her off the dance floor and toward their booth. He pulled out his wallet and threw a few hundred-dollar bills on the table.

"I'm paying," she protested.

He ignored her, lunging across the table to grab her purse and his suit jacket from the booth. Draping his jacket over his arm to hide his erection, he passed the little purse to her and wove his fingers through hers.

They headed toward the double doors at a sedate pace. He wasn't going to drag her around in those shoes and risk breaking her ankle. They passed the hostess desk, and he stabbed the Down button on the elevator.

When it arrived, he held the doors for her. "What floor?" he asked, his voice barely a growl. There were so many things swirling in his head, he could barely speak.

She pushed the button for the twenty-third floor. The elevator descended, and seconds later, the doors swooshed open. He gestured for her to precede him, and she exited the elevator and headed down the hallway.

With his hands in his pockets, he slowly walked behind her, watching the sway of her ass under her dress and the flex of her calf muscles in those fuck-me heels. He had every intention of having those lean legs wrapped around his waist tonight, and he was going to make sure she left her shoes on.

She came to a stop at a door toward the end of the hall, and he wondered if the rooms next to theirs were occupied. He sincerely hoped not, since he planned to make her scream all night long.

Using the key card, she quickly let them inside the room and flipped on the light switch. A floor lamp flared to life in the corner, along with the modern metal sconces on either side of the king-size bed.

As he closed the door behind them, she turned to face him, her eyes glinting gold and amber in the mellow lighting. "So tell me, *pahale*, what do you want?" she asked with a smile, placing her purse on the long wooden dresser.

He wanted a lot of things. The only question was what she was willing to give.

He tossed his suit jacket on the dresser before leaning his shoulder against the wall. "When you said anything I want and any way I want you, did you really mean that?"

She bit her lip. "Umm . . . yes?"

"Are you asking me or telling me?"

She blew out a breath. "I meant it when I said it, but now I'm a little worried because you have that look on your face."

"What look?"

"The one that says, 'By the time I'm done with you, you'll barely be conscious, and if you are, you'll be too embarrassed to look me in the eye.'"

"Oh. *That* look." He chuckled. "I'm glad you recognize it."

She laughed softly. "You obviously know exactly what you want, so why don't you tell me and end my suspense?"

He sat down on the end of the bed and spread his legs. "Come here."

She did as he asked, stepping between his knees, and he slid his hands under her dress to fondle her ass. By the feel of things, she wore his favorite kind of panties, lacy ones that showed just a hint of cheeks.

With him seated, they were nearly eye level, and she stroked a hand over his hair. "Whatever you want, I want to give it to you," she told him softly, settling her hands on his shoulders.

Her offer made his blood flow hotly through his veins. It wasn't just the idea of being able to do anything with her, but the fact that she trusted him enough to make the offer . . . that she trusted him to take care of her.

Leaning forward, he trailed his tongue along her collarbone until he reached the hollow of her throat. She let her head drop back, and he sucked lightly on the smooth skin. She tasted delicious, all of his favorite flavors in one lick.

"Do you remember when we visited the apple orchard?" he asked.

"Of course."

"Was that your first orgasm?"

She met his eyes. "Yes. It was my first."

He had a hard time believing she had never given in to the innate curiosity and physical need that drove humans to masturbate.

"You'd never had one? Ever?"

She shook her head, her cheeks dusky with a blush. He eased his fingers into the crevice between her ass cheeks and thighs, and she shifted on her heels, widening her legs to give him better access.

"Not even one you gave yourself?" he persisted. "You never touched yourself?"

Again, she shook her head. He stroked his fingers along the edge of her panties. "Why not?"

"I was unaware of my sexuality. My body wasn't a source of pleasure. It was just there . . . like a household appliance." She licked her lips, and he felt it in his cock. "I wasn't interested in sex until I met you. Now it's all I think about."

He slid his fingers beneath her panties, petting the damp hair of her pussy. "You touch yourself."

"Yes," she replied, her voice barely audible.

She was trembling against him, her breath coming in shallow pants. He slipped his fingers between the folds of her pussy, and slippery wetness drenched his hand.

"That's what I want, baby. I want you to show me."

"Show you what?" she asked breathlessly.

Confusion filled her face, and tenderness flooded him. She still was innocent in so many ways.

"I want to see you touch yourself," he explained, the thought of it making his temperature increase by a million degrees. "I want you to tell me how good it feels . . . what you're thinking about. I want to watch you make yourself come." Gently, he touched her clit, finding it stiff and swollen. "That's what I want for my birthday."

Chapter 27

CAL WANTED HER TO TOUCH HERSELF. HE WANTED HER TO touch herself in front of him.

Oh, God.

Giving him the gift of Bebe for his birthday suddenly seemed liked a bad idea. *A very bad idea.*

"Are you sure you don't want a blow job instead?" she asked, unable to hide the desperate note in her voice. "Wouldn't that be more fun for you?"

"I love it when you go down on me, but watching you is going to blow my mind."

The thought of masturbating in front of him made her hot with embarrassment, but she was going to give him what he wanted. She wanted to blow his mind.

Taking a deep breath, she nodded. "Okay, birthday boy. You got it."

She wiggled a little, a silent demand for him to remove his hands, and he let go. Reaching for the zipper hidden in the side of her dress, she pulled it down. Her dress pooled at her feet, and she held on to his shoulders as she stepped out of it.

"*Fuck*," he muttered. "Your underwear is a fucking wet dream waiting to happen."

She smiled, glad she had splurged on new underwear for

tonight. The lacy bustier matched her coral-colored dress, and a thin navy-blue ribbon was woven into the edge of the cups and laced up the front. Her panties matched, even down to the navy-blue ribbon.

She bent over to pick up her dress, and he groaned. "*Goddamn*, Bebe. Are you trying to kill me?"

She laughed as she straightened. "I'm trying to make you hard."

Rising from the bed, he took her hand and pressed it against his erection. "Mission accomplished."

She stroked him through his pants, and the feel of him under her hand made her even wetter than she already was. Suddenly she realized the sooner she gave him what he wanted, the sooner she could get what she wanted. Perching on the edge of the bed, she crossed her legs and reached for the buckle of her sandal.

"No. I want you to leave the shoes on."

His demand surprised her, and her eyebrows went up. "Leave them on," he repeated.

"Whatever you want, *pahale*."

She set to work unlacing her bustier. It had been such a pain to put on, but it was much easier to get off. Once she had pulled it away from her breasts, she stood up so she could shimmy out of her panties.

She glanced toward Cal as she stepped out of the stretchy lace. He was motionless, his eyes hot on her body, especially the space between her legs. She fought the urge to cover herself with her hands.

Her pulse pounded in her ears, and she worked to pull in a deep breath. She was so nervous, her tight throat constricted her voice.

"*Pahale*," she whispered, "I'm embarrassed."

Leaning down, he kissed her cheek. "There's no room for embarrassment between us," he countered softly, rubbing circles on her stomach with his big hand. "There's no room for anything but you and me."

His scent and warmth wrapped around her, both exciting and calming at the same time. She focused on her breathing, willing herself to relax.

Trailing his finger across her stomach to her breast, he rolled her nipple between his thumb and forefinger. The feel of his roughened fingers sent a shock through her body, and she couldn't hold back a moan.

He kissed the corner of her mouth. "Get on the bed, baby."

She took a moment to pull back the fluffy white down comforter and arrange the mound of pillows near the head of the bed before sliding onto the cool sheets. Settling on her back, naked except for her heels, she met his eyes where he stood at the foot of the bed.

He reached for his tie and slowly unknotted it. She watched as his long fingers worked the silk, pulling it from his neck.

Holding the tie loosely in his hand, he asked, "Do you ever fantasize about being tied up?"

She shook her head.

"I think you'd like it." He chuckled softly. "I know I would."

After a moment of consideration, she nodded in agreement. "Now?"

"No. I want your hands to be free tonight."

His eyes never wavered from hers as he tugged his shirt free from his pants, removed his cuff links, and undid the line of buttons down his chest. He shouldered off his shirt, letting it drop to the floor, before slowly stripping off his white undershirt.

Naked from the waist up, he rolled his shoulders a little. The light gleamed on his sculpted biceps as he leisurely ran a hand over his chest to his stomach.

She abruptly realized he was giving her a striptease, probably with the goal of easing her embarrassment. And it was working because she wasn't embarrassed any longer; instead, she was so turned on, she could feel her clit throbbing with her heartbeat.

Cal rubbed his palms across the ridges of his abs, and her own palms tingled with the desire to touch him. His hands hovered over his belt buckle, and she held her breath as he traced the metal with the tip of a forefinger.

"Enjoying the show?" he asked.

Somehow she managed to drag her eyes away from his hands to look at his face. "Yes."

"Want me to keep going?"

"Yes."

"Are you sure?" he prodded, a teasing note in his voice.

"Yes."

She watched avidly as he unbuckled his belt and unfastened his pants, knowing exactly what was hidden behind that expensive wool. She tracked the movement of his fingers as they grasped the tab of his zipper and inched it down at a torturously slow pace.

"Do you think about me when you touch yourself?" he asked, his deep voice swirling around her like smoke.

"Always."

"I think about you, too. When I wake up hard, and you're not there to take care of me, I do it myself."

Hooking his fingers in his waistband, he shucked his pants and underwear and kicked them to the side. He moved closer to the bed until his knees hit the mattress, giving her a better view of the massive erection jutting from the dark hair at his groin.

A whimper vibrated in her throat when she saw the fluid seeping from the tiny slit on the plump head of his penis. Cal swiped his fingers through his pre-cum and rubbed it along his thick length.

Fisting his erection, he said, "I wrap my hand around my cock, and I think about you." His fingers flexed as he moved his hand up and down. "I think about how hot and wet you are, and it makes me so hard, I hurt."

Cal talked during sex. *A lot.*

He never shut up unless his mouth was busy between her legs. He used nasty words, too—pussy, cunt, cock, dick, fuck. Nothing was off limits.

And she loved it.

"I think about how tight your pussy is," he continued huskily. "It sucks me in so deep, it's fucking unbelievable."

Arousal welled between her legs, wetting the insides of her thighs, and she squirmed against the smooth sheets. Her breasts shifted with the movement, and his eyes narrowed on them. Her nipples hardened under his gaze, and she smoothed a palm over one of the stiff peaks.

Cal made a sound in his throat, a deep growl that rumbled throughout the room. "Yes. Let me see how you like it . . . show me how you touch your nipples."

As he continued to stroke his erection, she gently pinched her nipple between her fingers. When she masturbated alone, she never focused on her breasts, but with Cal watching, she was suddenly aware of the different textures of her body: the velvety softness of her areolas and the pebbled skin of her nipples.

The rhythm of Cal's breathing increased. "Use your other hand to play with your pussy."

She immediately dipped her fingers between her labia, a heightened awareness of her own body sweeping over her. She was shockingly wet . . . so soft and slick. Swirling her fingers around, she coated them with her arousal.

Cal groaned. "You're so wet . . . I can see it from here." He moved his hand rougher and faster along his erection. "When I think about the way your juice tastes and the sounds you make when you're about to come, I shoot off like a fucking rocket."

Stroking deeper, she trailed her fingers from the entrance of her body toward her clit. She circled the delicate flesh around it, edging her fingers closer and closer until she grazed the knot of nerves with the tip of her finger. A zing shot down her legs, and she gasped.

"Spread your legs," he rasped. "I want to see your fingers in your pussy."

She brought her knees up with her feet flat on the bed and let her legs fall open. Shifting her hand, she pushed two fingers inside her. "*Oh, that feels good.*"

She pumped her fingers, sliding them in and out and pressing her thumb against her clit. The tension built inside her, fiery and edging toward pain.

She had never been so turned on, and it was solely because Cal was watching her and pleasuring himself at the same time. While she continued to work her fingers inside her, she zeroed in on the jerky movement of his hand.

An agonized sound rumbled from his chest. "Bebe." Glancing up, she met his eyes. "I want my birthday present. I want to see you come."

CLENCHING HIS PALM AROUND HIS HARD-ON, CAL SLOWED THE rhythm of his hand. He wanted to see Bebe come first and then he was going to push inside her and make her come again, all over his cock.

Against the backdrop of the snowy white sheets, her bronzed skin gleamed with a light sheen of sweat. Her lean legs were splayed, giving him a clear view of her hand and her glistening pink folds. He could see and smell her arousal, and he wasn't sure how much longer he could hold off before he erupted into his fist.

"Do you have a favorite fantasy that you think about—something that gets you off every time?" he asked.

She shook her head.

"I have one."

"Tell me. Please."

"Actually, there are two versions. I'm in my office, working at my desk, and you walk in wearing a beige trench coat and shiny black leather knee boots with a skinny heel. You unbutton the coat as you walk toward me, and you're naked under it. You spin me around in my desk chair, unzip my jeans, and straddle me. And then you fuck me, fast and hard. That's my go-to fantasy. When I think about it, I come in less than a minute. It gets me that hot."

"What's the other version?" she asked, her voice breathy like a starlet's.

"It starts the same, but instead of straddling me, you sit on the edge of the desk, and I eat your pussy before laying you out on top of my desk and doing you really slow. That version is my all-time favorite, but I only think about it when I have plenty of time to enjoy it."

Her eyes fell to his hand again, glazed with desire. He squeezed his shaft.

"Do you want this, baby?" She nodded, her hand working furiously between her legs. "As soon as you come, I'll give it to you."

She whimpered, and then she was coming, her torso arching off the bed and her legs stiffening. A husky cry spilled from her mouth, and her head fell back, exposing the smooth skin of her throat.

When she removed her hand and let it fall limply to her side, he lunged forward and grabbed her ankles. She yelped a little in surprise, and he tugged her toward the foot of the bed. He wasted no time flipping her over, and grabbing her hips, he lifted her onto her knees.

She glanced behind him, her eyes wide. He had never

been so rough with her, but he couldn't be gentle right now. He jerked her backward onto his cock, grunting as her slippery flesh opened to him.

His vision blurred around the edges. "Okay?" he asked, barely able to speak.

Her breath whooshed out. "Yes."

He pulled back and plunged into her again and again. He couldn't stop. He never wanted to stop.

She rocked backward, forcing his cock inside her until he couldn't go any deeper. Reaching between them, he found her clit. He gave it a gentle pinch, and then a not-so-gentle pinch.

She screamed hoarsely, the supple muscles of her pussy pulsing rhythmically as her climax pulled her under. And that was all he needed. Digging his fingers into her ass, he held her against him as his release burst through him.

"*Fuck*," he groaned harshly, his cock exploding inside her.

Her vaginal muscles flexed around him. He couldn't tell if she was coming again or just trying to make it better for him, but he almost passed out from the pleasure.

He fell forward, and somehow he managed to avoid crushing her by shifting to the side. They collapsed onto the bed with his front plastered against her back.

He was still inside her, still semi-erect. That was his perpetual state around Bebe. He barely got inside her before he came, and even when his orgasms made him deaf and blind, he wanted more.

It took a long time for his heartbeat to return to normal, and finally he withdrew from her body. She rolled to face him, and he rubbed his thumb over her lush bottom lip.

"Happy birthday to me."

She giggled. "Happy birthday to you."

"Thank you."

"You're welcome," she said softly.

"This is definitely the best birthday I've ever had."

"Really?"

"No. My best birthday was when I was eight years old and had the chicken pox. I got to eat ice cream all day."

She poked him in the ribs. "I can't tell if you're teasing me or not."

"Of course I am," he replied with a laugh. "Teasing you is one of my favorite things to do."

"What's your *favorite* thing to do?"

"You are."

She laughed softly. "I'm being serious, *pahale*."

"So am I."

She sighed in exasperation. "What's your second favorite thing to do, then?"

"Talk to you." He kissed her nose. "That's tied for first, actually."

"Really?"

"Yes."

He could list his top thousand favorite things to do, and she would be part of them all.

"I need to ask you something, Cal."

The tone of her voice and use of his name let him know she was serious. He tried to keep his muscles loose, but he was a little worried. He had no idea what she was going to say.

"When you offered to help with my de-virginization plan, I asked why, and you said, 'What would you say if I told you that I've wanted you since the first moment I saw you?' Do you remember saying that?"

Yeah, he remembered. He had been honest with her, and when that hadn't worked, he had given her a reason she wouldn't doubt.

"I thought you were joking. Were you?"

"No."

Her eyes widened. "No?" she repeated incredulously. "You weren't joking?"

"No." He figured he might as well lay his cards on the table. "I took one look at you and wanted you under me, on top of me, against the wall, any way I could get you. Every time I saw you, I wanted you."

She shook her head. "Why didn't you say anything?"

He couldn't help laughing at her ridiculous question. "Because you hated me."

She eyed him for a moment. "What would you say if I told you that I've wanted you since the first moment I saw you?"

He frowned. "Yes, I said that."

"I know. And now I'm saying it."

What?

"I didn't hate you," she continued. "I liked you, and I

didn't want you to know. I never imagined you would ever feel the same, and I was embarrassed."

"Are you fucking *kidding* me?"

"No. I wanted you, too. I turned you down when you offered to help with my de-virginization plan because I liked you too much to have sex with you."

"What the fuck does *that* mean?"

Her forehead furrowed with a frown. "Are you mad?"

So many emotions were swirling through him that he didn't know what he was. "I'm having a hard time understanding what you just said."

"Which part?"

"The part where you said you never hated me. The part where you said you've wanted me since the first moment you saw me. The part where you said you *liked* me but didn't want me to know. Did I hear all that correctly?"

She nodded, her dark hair brushing against her bare shoulders. "Why does that make you upset?"

He was torn between kissing her and shaking her. How could a woman as smart as Bebe be so damn stupid?

"Because right now it feels like I wasted four years of my life."

A mental slideshow of the last four years passed in front of his eyes. He saw himself, obsessing over Bebe, wanting her, but never having her.

He saw the women he had fucked, women who hadn't meant anything to him. And he saw Saika, a woman he had asked out because he couldn't have the one he really wanted.

In some small way, Bebe was responsible for him getting involved with Saika in the first place. If he'd known he had a chance with her, he wouldn't have fallen in love with Saika and Valerie and ended up with a broken heart.

"Wasted four years of your life?" Bebe repeated. "What do you mean?"

"If you hadn't been so damn stupid, we could have been together."

His voice was harsh, and her head jerked back as if he had slapped her. Calling his girlfriend stupid was not a nice thing to do, but he didn't feel like being nice right now. He felt like spanking her ass . . . *hard*.

"Did you just call me stupid?" she asked, her beautiful eyes narrowed with anger.

"Yes, I did." He sat up and wrapped his hands around her upper arms to pull her over him. "I suffered through four fucking years without you, and you're going to make up for every fucking day I suffered. Starting right fucking now."

Chapter 28

BEBE HAD TO TELL CAL ABOUT AKASH. SHE HAD TO TELL HIM because she believed that maybe . . . possibly . . . unbelievably . . . she and Cal might have a future together.

She had no idea how he would react. Would he understand? Would he offer to help her find a solution? She didn't know. But she knew she had to tell him, and she had to do it soon because she couldn't continue to keep it from him.

She never again wanted to lie to Cal the way she had lied to him this morning.

He usually rose before she did, and more often than not, he woke her with good coffee and great sex. This morning, she had been out of bed before him, and when he'd asked why she was leaving the house so early, she'd told him that she had an early breakfast meeting. The truth was that she had to have her monthly video chat with Akash.

She had skipped their last video chat, and she knew she couldn't risk doing that again. The day after they had been scheduled to talk, Akash had sent her a warning: an Excel spreadsheet of all the people in her extended family who worked for Mehra or lived in Mehra buildings.

There were two hundred and four people on the list, and he included details about each one. "Vijay's wife just had twins. What a blessing!" and "Divya's mother was just diagnosed with breast cancer. How unfortunate!"

She'd read every single name and the details Akash had provided. And when she had finished, her head pounded with a headache and her stomach churned with nausea.

"Good morning, Ms. Banerjee."

Bebe waved to Javier, the daytime concierge in her loft building, as she walked past him on the way to the elevators. As the elevator ascended, she mentally prepared herself for the chat with Akash.

It was the first week of March, and Akash and his parents expected her to come to India this month. She had told her unwanted fiancé that she had no plans to make the trip, but he had ignored her.

The elevator reached her floor, and she quickly made her way to her loft. Once she was inside, she dumped her leather messenger bag on the sofa and grabbed a carton of chocolate milk from the fridge. She hadn't eaten breakfast, and she was starving. Hopefully, the milk would satiate her hunger until she could grab some yogurt on the way to work.

She decided to do the video chat on her desktop computer in her study instead of unpacking her tablet, and at eight o'clock on the dot, she logged into Skype and hit the Call button. Moments later, Akash's face filled the screen.

"Bindu," he said flatly.

"Akash."

"I am pleased you decided to honor your commitment to me today."

She chose not to reply to his sarcastic comment, and after a few seconds of silence, Akash spoke again. "*Pitaa* and *Maataa* have been asking about your travel plans, and I have been unable to answer their questions."

"I'm not coming to India. I've told you that several times."

"If you refuse to come to India, Bindu, my parents will insist on visiting you. Is that what you want?"

Bebe sighed. "Akash, you must stop this. I don't want to marry you. You're blackmailing me by threatening my family. You must tell your parents the truth. They will not blame you. They will blame me."

"They will blame *me*," Akash snarled. "I will lose everything. I will be stripped of my position in Mehra. My father has already advised me of my replacement if we do not marry."

He pointed at her. "I have no idea why my parents are so determined that you be my wife. I have never understood why they want you to be a Mehra. There are many other women who are from better families. Women who are charming, beautiful, and accomplished. You are none of those things, yet I am forced to accept you."

Even though she knew he thought very little of her, his assessment still stung. For a brief moment, she wondered why Cal wanted to be with her, but then she managed to focus on the problem at hand.

"Akash, we should work together to change your parents' minds. We need to make them see that I am not a suitable wife for you."

He shook his head. "It's too late for that. We have perpetuated the lie that we are happy with the marriage—that we have genuine affection for one another. *Maataa* believes you will treat me as she treats *Pitaa*, and *Pitaa* believes you will be a shining star in the Mehra organization. If you break things off, they will think it is because I have done something wrong."

"Then we have nothing left to talk about," Bebe replied curtly.

"I am warning you now, Bindu, if you do not come to India, we will come to you."

She didn't bother to respond. Instead she clicked the button to end the chat.

Leaning back in the chair, she studied the exposed ductwork above her. There was a part of her that understood Akash's unwavering determination to marry her. Mehra was his life, and if he didn't marry her, he would lose everything he had worked for.

Akash only wanted to marry her because his parents were forcing him to do so. But if they changed their mind about her suitability as a bride, Bebe would be free.

She needed to make Ishani and Tushar think of her as a liability to their family rather than an asset. There were a lot of things she could do that would embarrass them and make them feel like she had dishonored their family. Unfortunately, those things also would humiliate her and put her professional reputation and career in jeopardy.

As she took a sip of chocolate milk, the straw malfunctioned, and brown liquid splashed across her white shirt and down her gray suit pants. She hastily dumped the carton on her desk and jumped to her feet, but the damage was done.

Great. Just great.

As if Akash wasn't enough to ruin her morning, now she had to change. She checked the clock and was horrified to realize it was past nine. She hadn't realized it was so late.

Her assistant was going to be very annoyed with her. Tara didn't like it when Bebe didn't let her know if she was going to be late.

Hurrying to her bedroom, Bebe made a beeline to her walk-in closet. Although she had kept her personal promise to spend Thursday night at her place, most of her stuff had migrated to Cal's condo.

Last week when she had stayed at her loft, she'd woken up the next morning and realized all her nice work clothes were at Cal's place. She was forced to wear a suit she hadn't worn in at least three years. Fortunately, it still fit, which was somewhat surprising, since she had gained a couple of pounds. Cal kept her well fed, and her main form of exercise nowadays was sex instead of kickboxing.

She cursed under her breath as she evaluated her clothing options. She really needed to buy some new suits and divide them between her place and Cal's condo.

Finally, she found a navy-blue suit that wasn't too worn and a light blue shirt that was nice enough to wear to work. She quickly changed her clothes and then cursed again when she realized she wore black shoes.

She hoped Teagan wouldn't stop by her office today. She didn't want to suffer another lecture from her best friend on the horrors of mixing navy-blue and black.

Jogging down the short hall to the living area, she scooped up her messenger bag. Her phone vibrated in the side pocket, but she didn't bother to check it. She knew it was Tara calling to harangue her.

She cast a frantic look at the clock on the wall: 9:42 a.m. Her day had just blown up.

THE FINAL STORYBOARDS FOR THE NEW TELEVISION COMMER-
cial looked good, and Cal gave an internal sigh of relief.
They were scheduled to shoot the commercial in two weeks,
and they were running out of time to make changes.

Before he could thank the team from the advertising
agency, the door to the collaboration room opened. Teagan's
dark head popped around the door frame, her blue eyes wide
behind her black-rimmed glasses. She beckoned to him before
shutting the door, and he frowned in confusion.

Teagan never interrupted his meetings. In fact, she never
interrupted anyone's meetings because she hated for people
to interrupt hers.

"Give me a second," he said, addressing his request to all
twenty people in the room.

He hurried to the door, making sure to close it behind him.
He turned to face Teagan and was surprised to see Priest,
Quinn, and Amelia in the hall with her.

"I'm kind of busy for an impromptu family reunion," he
quipped.

No one smiled at his joke. They just stared at him, their
faces blank.

"Cal, have you talked to Bebe this morning?" Teagan
asked.

The look on her face, combined with the desperation in her
voice, made the bottom drop out of his stomach. "Not since she
left for work. I've been in meetings. Why? What's going on?"

Teagan turned to Priest, burying her face against his
chest, and Quinn blew out a rough breath. His brother settled
a big hand on Cal's shoulder.

"A bomb went off in the lobby of GGB's headquarters this
morning right as people were coming in to work. Hundreds are
injured or dead." Quinn squeezed his shoulder. "Cal, no one
has heard from Bebe. Her assistant said she didn't come in this
morning. She's been trying to reach her. T has been calling
Bebe's cell phone, but she isn't answering."

A loud roaring noise in his ears drowned out the rest of
what Quinn said. He could see his brother's mouth moving,
but he couldn't hear anything.

Bebe. Bebe. Bebe.

Her name echoed with his every heartbeat.

"Cal." Quinn shook him. "Cal. Listen to me. Even if she was there, she could be okay." His fingers dug into him. "She could be okay."

Adrenaline flooded Cal, and he jerked away from Quinn. "I need to be there."

"Cal, no," Amelia said gently. "The police have blocked off the streets. No one can get through. They don't know if it's a single attack or if there will be more. They're trying to evacuate GGB's building and the buildings nearby so they can search them. They don't know anything right now. It could be terrorists. It could be a psycho employee. They just don't know."

"We're on lockdown," Quinn added. "Our building has been searched already because it's a high-profile target. We're clear. No one can get in, and we're advising everyone to stay here for now."

"*Jesus,*" he whispered. "This isn't happening."

He couldn't feel his legs, and he leaned heavily against Quinn. His brother staggered a little under his weight, and Cal tried to straighten, but he couldn't seem to stand on his own.

"Priest, help me," Quinn requested, grunting a little as he wedged a shoulder under Cal's armpit. "Damn it, Cal, keep it together."

Priest hooked an arm around Cal's waist, and they propped him against the wall. Cal stared into his brother-in-law's eyes. They were filled with sadness, maybe even grief. Priest thought Bebe was gone.

"She's fine," he insisted fiercely. "She's fine. I would know if she wasn't. I would feel it. Wouldn't I feel it?" He pressed his hand to his chest, over his heart. "She's inside me. She's part of me. I would know if she wasn't okay."

He couldn't imagine a world without Bebe, and he didn't want to think about how his life would be without her. Now that he knew what it was like to be with her, he refused to consider the possibility of losing her.

"Shit," Quinn muttered.

"Maybe she wasn't there," Amelia speculated, her voice soothing. "Maybe she's been trying to call, but the cell towers are overwhelmed."

Teagan began to cry, big gulping sobs that made him want to throw up. "Stop it!" he shouted. "Stop crying! There's no reason to cry. She's fine."

Priest roughly shoved his shoulder. "You're n-n-n-not the only p-p-p-person here who loves Bebe."

"Help me get him to his office," Quinn directed. "He's falling apart."

"I'm not falling apart!" he yelled. "There's no reason for me to fall apart! She's fine."

Quinn ignored him and grabbed his arm. Priest took the other one, and they half carried, half dragged him to the elevator. Suddenly they were in his office on the second floor. He was on his sofa, and his family surrounded him.

Tears burned his eyes. "She left earlier than usual. I was still in bed because we stayed up late. I don't remember if I kissed her good-bye." He swiped his hand across his watery eyes. "I'm in love with her. We wasted years when we could have been together."

Amelia made soothing noises as she rubbed his back, and he sucked in a shaky breath. "I haven't had enough time with her. I want more. I want a lifetime. She has to be okay."

Quinn roughly scrubbed his hands over his face. "I've called in as many favors as I have, and the fire chief has promised me that his team is looking for Bebe. We'll be the first to know when they find her."

A loud knock sounded on the door, and Priest opened it to admit Quinn's young assistant, Jeff. "GGB is the target," he announced. "A bomb just went off in its Phoenix R and D facility. They were in the process of evacuating it. The news outlets are saying the casualties are massive."

Teagan gasped. "This is horrible."

Quinn pulled Jeff aside, and they spoke quietly for a few moments before the younger man left. "Cal, when did Bebe leave exactly?" his brother asked. "The bomb went off just after nine."

"I don't know. Around seven fifteen, I think. She said she had an early breakfast meeting."

"Do you know where?" Teagan asked. "Was it at the office? At a restaurant? If it was at the office, she would have already been upstairs. The bomb was in the lobby, and sup-posedly most of the damage was on the lower floors."

He shook his head. "I don't know. *God*. I don't know. I didn't bother to ask." He glanced around his office, his gaze touching on the people he loved. "I feel like I should be doing something. What should I do? I can't just sit here."

"I feel the same way," Teagan said. "I don't know what to do. Quinn, do you think the fire chief would let Cal through the barricades?"

Quinn sighed. "I don't know." He grimaced. "From what I've heard, it's like a war zone."

Images of Bebe, injured, bloody, and helpless, flashed across Cal's vision, and his chest tightened. He struggled for air, and Amelia pushed his head toward his knees.

"Breathe, Cal," she crooned. "Just breathe. It's going to be okay."

As he sat there with his head hanging between his knees, his office line buzzed. He raised his head to look toward his desk.

"What the fuck?" Quinn muttered angrily. "I told Liza to hold your calls."

Just then the receptionist's voice floated over the intercom. "Guys? Bebe's on the line."

It took him a moment to comprehend what Liza had said, and when he did, relief made him light-headed. He vaulted to his feet, lunging toward his desk, and tripped over the round coffee table in front of the sofa.

As he crawled away from the table, Teagan snatched the phone from its cradle. "Bebe!" she cried. "Where are you? Where have you been? We were scared to death."

He scrambled to his feet. Grabbing the phone from his sister, he pushed her out of the way.

"I'm at the deli down the street from Riley Plaza," Bebe said. "I couldn't get into your building because the doors were locked."

The sound of her voice brought tears to his eyes, and he blinked them back. They clogged his throat, and he cleared it roughly.

"Baby, are you okay?"

"Oh, *pahale*," she replied softly, "I'm better now that I've heard your voice. I wasn't there when it happened."

Thank you, Jesus.

"Stay where you are. I'm coming to get you."

"I have my scooter. I'll be there by the time you get downstairs. Just let me in."

She immediately disconnected, and he slowly hung up the phone. When he turned around, his office was empty. That was his family—there when he needed them, out of sight when he didn't.

Rushing out of his office, he found Teagan waiting in the hall. "Will you bring Bebe to my office when she gets here?" she asked.

"Yeah," he agreed tersely as he passed her, understanding that Teagan and Bebe were closer than most sisters, and that Teagan needed to see Bebe almost as much as he did.

He jogged down the hall to the escalators that led to the first floor. By the time he got to the lobby, Bebe was out front. He quickly pushed open one of the side doors, remembering just in time to hold it with his foot so it wouldn't close behind him. Since the building was on lockdown, his key card wouldn't work.

She ran toward him, and when she got close enough, she threw herself at him. He caught her tightly against his body, burying his face in her hair, and took his first easy breath in more than an hour.

"I never want to go through that again," he murmured, dropping kisses on top of her head. "Would you be willing to have a tracking device implanted in your body so I know where you are twenty-four/seven?"

She burrowed closer. "Like the ones they put in Lamborghinis?"

Her voice was muffled against his chest, but he heard her. "Exactly."

She laughed, but it sounded like she was crying. "I'm not that valuable."

"You are to me."

Chapter 29

"LARS ENDICOTT, CFO OF GENERATION GLOBAL BIOTECHNOL-ogy, is with us today to talk about how the company is faring since the bombings at its global headquarters in San Francisco, as well as its R and D facility in Phoenix and its manufacturing facilities in Oklahoma and Nevada. Lars, thank you for joining us."

"Thank you for having me, Maria," Lars replied, nodding at Maria Belasquez, the anchor of the leading financial news program.

"First of all, Lars, how are you holding up?"

"Umm, well, umm . . ." Lars stuttered. "I'm okay, I guess."

Bebe winced at her boss's less than eloquent answer. They had put off the financial media as long as they'd dared, and this was the first interview he'd done since the bombings. She and GGB's vice president of corporate communications had prepped him for hours for this interview, and apparently they should have started with an answer to the basic question, "How are you?"

She and Lars had been in New York for more than three weeks trying to stop the financial hemorrhaging that GGB had suffered since the company had been attacked. They had flown out the night of the bombings and spent nearly every waking hour in meetings with large institutional investors, investment banks, and Wall Street analysts. Unfortunately, their efforts hadn't made much of a difference.

"I can only imagine how difficult things have been for you and the rest of the GGB family," Maria noted sympathetically. "Based on our research, the attacks on GGB were the worst any U.S.-based company has suffered in modern history."

"Unfortunately, you're right, Maria," Lars agreed. "This kind of attack on an individual company is unprecedented."

"What can you tell us about the attacks?"

"That's a difficult question to answer. The bombings are part of an ongoing federal investigation, and we are not allowed to comment on them beyond what the FBI has already said."

Maria nodded. "The FBI released a statement yesterday that Gordon Abernathy confessed to planning the attacks. They're still looking for accomplices. Abernathy has not been forthcoming about what help he did or did not have. He obviously couldn't have been in four places at once."

She gave Lars a moment to respond, but he stayed silent, as Bebe had coached him.

"Abernathy recorded several video messages and posted them on the Internet soon after the bombs went off," Maria continued. "He also emailed them to several news organizations. Here's a clip now."

The screen cut away to a video of Gordon Abernathy. With his sandy blond hair, unremarkable features, and wire-rimmed glasses, he looked just like the high school science teacher he was. He was also a murderer.

"My name is Gordon Abernathy. I want to tell you about my wife, Maggie. She was the love of my life. We were college sweethearts. She was a warm, generous, loving person, and Generation Global Biotechnology killed her."

The screen cut back to Maria and Lars, whose face was grim. He had watched that video hundreds of times.

"According to the videos, Maggie Abernathy was part of a clinical drug trial for Neuransa, a new therapy GGB developed to treat Parkinson's disease. Gordon Abernathy claims she had a fatal reaction to the drug."

Lars rolled his lips inward. "Maria, I can't talk about

Gordon Abernathy. I can't talk about the videos. I can't talk about his wife. I'm sorry."

Maria nodded. "What can you talk about?"

Bebe was surprised by Maria's question. It was a "softball" question, and softballs were easy to hit out of the park.

Lars tilted his head, and the new position emphasized the bags under his eyes. Since they had arrived in New York, they'd averaged three hours of sleep every night. They both looked like crap.

"I can talk about the four hundred and three employees GGB lost. We feel every one of those losses. We employ tens of thousands of people around the globe, and every one of those people is important to GGB. We feel the loss as an employer. We feel it as colleagues and friends. And we feel it as humans because losing even one person is a tragedy."

Bebe gave Lars a mental high-five. This interview was difficult for him, and he was doing a good job.

"I also want to tell you that this isn't something we're ever going to be able to forget. I think of GGB as a living, breathing organism, and these attacks wounded us. They didn't wound us fatally, but we're in pain, and we're going to feel it for a long time. These attacks are going to scar us. They're going to change the way we view ourselves and others. They've already changed us." Lars swallowed noisily. "We're never going to be the same company."

Maria was very obviously shocked by Lars's candor. "Lars, forgive me for saying so, but that doesn't give investors a lot of comfort."

Lars shrugged. "I'm not here to comfort investors. I'm here to tell them the truth. We have already relocated our corporate headquarters and R and D facility. We've revamped our security protocols so nothing like this will happen again. Our employees are doing their best to honor the people we lost by doing their jobs. We have six more manufacturing facilities spread across the globe, and plans are under way for them to pick up the slack from the two damaged facilities."

Lars took a deep breath. "That's the truth, but not the entire truth. The entire truth is that too many investors abandoned us, and now our stock is in the toilet. But we're still honoring our commitments to the investors we have. We are still making money. We still have people who come in to work every day to do their jobs. We are still producing drugs that save people's lives. We're still making lives better. We're doing what we're supposed to do."

Maria shook her head slowly. "What do you want to tell the financial community, Lars?"

Lars looked directly at the camera. "What are you thinking right now? Are you thinking, 'I'm glad I didn't lose money when GGB's stock tanked,' or are you thinking, 'I'm sorry so many people lost their lives when GGB was attacked'?"

"Lars, thank you for being here with us today."

"Thank you, Maria."

The cameraman gave them the green light that the segment was complete, and Lars rose from his chair. After shaking hands with Maria, he made his way to Bebe.

"Well? How did I do?"

She patted his shoulder. "Better than I thought you would."

He surprised her by hugging her to his side. "It was all because of you, Bebe. Those were your answers. I was just the mouthpiece." He sighed loudly. "Do you mind if we walk back to the hotel? I need some air."

"Fine with me."

When she and Lars had arrived in New York City, it had been much colder than she'd expected. She hadn't packed for such low temperatures, and she'd desperately needed a warm coat.

She'd mentioned it to Cal during a quick phone call, and early the next morning, the concierge had delivered a bright red Donna Karan coat, a pair of leather gloves, and a matching hat and scarf.

And Cal hadn't stopped there. Over the past three weeks, he'd sent her bouquets of flowers, baskets of fresh fruit and nuts, and bakery boxes full of cupcakes and brownies. He was doing his best to take care of her from nearly three thousand miles away, and she was grateful for his support.

Like everyone on GGB's executive team, she was reeling from the attacks, and nothing in her academic or professional career had prepared her to deal with a crisis of the magnitude that GGB had suffered.

When she thought about that terrible morning, she found it

both ironic and miraculous that her chat with Akash had saved her life. Her unwanted fiancé and his demands had kept her out of harm's way.

She hadn't had an opportunity to tell Cal about Akash, but she planned to come clean as soon as she got back to San Francisco. She knew it was going to be an awkward, difficult conversation, and it wasn't one she wanted to have when they were in different cities.

She had only managed to squeeze in a couple of video chats and a handful of phone calls with Cal because she had been so busy. Even finding time to send a text had been difficult. All their communication had been brief and consisted primarily of "How are you?" and "I miss you." Nonetheless, she thought about him constantly.

"What's on our schedule for this afternoon?" Lars asked as they shrugged on their cold-weather gear.

"We have three more media interviews, and tomorrow morning we have a breakfast meeting with the guys from Yale."

Prior to the attacks, several university endowment funds had been GGB investors. Yale was the only one that hadn't dumped its GGB stock.

They headed back toward their hotel at a measured pace even though the wind was blustery. New Yorkers hurried by them, their faces ducked against their chests.

"I'm ready to go home," Lars admitted as they turned onto the street where their hotel was located.

She nodded. "Me, too."

"I miss my wife," he confessed.

She smiled. "I'm sure she misses you, too, Lars."

"I don't think she misses me as much as Cal misses you."

Her cheeks heated, and she laughed self-consciously. "I definitely miss him."

It was a gross understatement to say Cal had been unhappy when she had flown to New York mere hours after the bombings. He hadn't said anything, but it was obvious he hadn't wanted to let her out of his sight. She hadn't wanted to go, either, but she had a responsibility to GGB. He not only understood that fact, but respected it, too.

He had wanted to come with her, but the big television commercial for Riley O'Brien & Co.'s new ad campaign had been scheduled to shoot. She had appreciated the thought, but even if he had been able to make the trip, it wouldn't have made any sense for him to come to New York.

If he had come along, she would only have seen him for a few waking minutes before she fell into bed. Even the weekends had been filled with investor meetings.

"We could go home tomorrow afternoon," Bebe suggested.

"I think that's a good idea. I don't think there's much else we can do."

"Unfortunately, I agree."

As she and Lars entered the lobby of their hotel, her gaze landed on a familiar handsome face. Akash sat on one of the gray damask sofas scattered near the entrance. The sight of him was such a surprise, she froze in the middle of the lobby. Lars turned to look at her, his eyebrows arched.

"Bebe?"

"I just saw someone I know," she replied, catching Akash's eyes across the lobby. "I'll meet you back here at two o'clock."

Nodding in agreement, Lars strode off to the elevators. She made her way toward Akash, and when she reached him, he rose to greet her. She hadn't seen him in more than a year, not since their engagement ceremony last January, and they hadn't video chatted since the day of the bombings.

Although most Indian men were small in stature, Akash easily topped six feet. Despite his height, he wasn't a large man, especially compared to Cal. Her fiancé didn't measure up to her boyfriend in any way, not just physically.

Akash was a dapper dresser, and today he wore a navy-blue Brioni suit with a sky-blue dress shirt and paisley-patterned tie. His dark hair was brushed away from his face, emphasizing his burnished skin and dark eyes.

Objectively, Bebe had no trouble seeing that her unwanted fiancé was a very attractive man. But he did absolutely nothing for her—unlike Cal, who could turn her on simply by smiling.

"Bindu, it's so lovely to see you. Have a seat," he invited, waving a hand toward one of the chairs in front of the sofa.

She ignored him. "What are you doing here, Akash?"

"I wanted to see my beloved fiancée."

"How did you know where I was?"

"That's a ridiculous question, Bindu. I always know where you are."

Akash's smile sent chills down her spine, and she abruptly realized that he scared her. Although she had always taken his threats seriously, she had never actively feared him. But she did now, and she wasn't sure what had changed.

"Why are you here?"

"My parents thought you could use my support during this difficult period. *Pitaa* and *Maataa* were so disappointed you weren't able to come to India as planned, and they suggested that I come to you."

She crossed her arms over her chest, stroking her fingers over the sleeve of the cashmere coat Cal had given her. Just the thought of him made her breathe easier.

"Are you happy to see me?" Akash asked silkily.

"No," she answered curtly. "I'm not happy to see you."

Without warning, his hand shot out, and he roughly grabbed her forearm. Pulling her over to one of the chairs, he shoved her into it.

"*I am a Mehra, and you will show me the respect I deserve,*" he snarled. "Now, I ask you again, are you happy to see me?"

As she stared up at Akash, she had an even greater appreciation for Cal. On paper, the two men had a lot in common. Both were from extremely prominent and powerful families. Both possessed unimaginable wealth, and both were intelligent, well-educated, and exceptionally good-looking.

But Akash and Cal were nothing—*nothing*—alike. Akash was an entitled, arrogant bully who lacked empathy. Cal was charming and funny, and he treated everyone with respect, regardless of their wealth or position in society.

Cal was an amazing, wonderful man, and she was in love with him. She had loved him for so long, but she had told herself it was a crush. Although she didn't really believe in love at first sight, she wondered if maybe she had fallen for him when they had first met.

She had been in love with him when she had lived in another city and pretended to hate him. She had been in love with him when she had turned him down and when they'd had sex for the first time.

She couldn't remember a time when she hadn't been in love with him. She hadn't wanted to admit it to herself, especially since she had never expected him to return her feelings.

But things were different now. They were a couple, and even though he hadn't said the words, his actions suggested that he loved her, too.

"When will your business here be finished?" Akash asked abruptly.

"I'm not sure," she prevaricated.

She didn't want to share her travel plans with him. She didn't want to share *anything* with him.

"I have one of the Mehra jets on standby." He returned to his position on the sofa. "When you are ready to leave, you will fly to Delhi with me instead of San Francisco."

She almost laughed at his ridiculous demand but managed to suppress it at the last moment. "That's impossible. This is the absolute worst time for GGB, and I am not going to shirk my professional responsibilities."

"You will come to Delhi with me, Bindu, and you will stay there. You will resign your position immediately, and we will ship your belongings to you. My father has grown suspicious of the authenticity of our relationship. He questions why you continue to live in the U.S. when your life should be in Delhi with me."

Akash leaned back, casually settling his arm along the back of the sofa and crossing his legs. "I wanted to wait until we could talk in person to discuss my expectations of you once we're married. My parents are eager for more grandchildren, and I want to begin trying for children as soon as possible."

Bebe worked hard to keep her face impassive. The thought of bearing Akash's children was so repugnant, she was sick to her stomach. There was only one man she wanted to have children with, and that man was Cal. She wanted sons and daughters who were just like him.

"It is my hope you'll get pregnant immediately," he added with a little moue of distaste.

All of a sudden, Bebe knew why Akash had been so willing to have an absent fiancée and an engagement of convenience. At last, she understood why he had no interest in finding another bride.

"You're gay," she stated with absolute certainty.

He smiled tightly. "Don't be ridiculous, Bindu. Homosexuality is illegal, according to the Supreme Court of India. And my parents would never condone criminal behavior."

Empathy welled within her. "I'm sorry," she apologized sincerely. "I'm sorry they cannot accept the person you are."

Uncrossing his legs, Akash scooted to the edge of the sofa until their faces were only inches apart. "It doesn't matter who I am or am not. The person I *will be* is your husband."

Chapter 30

TEAGAN'S OFFICE DOOR WAS OPEN, AND CAL POKED HIS HEAD around the door frame to see if his sister was there or if she had decided to move into the White House and take over the world. She was at her desk, talking into her headset, and when she saw him, she smiled and waved him inside. As he took a seat in one of the leather chairs in front of her desk, she wrapped up her call and pulled off the headset.

"I saw you booked a couple of hours on my schedule this afternoon," she said, tucking a tendril of wavy dark hair behind her ear. "What's up?"

"I want to get your opinion on the engagement ring I picked out for Bebe."

Her blue eyes widened. "Engagement ring?"

He nodded. "It's at the DeBeer's boutique in Union Square. I made an appointment for three p.m."

"You're going to ask Bebe to marry you?" she asked, the pitch of her voice falling somewhere between a squeal and a screech.

"That's usually what happens next after a man buys an engagement ring," he answered wryly.

A mischievous grin curved her mouth. "I thought it would

take you a few more months to find the guts to propose, since it took you four years to ask her out."

"It did *not* take me four years to ask her out."

"You're right. It was more like four and a half years."

He snorted, disgusted with himself. "I know. I was a pussy."

"Yeah, you were." She arched her dark eyebrows. "So how long did it take you to tell her that you loved her?"

Glancing down, he rubbed the back of his neck. To his shame, he still hadn't mustered the courage to say those three little words to Bebe. Other than his mother, Grandma Vi, and Teagan, he had said "I love you" to only one woman: Saika. Technically, he hadn't even said the words first.

He and Valerie had been watching TV while Saika cooked dinner. Valerie had snuggled up next to him and said, "I love you, Cal," in her sweet little girl voice, and he replied, "I love you, too, Ballerina."

When Valerie asked if he loved her mommy, too, he answered, "Yes." She shouted out to Saika: "Do you love Cal, Mommy?" Saika had looked at him for a long time from her position at the kitchen island before saying, "Yes, I love Cal."

Saika had loved him, but she hadn't been in love with him. And his feelings for Bebe were very different from what he'd felt for Saika.

"You've told Bebe you love her, right?" Teagan asked.

"No," he admitted.

She gasped. "*What is wrong with you?*"

"She hasn't told me she loves me, either," he responded defensively.

Her eyebrows shot up. "Are you waiting for her to say it first?"

He remembered a previous conversation with Quinn during which Cal had advised his older brother to "man up" and tell Amelia that he loved her. Cal needed to take his own advice. But he broke out in a cold sweat when he thought about all the ways Bebe could respond. She could destroy him with a handful of words—anything that wasn't "I love you, too."

"It takes a lot of balls to say 'I love you' when you're not sure if you'll hear it back," he pointed out.

Teagan frowned. "You're afraid to say 'I love you' but you're not afraid to ask her to marry you?"

"I'm thinking strategically. I'm going to tell her how I feel, and if she feels the same way, I'm going to propose. I figure there's a higher probability she'll say yes if she doesn't have time to think about it."

He had no idea how Bebe would respond to his proposal because they had never discussed marriage. He was taking a big risk, but he had wasted too much time already. He didn't want there to be any doubt that she belonged with him and he belonged with her.

He wasn't going to be okay with a long engagement, either. Maybe they could have a quickie wedding in Las Vegas.

Teagan eyed him thoughtfully. "You don't need to worry, Cal. Bebe is in love with you."

"Did she tell you that or are you making an assumption?"

She shook her head. "She didn't tell me, but it's obvious. I think she's loved you for a long time."

"I hope you're right because I've loved her for a long time, too. I think I've *always* loved her. It sounds horrible, but I loved her when I was with other women, even Saika," he confessed. "I would have married Saika even though a part of me wanted to be with Bebe. I just never thought I had a chance with her."

"I understand," Teagan replied emphatically. "I really do. I was in love with Nick, but I couldn't imagine he would want to be with me. I wanted to give myself a chance to be happy with someone else so I dated Marshall."

A long-forgotten memory tickled the back of Cal's mind. "When Quinn and I went to Miami for the Super Bowl, Quinn suggested that Priest check out Marshall to see if he was a decent guy, since we weren't there to do it. I didn't understand why Priest was so pissed off, but now I get it."

Her lips quirked. "Now you get it."

Pulling his phone from his hip pocket, he checked the time. "T, we need to get a move on."

Rising from her seat, she rounded her desk. She always dressed more businesslike than most Riley O'Brien & Co. employees, and today she had chosen a cropped black leather jacket, a pale pink silk shirt, a black skirt, and black leather boots.

He eyed the high-heeled boots, wondering how fast she could walk in them. Actually, they were so tall, he wondered how she could walk in them at all.

"Taxi?" he suggested.

She nodded gratefully, and they made their way out of Riley Plaza. Fortunately, a taxi had just dropped someone off right in front of the building, and they were able to nab it.

As they pulled away from the curb, Teagan said, "Did you hear that Quinn finally convinced Ava Grace to meet with Beck and the Trinity guys?"

"Really? When Quinn first mentioned it, she didn't seem that interested in Trinity."

"I don't think she's interested in Trinity at all."

"Then why . . ." She shot him a sideways glance, and he suddenly understood what she wasn't saying. "*Oh.* You think she's interested in Beck?"

Teagan shrugged. "I honestly can't think of any other reason why she'd agree to the meeting." She smiled slowly. "And Beck *is* finger-lickin' good."

"Finger-lickin' good?"

She snickered. "Well, he's from Kentucky. It makes sense."

Before they could further discuss Beck's finger-lickin' goodness or Ava Grace's motives for meeting with him, the taxi pulled up in front of the DeBeer's storefront. After paying the fare, Cal exited the taxi and helped Teagan out.

He ushered her toward the opaque glass building, which seemed almost translucent until you got close, and then the glass walls turned into mirrors. The DeBeer's boutique mimicked the building's exterior, and opaque glass panels were situated throughout the space.

He and Teagan stopped at the reception desk just inside the door, and he gave his name to the young blonde stationed there. Moments later, a short, rotund man hurried from a door near the back of the boutique. His speed, coupled with his dark suit and white dress shirt, made him look like a penguin skating across ice.

"Mr. O'Brien," he gushed, shaking Cal's hand. "I'm delighted to see you again."

"T, this is Branson Markham. He helped me pick out Bebe's ring. Branson, this is my sister, Teagan O'Brien-Priest. I brought her with me today because I wanted her opinion."

Branson extended his left hand to Teagan instead of his right. "Congratulations on your recent nuptials, Mrs. O'Brien-Priest."

After an awkward pause, Teagan offered her left hand,

and Branson took it in both of his. He immediately eyed her engagement ring and wedding band, turning her hand back and forth so the diamonds caught the light.

"Oh, my," he breathed. "What an exquisite example of vintage art deco design. Mr. Priest has excellent taste in jewelry." He looked up at Teagan. "And if I may be so presumptuous to say so, he also has excellent taste in women."

Cal chuckled when Teagan's face turned red. He happened to agree with Branson. His little sister was pretty damn fantastic, even if she did annoy the hell out of him at times.

"I have heard you possess one of the largest private collections of vintage jewelry in the country," Branson noted, stroking his fingers over the large round diamond in Teagan's engagement ring.

She nodded. "My grandmother, Violet O'Brien, left her collection to me when she died. We plan to showcase some of the pieces in her new museum."

Branson sighed blissfully, dropping Teagan's fingers and clasping his chubby hands beneath his double chin. "What a treat that will be!" He shifted his attention toward Cal. "Are you ready to see the ring, Mr. O'Brien?"

Cal nodded, eager to hear what Teagan would have to say about the ring he'd chosen for Bebe.

"Please follow me," Branson invited. "I've reserved a private viewing room."

They trailed after Branson as he weaved his way through several glass cases filled with sparkly, shiny jewelry. When they reached a door made of opaque glass, he placed his hand on a biometric security scanner to open it and gestured for them to precede him.

Branson shut the door and helped Teagan settle in the cream-colored leather chair next to Cal. A large glass-topped desk sat in front of them, and he took his place in the chair on the other side of the desk.

"As we discussed when you were here previously, once you make your final decision, we can have the ring sized and ready for pickup within forty-eight hours."

Opening a desk drawer, Branson removed a black leather ring case and placed it on top of the desk. He snapped open the small box and turned it so Cal and Teagan could see the ring within it.

Teagan gasped. "Oh, wow."

"Isn't it lovely?" Branson beamed. "As you know, yellow diamonds are the rarest and most precious of all diamonds. Mr. O'Brien expressed a desire for his future wife to have a unique, yet elegant engagement ring."

He took the ring from the case and handed it to Teagan. "The center stone is a four-carat fancy vivid yellow diamond. The fancy vivid is the darkest and rarest of all yellow diamonds."

Teagan evaluated the ring with the practiced eye of a jewelry connoisseur as Branson continued his description. "The center stone is a radiant square cut in a halo setting. It's surrounded by pavé-set white diamonds, and the platinum band features pavé-set white diamonds around the entire circumference. In total, there are nearly two carats of white diamonds in addition to the four-carat yellow diamond."

"What do you think?" Cal asked.

Teagan tossed him an amused glance. "I think you could send your first child to an Ivy League college for what this ring is worth."

He laughed. "Maybe so."

He extended his hand, palm out, and Teagan passed the ring to him. Holding it in front of his face, he looked it over. It was exactly what he had wanted for Bebe. She deserved a ring as special and unique as she was.

He nodded toward Branson. "Can you give us a minute?"

Branson hesitated, and Teagan laughed softly. "He's not asking to be left alone with the ring, Branson. He just wants to talk it over with me."

The jeweler exhaled noisily. "Very good," he said before replacing the ring in the case and exiting the room.

"Do you think Bebe will like it?" Cal asked Teagan.

She shifted slightly until she could look at him more directly. "Why did you choose a yellow diamond?"

"The color reminds me of her eyes."

Fancy vivid yellow diamonds reminded him of Bebe's eyes when he touched her. When she was turned on, her eyes glowed with a million different shades of gold and amber.

Teagan nodded. "If you hadn't brought me along, I wouldn't have understood what you meant, but I totally get it."

"If you think she would like another kind of stone better, we can ask Branson to show us something else."

"No, I think the yellow diamond is gorgeous. But the ring is *really* big. Bebe's hands are small, and it might overwhelm them."

"That's a good point. I hadn't thought about that."

"I'm not surprised," she scoffed. "You were thinking the bigger the ring, the more obvious it would be she was taken."

"Not really. I just wanted her to have a ring that would show her how much I love her."

Once he said it out loud, he realized how stupid it sounded. The idea that a ring would be able to convey the depth of his feelings for Bebe was laughable.

Quinn and Priest had warned him that one day he would be just as pathetic and pussy-whipped as they were, and they had been right. In fact, he wondered if maybe he was more pathetic, especially given how cranky he had been over the past three weeks while Bebe was in New York City.

"Trust me, women with smaller rings don't feel like their husbands love them less than women who have gaudy rings," she replied dryly.

He laughed. "How the hell would you know? Priest bought you a huge-ass diamond. Astronauts can probably see it from space."

She giggled. "He spoils me."

"Yeah, he does. But you deserve to be spoiled, T. And so does Bebe."

She nodded. "I agree. Get the ring, Cal. She's going to love it. Probably not as much as she loves you, but close."

Chapter 31

ACCORDING TO THE MONITORS HANGING IN THE BAGGAGE claim, Bebe's plane had landed, so she should walk through the revolving doors any moment. Cal's heart pounded with excitement and relief that she was almost within touching distance. He never again wanted to be away from her for such a long period of time.

His height made it easy for him to see through the crowd, but Bebe's petite frame made it difficult for him to spot her. A bunch of people flooded the baggage claim, and he scanned the crowd.

Finally, he found her near the back, and he barely controlled the urge to shoulder through the throngs of people like a linebacker to reach her. He waited until the crowd thinned out before making his way toward her.

When she saw him, she smiled one of those gorgeous smiles that always took his breath away, and she picked up her pace until she was nearly running. He opened his arms, and she threw herself at him, wrapping her arms tightly around his neck and hitting him in the back with her big leather bag.

He scooped her against him, letting her feet dangle in the air, and tucked his face into her hair. Her scent wrapped around him, and all the tension that had built within him over the past three weeks melted away.

He was so damn grateful she was home. He had been fucking miserable without her.

She leaned back a little, and he stared into her gorgeous face. If he was lucky, he would be able to see it every day for the rest of his life. The only thing he wanted more was to see her features in the faces of their children.

"Hi," she said softly.

"Nice to see you again, Cookie."

Her lips quirked in a small smile. "Aren't you going to kiss me hello?"

"If I start, I don't think I'll be able to stop."

Her smile widened. "I think it's worth the risk."

Dropping his head, he captured her mouth with his. He tried to keep things G-rated, but her lips were so smooth, he couldn't resist a small lick. And that small lick gave him a taste of her, and then he couldn't resist dipping his tongue inside her mouth.

Someone knocked into him, and he reluctantly raised his head. She licked her lips, and he let her slide down his body until her feet touched the ground.

A silky black-and-white dress clung to her curves, and he could feel her warm body under it. His cock twitched, and he wished they were already home so he could flip up her dress and slide into her where he belonged.

"I missed your kisses," she admitted softly.

"I missed your kisses, too."

He had missed more than her kisses. He had missed everything about her. He had missed *her*.

She tilted her head toward the baggage carousel. "I see my bags."

On the next revolution of the carousel, he grabbed her two red suitcases and deposited them on the ground near her feet. For the first time, he noticed her shiny black leather knee boots. With their skinny heel, they looked remarkably like the ones in his favorite fantasy.

"I like your boots."

She smiled. "I thought you might. I bought them with you in mind."

He shook his head in exasperation. She was going to give him a heart attack, he was sure of it. The only question was when.

"I had to park Belva on the fourth level of the parking garage, way in the back. Wait here, and I'll go get her."

Bebe shook her head, her glossy hair swinging into her eyes. "I'll walk with you," she replied as she brushed her dark bangs out of her face. "I need to stretch my legs after the long flight."

"I can help you stretch your legs when we get home," he suggested, widening his eyes to look as innocent as possible.

She laughed lightly. "You're so helpful."

"Maybe I can help you stretch other parts of your body, too," he added with a wink.

He chuckled when her cheeks turned red. He had missed teasing her almost as much as he had missed making love to her.

He pulled up the telescoping handles on her suitcases, and Bebe dropped her leather bag on top of one of them. "Are you sure you've got both of them?" she asked as he looped the straps of her bag over the handle.

"Are you questioning my manliness?" he asked with mock affront.

"What if I am? Would you feel compelled to prove it to me?"

"Yes. I would feel compelled to prove it to you all night long."

"In that case, I am definitely questioning your manliness," she answered with an emphatic nod.

He laughed and grabbed both suitcases, pulling them behind him as they made the trek to the parking garage. It was nearly one o'clock in the morning, and the tunnel was almost empty, since Bebe's flight had been the last one to arrive.

They took the elevator to the fourth floor of the parking garage, where only a few cars were still parked. When he had driven in, it had been completely full.

"This place emptied out in a hurry," he noted.

Bebe didn't reply, although she glanced around the parking garage as they headed toward Belva. Her boots made sharp clicks on the pavement with every step, and his senses were so overloaded by her proximity, the sounds echoed throughout his body.

They reached Belva, and he unlocked the trunk before stowing her bags in it. Bebe stood beside the passenger door, and he grimaced at his lack of manners. He quickly slammed the trunk closed and unlocked her door.

Before he could open it, she leaned back against it and looked up at him. Although the lighting wasn't all that great, her eyes glimmered brightly within the shadows.

"You have no idea how much I missed you, *pahale*."

If she had missed him even a fraction of how much he had missed her, she had barely been able to get through the day. Either he'd walked around in a daze of misery or he'd been a short-tempered asshole whom everyone went out of their way to avoid.

"You can show me how much you missed me when we get home."

"Okay," she agreed, hooking her fingers into the waistband of his jeans to tug him closer. "But I need another kiss to tide me over."

She puckered her lips, and he obligingly dropped a brief kiss on her mouth. He wasn't going to let himself get distracted in a poorly lit parking structure and end up carjacked or worse. He wasn't concerned about himself, but he had Bebe to think about now.

She frowned when he drew back. "I want a real kiss."

"That was a real kiss."

"It wasn't."

"I'm pretty sure we've had this conversation before," he noted with amusement before nodding toward his car. "Get a move on, Cookie. The faster you get into Belva, the faster I can get into you."

She made a funny noise, kind of a half laugh, half gasp, and shifted slightly so he could pull open the door. The sound of a car engine drew his attention, and he glanced toward the noise as a compact SUV made the turn to head to the lower levels.

By the time he brought his gaze back to Bebe, she had already climbed into Belva . . . or had she? She no longer stood in front of him, but the front seat was empty. Sticking his head into the car, he found her in the spacious backseat, her face lit by the dome light.

"What are you doing?" he asked.

She crossed her legs, the leather of her boots making a

squeaky noise as they rubbed together. The edges of her dress split, baring her smooth thighs and the dark hair of her pussy.

Holy fuck. She's not wearing any panties.

"Get in and lock the door."

CAL HESITATED, AND BEBE WONDERED IF HE WOULD DO AS she'd asked. Finally, he grabbed the door handle and slid into the backseat, pulling the door shut behind him and plunging the interior of the car into darkness. He pushed down the lock before lounging beside her against the dark blue cushion.

She immediately climbed over him, pulling up her dress and straddling his lap. The material of his jeans was rough against the insides of her thighs, and she squirmed a little to get more comfortable.

"Did you fly across the country without panties?" he asked, lightly gripping her hips.

It was too dark for her to see his face clearly, but she heard the amusement in his voice.

"Of course not. I took them off in the airport bathroom before I met you in the baggage claim."

"From a legal perspective, that would be considered premeditation."

"Don't worry," she assured him with a laugh, "I'm not planning to murder you."

"What *are* you planning to do?"

"What do you want me to do?"

He was long and hard between her legs, and she rocked against him. He dug his fingers into her hips, pressing her tightly to him.

"Me," he answered hoarsely. "I want you to do me."

Leaning forward until her mouth brushed his, she licked the inside of his top lip before sucking on the lower. She dipped her tongue inside his mouth, and he gave a long moan.

"How do you want me to do you?"

She nuzzled the underside of his chin before trailing her mouth toward his throat. He tilted his head to give her better access, and she tugged open the snaps on his long-sleeved plaid shirt as she nibbled the corded muscles where his neck met his shoulder.

Taking a deep breath, she filled her lungs with Cal's mouthwatering scent. She had missed his smell, his taste, the feel of him inside her, the rough sounds he made when he came.

"Fast. Slow. Hard. Easy. I don't care," he murmured. "Just do it now. I need you."

"I need you, too. I thought about this the whole flight."

She had missed him so much while she had been gone. She had been in one of the most exciting, populated cities in the world, but she had been lonely and bored without him . . . not to mention sexually frustrated.

"My panties were soaked when I took them off," she added.

He groaned. "Let me feel how wet you are."

Bunching her dress in his hand, he wedged his forearm between them. She rose up on her knees so he could touch her, moaning when his fingers eased between the lips of her sex. He swirled them around her clit before moving toward the entrance of her body.

Pushing two fingers inside her, he stroked deeply, grazing a sensitive spot. Her vaginal muscles rippled, and she gasped as pleasure sparked through her.

"You've got the hottest, wettest pussy I've ever felt." He took a big breath, his broad chest moving against hers. "I can smell you. You are so fucking delicious." He pushed his fingers deeper. "*Fuck*. I wish I could taste you. When we get home, I'm going to shove my face in your pussy until your juice fills my mouth. Then I'm going to suck on your clit until you're screaming my name."

His words turned her on as much as they embarrassed her, and she tucked her face into his neck. Pulling his fingers from her body, he shifted under her, fumbling with his belt. She leaned back on his knees to give him room. His belt buckle made a hollow clink, followed by the rasp of his zipper and a rustle of clothing.

"Are you ready for my cock?"

She was more than ready. "Yes. Please. Give it to me."

Cupping her hips in his large hands, he raised her over his thick penis, placing the plump head at the entrance to her body. He tilted his pelvis as he pressed her down on him, and even though she was wet, her flesh resisted his intrusion for a heartbeat.

He nudged into her with tiny pumps until he filled her completely. They'd had sex in this position on his sofa, but he had never felt so big . . . never felt so thick and hard.

She widened her legs to settle more fully against him, and he slid deeper. He groaned loudly, the sound echoing throughout the dark interior of the car.

"*Goddamn,*" he gasped, "how can you still be so tight when I've had you so many times?"

She couldn't answer him. The scalding pressure of his huge cock had stolen her voice. She wanted to stay like this forever, her internal muscles stretched tightly around him.

"Slow and easy," he breathed into her hair, his voice barely audible.

Bracing her hands against his shoulders, she rose over him so slowly, she felt every ridge and vein of his cock as it slid out of her. She stopped with just the tip of him inside and oh-so-slowly sank down on his length.

He hissed as her flesh sucked him in, the sound creating goose bumps all over her body. Shifting forward, she forced him so deep she could feel his heartbeat inside her. It was fast and strong, and her heartbeat joined the rhythm of his. She had never felt so connected to anyone, and she wondered if he felt the same way.

"*Pahale,* was it like this with other women?"

"No, baby. It was nothing like this. It's different with you."

She slowly rose again, suspended over the tip of his thick penis. "Is it better?"

He exhaled loudly as she started the sweet, slow slide back down. "Yes," he gasped, raising his hips to meet her. "It's better. It's fucking mind-blowing."

"Why? Why is it different?"

"Don't you know why?"

She hoped it was different because he loved her, but she lacked the experience to know for sure. "You're the only one I've been with," she reminded him, doing a little shimmy and widening her legs so he could go as deep as possible.

"I know." He moaned, his fingers clenching on her hips. "I love being the only one who's been inside you. I love being the only one who knows how delicious you taste and the sweet little sounds you make when you're about to come."

She never wanted to be with another man. She never wanted to let another man into her body and into her heart.

She wanted to tell him how much she loved him, but she forced the words down deep, and not just because she was afraid of what he would say in response. She couldn't tell him today that she loved him and then blindside him tomorrow with the knowledge that she was engaged.

She needed to stick to her plan. She would ask him to come by her loft tomorrow after work. She would tell him about Akash, explain the situation from the very beginning, and then she would tell him that she had fallen in love with him.

She rose again, letting his hard length drag heavily against her slippery folds. Circling her hips, she let the plump head of his penis stroke her clit. Her orgasm was close, and she wanted to make this last as long as she could. She tightened her vaginal muscles to ease the tension thrumming through her.

The air in the car was humid and heavy, and every breath she took was perfumed with their arousal. She could almost taste it.

She lowered herself at an excruciatingly slow pace, her body welcoming him little by little. Under her, he panted harshly, his breath coming in burning gusts against her throat.

"Does this feel good?"

"*Fuck, yeah,*" he breathed.

"Are you close?" she asked breathlessly.

"Yes. I can't last much longer."

"I need you to touch me."

He knew exactly what she needed, delving between her legs to find her clit and rubbing the hard nub with just the right amount of pressure. Tingles radiated from her core until her entire body felt like it vibrated.

She rocked on him as his fingers worked her clit. The tingles turned into fire, and she was too far gone to ask if he was there with her. Her orgasm blasted through her, and she screamed his name as she clenched around his cock, milking him hard. He stiffened and made a deep growling sound in his throat as his cock throbbed inside her.

Collapsing against him, she tucked her head against his shoulder. He pulled his hand from between them and clasped her tightly within his arms.

"You're mine," he stated huskily. "All mine."

Chapter 32

CAL'S PHONE VIBRATED AS HE ENTERED BEBE'S LOFT BUILDING, alerting him to a new text message. He reached into his pocket to grab it, and his fingers brushed against the leather jewelry case that held Bebe's engagement ring.

He had left work early so he could stop by DeBeer's and pick up the ring. He was going to ask her to marry him tonight. He didn't want to wait until he could plan something grand and romantic. He loved her and wanted to spend his life with her, and he wanted her to know it.

It wasn't smart to walk around with six carats' worth of diamonds in his jeans, but she had asked him to meet her at her loft after work. She had said she wanted to talk with him about something important.

Things between them were good, so he wasn't worried she wanted to end their relationship. There was a tiny possibility she would tell him that she was pregnant. She had missed a pill several weeks ago because she had left her pill pack at her loft.

She had assured him it wasn't a big deal because she had taken it the next morning, but maybe one of his swimmers had hit the jackpot. Because she had been in New York, he didn't know if she'd missed a period or not.

The thought of Bebe being pregnant sent a tingle of pleasure through him. He wanted to have children with her, and imagining her slender body round and heavy with his baby actually turned him on.

His phone vibrated again, reminding him of the text, and he stopped in the lobby to read it. The message was from Bebe. She didn't believe in texting shorthand, and her texts were always complete sentences and grammatically correct.

> Lars pulled me into a meeting. I'm going to be 45 minutes late. I'm sorry!

It would probably be closer to an hour if Lars was involved. That gave Cal plenty of time to walk to the nearby Whole Foods and grab some ingredients to make dinner. Maybe fish tacos or beef stir-fry.

He quickly responded to her text. Not a problem. I'll make dinner.

She immediately replied. I'll make sure to thank you properly.

He laughed under his breath. He always enjoyed her thank-yous.

As he turned toward the door, he noticed a commotion at the concierge desk. A tall, dark-haired man loomed over Javier, gesturing wildly. The man's voice was raised in anger, and the concierge's face was etched with a combination of misery and fear.

Cal debated whether he should stick his nose where it didn't belong. He wasn't a fan of bullies, and it was obvious Javier was dealing with one. He slowly made his way over to the concierge desk, and he was only a couple of steps away when he heard Bebe's name.

"I'm sorry, sir, but you are not on Ms. Banerjee's approved visitor list," Javier said in a placating tone. "I cannot allow you entrance to the building without her approval, and she is not answering my call."

"Is there a problem, Javier?" Cal asked.

Javier's head snapped toward him, and he sighed in relief. "Oh, Mr. O'Brien, thank goodness. Maybe you can help. This gentleman is here to see Ms. Banerjee, but he's not on the list, and I cannot reach her."

Cal glanced toward the so-called gentleman, taking in his designer suit, bronze skin, and glossy dark hair. The man looked Indian, and Cal assumed he was one of Bebe's relatives.

The man turned to face Cal, and strangely, he experienced an immediate surge of dislike. He rarely had such a negative visceral reaction to someone. Nonetheless, he held out his right hand.

"I'm Cal O'Brien."

The man scowled and ignored Cal's hand. "Unless you can show me to Bindu's residence, I have no interest in exchanging introductions," he said in an upper-crust British accent.

Cal arched his eyebrows. *What a dickhead.*

"I might be able to help if you tell me who you are," he replied in a friendly tone. He didn't want to make enemies of his future wife's relatives, even if they were assholes.

"I am Akash Mehra," the man announced.

Cal cocked his head. He had heard of the Mehra family. Hell, everyone had heard of the Mehras, but he hadn't known Bebe had ties to one of the most powerful families in the world.

"Are you related to Bebe?"

"Bindu is my fiancée."

What?

He was sure he must not have heard Akash correctly. There was no way Bebe was engaged to this guy.

"Are we talking about the same woman?" he asked.

Akash rolled his eyes and turned back to Javier. "Is there anyone in this building who isn't an idiot? A supervisor perhaps? I am tired of waiting. I wish to see my fiancée immediately."

Cal grabbed Akash's forearm. "You're not talking about Bebe Banerjee?"

Akash looked down at Cal's hand. "Remove your hand from my person. *Now.*"

He ignored him. "Are you talking about Bebe Banerjee?"

Akash shook off his hand. "Her name is Bindu," he sneered, his lips curling with distaste. "Bebe sounds like a stripper, and I refuse to refer to my future wife by such a moniker."

Cal's heart thumped heavily. "Future wife?" he repeated faintly.

Akash's dark eyes narrowed. "Yes. We plan to marry

later this year. We have been engaged since she was in medical school. My parents and I made the trip from Delhi to visit with her. We are here to finalize the wedding plans."

All the blood rushed from Cal's head, and black spots danced in his vision. Bebe was engaged. She had been engaged for *years.*

All this time, she had belonged to another man. She never had been his. He had fucked another man's woman, something he had sworn never to do. Even worse, he had fallen in love with another man's woman.

Akash smiled suddenly. "Ah, I understand. You are Bindu's fling."

Fling? What the fuck?

"What did you say?"

"You are Bindu's last fling before we take our vows. We agreed to give each other a . . ." Akash waved his hand. "I forget the term. Free pass? Is that right?"

Cal's body flashed hot and cold. Nausea churned in his stomach, and he thought he might throw up on Akash's expensive dress shoes. He swallowed thickly, trying to ignore the pressure in his throat.

Was he just a fling? He suddenly remembered Bebe's condition that their arrangement last no longer than twelve months.

A fucking expiration date because she's getting married.

"When I saw her in New York, we discussed you," Akash said.

The knowledge that Akash had seen Bebe in New York almost sent Cal to his knees. While he had been here, miserable without her, she had been with her fiancé.

Had she fucked Akash? Had she been fucking Akash the whole time she and Cal were together? A tsunami of rage crashed over him, and he struggled to focus on the other man's words.

"She planned to end the affair," Akash continued. "Since you are here, it appears she has yet to do so."

Bebe must have asked him to come to her loft so she could tell him about her pending nuptials. He had planned to propose to her, and she had planned to kick him to the curb.

"Mr. O'Brien, what should I do?" Javier asked, looking back and forth between Cal and Akash.

Cal shook his head, unable to speak. Turning on his heel,

he headed toward the door. His phone vibrated in his pocket as he exited the building, and he automatically reached for it. Instead of finding his phone, his fingers clutched the box that held the ring he had picked out for Bebe.

An engagement ring he had bought for a woman who was already engaged.

BEBE HURRIED INTO HER BUILDING AND DARTED TOWARD THE elevators. Even though she had managed to wrap up the meeting with Lars faster than she had expected, she hated to keep Cal waiting. He never got impatient with her or resented the time she had to devote to her job, but she didn't want him to think she didn't value him or his time.

"Ms. Banerjee," Javier called out. "Ms. Banerjee."

His footsteps pounded behind her, and she stopped reluctantly. Mustering a smile for the friendly concierge, she turned to face him.

"You have a visitor," he announced breathlessly, pointing toward the sofas grouped in an alcove behind the concierge desk.

She frowned. She couldn't see anyone in the seating area.

"A visitor?"

"Mr. Akash Mehra. Your fiancé. He's not on the list, so I couldn't allow him to wait upstairs. Mr. O'Brien was here, too, and I asked him what to do, but he didn't know."

Oh, my God.

She grabbed Javier's hand. "Did Akash introduce himself to Cal as my fiancé?"

Javier nodded. "Mr. O'Brien was pretty surprised to hear you had a fiancé."

Oh, no.

"It's none of my business, Ms. Banerjee, but I feel compelled to let you know that Mr. O'Brien is a much nicer man than your fiancé."

A much nicer man?

Hysterical laughter flew out of her. Akash and Cal lived on different planets when it came to being nice.

"Where's Cal?" she asked desperately. "Did he go up to my loft?"

Javier shook his head. "No. He left."

"How long ago?"

"Maybe ten minutes."

Pulling her phone from her suit jacket, she popped open the text screen and frantically typed a message to Cal. Where are you? I can explain. It's not what you think.

She hit Send, praying he would reply. She had no idea if he would give her a chance to explain.

She slipped the phone back into her pocket and turned to Javier. "You did the right thing. Mr. Mehra is not welcome here. Please stay close in case I need you to call the police."

Javier's eyes widened. "Of course, Ms. Banerjee."

She made her way to the seating area, and even though Akash saw her coming, he didn't bother to rise from the sofa. She stopped in front of him, and he met her gaze.

"You seem surprised to see me, Bindu," he noted with a smirk. "Why is that? I thought I made it clear that if you didn't come to Delhi, my parents and I would come to you."

"Your parents are here, too?"

He nodded. "We are staying at the Fairmont in the penthouse suite. I have a car waiting outside to take us there."

"And if I go with you and visit with your parents, you'll leave me alone for the next six months?"

He shook his head. "I expect you to move to Delhi as soon as possible."

"Akash, you gave me twelve months to pay back the money you loaned me, and it has only been six months. I have six months left."

Akash frowned. "I do not care if it's only been six months, Bindu. I do not care about the money. You will marry me as soon as you move to Delhi."

She had suspected for a long time that Akash had no intention of honoring their agreement. He would never let her go, not even if she handed him a suitcase full of gold bars. There was no reason to fight him because she would never win. There was no hope of swaying him from the course he had set so many years ago.

"And if I don't marry you?"

"You know what will happen. More than two hundred members of your family will be homeless or jobless or both."

"Does it matter to you that I'm in love with someone else?"

"Are you referring to Cal O'Brien? He certainly is an

impressive male specimen. However did you manage to attract such a man?"

She ignored his insult. "What did you tell him?"

"I told him the truth," he answered with a mocking smile.

She took a deep breath, trying to calm the furious beat of her heart. "What did you tell him?"

He shrugged nonchalantly. "That is not important." He uncrossed his legs and stood. "My parents are waiting."

Akash ran his gaze over her. He grimaced, shaking his head in disgust.

"You need to change. It is my preference for you to wear a *sari* when you see them."

"I'll change and meet you at the hotel," she agreed.

"I will wait in your residence, just in case you need assistance, of course." He laughed sharply. "It has nothing to do with the fact that I don't trust you."

Chapter 33

CAL SHRUGGED OUT OF HIS LEATHER JACKET AND HUNG IT ON the vintage wall-mounted coat rack in his foyer. His mom had found the coat rack at a flea market, and she had given it to him as a housewarming present. Every time he hung up a jacket, he said a little prayer of thanks he was blessed with such a wonderful mother.

He toed off his tennis shoes before slowly making his way into the kitchen and grabbing a bottle of water out of the fridge. Taking a big gulp, he let the cold liquid wash away the bitterness that filled his mouth from the three beers he'd consumed earlier in the evening. Too bad it couldn't wash away the bitterness that filled the rest of him.

It was after eleven o'clock, and he was exhausted. After he had left Bebe's building, he'd turned off his phone and driven to a lighted driving range, where he'd hit golf balls for nearly four hours.

The monotonous action of teeing up a ball and swinging a club had taken his mind off Bebe, but now that he was home, all the hurt he had managed to push down earlier flooded him. His chest ached when he thought about her marrying Akash Mehra, bearing his children, and growing old with him.

After emptying the water bottle, Cal tossed it into the

recycle bin and turned off the kitchen light before heading to his bedroom. As he closed the door with a loud snick, he heard a rustle across the room.

One of the bedside lamps flared to life, and he blinked as Bebe sat up in his bed. The covers fell to her lap, revealing a long-sleeved USC T-shirt. More often than not, she slept in his old college gear. She said it was softer and more comfortable than any pajamas.

"Why are you in my bed?" he asked rudely, leaning against the door and crossing his arms over his chest. "Why aren't you with your fiancé?"

"Please give me a chance to explain," she implored, pushing her dark hair out of her face. "It's not what you think."

He laughed, the sound bitter rather than amused. "You have no idea what I think."

"I don't know what Akash told you—"

"He told me you're engaged . . . that you've been engaged for *ten fucking years*. Was he lying?"

He prayed Akash had lied, but when she looked down without answering, he knew the other man had told the truth.

"You've been engaged the *entire* time I've known you. You've been engaged the *entire* time I was fucking you." He pointed at her. "Were you fucking him while you were fucking me?"

She threw back the covers, springing from the bed and stalking toward him. "You *jackass!*" she swore loudly, slapping the palm of her hand in the middle of his chest. "You're the only man I've ever been with, and you know it. *You know it!*"

He gripped her upper arms and lifted her until her face was even with his. He had never been so angry. His blood scalded his veins, and he was surprised his hair wasn't on fire. She was the only person who made him feel so much, and in this moment, he hated her for it.

"You've been lying to me the entire time we've been together," he shot back, breathing hard. "I never would have touched you if I had known you belonged to another man!"

"I have *never* belonged to Akash!" She kicked him just above his left knee. "I belong to *you*. I never even kissed him. You're the only man who has touched me." She sucked in a huge breath. "You know you're my first everything, you *jerk!*"

"Not your first fiancé," he growled.

She leaned forward until her nose touched his. "I never wanted to marry Akash. It was arranged by my parents. I've been trying to get out of it."

He tried to feed his anger by reminding himself that she had lied to him. But those words—*I never wanted to marry Akash*—doused the wildfire raging inside him, leaving behind only a few smoldering embers.

"He was blackmailing me," she added.

"What?"

She squirmed. "Put me down."

Loosening his fingers, he let her drop to the floor. She looked up at him, her eyes burning with tiny golden flames.

"You gave me my first kiss. You gave me my first orgasm, and I *gave* my virginity to *you*. I've been engaged to Akash since I was twenty years old, and he *never* touched me. I never wanted him to, not even once. The first time you shook my hand, I wanted you to touch me all over. It was the first time I felt sexual attraction. The first time I wanted a man. *You* are my first everything, Cal. Everything that matters."

As her words wrapped around his heart and squeezed, he abruptly realized this tiny woman had a hold on him that was absolute and immutable. He would forgive her for anything—*anything*—as long as she wanted him.

He stared down into her eyes. "He said I was your last fling before you got married." He swallowed thickly, remembering the agony he had experienced as Akash's words had cut into him. "He said you agreed to give each other a free pass. He said the two of you talked about me when you were in New York."

She gasped. "*Oh, my God.* That's not true." She clenched his hand. "Cal, that is not true. He was lying. He didn't know anything about you."

"So you didn't see him in New York?"

She dropped his hand. "I saw him," she answered flatly. "He threatened me and demanded that I fly to Delhi with him instead of coming home."

She turned and climbed back onto the bed, arranging the

pillows behind her so she could lean against the headboard. Tucking her knees up to her chest, she pulled the long shirt over her legs.

"I was going to tell you about Akash. That's why I asked you to come over to my loft tonight. I didn't want to have the conversation here. I was worried you would react badly, and I wanted you to be able to walk out if you wanted to."

"React badly? Now why would I do that?"

"You're making jokes?" she asked incredulously.

"It's either that or slam my fist into the wall," he replied, utterly serious. "What were you going to tell me about Akash?"

"Everything. I was going to tell you everything."

"Do it now."

"When I was in my second year of medical school, my mother called me out of the blue. I hadn't heard from her in months. She said a family friend wanted a wife for her youngest son. She and my father had talked it over, and they thought it would be a good match because the son was from a good family and well-educated. I didn't even know his name until we flew to India to meet him and his parents."

He perched on the edge of the bed. "What happened when you and Akash met for the first time?"

"It was dislike at first sight." She laughed sadly. "It was the total opposite of how I felt when I met you."

"Why did you agree to marry him?"

"All my life, I wanted my parents to love me the way they loved my brothers. That's why I accepted the marriage."

A wave of sympathy washed over him. He knew how horrible her parents were, and he understood why she had agreed to an arranged marriage, hoping to gain their approval.

"Oh, Cookie," he murmured, "you know it doesn't work that way."

"I know. It was stupid and pathetic. But I was so desperate for their love." She dropped her head to her knees. "It took me a while to realize they would never love me. I had an epiphany when my mother told me that she and my father weren't going to attend my graduation ceremony from Johns Hopkins. I had gone to medical school for them, and I didn't even want to be a doctor. That's why I turned down my residency." She pulled the covers over her legs. "My parents were furious, especially my mother."

He slouched against the footboard, swinging his legs up onto the bed. His sock-covered feet brushed against Bebe's legs, and she covered one with her hand, caressing it lightly. That small touch soothed him enough that his tight muscles finally began to relax.

"When I realized there was nothing I could do to make my parents love me, I called Akash and told him that I wanted to break off our engagement. He was upset."

"Why was he upset? I thought he disliked you."

"He did dislike me," she stated emphatically. "But he *liked* the convenience of having a fiancée who was seven thousand miles away. He could live his life without his parents bothering him about getting married. He was so determined that our engagement continue, he offered to pay for Harvard."

He studied her for a moment. "You took his money?"

His disapproval must have been obvious because she frowned. "Yes, I took it. Are you worried I'm interested in your big bank account?" she asked snidely.

Her sarcasm pissed him off. He wasn't the one who had kept secrets.

"No. That thought never crossed my mind. In fact, I'm sure you're a lot more interested in my big dick." Her eyes narrowed, but before she could skewer him, he continued. "I'm surprised you were willing to sacrifice yourself for a Harvard education."

"I didn't sacrifice myself. Akash swore he didn't want to marry me. He just wanted to be engaged to keep his parents happy. I needed the money for school, so I agreed. He gave me nearly six hundred thousand dollars. He never asked me to visit, and we talked for five minutes every month so he could report back to his parents that we had spoken recently."

He nodded. "That actually sounds like a sweet deal. I probably would have taken him up on it."

"It *was* a sweet deal until his parents started to get impatient with our long engagement. Akash was convinced they would leave him alone if we had an engagement ceremony. Engagement ceremonies in India are sacred. They're almost like weddings here."

He frowned. He didn't like the sound of that.

"He begged me to come to India for the ceremony, and I felt obligated to help him. I felt like I owed him for Harvard."

She cleared her throat. "I flew to India last January, and I spent three weeks pretending to be his adoring fiancée. It was horrible. I hated lying to everyone, but Akash was so relieved, and his parents were so happy."

"What a fucking mess," he muttered harshly.

She flinched a little. "Six months ago during our monthly video chat, Akash told me that his parents were pressuring him to set a wedding date. The engagement ceremony had made them more eager for him to marry. He said we had to get married."

"Why didn't he just find another woman? Are you really that special?" He didn't realize how insulting his question was until the blood drained from her face. "Bebe, I didn't mean it like that. I just—"

"It's fine, Cal, just forget it," she said flatly, waving her hand. "His father made it clear he couldn't take over Mehra's real estate holdings unless he married *me*. I didn't know that, and when he told me that we had to marry, I refused. At that point, he demanded that I repay the money he had given me. I would have given him the money if I'd had it, but I didn't. When I pointed out he couldn't force me to marry him or repay the money, since it was a gift instead of a loan, he threatened my family."

"How did he threaten them?"

"You have no idea how powerful and wealthy the Mehras are. They can do anything they want. More than two hundred members of my extended family work for Mehra or live in Mehra buildings. Akash threatened to fire them or kick them out of their homes."

"What an asshole."

"I knew he would do it. He's ruthless."

He had been in Akash's presence for less than ten minutes, and he had no doubt the man would have followed through with his threats.

"I negotiated a deal with him," she continued. "He agreed to give me twelve months to repay the money he gave me plus interest. If I didn't repay it, I had to marry him."

Tears welled in her golden eyes. "I didn't know what else to do. I needed time to find a solution. I needed time to do all the things I had never done. There was a chance I would be forced to marry him, and I didn't want him to get my firsts. That was the morning I went to Teagan's office—the morning you eavesdropped."

"*Goddamnit, Bebe.* You could have asked T for the money. You could have asked me for it."

She shook her head. "Think about it, Cal. Would you ask your best friend for six hundred thousand dollars? How would you have reacted if I had asked you for that much money? In the back of your mind, you would have wondered why I suddenly wanted to be with you. You would have wondered why I suddenly wanted to have sex with you."

He considered her questions for a moment before rolling his shoulders. He hated to admit that she might be right.

"My best friend is my brother, and I honestly don't know if I would have asked him for the money. And I don't know how I would have reacted if you had asked me for the money."

She smiled sadly. "Exactly."

"I'll give you the money. I'm offering. You're not asking."

She stared at him for a long time, and panic welled in his chest. He would do anything to keep her with him, even if it meant giving Akash Mehra every single penny he had.

"You are *not* going to marry him."

BEBE STROKED CAL'S FOOT, THE ONLY PART OF HIM SHE COULD reach. She was so grateful he had given her a chance to explain. She hadn't been sure if he would listen or if he would forgive her, but she could tell he wasn't angry any longer.

"Cookie, I won't let Akash hurt your family," Cal promised. "I'll talk to him."

"Akash doesn't listen to anyone but his parents."

"He'll listen to me."

The tone of Cal's voice, coupled with his ferocious scowl, made it clear that his idea of *talking* to Akash would involve fists rather than words. Maybe she should be appalled by the threat of violence, but she wasn't. More than once, she'd fantasized about using her kickboxing skills on Akash's testicles.

"I appreciate the offer, but my family is going to be fine," she assured Cal. "It took me a while, but I figured out a solution.

Akash's parents came to San Francisco with him, and when he took me to see them, I revealed our fake engagement and told them about his threats."

"*Holy shit!* You torpedoed him."

"I totally did," she confirmed gleefully. "His parents are the only people who have any control over him. Actually, his father controls him completely. I finally realized they were my only hope. They were devastated when I told them our engagement wasn't real."

He snorted. "I was devastated when I found out you were engaged, so I don't feel a lot of pity for them."

"You were devastated?"

He nodded. "That's a pretty good description for what I felt."

His admission gave her hope. He wouldn't have been devastated about her engagement unless he thought they had a future together.

"I'm not engaged anymore. And it was never a real engagement, not to me."

"Is that why you didn't tell me about it?"

"No."

"Then why didn't you tell me?"

She knew her answer would offend him, but she wasn't going to lie anymore. "I didn't think you needed to know."

His glacier-blue eyes narrowed. "Why not?"

"Because I thought we would be over by the time I had to make a decision about Akash."

He stared unblinkingly at her for several heartbeats. "You were going to tell me about Akash tonight," he pointed out. "Why?"

"Because I thought you needed to know."

He dropped his feet to the floor and leaned toward her. "Why?"

"Because I don't want us to be over." She licked her dry lips. "Ever."

Cupping his hand around the back of her head, he brought her face close to his. "You don't?"

"No." Her heart raced from the adrenaline pumping through her body, and she sucked in a deep breath. "I'm in love with you, Cal. I've loved you for years. I think I fell in love with you the moment I met you. I loved you when—"

He covered her mouth with his, his lips soft against hers. He kissed her until she couldn't breathe, licking and nibbling her lips and sucking on her tongue. When he finally pulled back, she was dizzy.

"Another first," he mused, rubbing his thumb over her bottom lip. "I'm on a roll."

"What?" she asked dumbly.

He smiled slowly. "I'm your first love."

"Yes."

He gently stroked her cheek, and she turned her face into his hand. Squeezing her eyes shut, she tried to keep the tears from spilling over.

"Why are you crying?"

Because I told you that I loved you, and you didn't say it back.

"I had a rough day."

"I know you did, baby. I did, too. Maybe I can make it better."

He always claimed sex made everything better. She usually agreed, but right now, she didn't want sex.

She wanted love.

She ducked her head to wipe her eyes, ashamed of her tears. She had no reason to cry. She should be happy he had allowed her to explain about Akash instead of kicking her out of his condo.

Tugging her hand away from her eyes, he began to pull the rings from her fingers, one by one. She looked up into his face.

"The night I picked you up from the Fairmont, you told me what these rings mean to you."

"I did?" She had no memory of talking about her rings.

"You did," he confirmed softly, dropping the thin gold bands on top of the striped duvet as he removed them. "You told me every ring represents something mean your parents or your brothers said to you."

She pulled in a shaky breath. "If I had a ring for every time they told me what a disappointment I am . . ." she said, trying to make a joke.

"I used to love the way they looked on your fingers, but once I knew why you wore them, I hated them." He caressed her bare fingers. "You also told me what your mother said to you that night."

She winced, reminding herself never to drink a double martini again. The hangover went away, but the humiliation went on and on.

"You asked me if it was impossible to love you, and I want you to know it's not impossible." Raising her hand, he kissed the tips of her fingers. "I love you. I think I've always loved you. The first time I looked into your eyes, I felt something. I don't know how to describe it . . . kind of a click. I had never felt anything like it."

He wove his fingers through hers. "I didn't know what it was, but I do now. It was recognition. My soul recognized yours. You might not believe in soul mates, Bebe, but I do, and you're mine."

Shifting to the side, he reached into his jeans pocket and pulled out a small black leather box. She had an idea of what was in that box, and she began to tremble. He flipped open the top and removed a ring that sparkled so brightly, it created colorful prisms all over the room.

"This ring means something." He held it in front of her face. "It means I love you. It means you have never disappointed me. You never *will* disappoint me. It means you're mine, and I'm yours. It means you are the woman I have chosen to be the mother of my children. It means you are the woman I want to be with until I take my last breath."

He took her left hand in his. "I want you to throw away your rings and wear my ring. And every time you look at it, I want you to remember what it means." He tilted his head. "Will you wear it?"

Her vision darkened, and she realized she had been holding her breath. Exhaling loudly, she took several deep pulls of air until she could see his face clearly. He was all she wanted . . . all she would ever want.

"Yes, I'll wear your ring."

He grinned, the dimple in his cheek flashing briefly. "That's what I wanted to hear," he murmured, sliding the ring onto her finger.

She held out her hand, studying her new engagement ring. It was the most beautiful piece of jewelry she had ever seen, and thanks to her shopping expeditions with Teagan, she had seen a lot.

"This means you're going to get all my firsts, *pahale*."

"Firsts are good, but onlys are better," he replied with a laugh.

"Onlys?"

"Yes, onlys." He dropped a kiss on her lips. "The only man you want. The only man you love. The only man you kiss hello. The only man you throw your panties at."

"Do I get to be any of your onlys?"

"You're my one and only."

Epilogue

Ten Years Later

THE BUTTERFLY NIGHTLIGHT PROVIDED ENOUGH ILLUMINA-
tion for Cal to see the toys blocking his path. He stopped to
pick up a couple of stuffed animals along with a Barbie and
several children's books and placed them in a wicker basket
at the end of the hallway before peeking into Gemma's room.

As usual, his firstborn child had kicked off her covers, and
he took a moment to pull the lavender sheets and quilt over
her. Like her mother, Gemma's favorite color was any shade
of purple.

Smoothing the tangle of dark hair from her face, he
dropped a kiss on her forehead. Her eyelids fluttered open to
reveal her sleepy golden gaze. She was the only one of his
girls who had her mother's eyes.

"Love you, Daddy," she sighed.

"I love you, too, *priye*. Go back to sleep."

She rolled over, and he quietly left her room and headed
next door to check on Kinley. As usual, his six-year-old daughter was awake, sitting cross-legged on her bed and studying her
e-reader.

All his girls were smart, but his middle child had a turbo-
charged brain just like her mother. But no matter how smart
she was, his little girl wasn't going to college until she was

eighteen. He wanted to keep her with him as long as he could, and Bebe felt the same way.

As he walked into the room, Kinley smiled, her blue eyes shining in the glow from the screen. She and her little sister had his eyes.

"Hi, Daddy."

"*Chatur*, you're supposed to be asleep."

She tilted her head, her glossy braid swinging over her shoulder. "I wanted to finish my book."

He held out his hand, and she reluctantly passed over the e-reader before scooting down in the bed. Tucking the e-reader under his arm, he pulled the floral sheets and apricot-colored quilt over her.

"I love you," he said as he leaned down and kissed her forehead. "Now go to sleep."

"Love you, too."

He pulled the door shut, shoved Kinley's e-reader in the fabric pouch hanging on it, and crossed the hall to Neela's room. As usual, his baby girl was passed out, her little body turned sideways in her pastel-pink-canopied bed. Apparently, preschool was hard work.

He debated whether he should move her, knowing it might wake her, but decided that would be better than her falling out of bed. That had happened way too many times, and he preferred to get through the night without any crying.

Gently grasping her legs, he turned her until she was stretched out. She awoke just as he pulled up the covers.

"Daddy," she chirped in her sweet little voice, "will you make blueberry pancakes for breakfast?"

"I sure will, *shishu*."

She frowned. "I'm not a baby anymore, Daddy. I'm going to school now. You need to stop calling me *shishu*."

"You're always going to be my baby." He smiled and tapped her on the nose. "I love you."

"Love you, too."

He closed Neela's door and stopped to pick up a few more toys, tossing them in the basket before making the trek downstairs. He and Bebe had bought their big Victorian when she had been pregnant with Gemma. It was only a few blocks away from Priest and Teagan's house in Pacific Heights, and it was perfect for their family.

Once he reached the main floor, he double-checked the front and back entrances to make sure they were locked and put Bebe's phone on the charger in the kitchen. Pascal's water bowl was empty, and as he filled it, he made a mental note to tell his girls to take better care of the dog they had wanted so badly.

He grabbed Kinley's fleece from one of the stools surrounding the kitchen bar, hanging it on the hook next to the back door so she wouldn't forget it tomorrow, and tucked Gemma's homework into her cubby so she wouldn't overlook it in the morning rush. Taking one last glance around the spacious kitchen, he flipped off the light and made his way to the master bedroom.

It was time for him to tuck in his favorite girl.

Bebe smiled widely when he walked into the room. She had given him thousands of smiles during their ten-year marriage, but they still stole his breath.

"How are the girls?" she asked as she smoothed sweet-smelling lotion onto her hands.

"Perfect."

She laughed softly, leaning over from her place on top of the fluffy down comforter to drop the tube of lotion onto the nightstand. The ancient USC T-shirt she wore bunched around her smooth thighs, revealing her bright pink panties, and his cock twitched with the need to be inside her. Even after all this time, she still was his favorite thing to do.

"That's not what you said when Gemma gave the neighbor's poodle a buzz cut or when Kinley tried to melt rocks in the microwave or when Neela flooded the laundry room."

He shook his head in exasperation. His mom claimed the girls were just like him when he was a kid: rascally. When he had asked if they would grow out of it, she'd laughed herself silly.

"They're perfect when they're asleep," he replied, amending his previous statement.

She laughed lightly, a musical sound that always filled him with joy. "I agree," she said, slipping her wedding band back onto her finger. She slid the ring that featured the birthstones of their children onto her other hand. He had given the jewelry to her after she had delivered Neela four years ago.

After tugging off his navy-blue T-shirt, he draped it over

one of the gray upholstered chairs situated in front of the bay window. He shucked his Rileys and boxer briefs before grabbing a pair of pajama bottoms from his drawer. Sleeping in the nude was not an option with three little girls in the house.

"*Pahale*, how it is possible for you to be hotter today than you were when I met you?"

He looked over his shoulder at his wife, whose eyes were focused on his ass. "You think I've still got it?"

"You've still got it," she answered emphatically. "All the other mommies want you."

He didn't care about the other mommies. He only cared about her.

"They want you, but you're mine." Her pink lips turned up in a satisfied smile. "All mine."

Yes, I am. Always.

He was thankful he still had what it took to turn her on because she still made him hard without even trying. With the exception of a few strands of silver in her dark hair, she looked almost exactly the same as she had when he had fallen in love with her.

Her face was smooth and unlined, and her eyes were as clear and gorgeous as they had been when he had first looked into them so many years ago. And despite having birthed three children who had tipped the scales at more than eight pounds, she was as slender as she had ever been.

"You know, Cookie, you're hotter today than you were when I met you," he noted as he stepped into the pajamas and tied the drawstring waist.

She blushed. "You're crazy."

"No, I'm not."

She really was hotter now than she had been in her twenties. She was hotter because of the happiness that radiated from her. She was loved, and she knew it. He told her how much he loved her every day, and so did their girls. She no longer worried about being unlovable.

"I talked to Teagan about the family portrait for Dad's birthday," he informed her, bending to scoop up his jeans and underwear. He nabbed a pair of black heels in his other hand and took everything to the walk-in closet. "We're going to meet in Golden Gate Park on Saturday at eleven o'clock for pictures, and then we'll have a picnic."

By God's grace, his dad had beaten the odds. He was still cancer-free, and Cal continued to say a prayer every night that he would stay that way. Luckily, his mom was healthy, too.

Bebe's parents were still alive, but she hadn't spoken to either of them in more than five years. They had never met Kinley or Neela.

Although Bebe had made peace with their indifference, his parents tried to make up for their absence, and surprisingly, Tushar and Ishani had stepped in as honorary grandparents to the girls. They came to San Francisco every couple of months to see them and to check in on Mehra's biotech investments, which Bebe managed.

"How are we going to corral ten young children for a photo?" Bebe asked, her voice floating from the bedroom. "It's going to be nothing but chaos. Patrick is going to be wild."

He laughed at her prediction. Without a doubt, Teagan and Priest's five-year-old son took after his mother, both in looks and temperament. Fortunately, Priest still had quick reflexes from his days playing pro football, and he put them to good use with Patrick.

"Letty is going to be there, and Valerie is stopping by to help out," he said as he exited the closet.

Saika and Noble's seventeen-year-old daughter was the O'Brien family's preferred babysitter. They kept her busy every weekend. Cal didn't know what they were going to do when she headed to the University of Oregon next fall.

"Everyone is supposed to wear Rileys and shirts with red as the primary color," he added.

"Other than her school uniform, I'm not sure Gemma owns a shirt that isn't purple," Bebe noted as he walked into the en suite bathroom.

He quickly took care of his get-ready-for-bed business, and by the time he finished, his wife was stretched out under the covers. After switching off the lamp on his nightstand, he climbed in beside her. She immediately snuggled up to him, placing her hand on his heart and throwing her leg over him so her crotch nestled against his hip.

"Thank you for marrying me," he said, rubbing his fingers over her engagement ring.

"Thank you for loving me," she replied, stroking his chest. He had said the same thing every night since their wedding night, and she always responded the same way. It was their nightly ritual.

They relaxed in comfortable silence for several minutes, and he was just about to pull her on top of him when she spoke into the darkness. "Oh, I almost forgot to tell you . . . Gemma had her first kiss today."

What the hell?

Shocked, he pushed her away and leaned over to turn on the lamp. Rolling onto his side, he faced her.

"Please tell me you didn't say what I think you said."

"What do you think I said?"

"I thought you said our eight-year-old daughter had her first kiss."

"That's what I said, *pahale*."

Damn.

"Who was the boy? I need to have a talk with his parents."

And tell them to keep their lecherous son away from my perfect daughter.

"Matthew."

"The one who throws bugs at her?"

"The very same. She said he called her a smarty pants, chased her across the playground, pulled her hair, and then kissed her." She waggled her dark eyebrows. "On the lips."

He couldn't help but laugh. "That sounds remarkably familiar."

She snickered. "You never pulled my hair."

"I wanted to," he joked.

But his amusement evaporated as the gravity of the situation hit him. "*Jesus Christ on a pogo stick*," he groaned. "I thought I would have a few more years before I'd have to worry about this kind of shit."

Leaning forward, she gave him a soft kiss. "She obviously takes after her father."

Keep reading for a preview of
Jenna Sutton's first Riley O'Brien & Co. romance

All the Right Places

Available now from Berkley Sensation!

Chapter 1

DERRIÈRE. ASS. BACK PORCH. BADONKADONK. RUMP. NO MAT-ter what you called it, the butt was Quinn O'Brien's favorite part of the human body.

Yes, he had the typical male appreciation for the female form, but truly, most of his interest was professional. In fact, some would say it was part of his DNA. He was the fifth generation of O'Briens to be involved in the family business, Riley O'Brien & Co., proud designers and manufacturers of blue jeans since 1845.

"Pay attention to how our jeans conform to the wearer's body, especially the butt," his father had schooled him and his younger brother when they were kids. At the time, Quinn hadn't realized scoping out every backside within sight might cause problems, especially when he stared just a bit too long at a crooked seam on a stranger's rear.

And right now, that's exactly what he was doing—staring at a stranger's ass hard enough to make his eyes cross. Who could blame him, though, since it was right at eye level above him on the escalator? And oh, what an ass it was—high and tight, yet still nicely rounded.

He sighed. The woman in front of him might have a great

ass, but she wasn't wearing Rileys. That was a big mark against her in his book.

Shifting his gaze from her curvy backside, he reviewed the brown leather belt encircling her slender waist. Embellished with beads and intricate stitching, it was eye-catching, not gaudy at all.

But it wasn't nearly as eye-catching as the red corkscrews of hair that fell down her back almost to her waist. They glinted with gold and amber from the early-morning sun shining through the skyscraper's windows. Her hair was so curly it kinked in some places, creating sharp angles that made him want to pull on a strand just to see how quickly it would recoil.

The woman stepped off the escalator into the reception area of Riley O'Brien & Co.'s global headquarters, cutting his perusal short. Unlike most high-rises in downtown San Francisco, Riley Plaza's first floor was filled with retail space, including the requisite Starbucks and a small shop that sold Riley merchandise. From the first floor, an escalator brought visitors and employees to the mezzanine level, where they checked in with reception or headed to their offices.

He pulled his gaze from the woman in just enough time to avoid tripping over the escalator lip and crashing onto the floor. Yeah, ogling asses could be hazardous.

As the redhead made her way to the reception desk, Quinn held up a hand and called out a greeting to the security guard posted by the double doors that led to the executive offices.

"Hey, Frank, did you see the new commercial last night?"

Riley O'Brien & Co. had recently launched a new advertising campaign featuring several well-known male athletes. The first commercial highlighting Quinn's best friend, Nick Priest, had debuted last night during Sunday night football.

Priest and Quinn had played football together at the University of Southern California. While Quinn's football career had ended when he graduated from USC, Priest had gone pro. He was one of the best wide receivers in the NFL, and his talent transformed every team he joined.

"Yeah, I saw it," Frank answered. "If you wanted to make women all over America lust after Priest even more than they do now, you succeeded."

Quinn laughed. "So, you thought Priest looked hot?"

"Hell, no," Frank barked. "But the wife couldn't take her eyes off the TV while he was on-screen."

"Who can blame her? She's had to look at your ugly face for more than thirty years. She needs a break."

Frank grinned and shot him the bird. "Get to work, son."

Quinn pulled open one of the heavy wood doors to the executive wing, and as he did every morning, he took some time to enjoy the walk along the polished concrete floors to his office. A timeline highlighting the major milestones in Riley O'Brien & Co.'s history stretched from one end of the hallway to the other. It started with the founding of the company prior to the California Gold Rush, and old sepia images, black-and-white pictures, and a handful of color photos brought it to life.

He could see glimmers of himself in some of the images on the wall. All the men in his family had hair so dark it was almost black. And like his grandfather's, Quinn's hair was slightly wavy.

It was hard to tell from the early pictures what color his ancestor's eyes were, but legend had it that Riley O'Brien's eyes were so cold a glare from him could stop even the roughest of gold prospectors in their tracks. No doubt, he must have been one mean son of a bitch to build a successful business at a time when California was nothing but a territory full of wild and avaricious men.

Quinn turned his attention from the timeline and entered his office. Before he could sit down, a sharp knock sounded on his door, and his sister's dark head poked around it.

"Do you have a minute?" Teagan asked, slightly breathless. Her blue eyes were wide behind the black-framed glasses she wore.

"Sure. What's up, T?"

She slipped inside his office, shutting the door behind her. Her black dress crossed over the front of her body and tied on the side. Dotted with big red cherries, it was a perfectly nice piece of clothing, but he was immediately pissed off she wore it.

"Why are you always wearing a damn dress?" he growled.

"You don't like it?" she asked, feigning confusion.

"Our family fortune was built on jeans," he reminded her. "Can't you put on a pair once in a while?"

It was a discussion they'd had many times, and her answer

was always the same. He could have repeated it verbatim, and now he got to hear it again.

"Rileys look good on you. They look good on most men. But they do not look good on most women. They especially don't look good on short women. Or women with big butts, big thighs, or big anythings. Ergo, they don't look good on me."

Quinn held up his hands, sorry he'd brought up the subject. "I don't want to get into another argument about the women's division," he backtracked hastily. "Your dress is fine. You look very pretty."

Ignoring Teagan's rude snort, he settled in his chair and propped his feet on his desk. "What did you need?" he prompted her as he inspected his new boots.

She eyed him for a few moments before answering. "Amelia Winger has agreed to design our new line of accessories."

He dropped his feet to the floor and sat up. The accessories were all Teagan's idea, and the little sneak had gone behind his back to make them happen.

She had wanted to revamp the entire women's division, and when Quinn refused, she had persuaded their dad to give his stamp of approval for the line of accessories. Now Quinn had to suck it up and play nice with the new designer until their dad officially resigned and handed the reins over to him.

"So she's definitely going to do it?" he asked.

"I think so. She requested a meeting with you, since you're going to head up the project, but as long as you don't blow it, I think she's on board."

He huffed out a breath in annoyance. "Why would *I* blow it?"

"Quinn, you can be really intense about Rileys. It's . . . well, it's a turnoff to some people."

He nodded, agreeing with Teagan's assessment. He *was* intense. He was devoted to protecting the Riley O'Brien brand, and he never forgot every single pair of Rileys ever produced was branded with his last name.

He realized Teagan was still talking. ". . . knew you were going to be in the office today, so I told her it would be okay."

"Wait, what did you say?"

Looking down, she tapped her fingers against her bottom lip. He tensed. She was a terrible liar and an even worse poker player because she always tapped her lips when she was nervous or unsure.

He stood. "Tell me," he demanded when she stayed silent a beat too long.

"I told Amelia Winger you would be available to meet her this morning."

"Shit, Teagan! You know I hate it when you ambush me with things like this. . . ."

She stopped tapping her lips and started tapping her toe, never a good sign for innocent or not-so-innocent males nearby. "This is a priority, Quinn," she shot back. "I've already worked out all the legal details with Amelia. All she wants is a meeting with you. So it's not on your calendar. Deal with it."

"When will she be here?"

"She's already here."

"Of course she is," he said dryly. He ran a hand through his hair before smoothing the mess he had made. "Let's go get her."

With Teagan click-clacking alongside him, he made the trek down the hall. He wasn't looking forward to this meeting, and not just because his sister had sprung it on him. The women's division limped along like a three-legged dog, and he doubted some new belts and purses would make a difference.

"Are you sure Amelia Winger is the right person to design our accessories?" Quinn asked.

He'd reviewed the information Teagan had provided about the designer, but he still had his doubts, especially since Amelia Winger had no formal design training, and she'd never done any work for a company like Riley O'Brien.

"I'd never heard of her before you mentioned her," he continued. "Just because her best friend is a country music star and wears her designs doesn't mean Amelia has any real talent. It just means she's smart enough to capitalize on Ava Grace Landy's success."

"Ava Grace doesn't wear Amelia's designs just because she's her best friend. She wears them because they're incredible."

Pushing open the door to the reception area, he ushered his sister through it before following. Frank turned at the sound, winking at Teagan.

The security guard tilted his head toward the only person sitting in the reception area. "There's your girl," he said with a smile.

Teagan hurried toward the woman with her arms outstretched. "Amelia, it's so nice to see you again!" she exclaimed.

The woman dropped the magazine she'd been reading and quickly rose from her orange chair. It clashed horribly with her long red hair, and his heart kicked in his chest as Teagan gestured toward him.

"Amelia Winger, this is my brother, Quinn O'Brien. Quinn, this is the fabulous designer we talked about."

Amelia released Teagan's hands and stepped forward to greet him. "It's nice to meet you," she said, offering her hand to him. Her voice had a slight twang to it, betraying her Texas roots.

Clasping her hand, he gazed down at her. She couldn't have been more than an inch or two above five feet tall because the top of her curly head didn't even reach his shoulders. Her brown eyes crinkled as she smiled, and he noticed a slight gap between her top front teeth.

Her smile wobbled a bit as he stood there silently, staring into a face sprinkled with freckles that reminded him of brown sugar. Finally, he spoke, but when he did, it wasn't exactly what he had intended.

"Nice ass," he said.

Damn. Did I really say that out loud?

All the Right Places

A Riley O'Brien & Co. Romance

Amelia Winger is a small-town girl with big dreams of becoming a successful designer. So when she gets a gig designing accessories for denim empire Riley O'Brien & Co., it's a dream come true. Amelia can handle the demanding job, but she isn't quite prepared for sexy CEO Quinn O'Brien. She's doing her best to keep things professional, but the attraction sparking between them makes it personal. And so does the secret project she's working on behind his back...

Quinn's not interested in the new accessories, but he is interested in the woman designing them. Amelia is smart, sexy, and talented, and he hasn't been able to stop thinking about her since they met. Mixing business and pleasure isn't wise, but that doesn't stop him from coming up with excuses to spend time with her. He thinks he understands the risk he's taking when he gets involved with Amelia. But he doesn't know he's risking a lot more than his heart.

jennasutton.com
facebook.com/jennasuttonauthor
penguin.com

Also From

JENNA SUTTON

Coming Apart at the Seams

A Riley O'Brien & Co. Romance

Teagan O'Brien, heiress to the Riley O'Brien & Co. denim empire, is anything but a spoiled rich girl. She's worked hard to secure her place in the family business and can hold her own, in and out of the office. Only one man has ever been able to get under her skin—sexy football star Nick Priest. Years ago they crossed the line from friends to lovers, but he left her heartbroken. Since then, she's been determined to keep him at arm's length—no matter how tempting he looks in his jeans...

Nick has fortune, fame, and looks that make most women hot and bothered. But he doesn't have the woman he really wants. He knows he screwed up when he walked away from Teagan, and now that he has a second chance, he'll do whatever it takes to win her over—no matter how tongue-tied he gets...

jennasutton.com
facebook.com/jennasuttonauthor
penguin.com